LEN DEIGHTON

Violent Ward

HARPER

This novel is entirely a work of fiction.
The names, characters and incidents portrayed in it are
the work of the author's imagination. Any resemblance to
actual persons, living or dead, events or localities is
entirely coincidental.

Harper
An imprint of HarperCollins*Publishers*
1 London Bridge Street,
London SE1 9GF

www.harpercollins.co.uk

This paperback edition 2016
1

First published in Great Britain by
HarperCollins*Publishers* in 1993

A catalogue record for this book is
available from the British Library

ISBN: 978 0 00 816225 2

Typeset in Ehrhardt MT Std by Palimpsest Book Production Ltd, Falkirk, Stirlingshire

Printed and bound in Great Britain

MIX
Paper from
responsible sources
FSC® C007454

FSC™ is a non-profit international organisation established to promote
the responsible management of the world's forests. Products carrying the
FSC label are independently certified to assure consumers that they come
from forests that are managed to meet the social, economic and
ecological needs of present and future generations,
and other controlled sources.

Find out more about HarperCollins and the environment at
www.harpercollins.co.uk/green

Cover designer's note

Prompted by seeing the renderings of my two murals for Cunard's new ship, *Queen Elizabeth*, Len Deighton suggested that I illustrate some of the covers of this next quartet of re-issues. I am delighted to be given the opportunity to draw once again, as it has been well over thirty years since my days as a regular illustrator for the *Sunday Times*.

It is amazing to think that it is also nearly twenty years since the 1992 Los Angeles riots, an event which looms large in this book. When first reading *Violent Ward*, it struck a chord with my wife and me as we had just moved into our new apartment in Hollywood when the riots took place.

On the first night we were awoken by loud shouting: 'Get out, get out, your building is on fire!' The warning came from a police officer who was banging his night-stick against our building's wall. In the alley behind us were a couple of LAPD black-and-white patrol cars, and I could hear an officer speaking on his radio urging the fire department to come as quickly as possible. Meanwhile my wife, wielding a garden hose, attempted to douse the flames that were engulfing our neighbouring garages.

The next night, along with several neighbours armed to the teeth, we formed a vigilante watch on the roof of our remaining garage. Apart from the sounds of a stray cat I am pleased to report that it was an uneventful night.

In the morning I visited Samy's, the professional camera store across from our home, to purchase a few rolls of film in order to record the damage of the previous day. A couple of hours later, while sitting at my desk, I heard three loud explosions. Looking out of the window, I saw an enormous mushroom-cloud rising up from the camera store, which had been torched. It appears that their large stock of photographic chemicals were responsible for the enormity of the explosions.

The following morning I ventured to the scene of the crime to discover the burnt-out shop front strewn with the remnants of expensive cameras, including a gold Leica that had become molten by the inferno, and a large shattered fish-eye lens. These later became part of an exhibit in the store's new premises.

The composition on the front cover draws upon all these events, with the addition of a National Guardsman who stands ready, and perhaps too eager, to respond to the civil unrest and general chaos that is unfolding. For the book's title I chose a bold font within which could burn the flames of civil unrest; the falling 'D' an apt symbol of the city's descent into 'war'.

The back cover collage includes a book match cover from the Beverly Hills Hotel, a valet parking stub with Murphy's Cadillac circled, a couple of Hollywood postcards, and a movie clapper board. Sitting behind all these is an edition of the 'Los Angeles Messenger', beneath whose fictional masthead shouts a contemporary headline that was all too true. When applying some authentic fire damage, we did not realize how flammable the newsprint would be, and nearly ended up burning our apartment down – it's a good job Isolde was standing by with a bucket of water! Each item in the montage has been selected to convey a facet of the City of Angels, its glamour and charm that is always just a hair's breadth away from a seedy underbelly full of corruption and violence.

The book's spine features an LAPD badge. Observant readers

will notice that each of the spines in this latest quartet of reissues features a metallic object; a subtle visual link that draws together four books written and set in very different times and places.

I have taken the photograph for this book's back cover with my Canon 5D camera, and my illustration was drawn with a HB Staedtler pencil.

Arnold Schwartzman OBE RDI
Hollywood 2011

Introduction

Not all of the world's greatest cities are old. Paris (where I set *An Expensive Place to Die*) is a great city. Cairo (the setting for *City of Gold*) is indisputably great but so is Los Angeles. People frown and argue when I say that but I stand by my assessment. And Los Angeles is dynamic; no sooner than you start to think you understand something of it you find it has substantially changed yet again. It is big, a vast sprawling city of low buildings that follow the freeways so that you can drive all the way to Mexico while believing you are still in the city. It is only when you fly over it that you see the uninhabited expanses that lie behind the freeways. The off-ramp signs offer a wonderland of realtor's poesy: Tarzana, Hidden Hills, Thousand Oaks, Malibu Canyon, Lake Sherwood, Woodland Hills. But you are never far from the wild outback; listen to the raccoons pattering across the roof to invade your attic; hear the noise of a rattlesnake lurking in your woodpile, go into the yard and see a coyote rummaging through your garbage; go for an early morning round of golf and be confronted with an impudent mountain lion in no hurry to depart. This is Los Angeles County.

I had first visited Los Angeles as a very young man but it was meeting Bill Jordan, a detective with the LAPD intelligence division, that enabled me to see the inner life of the city. Bill arranged for me to go out with the police cars on such expeditions as raiding the home of a drug dealer. Bill showed me the downtown streets and alleys he had walked as a young police officer, a Pacific war veteran just out of the US Marine Corps. Eventually Bill became a private detective and he is as near to being Raymond Chandler's Philip Marlowe as anyone could be. But although also armed with a Law Degree, Bill Jordan is a very far cry from Mickey Murphy. Bill is a sober and reflective man whose honesty, skills and charm combined to make him into a very successful investigator. As I witnessed one night when riding in a police car, he could even make a drunken driver believe that being taken into custody was an act of goodwill. 'How would you face your family if tonight you killed someone on the road?'

Bill showed me the many faces of Los Angeles, including the comfortable suburbia where a lot of this story is set. I returned many times and I was in Los Angeles during the days of the riots. It was a devastating time when mild-mannered citizens were suddenly brandishing guns. But writers are always apt to be opportunistic and I decided that the acrid smoke, drifting across the city's stately skyscrapers like a net curtain, should become the climax of this book. The description of the riots is as accurate as I could make it. It was my publisher who provided me with a close view of Los Angeles at the height of the violence. Due at a book fair in Anaheim, I was collected by an out-of-town driver who carelessly took the direct route through the smouldering streets of South Central.

Many of my stories are written in the first person. Eight of nine of the Bernard Samson books are in the first person and this one is too. Deciding to set a story in the first person is a major decision in the planning of a book. Some authors prefer to have their first-person narrative written in what is sometimes called the authorial voice. Somerset Maugham did this and did little to change the idea that his tales are that of an author gathering material and reporting on the follies and misfortunes of his friends and acquaintances. Other writers use the voice and actions of the main character to create a person quite different to themselves. Bernard Samson exaggerates and distorts the world he tells us about. Without deliberate, self-serving lies he is apt to parody his superiors and ridicule his father in law. Well, this is not unknown in our real lives and it provides a chance to see into Bernard's mind and judge his skills and his courage. Just as we love our friends and relatives as much for their failings as for their virtues, so we love and admire Bernard. The anarchic Mickey Murphy is also depicted by means of the first-person narrative and few men could be quite as different as Mickey is to Bernard. I hope that these characterisations provide something you enjoy for I devote a great deal of thought to creating these first-person people.

I am the luckiest of lucky men and I take pleasure in my work but I am a very slow worker. I envy those writers who find their characters speak to them and are able to dash off books at lightning speeds. I plod; writing books demands more than a year; no vacations, seven days a week and that includes wide-awake nights as I worry about whether to slim down characters, dump chapters or move them all to another town and start again. It is my family who deserve sympathy and have to be thanked for their understanding. *Violent Ward* was a specially happy book for me. Reading it again to write this introduction reminded me of all the fun I had creating the maverick Irish lawyer who has to be the hero because there is no one else around to play that role. More than one of my friends said that Mickey Murphy was exactly like me; quick to anger; quick to repent and tormented by self-doubt. Perhaps they were right. I admit to finding it relatively easy to create this rebellious Irish sinner; I admired him. Mickey's abrasive, cynical manner cloaks the fearless morality that arms those with little or nothing to lose.

Most of my stories are love stories. And most of these love stories are set in a commanding environment such as Cairo, Los Angeles or Berlin; or an environment of hazard, such as war or espionage. Or both. And the love is tempered by the asserted masculinity of men who declare their failure to understand women. Mickey Murphy does not resemble Bernard Samson in any way other than a failure to understand the women he loves, but this failure can be a fatal one. The theme of what might have been is a sub-text of fiction and of life. This story was different to all the other books I had written. Mickey was different so when I finished the first draft of *Violent Ward* I asked Mickey to write to my publisher to explain the change:

Hear me out, buddy. They say if America is a lunatic asylum then California is the Violent Ward. My name is Murphy and I'm a Mick lawyer with an ex-wife who sends her astrologer around demanding money so she can pay off her orthodontist. My kid has hocked his 9mm Browning using false ID. I'm in love with the wife of my wealthiest client and the cops are trying to pin a nasty homicide on me.

But there's no recession in the crime industry and my business is fine, or it might be if my German secretary could write and speak English, and my clients didn't get wasted before they paid my bills. The kind of crooks I defend never plead the Fifth because they can't count that far.

Okay, Okay. So nobody loves a lawyer.

See ya in court.

Len Deighton, 2011

If America is a lunatic asylum
then California is the Violent Ward.

1

'There's a woman sitting on my window ledge,' I said quietly and calmly into the phone.

'I can't see you, Mr Murphy!' said Miss Magda Huth, my secretary. Her German accent was more pronounced when she was agitated, like now, and her voice was strangled whenever she stood on tiptoe to see into my office over the frosted glass partition.

'There's a woman sitting on my window ledge. You can't see me because I'm behind my desk.'

'You must be on the floor.'

'Yes, well, I'm trying not to frighten her,' I said. 'Will you please just do something about it?'

Miss Huth has no sense of urgency except when she is leaving work. 'Your coffee is losing its froth out here,' she said. 'Perhaps if I brought it in to you—'

Jesus! 'Are you listening to me?' I said. 'She didn't come by for a cup of coffee and a Danish. She's going to throw herself into the street. Any minute.'

'There is no need to become belligerent.' Magda Huth wasn't young. She'd been some kind of schoolteacher in Dresden until reunification gave her a chance to leave, and at times she treats me like a backward pupil in a totalitarian kindergarten. That's the way she was treating me now. 'I will see if I can reach the Fire Department,' she said primly.

'Yes, you do that,' I said.

Miss Huth had not been with my law partnership very long. Previously, for five years I'd had Denise, a really sensible woman and an efficient secretary. Then she went off on a package-deal skiing weekend in Big Bear – I must have been soft in the head to give her so much time off – and within eight weeks she was married to a Mexican orthodontist she met in a singles bar there. For a long time I kept hoping she'd tire of living in Ensenada and ask for her job back. But then last Christmas I had this long chatty boilerplate letter, plus a blurred snapshot of her and her husband and twin bambinos, and now I was trying to get used to Miss Huth all over again. It wasn't easy.

'That's right,' I said. 'Get the Fire Department, and tell them to make it snappy or they'll be hosing her off the sidewalk.'

'You should not talk that way,' Miss Huth said, with a sniff, and cut me off before I could reply. I hung up so gently it didn't make a sound.

I looked through the kneehole of the desk so that I could see the window. The woman was still there, fidgeting around, trying to look down into the street below her. This *would* happen today of all days. My new boss, the mighty Zachary Petrovitch – el supremo, ichi-ban, tycoon extraordinaire – was spending a few days at his Los Angeles mansion so he could be guest of honor at the 'surprise party' his minions had been planning for weeks. Petrovitch wanted his own little law firm here in the city, and he was bringing to this partnership something it had never had before – money. By putting one of his tame in-house lawyers behind Korea Charlie's empty desk he'd found a legal way of getting control of a law practice. It had been decreed that I should be at his party tonight, tugging

2

my forelock and bowing low and telling everyone how grateful I was to become a toiler ant in the Petrovitch zoo.

The phone buzzed and I snatched it up. It was Miss Huth again. 'The people from Graham's builders' discount store have come out into the street; they are all staring up here, Mr Murphy.'

'So?'

'I thought you would wish to know.'

'What did the Fire Department say?'

'They've put me on hold,' she said.

'On hold?'

'I've got them on the other line. They asked was it a fire, and I said no, it was not a fire.'

'Well, that's dandy. I'll throw a lighted cigar butt into the shredder basket, and then maybe they'll discuss the possibility of dropping by sometime.'

'They are on the line now!' she said urgently and cut me off again. I had to crouch real low to see properly. The woman outside my window was still shifting her ass about. Maybe the rubbernecks in the street thought she was getting ready to throw herself off the ledge, but I had my reasons for guessing that she was getting a cramp in the gluteus maximus and moving around to be more comfortable.

There was a tapping noise – imperious and persistent – on the frosted glass panel. It was Miss Huth, making a menacing shadow against the whitened glass with just her fringed hair and beady eyes peeping over it. She signaled to tell me that I'd put the phone down without putting it properly on the hook. I picked it up and she said, 'They are coming. The firemen. They are coming – right away.'

'I should hope so.' There was the sound of a siren, but it grew fainter and went north up Western Avenue toward Hollywood. 'Maybe I could use that cup of coffee,' I told her.

3

'If you put it on the mat inside the door, I'll crawl over and pull it toward me.'

'I don't see what good you think you're doing sitting there on the floor, Mr Murphy.' She was peering over the frosted glass again; I could hear it in her voice.

'I'm trying not to alarm her.'

'The firemen will arrive and the woman will see them, won't she? Why don't you get up and go over and talk with her?'

'And if she jumps, I take the blame? *You* come in and talk to her. Maybe you've got an insight into the motivation of women who jump off ledges.'

She let that one go and busied herself with placing two tall polystyrene cups on the mat, together with a Bear Claw on a paper napkin. I'd ordered one coffee and an almond croissant; the Bear Claws were too big and had brightly colored strawberry jelly inside, and I didn't like them. The little old Vietnamese guy who had taken over Tony's Deli employed his relatives, and some of them couldn't understand a word of English. When Big Tony and his brother ran that place, Tonichinos – large cappuccinos to go – had froth you could cut with a knife. Now it withered and died within five minutes; I guess the Vietnamese didn't understand the froth machine. Even so, Tony's Deli still made the best cappuccinos in this part of town. Thank God those guys had passed on the recipe to their successor, because I was hooked on them.

Gently I pulled the mat over and grabbed the coffees. They were still warm; I savored them. Sitting there on the Persian carpet, the final sixteen payments for which had now been underwritten by our new owner, gave me a chance to reflect on the arrangements for the party that night. It had to go well. I needed the money, really needed it.

Before I'd finished the second cup of coffee I heard a siren

4

coming along Olympic. I looked under the desk to see the window. The woman outside must have heard it too, for she was slowly and painfully getting up. First she brought one foot up onto the ledge, then she was kneeling there. Finally, moving like someone terrified of heights, she stood up and leaned back against the window, with both arms pressed flat against the glass. She was wearing an expensive light-weight tweed pants suit and a gold and blue Hermès scarf around her head, the kind of outfit a choosy woman would need to throw herself out of a Los Angeles window in springtime. I watched her cautious movements with great interest. Considering the way she'd been acting out there on the ledge, enjoying all the motions of a would-be suicide, she was certainly taking great pains now to make sure she didn't lose her balance.

I went across the room. She had her back to me now. I slid the window up and said, 'For God's sake come on in.'

She swung her head around and stared at me with hate in her eyes. 'Did you send for the Fire Department?' She coughed to clear her throat. Her cheeks had reddened; I could see she was cold. Maybe that was why she'd decided to come in.

'Why me?' I said. 'Any one of those people down there might have sent for them. The whole neighborhood's been watching you.' This was one of the few tall buildings in a street of one story shacks; everyone could see her. 'Come in!'

'You're a shit,' she said, and moved suddenly, swinging her feet into the room with commendable dexterity. Spotting the polystyrene cups on the mat, she went across to get a hot drink. Finding that both cups were empty, she tossed them across the room with a violence that made me shudder. She didn't seem to fancy the Bear Claw; I suppose it was the strawberry jelly. She made for the door.

'The Fire Chief is going to be asking you some questions,' I called after her.

'You answer them, you goddamned lawyer,' she yelled. 'You've always got an answer for everything!' She slammed out through the door that leads to the back stairs, just as the sirens were dying outside in the street. She knew the way to the back entrance; it was the way she got in.

The next moment the whole room was filled with burly men in shiny oilskin coats, rubber boots, and yellow helmets. They were mad at me. 'How is it my fault?' I yelled back at them. 'You let her get away.'

'Where'd she come from?' said a burly fire fighter, picking up the Bear Claw and chewing a piece out of it.

'How should I know where she came from? Maybe she escaped from the zoo.'

'You called in and said this was an emergency,' said a rat-faced little guy who seemed to be the chief. He smelled of metal polish and mint digestive tablets.

'Is that so? Did I interrupt a poker game or something? What am I supposed to do when someone comes into my office and wants to leap out of the window, get an entertainment license?'

The burly one tossed the remains of the Bear Claw into the wastebasket, where it landed with a loud clang. No wonder they give me indigestion: toss away an almond croissant and it makes only a soft *swoosh*.

Maybe if I'd been a little more diplomatic, Ratface wouldn't have turned nasty and sent two of his men to search out violations of the Fire Department Code. 'You should have been doing that before your own block burned down,' I said. But these guys were young kids; they hadn't been with the department long enough to remember that scandal. Finally Ratface came up with a clipboard reading aloud what he said were twenty-two infringements. 'The fire escape is rusty,' he said, jabbing at the clipboard with his finger.

'We just ran out of Brillo,' I said. I looked over his shoulder and read the sheet. Most of the faults were minor ones, but it looked like someone was going to have to renew the sprinkler system, put up new smoke detectors, and install some kind of fire doors. If I knew anything about the small print in the lease, it wasn't going to be my rapacious landlord, but no matter. It wasn't my pigeon. Two months earlier, the bottom line on that kind of work might have been enough to bankrupt me, but now it was just something to pass on to the new owner: the mighty Petrovitch. 'These old firetraps should be torn down,' said the guy who didn't like Bear Claws to his buddy. 'The whole block should be flattened. It's just a shantytown.'

'We can't all live in Bel Air, buddy.'

After they all trooped out, I examined the carpet and the dirty marks that their boots had left. The carpet needed cleaning anyway, but the extra stains were not going to help me when Zachary Petrovitch came to see what kind of premises he was getting for his money.

When at last I was free to sit down behind my desk and leaf through all the work outstanding, I found there was plenty to do. A new client, hooray. A one-time soap star, drunk and resisting arrest. It took me a minute to recognize her name; there is no limbo more bleak than the oblivion to which the soapers go. Then there were two movie scripts, one dog-eared and the other pristine. This client was a writer – a nice intelligent guy until now – who had worked himself up into a roaring frenzy about a movie that was being made by a producer he used to work with. He wanted me to read the two scripts and sue the production company for plagiarism. Plagiarism! He must be living on another planet. Start seeking injunctions for that kind of larceny and Hollywood would slither to a complete standstill. Did he think those guys with the Armani suits could

7

write connecting the letters just because they had Montblanc fountain pens? Original ideas?

None of it was more urgent than the red box file marked Sir Jeremy Westbridge. A lawyer gets used to the idea that most of his clients are on a course of self-destruction, but this Brit was something else. Every mail delivery brought word of some new and more terrible misdeed. I could see no way of keeping him out of prison, it was just a matter of whether he got ten or twenty years. The only consolation was that he had me on retainer and paid up like a sweetheart. How did I ever get into this crock? When I left high school I had everything set for a career as a car thief.

Dumping the whole stack of work back into the tray, I found myself looking at that damned window ledge, so finally I decided to go see Danny. I picked up the phone and told Miss Huth, 'I have to see my son.'

'No. You have an appointment at eleven-thirty.'

'Cancel it.'

'It's far too late to do that, Mr Murphy. It is already eleven-twenty-two.'

'Who is it?'

'Mr Byron.' She purred: she recognized his name. Women always knew his name. Budd Byron was now old enough for his early shows to be on daytime runs.

'Oh,' I said. I guess his old shows were on TV in Germany too.

'I think he's here,' she said, and I heard the outer door buzz. 'Shall I show him in?' I could hear the emotion in her voice. No woman could catch sight of Budd Byron without losing her emotional equilibrium.

'Yes, do that, Miss Huth . . . Budd! It's good to see you.' Budd was slim and tanned. He came into my office with the kind of cool, calm confidence of General MacArthur wading ashore in the Philippines, Newton demonstrating the force of gravity, or Al Capone denying that he owed income tax.

Budd had been a college classmate; you maybe would not have guessed that from the hellos. Budd has a certain sort of Hollywood formality. He fixed me with a sincere look and gripped my hand tight while giving my upper arm a slap: a California salutation.

'You're looking great,' I said. 'Great.' He was wearing Oxford brogues, custom-made gray-flannel slacks, and a jacket of Harris tweed, the heavy sort of garment worn in the winter months by Southern California's native male population. His shirt was tapered and his collar gold-pinned to secure the tight knot of a blue-and-red-striped Brooks Brothers silk tie. The effect was of a prosperous young banker. It was the look many Hollywood actors were adopting now that so many of the bankers were going around in bleached denim and cowboy boots.

'Coffee? A drink?'

'Perrier water,' said Budd. To complete the costume, he was wearing a beautiful gray fedora, which he took off and carefully placed on a shelf.

I went to the refrigerator hidden in the bookcase and brought him a club soda. 'Cigarette?' I picked up the silver box on my desk and waved it at him.

He shook his head. I can't remember the last time someone said yes. One day someone was going to puff at one of those ancient sticks and spew their guts out all over my white carpet.

'I read the other day the UCLA School of Medicine calculated that one joint has the carbon monoxide content of five regular cigarettes and the tar of three,' Budd said.

'These are not joints,' I said, shaking the silver box some more.

Budd laughed. 'I know. I just wanted to impress you with my learning.'

9

'You did.'

Budd didn't have to work hard at being a charmer: it just came natural to him. We'd stayed in touch since he abandoned Social Sciences in favor of Actors' Equity. He'd made a modest rep and his face was known to those who spent a lot of time in the dark, but he expended every last cent he earned keeping up a standard of living way beyond his means because he had to pretend to himself and everyone else that he was a big big star. I suppose only someone permanently out of touch with reality tried for the movie big time in Hollywood. The soup kitchens and retirement homes echo with the chatter of people still talking about the big chance that's coming any day. But Budd was not permanently out of touch with reality, just now and again. As the smart-ass student editor of our college yearbook wrote of him, his head was in the clouds but his feet were planted firmly on the ground. He really enjoyed what he did for a living, whether it was first class acting or not. Back in the forties, when movie stars were youthful and wholesome and gentlemanly, Budd might have made it big – or even in that brief period in the sixties when the collegiate look was in style – but nowadays it was stubble-chinned mumbling degenerates who got their names above the title. Budd was out of style.

'You *are* coming to my little champagne-and-burger birthday bash?' said Budd.

'You couldn't keep me away,' I said. I'd received an elaborate printed invitation to a luncheon party at Manderley, his old house perched up in the Hollywood Hills, near the Laurel Canyon intersection. Budd was one of those people who keeps in touch. He always knew what all his old classmates were doing, and when reunion time came round he was there addressing the envelopes.

'Lunch, a week from Sunday. We'll keep going until the champagne runs out.'

'Sounds like a challenge.'

He shifted in his chair, ran a fingernail down his cheek, and spoke in a different sort of voice. 'Mickey, I need advice. You're my attorney, right?'

'You don't need an attorney,' I told him. 'You're too smart. If all my clients kept their noses clean the way you do, I'd be out of business.' It was true. I sent hurry-up letters and sorted out the occasional misunderstanding, but most of what I did for Budd could have been done by a part-time secretary. Maybe I didn't charge him enough.

He nodded and smiled some more and looked out of the window. 'This is a lousy neighborhood, Mickey.'

'I know, all my visitors tell me. But we got cops on every corner and great ethnic food. What can I do for you, Budd?'

A pause, a tightening of the jaw. 'Would you get me a gun?'

'A gun? What do you want a gun for?' I said, keeping my voice very steady and matter-of-fact.

'No special reason,' he said, in that nervous way people say such things when they do have a special reason. Then came the prepared answer: 'The way I see it, the law will be putting all kinds of new restrictions on gun sales before long. I want to get a gun while it's still legal to purchase them over the counter.'

'I guess you saw that TV documentary on the Discovery channel. But you don't need a gun, Budd.'

'I do. My place is very vulnerable up there. There have been two stickups in the doughnut shop since Christmas. My neighbors have all had break-ins.'

'And having a gun will keep you from being burglarized? Listen, the chances of someone breaking in while you're there are nearly zero. When you're not there, a gun won't be any good to you, right?'

'It would make me feel better.'

11

'Okay. So you made up your mind. Don't listen to me; buy a gun.'

'I'd like you to purchase it.'

'Come on, Budd. What's the problem?'

'I'll be recognized. My face is known. Maybe it will get into the papers. That's not the kind of publicity I want.'

'Buying a gun? If that was the secret of getting newspaper publicity, there'd be lines forming outside the gun shops and all the way to the Mexican border.'

'The paperwork and license and all that stuff. You know about that, Mickey. You do it for me, will you?'

'You mean within the implied confidentiality of the client-attorney relationship?'

He nodded.

I sat back in my swivel chair and looked at him. Just as I thought I'd heard everything, along comes a client who wants me to buy a heater without his name on it. Next he's going to be asking me to file off the identity marks and make dum-dum cuts in the bullets. 'I'm not sure I can do that, Budd,' I said, very slowly. 'I'm not sure it's within the law.'

He caught at the equivocation. 'Will you find out? It's the way I'd like it done. Couldn't you say it was for a well-known movie actor who wanted to avoid the fuss?'

'Sure. And I'll promise them signed photos and tickets for your next preview.' As he started to protest, I held up a hand to deflect it. 'I'll ask around, Budd.'

'A Saturday-night special or a small handgun would do. I just want it as a frightener.'

'Sure, I understand: no hand grenades or heavy mortars. Can you use a gun? You were never in the military, were you?'

'I was in ROTC,' said Budd, the hurt feelings clearly audible in his voice. 'You know I was, Mickey.'

'Sure, I forgot.'

12

'I can shoot. I've had a lot of movie parts using guns. I like to get these things exactly right for my roles. I do an hour in the gym every day. I jog in the hills, and sometimes I go to the Beverly Hills Gun Club.' He slapped his gut. 'I keep myself in shape.'

'Right,' I said. Well, wind in the target; he sure scored a bull's-eye with that one. The only thing I could sincerely say I devoted at least one hour every day to was eating.

'Am I keeping you too long?' he said, consulting the Rolex with solid gold band that came with every Actors' Equity card.

'No rush. I'm going to see Danny: my son, Danny.'

'Sure, Danny. You brought him and his girlfriend along to watch me on the set of that Western I did for Disney last year.'

'That's right.'

'Give Danny my very best wishes. Tell him if he wants to visit a studio again I can always fix it up for him.'

'Thanks, Budd. That's really nice of you. I'll tell him.'

Budd didn't get up and leave. He reached out for his glass and took a sip, taking his time doing it, as I had seen so many witnesses on the stand do, buying time to think. 'I haven't told you the whole truth. There's something else. And I want to keep it just between the two of us, okay?'

'The client-attorney privileged relationship,' I said.

He got to his feet and nodded. All my clients like hearing about the confidential relationship the attorney offers; I always remind them about it just before I give them my bill. Prayer, sermon, confession, and atonement: in that order. I figure the whole process of consulting an attorney should be a secular version of the mass.

'How could I get a gun without anyone knowing?'

'Without even me knowing? Buy it mail order under an assumed name, I guess.'

'Could I have it sent to you?' he said.

13

'But then I would know,' I said, keeping my tone real negative. I didn't want him mailing guns to my office.

'It's like this,' Budd said, making a futile gesture with his hand. 'I have a friend who is being threatened. She needs a gun.'

'Well, you tell her to order one through the mail and have it sent to a post office box,' I said. I guessed we were into some kind of show-biz fantasy, and I wasn't in the mood for that kind of crap. I looked at my watch. 'I'm going to have to kick you out of here. I've got a heavy schedule.'

'Sure, Mickey, sure.'

He reached for his hat and went to the mirror to be sure it was on exactly right. Then he turned to shake hands firmly and say a soft goodbye. There was something he still hadn't said, and I plowed my brain to guess what it might be. What new bullshit was he going to hang on me now?

His dark, lustrous eyes focused and he said, 'If an intruder was shot on my premises . . . what could happen?'

'Stay out of it, Budd,' I advised sincerely. 'Buy your friend a subscription to *Shooter's Monthly* and call it a day.'

'Okay,' he said, in a way that made it clear it wasn't advice he was likely to heed. Then, hands raised Al Jolson style, he struck a pose. 'What do you think of the snazzy outfit?'

'You got a portrait painting somewhere in your attic, Dorian old buddy?'

'Just termites,' said Budd. He was in an entirely different mood now. Lots of actors are like that; they go up and down with disconcerting suddenness.

When Budd had departed I went and looked out the window. That was enough to make anyone want to buy a gun. It was indeed a lousy block. My neighbors were mostly immigrants who quickly became either entrepreneurial, destitute, or criminal. I shared this ancient office building with a debt collection agency, an insurance agent, a single mothers advisory center, and an architect. These law offices were the best in the building. Miss Huth's reception area gave onto three rooms. Mine was the only one with a white carpet, but the others had two windows each. Equipped like that they could handle two suicides at a time.

I'd moved in right after my divorce, to share expenses with two Korean immigration lawyers who had a sideline in fifty-dollar flat-fee divorces. People all said we'd never get along together, they said Koreans were combative people, but I found Billy Kim and Korea Charlie to be congenial partners. We would share our business, each passing our most trouble-some clients to the other. Then we'd compare notes and have some great laughs together. Korea Charlie was the founding member of the partnership. He was a fat old guy who knew everyone in the neighborhood and built up a colossal reputation getting green cards for local illegals. Then, just as everyone was saying that Korea Charlie was the richest, happiest lawyer in town, one of his grateful clients accidentally shot him dead during a drunken celebration in a bar in Crenshaw.

Now, apart from the token lawyer whom Petrovitch would assign to us to make the takeover legal, I had only one partner, Billy Kim, a thirty-year-old go-getter who was attending his brother's wedding in Phoenix. He'd been due back this morning, but there was no sign of him so far and no message either. Either his brother had chickened out or it was one hell of a party.

On all sides of this block were single-story buildings that in any other city would have been temporary accommodation. From ground level LA may be a paradise, but from this height it's hell. The paved backyards of these cheap boxlike buildings were littered with dented cars and pickups, and their rooftops were a writhing snakepit of air-conditioning pipes. Directly

15

across the street was a parking lot surrounded with a chain-link fence; parked up tight against the entrance, a converted panel truck was selling soft drinks, tacos, and chili dogs. Now that we were to become a part of the Petrovitch organization I was going to press them to finance for us a proper office with Muzak, up-to-date magazines in the waiting room, distressed-oak paneling, and yards of antiqued leather books behind glass doors on stained wood shelving.

I tidied my desk and reminded Miss Huth that I was going to see my son. I didn't give too much thought to the task of getting a gun for Budd. I figured by next week the desire for a gun would have worn off. Budd was like that.

I went down to the garage. That was the best facility of this ancient building: it had a lockup garage so I could come back to my car and find it complete with radio antenna and hubcaps. Since I drive a beautiful 1959 Cadillac, that means a lot to me. It was one of the reasons I came here. I wouldn't move to another building unless it had an equally dry, airy garage with someone guarding it. This one was not really subterranean, it was a semi-basement with ventilation slots that let air and daylight in. Ventilation is important for a car: condensation can do more damage than the weather, especially in California. The story was that the landlord had wanted to make this lowest floor into accommodations but the city ordinances forbade it.

When I got down there I saw Ratface talking to the janitor. They both stopped talking as I went past them. I had a strong suspicion that they were comparing my shortcomings. They watched me without speaking.

'You're still dripping oil, Mr Murphy,' the janitor called as I was getting into my car. I pretended I hadn't heard him, but as I pulled away I glanced in the mirror and could see the dark patch shining on the garage floor. Okay, so it's an old car.

*   *   *

16

My son, Daniel, is studying philosophy at USC – the University of Spoiled Children – and living with a girl named Robyna Johnson. They share an apartment in a rooming house off Melrose near Paramount Studios. Melrose is a circus, but the kids think it's smart to be near where the movies are cranked. When you reach the studios, the first thing you see is that vast rectangular slab of blue sky that is the backdrop for the Paramount water tank. And if you know where to look inside the back lot you can spot the old Paramount Gate, the most evocative landmark still left of real Hollywood. That gate is the same way it was in the old days. I never see it without remembering when Gloria Swanson's Rolls-Royce purred through it in *Sunset Boulevard*.

My son doesn't live on the posh side of Melrose. Where he lives is as bad as where I work. They have steel gratings on the liquor stores and fierce guard dogs in the hallways. When I was a kid it was an Irish area and there was a great neighborhood atmosphere, but when Grace Kelly married into Monaco, the Irish here got big ideas and bank mortgages and bought homes with pools in the Valley, and the area filled up with weeds, rust, and sprayed graffiti. I waved to Danny's landlady, Mrs Gonzales, as she dragged the curtain aside to see who it was. She was a whiskery old crone: she scowled and ducked out of sight.

Danny shared a two-room apartment on the second floor. The buzzer didn't work, so I rapped on the door with my knuckles. They were watching a game show on TV, *The Price Is Right*: I could hear it through the door. *The Price Is Right*! After all that griping these kids are always giving me about materialism.

'It's your father,' said Robyna, after she'd undone the mortise lock, slipped the bolts, and opened the door as far as the chain would allow. She stared at me for a long time before unhooking the chain to let me in. She never says, How nice to see you, or anything. I always get the same treatment: she snaps her head around, so her long, straight blonde hair swings in my face, and calls over her shoulder, 'It's your father,' in a voice marine color sergeants use to announce the arrival of incoming artillery fire.

'Hello, Robyna,' I said affably. 'Do you mind if I talk to Danny in private?' She shook out her skirt – a long cotton one with African tie-dye designs – slipped her feet into jewel-encrusted sandals, picked up her makeup box, tossed her head to make her hair shake, and strode past without looking at me. She didn't even say goodbye. 'Come back, Jane Fonda, you forgot your muesli!' I called.

'Drop dead!' she snapped over her shoulder as she flounced out and slammed the door.

'Is your girlfriend always so charming?' I asked Danny.

'I don't know,' said Danny. 'I don't tell her to get lost the way you do every time you arrive. She pays half the rent, you know.'

The TV was still going, and Danny was searching to find the remote control to turn it off. Eventually he grabbed a pair of jeans from somewhere and draped them over the screen. He just couldn't bear to switch the damned thing off: he'd always been like that about TV; he just had to have it going all the time.

'Robyna must have the remote in her pocket,' he said apologetically.

There was a smell of burning incense in the room. It had a sweet flowery smell. I sniffed here and there. Although I looked all around, I couldn't see where the smoke was coming from. 'She's not on drugs, is she?'

'You always ask me if she's doing drugs,' said Danny wearily. 'We're vegetarians.'

'So maybe she passes on red meaty drugs.'

18

'She won't even drink tea or coffee because of the caffeine. No, she's not on drugs.' His search for the remote finally forced him to get up on his feet. Under some schoolbooks he discovered two paper plates containing a half-eaten burrito and a squashed package of tofu. He gave up trying to find the TV control and sank back, dropping his weight into the sofa with spring-shattering force. He'd wrecked all the best chairs at home doing that, but I tried not to remark on it this time. I hate to fight with him.

'Is your mother here?'

'Betty?' He always called her Betty. He never said Mom or Mother even when he was small. I blamed Betty for that. She never disciplined him. That's why he was slouching here with a stubbly face, long unwashed hair, and a dirty T-shirt printed with the slogan *Go away, I'm trying to think.* 'You can see Betty's not here; I don't know where she is.'

'How would it grab you if I told you she just now forced her way into my office and climbed out onto the window ledge?'

Danny took the news very calmly. I mean, this was his mother. He nodded. 'She did that with Uncle Sean in Seattle. He called the Fire Department.'

'So did I. I called the Fire Department, but she made herself scarce before they arrived. So of course they prowled through the office trying to find ways to give me a bad time.'

'Why?' He was always unnaturally calm with me. Calm in a studied and exaggerated way so I sometimes wondered if it was an effect I had on him. With other people he always seemed more animated. Did I make him ill at ease or something?

'Why did I call the Fire Department?' I said to clarify the question.

'Why did they want to give you a bad time?'

'It's a long story. The sprinklers never did work.' The more I thought about it the more angry I became. 'Soon after we

19

first moved in, Denise – remember Denise, my old secretary, who used to send you those religious cards with St Daniel and lions on your birthday? – when Denise felt like celebrating, she used to buy those throw-away barbecue packs and grill some steaks for our lunch. It's a wonder she never set the office ablaze. A couple of times she threw out the charcoal while it was still hot and set fire to the trash. Now I come to think of it, I remember those sprinklers never did work; the whole building is like that. Why pick on me? Those firemen were out to make trouble, and that Huth woman was no help; she said no one had ever told her where the fire exits were. I'll have to get rid of her. Thank goodness she didn't discover that Betty was my ex.'

Danny looked at me solemnly. He doesn't like me referring to Betty as my ex. 'What did she want?'

'Are you kidding?' Betty only came to see me when she wanted money for something.

He pulled a face and ran his hands under the cushions as if he was still trying to find the remote.

I said, 'Have you been encouraging her?' Yes, yes, yes, of course. I should have guessed it was Danny who kept sending her around to dun me for money. They both thought I had some kind of bottomless pit replenished daily with bullion.

'She had to have two root canals done, and she needs clothes and stuff. She doesn't earn any money working for that aroma therapy workshop.'

'Look at me. Look at me. If you're going to go to bat for her, look at me.'

He looked up.

I said, 'Are you doing her accounts or something? Why doesn't she get a paying job?'

'The aromatherapy workshop is a charity. It's for poor people. No one pays. She wants to help people.'

'She wants to help people? She works for nothing and I give her money. How does that make her the one who helps people?'

'She's really a wonderful person, Dad. I wish you'd make a little more effort to try and understand her.'

'It's always my fault. Why doesn't she make an effort to try and understand me?'

'She said you're getting millions from the takeover.'

'You two live in a dream world. There are no millions and there is no takeover. You can't buy a law partnership unless you are a member of the California bar. Petrovitch picked up the pieces, that's all that happened. He simply retained our services, put in a partner, and absorbed nearly a quarter of a million dollars of debt. I told you all that.'

'She clipped a piece about Zach Petrovitch from the *Los Angeles Times* Business Section. It said in there that he'd paid a hundred million—'

'But not for my partnership. I've heard all that talk. He picked up a Chapter Eleven recording company with a few big names on the labels and sold it to the Japanese. That all happened nearly three years ago. There's been a goddamned recession since then.'

'Petrovitch only buys companies he has plans for.'

'Is this something they tell you in Philosophy One-oh-one, or did you switch to being a business major?'

'You can't keep that kind of pay off secret, Dad,' he said. 'Everyone knows.'

'Don't give me that shit, Danny. I'm your father, and I'm telling you all we got is a retainer with a small advance so I can pay off a few pressing debts. Who are you going to believe?'

'You want a beer?' He got up and went into the kitchen.

'You haven't answered the question,' I called. 'No. I don't want a beer, and you're too young to drink beer.'

'I thought it was a rhetorical question,' he called mournfully

21

from the kitchen. I heard him rattling through the cans; I don't think he'd ever thought of storing food in that icebox, just drink. 'I've got Pepsi and Diet Pepsi; I've got Sprite, Dr Pepper, and all kinds of fruit juices.'

'I don't want anything to drink. Come back here and listen to me. I'm not a philosophy major; I haven't got time to sit around talking for hours. I have to work for a living.'

I found a cane-seat chair and inspected it for food remains and parked chewing gum before sitting down. This was just the kind of chaos he'd lived in at home, like someone had thrown a concussion grenade into a Mexican fast-food counter. On the walls there were colored posters about saving the rain forest and protecting the whales. The only valuable item to be seen in the apartment was the zillion-watt amplifier that had made sure his guitar was shaking wax out of ears in Long Beach while he strummed it in Woodland Hills. Near the window there was a small table he used as a desk. There was a pile of philosophy books, an ancient laptop computer with labels stuck all over it, and a paper plate from which bright red sauce had been scraped. There was a brown bag too, the kind of insulated bag take-away counters use for hot food. I looked into it, expecting to find a tamale or a hot dog, but found myself looking at a stainless steel sandwich.

'What's this?' I said.

Danny came out of the kitchen with his can of drink and a package of non-cholesterol chili-flavored potato chips. 'It's only a gun,' he said.

'Oh, it's only a gun,' I said sarcastically, bringing it out to take a closer look at it.

It was a shiny new Browning Model 35 9-mm automatic. I pulled back the action to make sure there were no rounds in the chamber. The action remained open, and from the pristine orange-colored top of the spring I could see it was brand new.

'And what the hell are you doing with this?' I took aim at Robyna's save the whale poster and pulled the trigger a couple of times.

'Relax, Dad. I loaned a Jordanian guy in my religion class two hundred bucks. He was strapped, and instead of paying me back he gave me the shooter and a stereo.'

'You were ripped off,' I said.

'You're always so suspicious,' he said mildly. 'A gun like that costs about five hundred bucks. I can pawn it for three hundred.'

'How do you know it's not been used in a stickup or a murder?'

'His father had just bought it for him; it was still in the wrappings. So was the stereo.'

'His father bought it? What kind of dope is his father?'

'Don't keep doing that, Dad. It's not good for the mechanism.'

'What do you know about guns?' I said and pulled out the magazine and snapped it back into place a couple more times just to show him I wasn't taking orders from him. 'You're talking to a marine, remember. Have you ever fired this gun?'

'No, I haven't.'

'Budd Byron was in the office today asking me how he could buy a gun. This whole town is gun crazy these days.'

'What does he want a gun for?'

'Budd? I don't know.' I looked at the gun. It was factory-new. 'In the original wrappings, you say? In the box? Then this is part of a stolen consignment.'

'It's not stolen. I just told you I got it from a guy I know at college. He does Comparative Religion with me. Next week he'll probably want to buy it all back. He's like that. He's an Arab; he's a distant relative of Kashoggi the billionaire.'

'Do you know something? I'm still looking for some Arab in this town who is not a relative of Kashoggi. My mailman

23

mentioned that he is Kashoggi's cousin. The guy in the cleaners confided that he is Kashoggi's nephew. They're all just one big happy family.'

The TV was still muttering away: the ads are always louder than the programs. 'You're in a crumby mood today, Dad. Did something bad happen to you?'

'Something bad? Have you suddenly gone deaf or something? Your mother dropped by to throw herself out of my office window.'

'That was just a cry for help. You know that.' He ate some chips, crunching them loudly in his teeth; then, leaning his head far back, he closed his eyes and held a cold can of low-cal cranberry juice cocktail to his forehead.

He wouldn't hear a word against Betty. Sometimes I wondered if he understood that *she* walked out on *me* – walked out on *us*, rather. Yet how could I remind him of that? I said, 'Will you find out where your mother is crashing these days? If she keeps pulling these jumping-off-the-ledge routines, she'll get herself committed.'

He came awake, snapped the top off his cranberry juice, and took a deep gulp. He wiped his lips on the back of his hand and said, 'Yah, okay, Dad. I'll do what I can.'

'Tell her I'll maybe look at her dentist bills. I'll pay something toward them.'

'Hey, that's great, Dad.'

'I don't want you getting together with her and rewriting the accounts, trying to bill me for a Chanel suit or something.'

'What do you mean?' Danny said.

'You know what I mean. Do you think I've forgotten you using the graphics program on my office IBM to do that CIA letterhead that scared the bejesus out of old Mr Southgate?'

'He deserved it. I should have gotten an A in his English class. Everyone said so.'

'Well, I had to calm him down and stop him from writing to his senator. You promised you'd be sensible in future, so leave it between Betty and her dentist, will you?'

'She wouldn't gyp you, Dad.' He gently eased the gun out of my hand and put it back in the bag and put the bag in a drawer.

'Well, I've known her longer than you have, and I say she might.' I got up. 'Leave her address and phone number on my answering machine. Maybe this afternoon?' He knew where to get hold of her, I was certain of that.

He nodded and came with me to the door. 'Is our Sunday brunch still on?' he asked.

'Sure,' I said. 'The Beverly Hilton at noon. I'll get a reservation.' I gave him a hug; he was a good kid. 'You can always come and use your room again,' I told him. 'I wouldn't want rent or anything. I rattle around all alone in that house.'

'We tried it twice, Dad.' He bent down to open the door: three deadbolt locks they now had! What kind of neighborhood is that? 'Could you let me have fifty until the weekend?'

I peeled off a fifty for him. 'Don't change to being a business major,' I said. 'You're doing just great in philosophy.'

Before I drove away from Danny's place I opened the trunk of my Caddie. Hell! There should have been a case of booze there. One of the commissars in Petrovitchgrad had left a message asking me to get some wacky brand of tequila. It was for the welcome party. She was organizing the refreshments, and this poison was apparently Petrovitch's favorite drink. Miss Huth had worked her way through the yellow pages and found out a Mexican liquor store on Broadway was the only place that stocked it. They were supposed to have sent it around for the janitor to put into my trunk. I should never have trusted her with my Visa card number. Maybe it was a rip-off by the liquor store, or maybe it was the janitor. He was an unreliable bastard. Why hadn't she double-checked it?

I looked at the empty trunk like the booze would suddenly appear there but it didn't. The trunk of my lovely old gas-guzzling Caddie convertible remained empty, so there was no alternative to driving back to the office to pick it up. When I got there I swung into the entrance and down the ramp into the basement. Can you imagine it? Ratface was still there, talking with the janitor. What did they find to talk about all that time? I saw a vacant parking place nearer to the elevator than the lousy place they'd assigned to me. Ratface had parked his little car alongside it. It was a Honda Accord: a bumper sticker on it said MY OTHER CAR IS A FIRE ENGINE.

As I pressed the call button for the elevator, the janitor said, 'If you're going up for the tequila, I've got it right here for you, Mr Murphy. They delivered it this afternoon.' He kicked the carton at his feet.

'I figured you would have loaded it into my trunk,' I said. The residents all paid the guy an extra ten a month in the hope that he would be helpful. Some of them gave him more than that. He made a fortune from us.

'Ah, my back is playing up again, Mr Murphy,' he said. 'My doctor says I should be real careful about lifting and that kind of work.' He said this slowly and carefully while both of them watched me struggling under the weight of a dozen bottles of tequila. That Mexican hooch was heavy; what do they put into that poison?

I cleared space for it in the trunk and then stood up and got my breath. 'Maybe you should get a job with the Fire Department,' I said. 'You could take it easy there.' Ratface glared at me. I lifted the crate, put it into my trunk, pulled the lid down, and watched it close automatically. I loved that old Caddie; it was a part of me. The trouble was, the old lady really was dripping oil and leaving a pool of it everywhere I stopped, and the way things were at present I didn't have time enough to take her to the service station.

'And that's a parking place for the disabled,' called Ratface. I pretended not to hear him.

2

That was some bash, that party for Petrovitch. The little girl who organized it for Petrovitch Enterprises International was a professional party fixer. I didn't know there were such jobs, even in Los Angeles. She'd rented the Snake Pit for the whole evening, and that takes money. Alternating with the Portable PCs, who had an album at number three that week, there was a band playing all that corny Hawaiian music. The waitresses were dressed in grass skirts, leis, and flesh-colored bras, and one wall was almost covered with orchids flown in from Hawaii. There were dozens of miniature palm trees standing in huge decorative faience pots. The ceiling was obscured by hundreds of colored balloons; from each one dangled a silver or gold cord, the end supporting an orchid bloom, to make a shimmering ceiling of orchids just above head height.

The place was packed. I had trouble parking my Caddie. I can't get the old battle wagon into the spaces they paint for lousy little imported compacts. So I left it in a slot marked RESERVED FOR SECURITY and wrote *Mr Petrovitch* on a slip of paper that I propped behind the windshield. I didn't want my new boss screaming for his fix of special-brand tequila and me blamed for his deprivation. I heaved it out of the car, put the crate on my shoulder, and staggered across the underground parking garage to where the entrance was located. It was so crowded there were guests talking and drinking and dancing right out there on the concrete. They were waltzing around on the red carpet and through the crushed flowers that had been strewn around, and I had to push my way past them to get inside the place. I gave the crate of tequila to the bar man, got a Powers whisky with soda and ice, and started to circulate. The last thing they needed was more booze. Most of them seemed tanked up to the gills. I was frightened to strike a match in case the air exploded.

'Mickey Murphy! I saw you were on the guest list.'

The deep, lazy voice came booming from a corpulent individual named Goldie Arnez. He'd been watching two video monitors from cameras trained on the lobby to show the guests as they arrived.

'What are we tuned to, *Lifestyles of the Rich and Famous?*'

'That's about it,' he said, taking his eyes from the screen to scrutinize me carefully.

When I first met Goldie he was slim — a movie stuntman, can you imagine? We used to work out together at Gold's Gym, when there was only one Gold's Gym and it was on Second Street in Santa Monica. That was where Goldie had acquired his nickname. The stuntwork dwindled as he wrestled with the scales, and the last time I met him he was a 250-pound bail bondsman with a reputation for playing rough with the fugitives he brought in. Now he looked like he'd gone to seed: where he used to have muscles, he had flab, and there were dark rings under his eyes. Maybe I wouldn't have recognized him, except for that full head of brown wavy hair. He still had his hair — or was it a rug? In this light I couldn't decide. 'What are you doing nowadays, Goldie?'

'You don't know?'

'No, I don't know. Would I be asking you if I knew already?'

'That's my Mickey,' he said. 'You say good morning to the guy, and you get maimed in a riot.'

'Cut it out, Goldie.'

'I'm muscle for Mr Petrovitch.'

'You're what?'

'Don't be that way. You might need a buddy who can put in a good word with the man at the top.'

'Muscle?' I could see it wasn't all flab; the bulge under his armpit had square edges.

'I run a team of twenty.'

'Does Petrovitch need twenty bodyguards?'

'I'm not a bodyguard. I have guys to do the day-to-day work. I'm head of security for Petrovitch Enterprises International. I'm responsible for the vice presidents and everything in the continental U.S. It's a big job.' He gave me one of his business cards.

I looked at it and put it in my pocket. 'Is that why you're drinking Pepsi?'

'Mr Petrovitch cracks down on drinking by staff on duty. He'll tell you that.'

'I might find that a little difficult to adjust to,' I said.

'Not after Mr Petrovitch has talked to you, you won't.' Goldie took a sip of his cola and looked me over. 'It's the cost. When he takes over a company he strips all the surplus fat from it and makes it into a lean and trim earnings machine.' Goldie looked at me as he said it with relish. It sounded like something he'd read in a prospectus, and I didn't like it. And what kind of lean and trim earnings machine was Goldie?

'You want to lend me your phone, Goldie?' I said, eyeing the cellular clipped to his belt. 'I need to get hold of my partner in Phoenix. I'll call collect.'

'Haven't you got a phone in your car?' said Goldie.

'Are you crazy? I drive a beautiful 'fifty-nine Caddie with the original interior and paintwork. I don't want some guy drilling holes in her and bolting phones and batteries into the bodywork.'

30

'There's a phone upstairs,' said Goldie. 'Come with me, or you won't get past my security guys.'

Goldie led the way to a messy little office with a fax machine and word processors and a bulletin board displaying half a dozen bounced checks, a buy-one-get-one-free coupon from Pizza Hut, and a signed photo of Arnold Schwarzenegger. He lingered out in the hallway for a moment. I thought he was being discreet and allowing me a little privacy, but I should have known better. He came right in.

'Make your call and let's get out of here.' He seemed to disapprove of my looking around the place, but that was just my natural curiosity.

I sat down behind the desk, picked up the phone, and was about to start hitting the buttons when I noticed there was an extra wire coming from the phone and going into a hole freshly drilled in the desktop, a hole marked by a trace of sawdust. 'Goldie,' I said, 'you got a scrambler on this phone or something? What's this wiring deal? Are you bugging someone's calls?'

'Don't hit that button!' he barked, showing an alarm in sharp contrast to his previous doleful demeanor. 'Stay where you are. Put the phone down on the desk and let me come round there.' He grabbed me by the shoulder as I got to my feet. Then he grabbed the scissors from the desk and cut all wires leading to the phone.

'What is it?'

'Jesus!' said Goldie, talking to himself as if he'd not heard me. 'The bastards!'

'Is it a bomb?'

'You bet it is,' said Goldie. He followed the wires that went through the desk and kneeled down on the floor under it. I crouched down to see it too. He tapped a brown paper package that had been fixed to the underside of the desk. 'See that?

There's enough plastic there to blow us both into hamburger,' said Goldie. Carefully he stripped the sticky tape from the woodwork and revealed the detonators. It looked as if he had done such things before. 'Maybe it was set to make a circuit when triggered by the buttons, or maybe it was one of those tricky ones that detonate with an incoming call.'

'What's it all about, Goldie?'

'Say an extra prayer when you go to mass tomorrow morning,' said Goldie. He was still under the desk fiddling with the bomb. 'Go back downstairs and circulate. I can deal with this.'

'Are you sure you don't want the bomb squad?'

His glowering face appeared above the desktop. 'Not a word about this to anyone, Mickey. If a story like this got into the papers, the shares would take a beating and I'd pay for it with my job.'

'Whatever you say.' I decided to leave my call to Phoenix for some other time and went back to the party for another drink. I could see why Goldie was so jumpy about publicity. The media crowd was well in evidence. Some of them I recognized, including two local TV announcers: the guy with the neat mustachio who does the morning show and the little girl with the elaborate hairdo who stands in for the weatherman on the local segment of the network news. They were standing near their cameras, paper napkins tucked into their collars like ruffs and their faces caked with makeup.

The one I was looking around for was Mrs Petrovitch. When I knew her we were both at Alhambra High, struggling with high school mathematics and preparing for college. High school friends are special, right? More special than any other kind of friends. In those days she was Ingrid Ibsen. I was in love with her. Half the other kids were in love with her too, but I dated her on account of the way she lived near me and I could always walk her home, and her dad knew my dad and did his accounts.

She lived only a block from me on Grenada. We used to walk down Main Street together, get a Coke and fries, and I'd think of something I had to buy in the five-and-dime just to make it last longer.

In my last year Ingrid was the lead in the senior play and I had a tap dance solo in the all-school production of *The Music Man*. I remember that final night: I danced real well. It was my last day of high school. It was a clear night with lots of stars and a big moon so you could see the San Gabriel Mountains. Dad let me have the new Buick. We were parked outside her house. I'd got my scholarship and a place at USC. I told her that as soon as I graduated I was going to come back and marry her. She laughed and said, 'Don't promise' and put her finger on my lips. I always remembered the way she said that: 'Don't promise.'

Ingrid spent only one semester at college. She was smarter than I was at most subjects, and she could have got a B.A. easily, but her folks packed up and went to live in Chicago and she went with them. I never did get the full story, but the night she told me she was going, we walked around the neighborhood and I didn't go home to bed until it was getting light. Then I had a fight with my folks, and the following day I stormed off and joined the Marine Corps. Kidlike, I figured I'd have to go to 'Nam eventually and it was better to get it over with. Now I've learned to put the bad ones at the bottom of the pile and hope they never show up. It was a crazy move because I was looking forward to going to college and almost never had arguments with my folks. And anyway, what does joining the service do to solve anything? It just gives you a million new and terrible problems to add to your old ones.

The next I heard of Ingrid was when her photo was in the paper. Budd Byron, who'd known us both at Alhambra, sent me an article that had been clipped from some small-town paper. It was a photo of Ingrid getting married. That was her first husband, some jerk from the sticks, long before she got hitched to Zachary Petrovitch. It said they'd met at a country dancing class. I ask you! I kept the clipping in my billfold for months. They were going to Cape Cod for their honeymoon, it said. Can you imagine anything more corny? Every time I looked at that picture it made me feel sorry for myself.

Soon after I met Betty, I ceremonially burned that clipping. As the ashes curled over and shimmered in the flames I felt liberated. The next day I went down to Saturn and Sun, the alternative medicine pharmacy where Betty worked, and asked her to marry me. As a futile exercise in self-punishment it sure beat joining the Marine Corps.

Then in the eighties I heard about Ingrid again when she upped and married Petrovitch. I knew the Petrovitch family by name; I'd even met Zach Petrovitch a few times. His father had made money from Honda dealerships in the Northwest, getting into them when they were giving them away, a time when everyone was saying the Japanese can maybe make cheap transistor radios, and motor bikes even, but cars?

The first time I met Petrovitch Junior he was with his father, who was guest of honor at an Irish orphanage's charity dinner in New York. I guess that was before he knew Ingrid. At the end of the evening a few of us, including Zach, cut away to a bar in the Village. The music was great, and we all sank a lot of Irish whiskey. Petrovitch passed out in the toilet and we had a lot of trouble getting him back to the Stanhope, where he was staying. Cabs are leery of stopping for a group of men carrying a 'corpse,' and the ones that do stop, argue. I got into a fist fight with a cabbie from County Cork; it wasn't serious, just an amiable bout with an overweight driver who wanted to stretch his legs. When I told him we were coming from the Irish orphanage benefit, he took us to the hotel and wouldn't accept the fare money. The crazy thing was that when Petrovitch recovered someone told him I'd strong-armed the cabbie to take him that night. I suppose Petrovitch felt he owed me something. I never did explain it to him.

I moved over to the bar to sneak a look at Ingrid. She was standing with her husband at the end of the red carpet, welcoming guests as they arrived. I studied her through the palm tree fronds, making sure she didn't see me. She looked as beautiful as ever. Her hair was still very blonde, almost white, but cut shorter now. She had on a long black moiré dress with black embroidery on the bodice and around the hem. With it she wore a gold necklace and a fancy little wrist-watch. I watched her laughing with an eager group of sharp-suited yuppies who were shaking paws with her husband. Seeing her laugh reawakened every terrible pang of losing her. It brought back that night sitting in the Buick when the idea of being married was something I didn't have to promise. To hear that laugh every day; I would have sold my soul for that. So you can see why I didn't go across to say hello to them. I didn't want to be shoulder to shoulder with those jerks when talking with her. It was better to see her from a distance and shuffle through my memories.

'Hello, Mickey. I thought you might be here,' chirruped the kind of British accent that sounds like running your fingernails across a blackboard. I turned to see a little British lawyer named Victor Crichton. He was about forty, with the cultivated look that comes with having a company that picks up the tab for everything. His suit was perfect, his face was tanned, and his hair wavy and long enough to hide the tops of his ears.

'Oh, it's you,' I said, in my usual suave and sophisticated way. Vic Crichton's boss was Sir Jeremy Westbridge, the client who was giving me ulcers. His affairs were in such desperate disarray that I could hardly bear to open my mail in the morning.

'Did I make you jump, old chap? Awfully sorry.' He'd caught me off guard; I suppose I looked startled. He gave a big smile and then reached out for the arm of the woman at his side. 'This is Dorothy, the light of my life, the woman who holds the keys to my confidential files.' He hiccuped softly. 'Figuratively speaking.'

I said, 'That's okay, Victor. Hi there, Dorothy. I was just thinking.'

'Wow! Don't let me interrupt anything like that!' He winked at the woman he was with and said, 'Mickey is Sir Jeremy's attorney on the West Coast.'

'Pleased to meet you,' she said. His wife was British too.

'It sounds good the way you say it, Vic. But we've got to talk.' I was hoping to make him realize the danger he was in. It wasn't just a matter of business acumen, they were going to be facing charges of fraud and God knows what else.

'He's really an Irish stand-up comic,' Vic explained to the woman, 'but you have to set a comic to catch a comic in this part of the world. Right, Mickey?'

'I've got to talk to you, Vic,' I said quietly. 'Is Sir Jeremy here? We've got to do something urgently.'

He made no response to this warning. 'Always together. Dean Martin and Jerry Lewis, Lennon and McCartney, Vic Crichton and Sir Jeremy. Partners.'

'They all broke up,' I said.

'I wondered if you'd spot that,' said Vic. 'Split up or dead. But not us; not yet, anyway. Look for yourself.'

He waved a hand in the direction of the bar, where I spotted the lean and hungry-looking Sir Jeremy. He was a noticeable figure: very tall, well over six feet, with white hair and a pinched face. He was engaged in earnest conversation with a famous local character called the Reverend Dr Rainbow Stojil, a high-profile do-gooder for vagrants who liked to be seen on TV and at parties like this. I guessed that Stojil was trying to get a donation from him. Stojil was famous for his money-raising activities.

'Don't interrupt them,' advised Vic.

'Why not?' I said. 'We've got to have a meeting.' Vic didn't reply. He was drunk. I wasn't really expecting a sensible answer.

Vic and his master were well matched. They were as crooked as you can get without ski masks and sawed-off shotguns. They called themselves property developers. Their cemeteries became golf courses; their golf courses became leisure centers, and leisure centers became shopping malls and offices. They had moved slowly and legally at first but success seemed to affect their brains, because lately they just didn't care what laws they broke as long as the cash came rolling in.

'Look,' I said. 'The game's up with all this shit. I know for a fact that an investigation has begun. It's just a matter of time before Sir Jeremy is arrested. I can't hold them off forever.'

'How long *can* you hold them off, old boy?'

He wasn't taking me seriously. 'I don't know, not long. One, two, three weeks . . . it's difficult to say.'

He prodded me in the chest. 'Make it three weeks, old buddy.' He laughed.

'Look, Vic, either we sit down and talk and make a plan that I can offer to them—'

'Or what?' he said threateningly.

I took a deep breath. 'Or you can get yourselves a new lawyer.'

He blinked. 'Now, now, Mickey. Calm down.'

'I mean it. You find yourself a new boy. Some guy who likes fighting the feds and the whole slew of people you've crossed. A trial lawyer.'

'If that's the way you feel, old boy,' he said and touched me on the shoulder in that confident way that trainers pat a rottweiler.

Maybe he thought I was going to retract, but he was wrong. With that decision made, I already felt a lot better. 'I'll get all the papers and everything together. You tell me who to pass it to. How long are you staying in town?'

'Not long.' He held up his champagne and inspected it as if for the Food and Drug Administration. 'We've come to hold hands with Petrovitch about a joint company we're forming in Peru. Then I'm off for a dodgy little argument with some bankers in Nassau and back to London for Friday. Around the world in eight hotel beds: it's all go, isn't it, Dot?'

'What about Sir Jeremy?'

'Good question, old man. Let's just say he has a date with Destiny. He's modeling extra-large shrouds for Old Nick.' He held out a hand to the wall to steady himself. Any minute now he was going to fall over.

'What do you mean?' I said, watching his attempt to regain equilibrium.

'Don't overdo it, old sport.' He put his arm around my shoulder and leaned his head close to whisper. 'You don't have to play the innocent with me. I'm the next one to go.'

'Go where?'

'You *are* the one arranging it, aren't you?' His amiable mood was changing to irritation, as is the way with drunks when they become incoherent. 'You buggers are being paid to fix it.' He closed his eyes as if concentrating his thoughts. His lips moved but the promised words never came.

'I think we're boring your wife, Victor,' I said, in response to the flamboyant way she was patting her open mouth with her little white hand.

'Victor always gets drunk,' she said philosophically. She didn't look so sober herself. She'd drained her champagne and experimentally pushed the empty glass into a palm tree and left it balanced miraculously between the fronds.

Victor didn't deny his condition. 'Banjaxed, bombed, bug-eyed, and bingoed,' he said without slurring his words. 'Wonderful town, lavish hospitality, and vintage champagne. Very rare nowadays . . .' He drawled to a stop like a clockwork toy that needed rewinding.

'Better if you don't drive,' I advised him. At least he didn't call it Tinseltown, the way some of them did.

'Dot will drive,' said Vic. 'She's wonderful in the driving seat, aren't you, Dotty? Unless we can find a motel, that is.' He slapped her rear gently, and she bared her teeth in an angry smile. He finished his champagne. 'I think I need another drink, a real drink this time.'

'You've had enough, Vic. We've got to go,' she said.

She took him by the arm, and he allowed himself to be guided away. 'When you've got to go, you've got to go. Right, Mickey, my old lovely?'

'Sure,' I said. 'See you around, Victor. 'Bye, Dot.' He turned and, with one hand on her buttocks, shepherded her toward the bar. I wondered if he knew that Petrovitch had put a partner into my law business. If not, this didn't seem to be the right time to discuss it. Victor waved a splay-fingered hand in the air. He didn't look back. He seemed to know I'd be watching him go and calculating how much I was going to lose in fees next year. Oh, well, I hate crooks. I should never have become a lawyer.

The reception line was still going, but people were no longer coming through the door. This was a celebration for employees and associates, and these guests didn't come late to a Petrovitch bash if they knew what was good for them. I decided to get a closer look at Peter the Great, whom someone seemed so keen to murder, and inched my way across the room to where the

39

bright lights and TV cameras had been arranged just in case Petrovitch deigned to step over and tell the hushed American public the secret of making untold millions of dollars while still looking young and beautiful enough to run for President. He was dressed in a dark blue silk tuxedo with a frilly blue shirt, floppy bow tie, and patent shoes with gold buckles. He had a loose gold bracelet and lots of gold rings and a thin gold watch on a thin gold bracelet: more jewelry than his wife, in fact. He was tall and well-built and didn't look as if he'd need the help of Goldie or any of his muscle men to look after himself. His face was bronzed and clear, almost like the skin of a young woman, and his eyes were blue and active, moving as if he was expecting physical attack. Maybe Goldie had told him about the bomb in the phone.

As I got near the people thronging around him, the thin elderly man at his side said, 'And this is Mr Murphy of the law partnership downtown.'

'Mickey!' said Petrovitch. 'It's a long time.' He extended his hand and gave me a firm pumping shake while grabbing my elbow in his other hand. It was another of those Hollywood handshakes, and with it he gave me a Hollywood smile and that very very sincere Hollywood stare too. I wonder if he did it the same way in New York. 'How are tricks, buddy?'

'What a memory you've got,' I said.

'You fighting the taxi driver, to make him take me to the hotel? How could I forget?' Another big smile. 'You drank me under the table. It doesn't happen often.' The thin elderly sidekick smiled too, both men operated by the same machinery.

'Just hold it like that!' It was a photographer crouching down low to sight up one of those shots that make tycoons look statuesque.

'It's okay,' Petrovitch told me, indicating the photographer.

'He's one of our people.' With that comforting reassurance, he grabbed my hand again and held it still so it didn't blur, while turning his head away from me to give the camera a big smile. A flash captured this contrived moment for history.

'Murphy,' I heard the elderly man tell the photographer. 'Mickey: business associate and old Marine Corps friend.' The photographer wrote it down.

The thin elderly man smiled, and a gentle pressure upon the small of my back propelled me out of the shot as another business associate and old friend of Mr Petrovitch was given the handshake and smile treatment.

With the benediction still ringing in my ears, I shuffled off through the crush. I saw Goldie standing guard just a few paces away. He met my eyes and grinned. That guy really earned his salary, judging by the matter-of-fact way he defused bombs. Wondering how often such things happened to them, I went to the bar and got another whisky. 'Old Marine Corps friend.' What was that guy talking about? I looked around. This wasn't really a party, it was a press call with drinks and music. Petrovitch had the clean-cut film-star image and the rags-to-riches story that America loves. Tonight he was showing once again that he knew exactly how to turn a few thousand dollars' worth of tax-deductible entertaining into a message to his stockholders that sent his prices soaring when the rest of the market was struggling to keep afloat.

'Did you get your press kit?' A pretty girl in a striped leotard tried to hand me a bulky packet while her companion offered me a pink-colored flute of champagne.

I declined both. 'I'm drinking,' I said, holding my whisky aloft.

'Everyone has to have champagne,' said the girl, pushing the glass into my free hand. 'It's to toast Mr Petrovitch's health and prosperity.'

41

'Oh, in that case . . .' I said. I took it, held it up, and poured it into a pot where miniature palms were growing.

The girls gulped, smiled, and moved on. Dealing with folks who don't want to drink to the health and prosperity of Mr Petrovitch had not been part of the training schedule.

'I saw you do that, Mickey.'

I looked up; it was Ingrid Petrovitch, née Ibsen, standing on the rostrum behind me. She looked ravishingly beautiful, just the way she'd been in my fevered high school dreams. She gave me a jokey scowl and waved a finger, the way she'd done back in those long-ago days when I'd pulled up at night in my father's car and suggested we climb into the back seat.

'Hello, Ingrid,' I said. It sounded dumb and I felt stupid, the way some people do feel when confronted by someone they love too much. I'd always been a klutz like that when I was with her: I never did figure out why.

'Hello, Mickey,' she said, very softly. 'It's lovely to think that some things never change.' She turned away and kept moving to where a line had formed to get a smile from her husband.

'Ingrid . . .'

She stopped. 'Yes, Mickey?'

'It's good to see you again.'

She smiled sweetly and moved on. I guess she was telling me I'd had my chance with her and blew it. And that was long ago. It was nice of her not to say it.

3

I drove back from the Petrovitch bash with a lot of worries on my mind. The Ventura Freeway, U.S. 101, runs west to Woodland Hills but it doesn't run far enough or fast enough, because when you get there you might as well never have left the city.

When we first went to live in Woodland Hills it was a village. Betty loved it. It was country-style living, she said, a great place to bring up children. A village, did I say? Now it's got all your user-unfriendly banks, plastic fast food, international high-rise hotels with atriums and shopping malls with floors made from Italian marble, indoor palm trees, and fountains with colored lights, not to mention vagrants sleeping out-doors in cardboard boxes.

They say this is a early-go-to-bed town, so who are all these guys doing the Freeway 101 assignment in the small hours? Newly waxed Porsches, dented Mazdas, Chevy pickups, stretch Caddies with dark glass and TV antennas – who are these guys? Tell me. That journey home took me the best part of an hour, crawling along in a pox of red lights. I tuned in to the news on the car radio. It was a litany of violence: a decomposing corpse found in a closet in Newport Beach, a liquor store stickup in Koreatown, a drive-by killing in Ramparts, and if that wasn't enough you could join the crowds in Westwood flocking to see a movie about a cannibalistic serial killer. That's show business?

As I got near my house I saw blue-colored flashes illuminating the trees. Uh-huh? There were two black-and-whites parked on my frontage. One of them still had the beacon revolving and its doors open.

I drove up and parked on my ramp. As I stopped and lowered the window, a young nervous cop came at me out of the darkness waving a handgun. 'Are you the resident here?' He was a thin kid – straight out of the Police Academy, unless I'm very much mistaken – growing a straggly mustache to make himself look old enough to buy a beer without flashing ID.

'You got it, kid. You want to point that thing away from me?'

'Mr Murphy?' He looked up as the second car started up and pulled away.

'That's right.' As I said it, another cop arrived panting from somewhere behind my house. He was a plump old fellow with his pistol in his hand. He was oriental-looking. You don't get many oriental cops, do you? Hispanics, yes; black guys, even; but how many Asian cops do you see?

'What's going on?' I asked. I went to the door and got out my keys.

'There was a prowler,' said the plump one. 'A neighbor called it in. Saw someone in your yard. Do you want to go inside and see if he got entry?'

'Confucius say, Cop with gun go first,' I told him.

Before anyone could go anywhere there was the sound of a nearby door catch, and the prowler light illuminated the doorstep of my next-door neighbor, Henry Klopstock. He'd come out to watch. He was some kind of English teacher at UCLA. His wife liked to call him Professor Klopstock. 'Is everything okay, Mr Murphy?' He was leaning across the orange trees, the flashing lights illuminating his lined face and five-o'clock

44

shadow and his slicked-down hair. When my son was dating the Klopstock daughter he was all smiles and Hello, Mickey. Then they split up – you know the way kids are – and suddenly he's giving me the 'Mr Murphy' syntax.

'Sure it is. Didn't you hear the sirens? I always have a police escort now I'm running for mayor.'

'Okay, okay. Sorry I asked,' he said. I saw him exchange rolling eye glances with the Asian cop. So why ask dumb questions, right?

I went up the path and unlocked my front door and waited while the fat one stepped past me into the entry. Rex, my terrier, suddenly awoke and came scampering from the kitchen to growl at both of us.

'It's me, Rex,' I said.

Rex crouched very low, crawled around, and watched resentfully. The cop looked at me, looked at Rex, and then stepped over him to jab the kitchen door with his nightstick. It moved just a little, but his second jab made the door open all the way. 'Mind my paintwork, buddy,' I said. 'Try a little tenderness, like the song says.'

There was no one there, just the little safety lights that switch on automatically when it gets dark. He went from room to room, all through the house. I followed him. It wasn't really a search and he didn't do it like in the movies; he wasn't agile enough. He knew there was no one there, and he was determined to make me feel bad about making him do it. He just plodded around, puffing, sighing, and tapping the furniture with his baton. He wound up inspecting the stuff I've got decorating all the walls. Broadway posters and signed eight-by-ten glossies of the stars. My dad left me his collection, and I added to it. It goes back to *Show Boat*. Forgive me, Dad; it goes back to *Rose Marie*. It's the greatest. My dad got signed photos of everyone from Cole Porter to Ethel Merman.

45

The cop inspected these pictures and posters without enthusiasm. 'Seems like your intruder didn't get in.' He said it like he was consoling me.

'Is that your professional opinion?' I said.

Having studied the titles of my books, the level of my whisky, the corn flakes supply, and the big colored photo of Danny that's on the breakfast counter, he turned to me, gave a grin, and hitched both thumbs into his gun belt. 'That's right. You can rest your head on your pillow tonight and enjoy untroubled sleep.'

'You must be the poet who writes for the fortune cookies,' I said.

He smiled. 'Just tickets.'

'For the police charity concert?' I said. 'Who are you having this year—'

'Yah, Miss Demeanor Washington and Felonious Monk,' he interrupted me. 'That's getting to be a tired old joke, Mr Murphy.'

I knew he was just trying to make me feel bad about having him go inside first. But what is a cop paid to do anyway? Don't get me wrong; I like cops but not at the fold of a tough day, right? And not when they are doing a Lennie Bernstein with their nightstick.

'Just you living in the house, Mr Murphy?'

'You got it.'

'Big place for just one person.'

'No, it's just the right size. Listen, wise guy, I've put this mansion on the market four times in a row with three different real estate dummies in different-colored blazers. Three times it went into escrow, and three times the deal fell apart. What else would you like to know?'

'Nothing,' said the cop. 'You explicated it just fine.' I followed him outside. Explicated: what kind of a word is that?

46

We were standing out front smelling the orange trees, and I was remembering that if I roust these guys too much they might Breathalyze me, so I was taken suddenly good-natured: smiling and saying good night and thank you, and without any kind of warning there comes a noise and a scuffle as some dumb jerk of a burglar jumps out of my best bougainvillea and runs down the side alley.

It was damned dark. The plump cop didn't hesitate for a second. He was off after him and moving with amazing speed for his age and weight and leg length. I couldn't see a thing in the darkness but I followed on as best I could, clearly hearing the clattering sounds of their feet and then the loud and fierce creak of my back fence as first the perpetrator and then the cop vaulted over it into my neighbor's yard. Behind me, I heard the scratchy sounds of voices on the police radio: the second cop was calling for backup. Then he changed his mind and said they were okay. What did he know? He was in the car with the heater on.

The fugitive was scrambling across the backyards to the street on the other side of the block. I knew the scam. Some other perp would be arriving there in a car to pick him up. The newspapers kept saying it had become a popular modus operandi for these suburban break-in artists. The papers said the cops should be countering it with random patrols and better intelligence work. Those newspaper guys know everything, right? Sometimes I wonder why these guys and gals writing in the newspaper don't take over the whole world and make it faultless like them.

Bam! Now I heard the noise of someone blundering into my neighbor's elaborate barbecue setup. Crash, crunch, and clatter; there go the grills and irons, the gas bottle thumps to the ground, and finally the tin trays are making a noise like a collapsing xylophone.

'*Owwwww . . . errrrrr!*'

I stood there hoping it marked the perpetrator's downfall, but the cry had the tenor trill of the plump cop. 'Watch out!' I shouted as loud as I could shout, but I was too late. Even before I reached the fence there was an almighty splash and another cry of anguish with a lot of shouting and gurgling.

The other cop, the young thin one, came rushing over to me with his gun drawn. He looked at the fence. 'What happened?'

'Sounds like your partner went into my neighbor's pool.'

'Holy cow,' he said quietly and glared at me. 'You son of a bitch, you let him do that?'

'Don't look at me,' I said. 'It's a pool, not a booby trap. We didn't dig it out in secret and cover it with leaves and twigs.'

'Are you all right, Steve?' he called into the darkness. I could hear his partner wading through the water.

There was the sound of a man climbing onto dry land. 'The bastard got away.' The half-drowned voice was low and breathless as he came back along the alley and opened my neighbor's side gate. Shoes slapped water; he was wringing it from his shirt. More water flooded off him as he squeezed his pants and continued cursing. He came very close to me, as if he was going to get violent: he smelled strongly of the pool chemicals that cut the algae back.

'You'd better come in and dry off,' I said. My neighbor was nowhere to be seen and all his lights were out. Professor Klopstock certainly knew when to make himself scarce.

'Why don't you drop dead?' he replied. You'd think they would have been mad at my neighbor, but the wet one was acting like I'd switched off the pool lights and lured him on.

'We'll get back to the precinct house,' the dry one said. 'We're off duty in thirty minutes.'

'Suit yourself,' I said. Now that we were standing in the dim antiprowler light from my porch, I saw how wet he was. Up to his waist he was soaked, but his shoulders were only partly wet. He must have gone in at the shallow end, where all the toys and the inflated yellow alligator are floating, and recovered his balance before going under.

'I should book you, smart-ass,' said the wet one.

Book me? 'What for?'

'Disorderly conduct,' he said.

'Next time you take a midnight dip,' I said, 'don't count on me for the kiss of life.'

'And next time you get burglarized, drop a dime to your interior decorator,' he said. I guess he was mad that I'd told him not to chip my paintwork.

They both got into the black-and-white, with the wet one moving carefully, and drove away. Once they'd sailed off into the night I went inside, poured myself a drink, sank down on the sofa, and kicked off my shoes. With a picture window in this town, who needs television? I looked around me; I should make more serious efforts to sell the house. Maybe if we swung a new office from Petrovitch I could rent a small service apartment somewhere nearby. If I could find a place real close, I could leave my car parked at the office. Why hadn't I sold years ago? I knew the answer. This is the house where I'd been happy. Betty had brought Danny back here from the hospital, and everything in the house reminded me of those days. Under the dining room table were two cardboard boxes containing ornaments and chinaware. When Betty first left me I decided to move out right away and started packing up the breakable stuff. But it was a dispiriting task and I soon gave up. Now the half-filled boxes were just collecting dust under a dining table I never used. I had to do something about my life; it was a mess.

What a tacky day I'd had. And then, just to make it complete, the phone gets up on its hind legs and warbles at me. 'Is that you, Mickey?' said a voice I recognized.

'No, it's his valet. I'll put you through to the solarium.'

'This is Goldie,' he said. 'Goldie Arnez.'

'Yeah, I knew which one it was,' I told him. 'I haven't got a confusingly large number of acquaintances named Goldie.'

'You slipped away without my seeing you go.'

'Did I? I do that sometimes, when the hands are creeping toward the witching hour and I've swallowed too many of those sharp little sticks they spear the cocktail wieners on.'

'Mr Petrovitch wants to talk with you.'

'Put him on.'

A polite little chuckle. 'Tomorrow. Nine A.M. sharp. At Camarillo airport. Bring all the papers concerning Vic Crichton's deal with the British lord. The British companies and all.'

'Camarillo?'

'It's a short drive down the freeway, Mickey. And at that time of day you should have the westbound side all to yourself.'

'I would have thought a rich guy like that would have a hangar in John Wayne or Santa Monica, some place with a fancy restaurant.'

'I got news for you. Rich guys like that have a chef right on the plane, cooking them all the fancy food they can eat.'

'In the main building? Where will I find him?'

'There's no main building. You'll spot his limo: white with tinted glass. Just make sure you bring the papers, like I said.'

'I'm not sure I can do that. Those papers concern a client. There is a matter of confidentiality involved.'

'Just bring the files.'

'Like I'm telling you, Goldie. This is a matter of confidentiality, client-attorney confidentiality.'

'Are you getting senile amnesia or something? One of the Petrovitch holding companies now owns your whole bailiwick. Remember, old buddy?'

'That makes no difference in law. You can't buy a law practice.

50

All that's happened is that we've taken on a new partner of Mr Petrovitch's choosing. And I haven't even met him yet.'

'You play it any way you choose, Mickey. You were always a maverick. But if I were in your shoes I'd be at Camarillo airport with my notebook under my arm and my pencil sharpened.'

'I'll have to think about it.' I was already thinking about it, and my thoughts were negative. That stuff went a long way back. Take the notebooks: Denise had filled them with that impenetrable shorthand of hers. Who knows what any of us might have said in some of those brainstorming sessions?

'Yes, you think about it,' said Goldie. 'But don't talk to Crichton or Lord Westbridge or any of their people. Got it?'

'Did Petrovitch tell you to insert that clause into this tacky ultimatum of yours?'

'It's not an ultimatum.' Then he amended it. 'But, yes. As a matter of fact, Mickey, yes, he did.'

'Tell him to get lost,' I said.

'I won't relay that message. You be there in the morning, and if you still feel the same way you'll be able to tell him in person.'

'Okay.'

He was reluctant to hang up; he wasn't sure he'd threatened me enough. 'Better still, what say we meet in Tommy's on Ventura? Do you still go there for breakfast?'

'Sometimes.'

'Seven-thirty?'

'Okay,' I said. I guess Goldie wanted time enough to send the hounds after me if I didn't show up.

'Sleep on it, Mickey. If you want to talk to me anytime at all, day or night, the eight hundred number on the card I gave you is my cellular phone.'

'Thanks.' Goldie was the only man I knew with his own personal eight hundred number.

'You'll see reason,' said Goldie.

When I'd sipped a little more of my whisky I had a sudden inspiration. I went to my dressing room – it's a walk-in closet, really – and to the place where my personal safe is hidden behind a locked panel. My heavy-duty fireproof-steel money box was alive and well and locked up tight. There was nothing in it that could be of much value to a thief. There were my insurance papers, the deeds of the house, and a dozen or so three-and-a-half-inch floppies that I copied from my computer each week and brought back for safekeeping. But now that I looked again at it, a closer inspection revealed faint gray streaks along the edge of the wooden outer panel. I couldn't think of any way those marks could have got there – I don't let the cleaning lady come into the dressing room – so maybe the intruder had got inside. Maybe he'd just started on the combination lock when my neighbor's 911 call had interrupted him. The sort of intruder who goes housebreaking equipped with watchmaker's tools would have brought with him a police scanner to monitor the call and would have got out before the black-and-white arrived. Maybe he'd stayed outside, stayed real still, hoping everyone would go away before his pal came to collect him. Wow! So who's been eating my grandmother?

I twirled the combination lock, opened the door of the safe, and looked inside. My stomach turned over. Flopped on top of a bundle of papers was an ugly brown withered hand, a severed hand. I jumped back like it was going to bite me. I looked again. There it was, like a huge tarantula poised to strike. It made me want to vomit. A hand! In a foolish and useless gesture I pushed the safe door closed while I went and got a flashlight from the garage.

With the light I could see right into the safe. Now that the light was shining on it I could see it was a glove, a heavy-duty protective glove used in factories and warehouses. I pulled the

52

papers forward, holding papers and glove under the ceiling light to see it better. It was a leather glove, bent, battered, and whitened in use, the kind that might have been rescued from some industrial garbage bin. Even now it took me a moment or two before I could touch it. It seemed to be pulsating with life, but then I realized my hand was trembling. There was no message with it, but it was just the kind of prank that Goldie would pull on a guy who might not at first see reason.

This was getting a little too rich for my diet. I flipped open my notebook and called the Century Plaza, where Vic Crichton was staying. They put the call through to his suite and it was answered immediately. I said, 'Can I speak to Vic?'

'He's not here. This is Mrs Crichton. What is it about?'

'Dorothy, this is Mickey. We were talking tonight, remember? I know Victor was pretty smashed but drag him out of bed and order some coffee from room service, honey. We've got to talk.'

'My name is not Dorothy. This is Mrs Crichton, and I've just arrived from London, and I'm waiting for him to get back. Who is this?'

Shit! All these British voices sound the same to me, especially after a long day at the office. 'Murphy. I'm Sir Jeremy's West Coast attorney. I'll call again when you've had a chance to settle in.'

'You say you saw Victor tonight?'

'No. I mean, it must have been someone else. It looked very like him, but it gets crowded at the health club, and I was in the pool with the chlorinated water getting in my eyes.'

'I planned to surprise him,' said Mrs Crichton. 'But there are no messages here, and the office number I have doesn't answer.'

Surprise him; she'd do that, all right, and surprise his girl-friend too if they both went back to his hotel. 'I'm sure he'll show up,' I said. 'Will you ask him to phone Murphy? Tell him it's a matter of life or death.'

'Life or death?'

'I'm exaggerating,' I readily admitted. 'This is Southern California; everything is a bit larger than life around here. And a bit smaller than death.'

'I'll tell him.'

'Thank you, Mrs Crichton.'

I hung up, and then I began worrying whether some bastard had tapped my phone. I would have unscrewed the handset and looked for a hidden microphone, the way they do in movies, except that this was a Japanese phone with a handset of welded plastic.

'What should I do about the paperwork, Rex?' I said, but Rex had disappeared. He always was a go-to-bed-early kind of dog.

I felt like going to bed too, but the Westbridge files, three boxes of them, were in my downtown office, some twenty-five miles away. And Camarillo was forty miles in the other direction. Why did I pick up that lousy phone? Why didn't I let Goldie leave his messages on my answering machine?

I had to have something to show that bastard Petrovitch. I mean, I wasn't in a position to tell him to drop dead. When the deal went through and my check was cashed then maybe it would be different, but not right now. Goldie was right; no matter about the fine print, the fact was that Petrovitch owned me and the whole kit and caboodle. Maybe the written record was secret, but all those sheets of paper, on which it was typed or written, were owned by him. So what did I do? I went and climbed back into my Caddie.

By four o'clock in the morning I was sitting in my office sorting out all the Westbridge stuff with a big industrial-size shredder at my side. It was spooky in that place in the dead of night. In the street there were some strange people patrolling, I'll tell you: hookers, drug dealers, and kids from the gangs, armed to the teeth and pupils dilated. The janitor was useless.

He has an apartment as part of the deal but he didn't budge from it. I could have rolled the whole building away without his coming down to see where we were headed.

I boiled some water and stole a little of Miss Huth's instant and found where she stashed the chocolate chip cookies. Then I went through the papers sheet by sheet. I made three piles: one, don't matter; two, grand jury for Vic Crichton; three, trouble for Murphy. And I'm telling you I made sure everything in the third pile was shredded into paper worms, shaken, and stirred too. As I sorted through that stuff I saw indiscreet little items that could have had me disbarred a dozen times over. I didn't take a deep breath until only two piles remained. Trouble for Westbridge, Inc., was something I could endure.

Then I crammed all the totally innocuous stuff into my best pigskin document case. With that done I sprinkled a few trouble-for-Westbridge items over them just to make it look kosher and stuffed it tight and strapped it down. Then I took the more delicate Westbridge material – one three-quarter-full Perrier-water box of it – and put it into my trunk and drove back home with it.

I put it on a rafter in the garage together with a lot of other cardboard boxes that had formerly contained my desktop computer, my microwave oven, my coffee maker, and all that kind of stuff, because if you don't keep the cardboard boxes the stores won't fix items that go on the blink. Did you know that? They won't fix them without the boxes.

The dust and dirt I dislodged from that garage made me dirty enough to need a good long hot shower. By the time I was through washing up there was no time for sleep. I changed into a sport coat and cords to show all concerned that this wasn't a part of my regular schedule and then went along Ventura Boulevard to Tommy's Coffee Shop.

55

4

Fancy Goldie remembering our breakfasts in Tommy's. It's one of those restaurants that open at dawn and close in the early afternoon. I parked at the back. The sun crept out of the darkness and peeked over the roofs, to be reflected in my lovely old Caddie. With its original gold-colored paint job, it was spectacular. I stood there admiring it for a long time; I love that car. Even the radio was original. It would have made a stunning color photo the way it looked that morning. Maybe I should buy myself a camera.

I went in through the back door. Already the dining room was crowded with men on their way to work. Brawny fellows in bib overalls and plaid work shirts, men who adjusted machinery, fixed appliances, and mended utilities; straight-speaking American heroes like my mother's brothers.

Goldie was already there, sitting near the window, watching the cook cracking eggs and flipping hash browns on the shiny steel griddle. We said our hellos. Goldie looked tired. Judging by the clothes he was wearing and the blue chin, he'd been up all night. The smell of bacon got my appetite roused and I went ape and ordered sausages, bacon, fried eggs, pancakes with butter and syrup, toast, honey, and coffee. It was just like being back with my folks. The coffee was fine, the eggs went over easy, and it was the only place around there that opens at five-thirty in the morning.

'Hello, Mr Murphy,' said Cindy. She picked up Goldie's empty plate and gave him a refill of coffee.

'Boy, are you looking great, Cindy!' I'd known Cindy Lewis for years. She was a hardworking, sensible woman with two grown daughters. Her husband had been a marine killed in 'Nam back in the early days. When Danny was very young she'd regularly come in to baby-sit for us.

'It's work that keeps me in shape,' she said, while she watched me eating. 'I tell the young ones that but they don't listen. People have forgotten how to work. My next-door neighbor is a nice old Japanese gentleman who works at Northrop. That poor man can't even go into his own front yard to water his flowers and plants without people thinking he's a gardener. They can't believe he gardens for himself; they pester him all the time with offers of work.'

Goldie nodded soberly. I had a feeling he was going to doze off at any moment.

'Can you beat that?' I said, but oh, boy, I could well believe it. The two dumb jerks doing my garden knew as much about gardening as they knew about nuclear physics, and they were charging me an arm and a leg. They popped in for ten minutes of grass-cutting every Friday morning and didn't even take the clippings and leaves away afterward. I tried to remember exactly where Cindy lived. I had driven her back there a million times. Next-door neighbor, eh? I mean: how much could they be paying him at Northrop?

'I've been waiting for you to look in, Mr Murphy; you can settle a bet for me. It was Frank Loesser wrote "Brother, Can You Spare a Dime?" Wasn't it? I was arguing with my young brother; he thinks he knows everything. Back me up, will you? I've got ten dollars riding on it.'

'Too bad. You lost your money, Cindy. Words by Yip Harburg, music by Jay Gorney.'

She didn't seem too devastated at losing her ten bucks. She shook her head in admiration. 'He should go on one of those TV quiz shows,' she told Goldie. Goldie nodded. She had an exaggerated respect for anything she perceived as education.

I dredged my memory: 'Written for a show called *Americana* sometime in the early thirties.'

Cindy refilled my coffee cup. 'I can't remember a darn thing these days,' she admitted cheerfully. 'I keep forgetting to tell you about your car, Mr Murphy.' She poured coffee for the guys at the next table and then came back to me. 'Maybe somebody else told you already. That old car of yours, it's dripping oil everywhere.'

'I know; it's nothing,' I said.

'I noticed it when you drove away last week. A big pool of oil.'

'It's nothing that matters,' I said. 'Probably a gasket.'

'Why don't you get yourself a nice new car? Now your company has been bought out and everything.'

'Are you crazy?' I said. 'That's a valuable vintage car.'

'Those Japanese cars are very reliable. My grandson has one. He's got a great deal: ninety-nine dollars a month. It's a lovely little car. Bright green. Four doors, radio, and everything. So comfortable and reliable.' Goldie was looking at me with a stupid smile on his face.

'And I haven't been bought out.' Maybe I said it too loudly.

'I didn't mean anything.' She poured coffee for me.

'Everybody keeps telling me I'm rich, except I don't get the dough. So don't go around saying I've been bought out.'

She looked at me and at Goldie and nodded. I could see what she was thinking. She was thinking I was making millions of dollars and hiding it away somewhere. 'I thought I'd better tell you about the oil,' she said, and walked away.

'Stupid woman,' I told Goldie. 'Japanese cars. I don't want to hear about Japanese cars.'

Goldie said, 'Did you bring everything?'

'I brought everything,' I said. Goldie nodded.

I devoured the whole breakfast and even wiped the plate with bread. Was it a sign of nerves? I always eat too much when I'm tense. I wish I was one of these skinny joes who go off food when they are under stress, but with me it works just the other way. Anyway, it was a delicious breakfast: cholesterol cooked just the way I like it.

Then I reached into my leather case and brought out the glove I'd found in my safe. I put it on the table. Goldie looked at it without emotion. 'Is this yours?' I asked him.

'Could be. I've got one just like it at home.'

'You son of a bitch.'

'Now we're quits,' said Goldie. 'Don't fool with my phones in future.' He raised those heavy-lidded eyes of his to look at me.

'I didn't plant that bomb, Goldie.'

'You just happened to want to make a call? You just happened to notice the wiring? Is that it?'

'Of course it is. I didn't plant that bomb.'

'Maybe not, but I think you know who did. And you made sure I found it. I get the message, Mickey. Is this something you dreamed up with Budd Byron?'

'What's Budd got to do with it?'

'He's the one you promised to get a gun for, remember?'

'This is too much! Are you bugging my office?'

'It's not your office any longer. You work for us now.'

I got to my feet and put some money on the table. Goldie reached out and grabbed my arm. 'These are big boys, Mickey. This isn't a Monopoly game, it's real life. Ask yourself, pal. When big corporations are pushing hundreds of millions of dollars around the board, they are not deterred by some little guy reading aloud the instructions on the box lid.' He looked at me. 'They'll squash you like a bug.'

'Keep your guys out of my house,' I said. I pulled away from his grip, picked up the glove, and tossed it at him. 'You pull a routine like that again, and I'll fix you in a way you won't like.'

'Turn off at the water tower,' said Goldie. 'It's a white limo with tinted glass, parked near the main hangar.'

Camarillo airport is a onetime military field with six thousand feet of concrete runway, one hundred and fifty feet wide, and that's more than enough to land Petrovitch's plane even if old Petey himself is at the yoke nursing a hangover. I knew the field. For years, when driving on Route 101, I'd stolen a glance at the old blue-and-white Lockheed Constellation that marked the end of the runway.

I recognized the freeway exit ramp. I used to take Danny up that way to buy strawberries. Danny loved strawberries. I remember the first time he saw the strawberry fields – miles of them all the way to mountains – he could scarcely believe it was all real. Betty liked them too. We regularly bought berries there and took along a big tub of ice cream and had a feast in the car.

I turned in at the water tower, I went past the huts that are now municipal offices and spotted the biggest of big white cars, a regular Moby Dick of a limo. The driver must have been told to watch for me; he flashed the lights. He was parked on the far side of the big red notice that said AUTHORIZED VEHICLES ONLY BEYOND THIS POINT. Where else would Petrovitch want to be?

The driver, a pugnacious youngster with a battered ear, jumped out of his seat brandishing what looked like a wire coat hanger fixed to a transistor radio. It was a metal detector, and he used it to locate a bunch of keys and three dollars' worth of coins in my pocket.

Seemingly unafraid of being assaulted with a handful of loose change, Petrovitch was leaning well back in the real leather and sipping hot coffee and looking like a million dollars. How do people do that so early in the morning? I had a splitting headache, red eyes, and disheveled hair.

'Hello, Mickey,' he said.

Maybe I've given you the idea that Petrovitch was a close buddy of mine. Not so. He was just a rich, glamorous personality who kept crossing my path, which is a zone into which not many glamorous personalities allow themselves to stray. I'd seen him a hundred times or more but always across a crowded room. And when I did find myself having a conversation with him, he needed a sidekick at his ear to tell him who I was. But today there was no sidekick: just the maestro himself, sitting in the back seat of his stretch, dressed in a World War Two-style leather flying jacket, open-neck silk shirt, zip-sided boots, and neatly pressed Bedford trousers.

'Hello, Zach,' I said, getting into the seat alongside him. 'What's on your mind?'

'Someone tried to kill me last night.' He looked at me with cold gray eyes. I recalled Goldie's warning about being squashed like a bug. No matter how civilized they looked, guys like Petrovitch and Westbridge had reached the head of the line by stepping over a lot of inert bodies.

'I know, I was the one who found the bomb.'

Without a flicker of emotion he said, 'Goldie thinks you were involved.'

'Goldie is out of his mind,' I said.

'You're wrong; Goldie is a good man. Very efficient.'

'How would a bomb in a back office endanger you?' I said.

'You weren't planning to spend the evening sitting there waiting for the phone to ring, were you? Someone rigs up a lethal gadget like that, it would kill one of your sidekicks.'

'Go on,' he said, without sounding very interested. 'You've got my attention. You think it was nothing to do with me?'

'Ask yourself. What client or associate do you have who is so important that you'd sprint upstairs to take the call in person? Were you expecting some special call last night?'

'No, I wasn't.' He waited and then said, 'Does this puzzle come with a solution, or do I have to wait till the next installment?'

'Who came out of it looking real good?'

'What do you mean?'

'Mr Super Efficient.'

'You think it's some kind of gimmick to make Goldie shine like bullion?' He laughed. Still speaking slowly, he said, 'How I'd love to believe that. The problem with that one is that Goldie tells me going up to that office was your idea, not his. He says you came in asking to use the telephone. Did he get that wrong?'

Ouch. He had me there. 'I wanted to phone my partner,' I said. I'd been about to put the poison in for Goldie, and complain about his breaking into my house, but now that didn't look like such a good gambit.

There was a long silence; then Petrovitch said, 'Well, it's darn nice of you to trail out here.' He made it sound as if I'd insisted upon doing it against his urgings. 'I'm about to finalize a little deal with Sir Westbridge, and I know you know him well.'

'Sir Jeremy,' I said.

'How's that?' He opened the door of a little veneered cupboard and pointed his finger. Built into the space between and behind the front seats there was a mirror-fronted bar, icebox, and coffee dispenser.

'Not Sir Westbridge,' I told him. 'Sir Jeremy. Sir is a title. It goes with the first name, not the family name.'

'Is that right? Coffee?'

'Yes, please.'

'Help yourself.' He settled back and watched me while I fiddled to get a cup off the little shelf without knocking the glasses over and poured hot coffee into it. I found a packet of nondairy creamer, tipped some into the swirling black mix, and stirred it well before sipping some. My God, it was a filthy concoction. I watched little islands of powdered milk substitute bumping into one another and spinning around at a dizzying rate. It made me want to throw up. I put the cup back into the little cupboard. Rich guys eat any kind of filth; I noticed that when I was a waiter downtown working my way through college. Any kind of filth as long as it costs!

'Well, Sir Jeremy came to me saying he lacked liquidity . . . that's the delicate way these European aristocrats say in deep shit.' Petrovitch grinned. 'I'm trying to make the shit he's in a little more liquid.'

'They don't confide in me,' I said.

'Now they tell me the old guy is dead. But I think he had to leave town in a hurry. What do you know about that?'

'It's news to me.'

'They may be friends of yours,' said Petrovitch, 'but these guys are crooks. Did you know Crichton carries a gun everywhere he goes? Why would a businessman be carrying a gun unless he figures on using it?'

'I don't know anything about them. They are not friends,' I said. 'They are clients.'

'Touché, old buddy.' He laughed grimly. 'Well, maybe we're in accord after all. I'm in the throes of a deal with these people and I plan to go through with it. But I don't like them and I don't trust them. Say, what is in that damned leather case you are hugging so tight?'

63

'Westbridge paperwork.'

'Jesus Christ, Mickey. Don't show me that stuff!' He gave a brief derisive laugh. 'You've got a professional relationship with them. You could get yourself thrown into prison.'

'Goldie Arnez told me to bring it.'

Petrovitch laughed briefly. 'Well, even Goldie gets a little too enthusiastic at times. He's a loyal guy but a gorilla at heart . . . No, put that document case away.'

I suddenly thought I might be able to make my rather hasty decision to fire Westbridge into Petrovitch's responsibility. 'Do you want the partnership to continue to act for Westbridge?'

'Why not?'

'Conflict of interests. Also, I think they are being investigated. It could spatter everyone.'

'Is that why you brought their paperwork?'

'I told you why I brought it.'

He smiled. 'Don't rock the boat until the deal has gone through. After that we'll think about it.'

I put the case back down on the beautiful carpeting. You sadistic bastard, Petrovitch. He just made me bring that bag full of documents out to him so I would know that when the chips were down Petrovitch called the shots. Now we had established that he was the boss. I was the hustler, but he would save my soul. And now he knew that any time he cracked the whip and held aloft the fiery ring, Mickey Murphy would run and jump through it for him. I won't forget this, you bastard!

'What do you know about California laws and charity setups?'

'Not a thing,' I said. I watched him. He savored that stale coffee as if it were Château Margaux.

'But you lowered the boom on two swindlers who were milking a phony charity last year. You got yourself an admirer in the prosecutor's office. She told me it was your discovery procedure that sent them away for fifteen years.'

Not only was this guy spying on me, he was boasting about it. He was bugging my office, burglarizing my home, and looking in my safe. How can you deal with people like that?

'Your informant was exaggerating,' I said. 'It was a little downtown Korean charity, and my partners did most of the preparation. They spoke the language and pried the papers loose. I would have had nothing to do with it except that my partner Charlie got killed in an accident. My other partner, Billy Kim, was busy being Charlie's executor so I took the case to court.'

Airplane noise made conversation impossible. A C-130 Hercules passed overhead, a snarling orange-and-gray monster that was in the circuit for the naval air base at nearby Point Mugu. We waited for the sound to abate.

'I need someone who knows his way around the charity business,' said Petrovitch. 'Ingrid is on a committee. I don't want her to get entangled with the law. Are you free this weekend? We'll be in Aspen.'

'I can be, Zach, sure.'

'Vic Crichton will be a houseguest. I'm hoping to catch him in the right mood and get some sort of agreement roughed out. And you can talk to Ingrid.'

A man in coveralls came over to the car and said the plane was ready to go. Petrovitch said, 'Has my own engineer checked it out?'

'Sure thing, Mr Petrovitch. He's over there now with your pilot. She's been running real sweet this morning.'

'Is that all?' I asked.

Leaning very close to me, he put his hand out, softly touching my necktie like he was searching for the beat of my heart. 'I hope I've got it right, about you being Mr Nice Guy,' he said in a hoarse whisper. For a moment the real Petrovitch was on display, and it was not a pretty sight. 'Because I hate myself if

I misjudge people. I kind of go ape and arrange for things to happen that I'm sorry about afterward.' His eyes were still and icy and unseeing, as if he was looking through me.

'I know the feeling,' I said and brushed his hand away.

As he started to get out, the driver jumped out of his seat and almost wrenched the door off its hinges in his excitement. 'Sit still and finish your coffee,' Petrovitch told me. 'Have something stronger if you want.'

'I'm cutting back on coffee,' I said. Coffee like this, I should have added. I was counting the minutes to getting to the nearest pharmacy for Alka-Seltzer on the rocks. Petrovitch straightened up and looked at something on the horizon. Flying very low I saw a navy Tomcat; there were fighters based at Point Mugu, and their circuit passed along the edge of the Camarillo field. This one flashed past behind the eucalyptus trees and was gone; the roar came afterward.

'Look at them go,' said Petrovitch admiringly. 'What wouldn't I give to change places with one of those navy jocks!'

'Semper Fi.'

'What's that? Oh, yeah, Semper Fi,' he said.

I watched Petrovitch walking out to the apron, waving his hands in the air as he shouted to a white-shirted engineer who was dancing around him all the way. Petrovitch was an inscrutable personality. I couldn't get the connections between mind and body. Talk about fly by wire – I'd guess Petrovitch would rather die than let anyone know what he was really thinking. Maybe that's what big money does to people, or what kind of people make big money. I wondered if Ingrid was like that now she was a part of the big bucks society. I watched Petrovitch standing arms akimbo as his jet was rolled out of the hangar. White, with a special red-stripe paint job with PETROVITCH ENTERPRISES INTERNATIONAL painted across the tail. 'A ship like that really costs,' said the driver, as if reading my thoughts.

'It sure beats Economy seating on Aero Mexico,' I said.

'They have to be sure,' explained the driver. 'They're worrying a lot right now. Ever since last month; they have to be sure.'

'That's right,' I said, wondering what the hell a good-looking guy with a gorgeous wife and money falling out of his shoes had to be worried about.

I suppose he was counting on my asking him about it, because before I could think of any way of delving deeper into the oracle he said, 'It was a wrench they found in the engine. A regular wrench from a tool kit, so there was no way of being certain that it was sabotage. But from then on, the plane gets a twenty-four-hour guard and is checked again from tip to tail before every takeoff.'

'You can't be too careful,' I said, opening the door and splashing the remains of my coffee onto the tarmac. 'A guy who finds a wrench in his engine compartment should go through his address book and see if he's been going to dancing class with someone his folks didn't invite to his parties.' I reached into the glittering little mirrored box and grabbed a fifth of Jack Daniels I'd spotted behind the decanters. 'Enemies with style, know what I mean?' As I upended the bottle and took a quick swig, I met the driver's eyes in the mirror. He was watching me, the snooping bastard.

'What causes a car to drip oil from the sump?' I asked him, wiping my lips, replacing the bottle, and closing the little door of the bar. 'Is that something simple to fix?'

'Did you look for a wrench?' he asked slyly.

Goddamned comedian.

It was then that I remembered something about the bomb. I'd asked to use Goldie's cell phone. Going to that office was his idea.

* * *

67

Coming from the airport at Camarillo along the 101 to town, you practically have to pass the front door of my house in Woodland Hills. But I didn't pass it. After a night without sleep I needed some shut-eye. I went home. After calling Miss Huth to tell her I had a number of important appointments near Woodland Hills and would come back to the office in the early afternoon, I closed the curtains, undressed, and went to bed.

I remember hearing the Klopstocks' gardeners arrive with all their noisy machinery but they didn't spend long on the job. These guys weren't dedicated horticulturalists; they weren't dedicated anything. It didn't take long before I was sound asleep.

I was awakened by the telephone and the operator asking me if I would accept a collect call from Phoenix.

'Mickey? It's Billy: Billy Kim.'

'Hi,' I said sleepily. 'How did you find me?'

'Magda said she thought you were at home sleeping off a hangover.'

'Miss Huth said that?' What a nerve she had, when I'd told her I was working.

'Mickey. I'm in a little trouble.'

'You didn't get into drag again and goose all the bridesmaids?'

'I've got no time for your Irish jokes. I was hit by an RV full of drunks on the freeway. My car is totaled and I'm in the hospital.'

'Jesus, Billy. You okay?'

'I'm just a little shaken, but they're doing tests. I wanted to fly back today, but then I suddenly figured that if I discharge myself from the hospital it might affect my legal position with the insurance company.'

'But you *are* okay?'

'Hairline fractures of the bones in my hand, nothing. But

they're still doing tests and stuff. You know what hospitals are like.'

'Is there anything I can do at this end?' I said. I wasn't looking for extra work, but Billy had done me so many favors I was in debt to him.

'Yeah, quite a lot.'

'Say the word.'

'If you look in the safe there is a packet of money there. I want you to pay off the Reverend Edgar Stojil: Rainbow, they call him. Do you know who I mean?'

'Sure, he's famous. I saw him at a party: tall thin guy with sideburns and a red face. He runs a shelter for the homeless, right?'

'The Rainbow's End Shelter for Homeless Men. That's him. Give him all the money in the package. There's about eight grand there. Get two grand more out of your account to make it up to ten. Cash; he won't take checks. I'll pay you back as soon as I get out. Can you do that?'

'Sure, Billy.' I wanted to ask him what it was all about, but I figured he'd tell me in good time. Billy Kim always had lots of action going, with his investments in restaurants and nail salons and so on.

'Go down to the shelter, and the Reverend will give you a new U.S. passport and tell you what else to do. It's complicated, but I don't want to go through it on the phone.'

'Okay.'

'It may take a little time,' he said. 'Half a day, maybe.' I think he was disappointed that he didn't have to talk me into it. 'Take my spare house keys from the safe too. You might need them.'

'How urgent is all this?'

'Could you see him today, Mickey? I was expecting to be there. Make sure you get the passport before you hand over the dough.'

'Okay.'

'And Mickey . . . you might recognize some of the people involved. Don't be mad at me.'

'We'll talk money later,' I said. Billy was always doing deals on the side, and snatching other people's clients was his specialty.

The Reverend Rainbow Stojil was the sort of freak created for TV talk shows – or maybe by them. His fluffy white sideburns made him easily recognized, and his well-modulated speaking voice was classless and without regional identification. And did he ooze charm! He was smoking a cheroot when I went in to see him. It went well with his black suit and clerical collar but the spilled ash showed.

The Rainbow Rooms – as the wags referred to the shelter for homeless men – was a once-grand hotel that Rainbow had bought when it could no longer function as a three-ninety-nine per night flophouse. He'd squeezed the purchase price from the city and from various charities and business people. Rainbow had become famous for the way he spent so much time going to charity dinners and talk shows and making emotional speeches at Rotary clubs and prizing donations from California's guilt-racked rich.

'My name is Murphy. I'm Billy Kim's partner.'

He looked at me, flicked ash, and nodded. 'Did you bring the money?' It was almost the first thing he said.

'Ten grand,' I said and passed it to him.

He stubbed out his half-smoked cheroot in the lid of a tin that held other butts and a great deal of ancient ash. 'We need it so badly. Take a seat.' He was sitting behind a scrubbed table in what had once been the hotel manager's office. On the walls were two colored prints of Matisse paintings and two posters that showed in graphic detail how you get AIDS from dirty hypodermic needles.

70

At one time this had been the heart of the city, a neighborhood of fine old homes and luxury hotels; now it was skid row. The street was littered with broken pieces of automobile and huddled slumbering men. Immediately outside on the sun-baked pavement that fronted the shelter I could see men in ragged clothes sitting with their backs against a chain-link fence. They had nothing to do but wait until it was time for the Rainbow Rooms to open its doors and serve the one and only meal of the day. They didn't talk or play cards or even fight or argue; they just sat.

Rainbow didn't count the money. He just riffled the corners of the bills, but he had the legerdemain of a bank cashier and I had the feeling that if the wad had been only $9,999 he would have detected it with his fingertips.

'Poor devils,' he said, following my gaze. 'They are not frightened of work, you know.' He said it accusingly.

'I guess not,' I said.

'They eagerly take turns being on my cleaning team, and that only pays a nominal dollar a day.'

I looked at my watch. 'What happens now?' I asked him.

'Do you have ID, Mr Murphy?'

I showed him my driver's license. He looked at me and at my photo carefully before handing it back. I could see he was suspicious. I said, 'My partner was in a freeway accident. Didn't he phone you?'

'He left a message. I'm not very good at operating these machines. I accidentally erased the message after hearing it once.'

'He was in the hospital when he called.'

The reverend looked at me. 'We usually keep it all very discreet. We don't use names in these transactions.'

'I didn't know that. I'm sorry.'

'I was expecting him to be collected two days ago. I got a

71

little jumpy.' He pulled a big register off a shelf that held phone books, street maps, and an old clock that had given up at two-thirty a long time ago. He opened the book and swung it around on the table. 'Would you sign there, Mr Murphy? Most all the other paperwork is done.'

I signed the ledger where it said I was donating ten thousand dollars to the shelter on behalf of a client who wished to remain anonymous. It seemed okay to do that.

He passed me some official-looking papers in a brown envelope. 'You'll need all this. There is the name of the deceased. There is the death certificate – natural causes: heart attack – and there is the letter from the doctor who was attending him.'

'Attending him?' What was all this?

'He died three days ago, Mr Murphy. The doctor attended him during the ten days prior to death, as prescribed by law. Otherwise we'd have to have a post-mortem.'

'You'll have to help me,' I said. 'My partner was in a hurry. He said you'd explain everything. Who died, a relative of Billy?'

'The deceased. One of our inmates. You're collecting the body, aren't you?'

'Am I? Is that what Billy . . . is that what was done in the past?'

He sighed. 'I wish your partner had come in person. He knows I don't like outsiders becoming involved.'

'I'm not an outsider,' I said. 'I'm a partner of the man we mentioned.'

'He's a tall man. You won't be able to take the body in that Cadillac of yours.'

'I'm not putting any stiff into my car,' I said. 'It already smells of tequila. Did the other party put them into his car?' I thought Billy only had a Porsche.

'He always brought a Jeep and a horse trailer,' said the reverend. 'You can get anything into a horse trailer.'

'What do you want me to do with the body?'

'The law says the deceased goes to a mortuary. The airline won't accept a body from people like you or me. He will have to be delivered to the plane by someone from the mortuary and collected by a mortuary employee at the other end. The airport officials are very stringent about that.'

'What airplane?'

'The body goes to London. I thought you would know that. They always go to London. Airline cargo, hermetically sealed, and charged four dollars per pound weight.'

'Billy did this?'

'You'd better come and see.' He got to his feet and took a key from his pocket. 'He'll have to be embalmed anyway,' he said. 'The airline won't accept him if he's not embalmed, so don't get any crazy ideas about taking him straight to LAX.' He opened a door that gave onto a dark corridor. I followed right behind him.

As we walked I said, 'So where do I take it if not to the airport?'

'I'll give you the address.' He went through a door marked STAFF ONLY, and I followed him down a flight of stairs to a dark cellar. At the bottom of the stairs he took his time unlocking the door; then he stood aside and ushered me into a cold and dimly lit room.

'Holy Mother of God!' I said. The only light came from four candles, but it was enough to see a body laid out there on a big table. The body was stiff, arms close by its sides and eyes staring at the ceiling, and was dressed in baggy pants and clean T-shirt. The clothes were simple but of good quality: the leisure clothes of a wealthy man rather than the rags you'd expect to find on a down-and-outer. He was a middleaged man of above-average height. His face was dark with the stubble that continues to grow after death. The candle flames flickered in a draft from the door, and with the movement of the light the shadowy face seemed to leer at me. Plastic sacks of ice had been wedged around the body, and enough of it had melted and escaped from the bags to form large puddles on the floor. There was a constant dripping sound as more ice melted. It was the only sound to be heard apart from my own breathing. On a shelf at the end of the room, along with the candlesticks, stood a large brass crucifix and two pots of cheap flowers.

'Who is this stiff?'

'I'd be obliged to you, Mr Murphy, if you would show more respect,' he said. 'I knew this man. He worked hard and feared God.' Rainbow's voice echoed in the little room. 'This is our chapel where so many others have found final peace. Don't forget you are in the presence of God.'

'A chapel? So many others? How many dead do you handle in the shelter?'

'County General reckons on about fifty bodies a night picked up on the streets of our city. Often a poor soul facing his maker chooses to come and spend those final few hours with us.'

I had recovered from my initial shock by now, and I took one of the candles and brought it closer to the body. The circulation had long since stopped, so that the dead man's skin was dull and gray. His face was set in a scowl and the hands – always the most revealing – were hard and scarred, with broken nails and calluses. The legacy of a lifetime of hard manual work. 'And who was he?' I said.

'He was Jeremy Westbridge.'

I became impatient with the reverend: it was not just his manner; I resented everything else about this deal into which I had been gently led and where I was now drowning. 'We both

74

know it's not Sir Jeremy Westbridge. I saw you talking to Sir Jeremy the other night. This body is maybe somewhere about his shape and size and age, but we know it's not him, don't we? We know this is not Westbridge.'

'You frighten me, sir,' said the reverend. He brought the packet of money out of his inner pocket and held it as if about to hand it back to me. Then he seemed to find new resolve. 'I have had a Jeremy Westbridge registered in this shelter for over three weeks, and this is him. I can show you the register if you like. What can be your motive in arguing otherwise?'

'Okay. I'm not arguing. Pretend I'm Billy Kim. What do I do now?'

'With ten thousand dollars I can comfort and shelter hundreds of souls. Don't look to me for any kind of contrition for breaking the letter of the law; I won't oblige you.'

'Okay, reverend. Put away the violin and tell me what to do. If you don't provide a little more help and explanation, I'm going to take my money and leave you with the stiff.'

He looked at me. He didn't like my attitude but he liked my ten grand, and that was the deciding factor. He said, 'Your partner would have taken him to the home – I mean, the private address – of the mortician he works with. That's what you have to do. They will do everything else. They will take him to the mortuary in a panel van. A mortuary panel van attracts very little attention in front of a mortician's home.'

'I don't like it,' I said.

'I don't like it either,' he said. 'But it's what you will have to do.' He looked at me to show me he knew far more than he was supposed to know. You have no secrets from Rainbow. I nodded. 'We'll have to move him soon, Mr Murphy. He has to be embalmed. He's been here too long already, and those bags of ice are not keeping him cold enough.'

'You're right,' I said.

75

'You'd better get the horse trailer from your partner's home. He tows it behind a Jeep that will probably be there with it.'

'It will take a couple of hours,' I said.

'Did I give you the passport?'

I'd forgotten about the passport. 'No, you didn't.'

He found the passport in his pocket and gave it to me. It was a brand new U.S. passport, the holder's name one I'd never heard before, but the photo was a recent one of Jeremy Westbridge. So that was it. No wonder the guy wasn't worried about the feds coming after him. He was changing identities with someone who had died on the street. Stojil and Billy were running quite a racket. They would have applied for a passport and no doubt all kinds of other paperwork while the guy was still alive. Now the real Sir Jeremy would have a new name, become a U.S. citizen, and his documentation would all be one hundred percent genuine.

'Don't worry about your car. I sent someone out to guard it.'

'Thanks,' I said. I was keeping very cool, but my mind was in a whirl. I was remembering what Vic Crichton had said at the party, about Sir Jeremy going away. Now I understood. I put the passport in my pocket. That Billy Kim! What other crooked capers was the son of a bitch up to? I was getting deeper and deeper into this business, but I couldn't think of any way of extricating myself. I owed Billy Kim a whole lot of favors. If I walked away from this one, he could end up in prison.

'Yes, I always do that. Too many kind and generous persons dropped in to donate a hundred dollars and went out to find their hubcaps missing. By the way, don't say I gave you the mortician's address,' he said. 'I'm not supposed to know who he is. But it's difficult to keep anything really secret in this town.'

'That's right,' I said. 'But fortunately for those of us with secrets, no one in this town gives a damn about anything anyway.'

'I must send out for some more ice. The liquor store will wonder what kind of a party we are having over here. Perhaps I shouldn't have said I wanted it for a celebration.'

5

I'd had it too long to trade it in. Maybe I hadn't treated it with due care and reverence, but what is 'fair wear and tear' anyway? I'd spent far more than I could afford on magic creams and maintenance. Dented, maybe, and sure the fillings showed; flaking in places and the original finish no more than a memory, but what does the bodywork matter? It's what's inside that makes a winner. So I sucked in the gut, dabbed on the after-shave, parted my hair, and tried to forget what I'd seen in the mirror until tomorrow morning came round again.

So the mastermind wanted me in Aspen: okay. For the time being I would dance to the Petrovitch tune, but once the money was paid over to me, and my debts were cleared, I'd be my own man. At present the partnership had only a 'deal memo,' and I'd squeezed too many slippery clients through the pliable bars of such preliminary contracts to believe it would force Peter the Great to go through with the deal. So yes, sir; no, sir; I'd be on the early flight out of LAX and bring my laptop computer with me.

I did my exercises. I touch my toes one hundred and fifty times and follow it with ten minutes of deep breathing. Yeah, that's right, it's a joke. Really I collapse onto the bed, gasping for air. I hate exercising: I hated it even back when I was on the football team; that's why I do it before I'm fully awake.

I wish I could have persuaded my dad to do a little bend and stretch. It would have prolonged his life. My dad smoked heavily. I read in a news magazine that habitual smoking reduces the average person's life by five to eight years. So why didn't you listen to me, Dad? We could have had another five years together. We could have talked. I would have told you all kinds of things I never got around to telling you because I was too young and stupid. Now I need you more than ever.

Sixty times touching the toes – reaching high into the air each time, not this flaky stuff of staying bent over and bobbing your head. Sometimes I do it holding cans of food in my hands like weights. I did that this morning with cans of dog food, and Rex came to me and dropped a ball at my feet. 'No can do, kid,' I told him. 'Rain check: I owe you another walk.' Then, if there's time, I do my tap routine. You've got to be warmed up for that.

Fly to Aspen. Klopstock, my next-door neighbor – the professor – drives there when he goes to see his married daughter. That's not the daughter Danny was dating; it's his younger daughter, who married a photographer from the *Times* who moved to Denver and bought a one-hour photo franchise. My neighbor drives to Colorado to see her. In a good car it's no big deal, right? Because if it was a big deal, Klopstock wouldn't be able to manage it.

But go there by plane and you arrive totaled, I mean completely frazzled. Getting through those security people at the airport here in town is more hassle than being inducted into the Green Berets. Stand in line! Buzzers sound. Red lights flash. Turn out your pockets! Is that really a camera? Where do you put the film in? What have you got inside your carry-on bag? Clean shirt and underwear; there's a surprise. A computer? So that's a computer! Is it really a computer? What kind of honest man would be carrying a computer wrapped in his

79

underwear? You must be some kind of kinky computer under-wear pervert and terrorist.

What a lot of malarkey. Just take a look out the airport window, and you see a bunch of guys in greasy coveralls strolling around the tarmac, climbing in and out of planes, work shirts bulging with guns and explosives, and not a security man – whoops! person – in sight. Right?

Anyone smuggling their personal possessions past the security personnel is punished with a ten-mile schlepp to the airplane. That will teach you to bring hand baggage, right? Then, with a pilot who looks like he's working his way through high school, we share the experience of conquering gravity. Ten thousand feet: wow, look down and you'll see the mountains!

Change planes at Denver, run and wait, run and wait. Denver is lovely too: they sell folk art right there at the airport. It's so convenient; it saves you from going into town for folk art. You finally arrive at Aspen drained. But Aspen is really worth the journey. You'll love it. I mean it: it says so right there in the flight magazine. Here is the place where the rock stars, the heroes and heroines of the daytime soaps, the unwashed guitar strum-mers and show-biz pixies meet billionaire property men, Arab princes, and European royals.

Aspen has a smart little airport, and the private jets were double-parked. I searched the concourse without catching sight of even one of this bewitching array of glitterati; I guess they had all gone for a piss.

Even without an airplane you're seven thousand feet high here in the mountains. For folks from ocean-level Los Angeles County it's ear-pop and fart time. And for those of us who forgot to bring confetti, it's snowing. I come out of the airport building and look around. Ugh! I get down and kneel, I promise I'll never complain about Los Angeles again, not ever!

I spotted a Chevrolet Suburban four-by-four waiting outside the terminal building. It's a shiny new Zach Petrovitch kind of a car. How did I know? I don't know how I knew; I just knew. These Petrovitch operators knew me too. A big bearded guy in a parka and a red woolly hat with a yellow pom-pom pitched his half-empty bag of hot popcorn into the trash, grunted my name, and wrestled my bag away from me. I followed him.

The freezing air slapped my face and the mountains glowered down like scorched cakes dusted over with too much sugar icing. Yellow pom-pom lobbed my bag into the back of the Chevy with admirable sangfroid. I always like to see my bag aboard: I've never been really comfortable with borrowed shirts, hastily bought underwear, and expendable plastic razors. Maybe this gorilla guessed my thoughts, for he turned and gave me a sullen grin as he slid into the driver's seat. The motor was running, and I stepped up to the Suburban and climbed into the front. The stereo was playing soft Mozart. The driver didn't look like your average Mozart aficionado, but they play a hell of a lot of soft Mozart in Aspen. You hear it in the antique shops and in the burger boutiques, the bars, and the toilets too. I think I read in the flight magazine that Amadeus and his agent both bought spreads up there on the slopes after he hit the big time with *Idomeneo*.

You can see the ski lifts and the skiers too, like bugs on a starched white sheet. The road, like all roads hereabouts, followed a river. It appeared to be frozen over, but looking closer I could see that here and there some of the smarter water escaped for long enough to bubble over the shallow rocks and make a noise and a splash or two; but no matter what shape it got itself into, eventually it all turned into ice. Maybe there was a moral there, but if there was, I still don't want to think about it.

We left the ski runs behind. Once outside the city limits,

the landscape was dignified and omnipotent: like the pictures on those five-dollar all-denominational Christmas cards that omit any references to God. The snow fell gently, making everything gray except where the snowplows whizzed past spewing clouds of white. There were tall green firs, and rocks shaped like something animate and only slightly deformed. Clumps of mature cottonwoods, bare and brown, looked like clouds of diesel-polluted air. While, breathing smoke in the snowy fields, there were horses wearing coats. I'm serious. Wearing little checkered coats! This was all heady stuff for a Southern California boy whose experiences with snow and ice ended for good when Sears put automatic-defrosting refrigerators into their catalog.

We continued down the valley made by Roaring Fork River. This is Route 82, and, as we got away from the million-dollar homes to the unfashionable side of town, things got a little more homely. Deep under snow here is the Aspen of the waiters, porters, and upstairs maids or, more precisely, the bartenders, short-order chefs, strippers, hookers, and disco hostesses. Cops live here too. Aspen cops can't afford houses within the city limits. The snow-laden mobile homes and trailer parks gave way to farms and ranches. Not film-star ranches either: spreads where men worked to earn a living. Maybe I had Big Pete all wrong; this wasn't the natural habitat of your jet-set millionaire.

You should have seen that Petrovitch spread. When finally I got there I could see why he'd bought land way outside of town. I'm only guessing but he must have had a thousand acres, at least a thousand acres. From the mountainside all the way down to the road and then as far as you could see along the valley, according to what the driver told me. At least a thousand acres.

It wasn't flashy. You could have driven right through the whole spread and thought it was no more than a well-maintained ranch, owned by some farmer who needed an Olympic-size heated pool and a twelve-bedroom house with annex accommodation for servants and was stashing a four-seat chopper in his barn for a friend.

Petrovitch was in the stable yard when I arrived. He was dressed in artfully faded jeans and a heavy woolen coat and tall patterned boots. With him, and wielding a big flashlight, was a man in a business suit, a *coiffure bouffante*, and rubber gloves. A timeworn ranch hand was holding the jaws open and keeping everything steady while they all looked into the mouth of a bored-looking horse.

'Go on in the house, Mickey,' Petrovitch called. 'Ingrid's in the kitchen; she'll fix you some coffee and tell you all about it. I need just five more minutes with Dr Wilson.' Upon hearing his name mentioned, Dr Wilson put down the flashlight and leaned closer to the throat.

It was cold, and I do mean cold. I was relieved that he didn't invite me to stand around and share whatever they were getting from the horse's mouth. I followed the driver, who opened the door of the kitchen, leaned inside, and dropped my bag with a crash that made me wonder if my underwear was still okay. He didn't step inside; I guess he didn't want to make marks on the tile floor. 'Thank you,' I said. He smiled. The Petrovitch people smiled a lot; it must have been all the wages he owed them.

That house was really something. From outside it could have been just a regular Colorado barn-shaped clapboard two-story, but inside it was something to gloat over. The kitchen looked like the flight deck of a 747, orange and red lights flickering in the gloom, and machines that ticked, and spotlit worktops. Once inside the kitchen you could see the dining room and the walk-in larder and the hallway. That was another world of shiny brass fittings, chandeliers conjured from elkhorn, carved

83

Victorian closets, handwoven carpets, lush potted plants, and valuable knickknacks on inlaid tables. And it was all squeaky clean and well kept. You could see these fittings were the real thing, antiques with a patina of age. The dining room lights were on, and the table was set for something pretty special. There was a huge carved mahogany fireplace with a log fire blazing. Above the mantelpiece was a doleful elk eyeing some antique Winchester rifles. On all the walls, even in the kitchen, were valuable paintings of the Old West: Remington and Russell, originals. Maybe it was a little like a film-set interior of a Wild West brothel, but it was stylish and comfortable and I had to confess I liked it a lot.

'I'll be right with you, Mickey,' said Ingrid, appearing from a paneled door. She gave me a big smile, waved a can of coffee, and began rattling around in the kitchen. I don't know if she was trying to convince me that she was the kind of little woman who fixed home-style meat loaf and hash browns for hubby Zach to come home to. I suspect she had an army of servants hidden in the cellar.

'Hello, Ingrid.' She was wearing a simple cotton dress, and her blonde hair was kind of messy. 'Quite a place.' I didn't know whether I was supposed to kiss her, shake hands, or reserve a table for dinner.

'Do you really like it, Mickey?' Her eyes were wide and wonderful, and she asked as if she really cared.

'It's overwhelming,' I said.

She saw me peeking into the dining room. 'We buy at auctions.'

'You dood good.'

She nodded and didn't smile. 'Everything in the house – the furniture and the fittings and everything – it's all authentic nineteenth century. Gathered from old houses around here. We love it.' So screw you, Mickey Murphy, horny-handed peasant from Alhambra High.

'Who wouldn't? I can't wait to see the bedrooms.' She gave me a not-amused look and I added, 'I mean . . . it's just great. I always liked cowboys.'

'I've been so looking forward to you visiting with us,' said Ingrid. 'Have you eaten?'

'No. I steer away from that airline garbage,' I said. 'It gives me acid indigestion.'

'I'll fix you a sandwich and coffee. Decaf – we don't drink ordinary coffee. Cream and sugar? Or maybe you'd prefer alcohol?'

I had the feeling I'd become a social outcast by preferring alcohol. 'I like decaf. And may I have hot milk instead of cream? I'm pounds over my regular weight. I've got to cut down on booze and butter and stuff like that.'

She looked at me as if seeing me for the first time. 'Hang your coat behind the door and sit down. You haven't changed at all, Mickey. I told Zach that, after I saw you the other night at the party. You haven't changed at all.'

I hung up my coat, sat down, and smiled my shy smile. I wasn't sure whether she was referring to my pouring her husband's imported champagne into the greenery, drinking decaf with hot milk, making sardonic comments, or weighing in at about fifteen pounds heavier than what the insurance companies say is healthy.

While she was setting up the percolator on the ceramic hot plate and reaching for the sliced Wonder loaf and the shrink-wrapped salami slices, Petrovitch in person came through the door that opened onto the stable yard.

'Doc's got to take Aunt Jemima to his surgery,' said Petrovitch without preamble. 'I'll have to go with him. Tell the girls in the office to phone around and cancel the dinner. They have a list of who was invited.' He noticed me sitting at the kitchen table. 'Hello, Mickey. I'm sorry about all this. Did Ingrid tell you about Vic Crichton?'

'No,' I said.

'He's got some kind of bug. He's in bed. Maybe you'd look in on him later, see if he's in the mood to talk business.'

Ingrid said, 'Darling, do you have to go? You should be getting a nap.' She posted two slices of bread into the toaster and explained to me, 'They got Zach out of bed in the middle of the night.' She went to the fridge to get milk.

Petrovitch mangled his face with his hand and then called after her, 'Doc's got all the equipment there, and he wants me along.'

'Do you have to, darling?' She turned a control, and the ceramic hot plate clicked, and the milk pan got a pink underlight.

Petrovitch made a little choking noise and said, 'There might be a vital decision to make. It's better I'm there.'

'Oh, darling,' said Ingrid with great emotion.

I looked at Petrovitch. If I hadn't known what kind of guy he was, I would have sworn he was on the verge of breaking into tears. Ingrid saw it too and stepped forward to put a hand on his arm, as if trying to help him through the moment of pain.

'Aunt Jemima is a horse,' she told me over his shoulder. 'She's one of Zach's favorites.'

'The first one I bought,' said Petrovitch.

'She's an old lady now,' said Ingrid. The toast popped up and bell rang.

'She's not old, not even four,' said Petrovitch in a loud voice, almost losing control of himself for a moment. But then he was over it. 'Wilson is a good man: the best,' he said, in the shrill way people praise their doctors and their lawyers and their dentists when they badly need reassurance and can't find it anywhere. 'I know he'll do everything he can. He was to speak at a fund-raising dinner in Denver tonight. He's canceled everything.'

'Of course he will,' said Ingrid. 'Remember what he did when Plantagenet Royale had that strange digestion problem?'

'Yeah, I reminded him about that.' They embraced some more.

I felt like an intruder. I just sat there and waited for the milk to boil over. When it made a noise and smoke, she jumped and shouted, 'Oh, dear, what a fool I am.' Petrovitch moved aside while Ingrid mopped up the spilled milk, using a cloth printed with a colored picture of the Grenadier Guards in fur hats marching around Buckingham Palace.

Petrovitch seemed not to notice her little calamity. He came across to me and said sonorously, 'There are all kinds of things I was going to talk to you about, Mickey, but it will have to wait for another time. Talk to Ingrid about her problems.' He went to the window as if checking on the weather and then reached into a closet near the door, got a waterproof mackinaw and a Stetson, and went out again. He didn't say goodbye either to Ingrid or to me. His mind was fully occupied with Aunt Jemima.

'Zach can be awfully sweet,' said Ingrid, as she put a toasted salami sandwich and a big mug of coffee in front of me. She poured the remaining milk from the pan. 'Will that be enough milk?'

'Oh, sure. I'm not too crazy about milk.'

She draped the milk-soaked tea towel across the sink, took off her apron, and sat down at the kitchen table. She sounded somewhat wistful, as if trying to forget the times when Zach was not trying so hard to be sweet. 'It's just dry toast.'

'Yeah, I know,' I said. 'About him being sweet, I mean.'

'Secretive and complicated but very sweet. I fell in love with him the moment I first saw him,' she said. 'I never knew it could be like that.'

'You're lucky, Ingrid,' I said. She touched her hair; she

looked wonderful sitting there in the shadows with golden light delicately outlining her features.

'I was never friends with Zach, the way you and I were friends. Talking about folks and school and sharing homework. With Zach it was serious – love right from the start.'

'I'm glad it worked out for you, Ingrid,' I said.

'It's a special kind of feeling . . . You know what I mean, Mickey. We always told each other everything, didn't we? You and me, I mean. I've always thought of you as if you were my big brother.'

'Yeah, I know.' Why did she have to torture me? Until this very moment I'd been able to persuade myself that Ingrid and I had shared the world's most perfect love affair, one that would have become torrid if she hadn't been snatched away by her folks to go and live in Chicago. I thought she'd loved me as I'd loved her: desperately, irrationally, and forever. I'd always told myself that her husbands were inadequate substitutes for that old love of ours. Now I had to sit and smile and hear her explain that we'd just been good friends. A brother? Me? Jesus Christ! Was that the way it really was, or was that the way she was now determined to remember it?

I drank from my coffee mug. It was decorated with a kind of fur design and said ANIMAL RIGHTS SYMPOSIUM, ASPEN, COLORADO 1990. Her mug said BEEF WITHOUT STEROIDS, HORMONES, OR ANTIBIOTICS. It was a sort of his-and-hers environmental-awareness decaf set. 'Have you got any sugar?' I needed sugar.

'We don't use it,' she said, but she got up and went to the dresser for an antique chinaware jug. She shook its dusty contents onto the table. There were two little packets of cane sugar bearing the slogan DANCE AND DINE AT THE LAZY NINE plus half a dozen Sweet 'N Low, a box of matches from the

Hotel Jerome, three bobby pins, and a pencil stub with a broken lead. 'It's bad for you,' she said.

'I know. Almost everything I really like is.' I ripped those packets open like an addict and tipped both into my coffee. If this was all the sugar they had in the house, I was going to have to arrange an urgent visit to the Lazy Nine.

'Here is what I want to talk about,' said Ingrid. She produced a concertina file out of nowhere, and from it she began bringing letters and receipts and account sheets and notes. 'Zach is frightened my charity may be breaking California law. Inadvertently.' She spread it all across the table. 'He said California has a lot of law. We are holding a kind of lottery, but when you see the way we do it you'll be able to tell him we are in the clear.'

'I'm not an expert, Ingrid,' I told her. 'Not on California lotteries.' She slid some of the typewritten papers along so they were in front of me in chronological order. She'd always been methodical. 'This is Ingrid the business major,' I said, reading the sheets. 'You had legal advice?'

'I went to the Los Angeles public library and looked it all up in the lawbooks.'

I guessed they were boilerplate examples she'd copied from a textbook, but I could find nothing wrong with them. 'Brilliant. I'll double-check it, of course, but it looks like you did everything right.'

'I think I did. I knew there were laws . . . Mickey,' she said in a different voice as she took the papers and put them away in the big brown folder, handling her work with a proud reverence. 'By the way . . . there is one other thing.'

This is it, I thought. It's always like this. They come into the office with some long story about their problems, their neighbors, their office, their boss, and it all comes to nothing. Then, as they are going out through your office door, they hang the real one on you: *boom, boom!*

'What's that?' I said, making it sound real casual. 'What's that, Ingrid?' I sipped a little coffee. It was very sweet.

'One of the people on the committee with me in the Los Angeles office is a nice man named Pindero: Albert H. Pindero.' It all came out in a rush like she'd rehearsed it. 'He's rich and charming. I liked him, and he was always very generous with his time.'

'What happened to him?' When a guy suddenly goes into the past tense like that, you can bet he's in trouble.

She was calm again now. 'He disappeared.' She tied the pink ribbon that held the concertina file together and then looked up and smiled.

'What do you mean, he disappeared? You mean he's not been able to get to your charity committee meetings lately? Maybe he's too busy.'

'Oh, no. He's gone. I went to his home, a big condo apartment on Wilshire. I wanted to return a book he'd loaned me. It's all closed down and empty. I traced the owners – a property company in New York – and when I called, a nice secretary there said the lease ended and the house was vacated. Nothing abnormal, this lady said. But it *is* abnormal; he's vanished. And there's no trace of his company, his factory, his office, or anything.'

'Vanished how? People don't vanish often, and factories never do.'

'I'm telling you, Mickey darling. There is no record of his company. I went through everything; a man at the library showed me how: California Manufacturers Register, California Services Register, and so on.' Ingrid had a sheet of paper in her hand. I could see it was a long list, all of the names ticked off in pencil. 'You want to hear?'

No, I didn't. 'Did you try the telephone company?'

'I'm not a fool; of course I did. First I looked at the

90

directories Zach has in his study: Standard and Poor's, and Dun and Bradstreet. Then I went back to the public library and went through the business directories and buyers' guides too. There is no record of Mr Pindero. I've become obsessed with it.'

'What does Zach say?'

A look of fear passed across her face. 'Oh, you mustn't tell Zach about it.'

'Why not?'

Her face was tense. 'He wouldn't like it. I never do anything that clashes with his business.'

'How would this guy suddenly going lost-and-found clash with Zach's business?' I said.

'You know what I mean, Mickey honey.' She smiled nervously. 'This is not anything that affects Zach. And Mr Pindero hasn't broken any laws.' She amplified that. 'You would like him. He used to arrive in a lovely old sky-blue convertible. He said it was a Dutch Packard. Are you still crazy about cars?'

She'd got my attention. 'A Packard Darrin? About 1941 or 1942?'

'It was old. He only took it on the road now and again.'

'Dutch Darrin was a designer who built car bodies on Sunset Strip. He did one-of-a-kinds for movie stars in the thirties. If that's what your guy has, it's a museum piece. It could be worth anything up to a million dollars.'

'Yes, he was so proud of that car. Mr Pindero was a gentleman. If you'd met him you'd know what I mean. He was like a college professor.'

'Is that right? I've got a college professor for a next-door neighbor, and I wouldn't trust him to pick up my dry cleaning.'

'You are funny, Mickey,' she said, without giving any sign of being amused. 'One of these days someone will take the things you say seriously.'

'There's no sign of that happening so far,' I said.

She touched her hair and smiled. She was about to try a completely different approach. 'It's just my feminine curiosity, Mickey. I have to know what happened to this Pindero gentleman. As long as he's not been hurt or anything.'

'There's no other reason?'

'I know you can find him. You must know someone who specializes in tracing missing persons. I'll pay you whatever it costs, and for your time too.'

'You don't have to pay me, Ingrid. We're old friends, aren't we?'

'I'm sorry.' She reached out and touched my hand. 'I wouldn't want to offend you, not for anything. That was stupid of me. But I need you to keep this little matter a secret between the two of us.'

'Pindero? You'll have to give me all the details you can remember.'

'I've written it all down,' she said, and passed me a sheet of paper. 'I was frightened you'd say you didn't do that kind of thing – criminal law.'

'Criminal law, commercial law, Gresham's Law – since the recession started to bite we take anything that comes along.'

I looked at the piece of paper. A name and a phony business address. I'd seen it all before: the phone number would lead me to a taciturn downtown bartender who knew where to get anything from bennies to a bent badge. There the trail would end. There wasn't much to go on. The chances were that this guy Pindero was some dishonest joe who had never given anyone a truthful answer in his life. I meet a lot of guys like that: they give false names, false ID, false social security, have checking accounts in assumed names, and a Panamanian passport, greenbacks, and an unmarked Magnum squirreled away in a deposit box ready for *der Tag*. I've got a long list of guys like that in my big fat unpaid accounts file.

'I'll do what I can,' I told her.

'And you won't tell Zach I gave you those notes?'

'No.' Notes? There were no notes. She hadn't written it down at all: she'd run it out on some kind of fancy laser printer. There wasn't even a letterhead or a signature. There was nothing to connect her to the anonymous sheet of paper, as she must have known. 'Tell me honestly, Ingrid. Did you arrange all this – having your husband tell me to come here to Aspen – just to ask me to find Pindero for you?'

'Of course not. What a silly thing to say.' She looked away from me. She could never look you in the eye when she was trying to conceal something. Ingrid had always been like that. 'Do you still practice every day, Mickey?' she said.

She wanted to talk. 'Practice? Law?'

'Law.' She laughed. 'No, tap. Tap dancing. You used to get up early and do two hours on that board you had in the garage.'

'I never did.'

'You did.' She laughed. 'Your folks complained about the noise you made tapping. You were waking them up. They told me about it. Every morning: two hours.'

'Naw. Anyway, that was years ago. I gave all that kind of stuff up long before I took the bar exams.'

'Okay.' She smiled and wrinkled her nose.

Ingrid knew me very well: now both of us had told our lies. She knew those A-plus marks I got in tapdancing classes had had a lasting effect on me. Even now that I'd become a middle-aged attorney, I still did my tap routines every morning and nursed a secret dream of turning pro.

'More coffee? Didn't you like the salami? It's real Italian. What about a homemade brownie?'

On the kitchen wall I noticed a photo of our class. It wasn't an original photo, it was one of the photocopies Budd Byron had sent as Christmas cards a year or so ago. She'd cut off the strip where he'd hand-lettered his greetings. The way in which this fuzzy little card was so beautifully mounted and framed said a lot about Ingrid's nostalgia.

'Just a little more coffee.' This was like old times. It was difficult to believe I was really here and with her. How many years was it since I had sat opposite Ingrid like this, looking at those big hazel eyes and deep dimpled cheeks, hearing that infectious laugh, doting on her and watching every movement. She brought the percolator and a big tin containing the brownies. I took one. 'You haven't changed either, Ingrid,' I said. 'You're just as young and beautiful as you ever were.'

She gave another one of those merry little laughs. 'That Irish blarney!' she said. 'I love it.'

The brownies were great. 'You make these?'

'I helped.' So I guess it was one of the kitchen staff: the brownie chef, maybe. She also took one, and as she bit into it she said, 'I wish I understood more about business. Zach gets me to sign all kinds of documents, and sometimes I have no idea of what they are about.'

'You shouldn't do that,' I said, the lawyer coming to the surface.

'All kinds of crazy offshore companies, in countries I've never even heard of. Millions and millions of dollars' worth of stock signed over to me, and then the next thing I know I'm signing it over to someone else. I guess that's a regular part of the way business is done these days?' In her voice there was a mixture of pride and anxiety. She sounded as if she just wanted to be reassured, but would it be right to reassure someone who was maybe going neck deep into what sounded like crooked dealings? Reassure someone you loved, I mean?

I was still trying to decide what to say when suddenly the

kitchen door crashed open. A cold wind came tearing into our cozy tête-à-tête. It was Goldie Arnez, looking very much out of place in a dark blue big-city overcoat. There were flakes of snow on his smart Madison Avenue felt hat and more of them forming white epaulettes on his shoulders. Clipped into his top pocket was his ever-present cellular phone. 'Mrs Petrovitch?' His voice was hoarse as if the cold air had got to his tonsils; his face was flushed and his eyes watery.

'What is it, Goldie?'

'Mr Petrovitch has gone into the operating room with the horse. He phoned. I'm bringing a dozen men up here to the stables. I didn't want you to worry if you saw them foraging around.'

'Men? What for?'

'My men, Mrs Petrovitch. Security guys. Mr Petrovitch wants all the feed taken out and loaded on a truck. He doesn't want the ranch hands to do it.'

'I don't understand,' she said.

'We'll have to search the rooms where the ranch hands sleep. They might object; my boys can handle that okay, but I didn't want you to worry if there was any kind of commotion.'

'The feed?'

'There's a laboratory in Denver with analysis clerks on standby. We're flying the feed over there and picking up fresh feed they will have already tested.'

'Denver?'

'It's beginning to look like Aunt Jemima was poisoned, Mrs Petrovitch. Your husband thinks the feed might have been tampered with.'

'How terrible! Who would want to do such a thing?'

'I can think of plenty of people,' said Goldie. 'It's not the first time, is it?' He bit his lip as he realized that wasn't the right answer. It was everyone-loved-old-Petey when you talked to Mrs Petey. He shuffled his feet and looked at me. 'Hello, Mickey,' he said. Goldie had always been good at putting his foot in his mouth.

'Hi, Goldie.'

'Well, I'd better get to work,' said Goldie. 'Mr Petrovitch said to tell you he'd phone you as soon as he could.'

She smiled sadly. 'I understand,' she said. Sure, we all understood the way it was. When it came to an emergency, Old Petey phoned his muscle man rather than his wife.

Goldie grinned. It was the confident grin of a man who can't be fired. For a moment I had a feeling he might have been listening at the door, but Goldie wasn't like that. Goldie was the kind of man who would have wired the house.

Ingrid said, 'I'll go over to Dr Wilson's place, Goldie. I'll drive myself in the Jeep.'

'Whatever you say, Mrs Petrovitch.'

After Goldie went out we both sat there, saying nothing. Then Ingrid leaned very close to me so she could whisper in my ear. 'It's all my fault,' she said. 'I'm bad.'

'What did you do?'

She put her arm around me and held me tight. I sat in my chair, wondering if Goldie was spying through the window. 'I'm very bad.'

'What?' I said again.

'I fed chocolate bars to Aunt Jemima. It made her ill before.'

'Jesus, Ingrid,' I said, only with effort keeping my voice very quiet. 'Why did you do that?'

'She loves them. Zach feeds her sugar lumps. I figured maybe a little treat now and again would be okay for her.'

'Chocolate bars? Hadn't you better call the vet?'

'No, Mickey, no. He'd kill me. You don't know how angry Zach can be. I told him I hadn't been near Aunt Jemima in weeks. If he found out . . .'

'What would he do?'

'Terrible things.' The way she said it made me want to cry for her.

I sat there until she let go of me. Suddenly she got to her feet and said briskly, 'I must go to him. Will you look in on your friend Mr Crichton? I don't want him to think we don't care about him.'

'He's not a friend,' I said, 'he's a client. I hardly know him.'

'Oh? He was so sweet about you. He thinks you're the smartest lawyer on the Coast. He said you'd become very close friends and he'd trust you with anything.'

'Vic Crichton said that?'

'You're a funny man. Why do you find it so hard to believe that people care about you?'

I looked at her. I didn't say anything.

'Dial Nine when you want dinner. Cook will fix you a steak or something. Tell her what you want.' She looked in the mirror and fluffed her hair.

'I think you should call them about the chocolate bars,' I said.

'Or' – another thought came to her – 'you could take the Audi: the keys are on the hook there. Have fun in town. Whatever! I'll see you in the morning. Mickey, I'm sorry about all this. I'm sure Zach is too.'

6

It wasn't like staying with friends. There was a sort of perfection to the Petrovitch house that deprived it of grace. The servant girl who showed me upstairs to the visitor's suite was dressed in a starched apron, and she spoke in a whisper. It was a small apartment with lithographs and cut flowers and an antique patchwork quilt that all added to the feeling of spending a night in a folklore museum.

From my window I watched Ingrid hurry across the yard and climb into a black Jeep Cherokee with a tall car-phone antenna and the Petrovitch Ranch brand painted on its door. She was wearing a striped fur coat. It was the kind of striped fur coat that looks very fake because real fur coats are not admired in Aspen.

Man, it was cold out there and the snow was coming down heavily, blowing in the wind to make whirlpools and covering the newly swept paths with fresh layers of white. I could tell it was cold from the clouds of steamy smoke the engine emitted as she started up. I spotted Goldie standing in the stable doorway. He'd put on heavy rubber boots, the kind of footwear worn by the men swilling out operating rooms after major surgery. He saluted solemnly as she passed him and then he went across the yard, heading no doubt to where his boys were rummaging through the ranch hands' quarters. As he reached the deep snow he began plodding, holding up the skirt of his coat so it didn't drag in the snow.

I closed the curtains, switched up the thermostat, and then phoned Danny. I was in luck; he was home. I said, 'Danny. You know that flaky kid who was trying to hang that old wreck of a Studebaker on you last month?'

'He's my best buddy,' said Danny guardedly.

'Okay, okay. Well, didn't he tell me that his dad rebuilt vintage cars?'

'That's right.'

'Danny, I'm looking for a guy with a restored Packard Darrin. Convertible. Blue coachwork. An old guy. He drives it. It should be in a museum, but this guy drives around in it. An auto like that is going to have a high profile, right? Phone around to some of your buddies, and see if anyone has seen it. If you locate this guy it's worth a hundred bucks to you.'

'You don't have to pay me,' said Danny huffily.

Like father like son. 'You might need to pay off someone. But you should be able to find it. It's got to be gassed up and serviced and garaged and waxed and looked after.'

'I'll do what I can.'

'Can you get on it right away? Over the weekend, I mean?'

'Where are you calling from?'

'I'm in Colorado. Aspen.'

'Aspen! Some guys have all the luck,' said Danny. 'Have you seen any movie stars?'

'A hundred dollars.' I told him again, in case he forgot the reward. Forgot a hundred bucks? That will be the day.

'So I won't be seeing you for brunch on Sunday?'

'No. I'm sorry, Danny. We'll have to fix another time.'

'It doesn't matter. It's work, I guess.'

'Yeah, it's work. We'll make it next weekend. Maybe Robyna

99

would like to come along too.' Robyna too – that was the ultimate sacrifice, and Danny knew it.

'Packard Darrin. I'll find it for you. We'll keep the hundred bucks in the family.'

'I said I was sorry.' I was never quite sure when he was riling me. 'Listen: brunch at the Beverly Hilton next Sunday. For sure.'

'With Robyna.' He brightened as he thought about it. The Beverly Hilton brunch was his favorite, and my boy Danny was an authority on all-you-can-eat brunches.

'Sure. Book a table. Not too near the food.' Danny always asked for a table near the food.

'Okay,' he said. 'I'll make it real early, so we can be first to cut into all the cakes and stuff.'

'Sure.' What kind of kid is this philosopher? Start talking food and he lights up and says tilt. 'Leave a message on my machine. 'Bye for now.'

''Bye, Dad.'

As I put down the phone, I heard a sound like someone moving around in the corridor. I went across the room, opened my door, and stepped out onto the landing. The whole house was in darkness apart from the glimmers of little emergency lights on the staircase. I had a feeling someone was nearby, listening and watching everything, but there was no one in sight. I stood very still. It was a big rambling place with creaky stairs and a clock that chimed. I stood there a long time, but there was no movement anywhere. Through the windows the snow reflected the moonlight so everything was underlit and kind of spooky.

'Mickey!' Looming out of the shadows like the ghost of Hamlet's father, and with a voice twice as plaintive, was Victor Crichton. He was wearing a silk dressing gown decorated with Chinese dragons and bedroom slippers embroidered with his initials.

'I was going to come and find you,' I said. I wondered if he'd been listening at my door.

'Do you want a drink?'

I followed him into his room. The bed was rumpled, with the bedclothes pulled back and business papers scattered on the counterpane. 'No, I don't want a drink. You look groggy.'

'I'm never going to eat Mexican food again,' he said. 'I'm on antibiotics.'

'They've canceled the dinner party. They both went into town to visit a sick horse.'

'How long have you known these people?'

'A long time.'

'I wish I'd never got into this.'

'Don't play the outraged innocent, Vic. I know about Sir Jeremy and his new passport.'

'Don't link me with that business,' said Vic angrily. 'Those bastards trapped me into playing along with them, just like they trapped you.'

'At the party—'

'At the party I was very boozed. And I'll tell you why I was so boozed. Sir Jeremy had just laid it on me that I was going into the firing line while he made himself scarce.'

I didn't believe him, and I suppose it showed.

Victor said, 'Have you seen what Petrovitch and Sir Jeremy have set up? The Peruvian company?'

'Tell me.'

'They'll put everything into the hands of nominees, who will then divest themselves of all those assets by means of bearer shares. The principals go down to Lima penniless and then, by means of the bearer shares, set up a company there. No tax at any stage of the transaction.'

'Why Peru?'

'All the Caribbean tax havens have just about had their day.

101

Washington has leaned on the governments down there with such energy that no one's using them anymore.'

'Do you have a company in Peru?'

'A small provincial bank that Sir Jeremy picked up for a song. It will be useful for the actual machinery.'

'You'll assign the necessary assets?' I suppose it was legal. Guys like Victor knew when to keep it all legal.

'Yes. And Mrs Petrovitch will do the same for the other side. It's all in her name, he tells me.'

'I hate bearer shares,' I said. 'They can be lost or stolen and there's no recourse.'

'There's no alternative.' He walked across the room. The red dragons were snarling.

'I think we should try to think of one,' I told him. 'Someone grabs those bearer shares, and you'll lose your zillions.'

'It comes to nearly a hundred million dollars if the real estate is included.' He sat down on the bed as if feeling weak. He shook some tablets from a bottle and swallowed them with a sip of water. Then he put a hand under his pillow in a furtive movement.

'What have you got under that pillow, Vic? That's the third time you've done that.'

He lifted the pillow to reveal a revolver. Oh, no! Not another one. He turned to me. 'I don't like what I see in this house. I feel better with a gun under my pillow.'

'What do you mean?'

'Listen, blue eyes. What I've told you is what Petrovitch *says* he's planning. But he could do it all much more elegantly if he had his wife murdered at exactly the right juncture. Furthermore, as a principal of the company acting on company business, she would be insured under the corporate insurance plan. That would give Petrovitch an extra couple of million.'

'Kill Mrs Petrovitch? Is this something Ingrid told you?'

'Mrs Petrovitch? I don't even know the woman. All I'm going by is Zachary Petrovitch's reputation.'

'Try to rest, Vic,' I said. 'Maybe you're getting some kind of fever.'

He kicked off his fancy slippers, took off his dressing gown, and got into bed. His face was very white, as if he'd seen a ghost or been feasted upon by a vampire. 'Maybe I will at that,' he said. 'We'll talk tomorrow.'

'You haven't been eating chocolate bars, have you?'

'No, I'm allergic to chocolate. It brings me out in spots.'

'Make sure the safety is on before you go to sleep,' I told him.

I suddenly wanted to get out of that place and stretch my legs. A steak in some noisy downtown dive would be preferable to sitting in this creaky old mansion working my way through a backlog of unintelligible notes I'd made on my laptop.

I took the Audi and drove into town. The streets were packed with visitors. I'd forgotten what Aspen could be like on a Saturday night when the powder snow is deep. I mooched my way from bar to bar until I found a place I used to like before they fitted it out to look like Sherlock Holmes's Baker Street apartment. There was glitter and tinsel everywhere as if they'd forgotten to take it down at Christmas, except that every day was Christmas for the folks who owned a place like this.

The customers were mostly dressed in cowboy style. Not cowhand style: not sweaty work shirts and stained jeans, but the silk-and-satin cowboy style that Hollywood invented for singers back in the thirties. There were four slim long-haired musicians: fiddle, bull fiddle, electronic keyboard, and a female vocalist with heavy white makeup. They were playing Country and Western, making good music, but the way it was coming over the amplifiers was enough to rattle the eardrums.

'Mickey!' It was someone I knew from college and one of the best friends of my ex-wife, Betty. I've got a terrible memory for faces. I knew her well; she'd been to the house for dinner many times. I knew her very well indeed, but what was her name – Fluffy? Fifi? Frances? 'Remember me, darling? Felicity?' Well, I was nearly right. 'Felicity Weingartner. Remember? USC.'

'Sure I remember, Felicity. Say, didn't I know you at USC? What were you: class of 'Forty-five?'

'You pig!' She gave a shrill little laugh but the loud music swallowed it. She leaned over and looped her arm through mine as if she was going to grab a stein and go into a drinking song. 'You do remember, don't you?' A waitress arrived and hovered over us expectantly.

'Easy does it, Felicity. Plonk your ass down and have a drink.'

'Already.' She held up a glass and rattled the ice in it. She'd been drinking, but not so much that she was in any way drunk. A six-foot-tall good-looker, she was wearing a navy blue cap-sleeve dress. Around her neck was a chain from which a big gold zodiac sign dangled. She had curly brown hair cut short and a golden tan, very white teeth, and a fixed, dotty kind of smile. She was cute.

'Have another,' I said.

'Just a Coke. I drink too much these days.'

'Irish whiskey on the rocks and a Coke,' I told the waitress. 'What are you doing in Aspen, Felicity? I thought you were in movies.'

'I am in movies. We're shooting here in town. I've been here two weeks. It's a dump. We've still got three locations to go: Denver, then a mountain hut, and then a train station or something. I can't wait to get out of here.'

'What do you do in movies?' I asked, more to be polite than because I wanted to know.

'I thought you didn't like movies,' she said. So she really did remember me. The waitress gave me my whisky and put a cold can of Coca-Cola on the table together with a tumbler containing ice. Felicity pulled the ringtop and drank from the can. Aspen is like that.

'Yeah, well, I'm not a movie person,' I admitted. 'I prefer videos. With videos you can get up and fix yourself coffee or a sandwich. And you can roll the same sequence again if you forgot what it was all about.'

'Video. That's like eating candy with the wrapper on. Video is for old folks.'

'I'm getting to be old folks real fast these days, Felicity, and that's the truth.'

'Are you kidding me? Old folks!' She gave me the kind of playful punch that leaves bruises. 'I'm with special effects: explosives, smoke, and stuff. You name it, I do it.'

'Yeah, I remember now,' I lied. 'That must be interesting.'

'You get to talk to the director. You see places and people. And with these location deals you make money. This shoot is a six-day week with lots of nights. That's good bread. I needed this one: I had a repo man come for my BMW. Can you imagine?' She gave another of those shrill laughs. They must have heard her across the room.

I looked around to see: there were a dozen or more men wearing zip-front jackets and baseball caps crowded around a table that was covered with cans and bottles. They were waving to her.

'Get lost!' she shouted. 'The crew,' she explained. 'A lot of no-good drunken bums. The last film, I was with real nice people. You never can tell.' She held the cold can against her cheek. 'What brings you here, Mickey?'

'Work.' I looked around the room. It was crowded; even the dancers were close together. You can tell the tourists from the ones with houses by the way they hold their heads. The visitors are always looking around hoping to spot some celeb, while the regulars are wearing shades and cowering in dark corners. And the people who live here have all got tucks in their faces, porcelain teeth, plastic hair, and ten-thousand-dollar wristwatches.

'Work?' she said. 'What kind?'

'I'm way down Route Eighty-two with a client,' I told her. I looked at her as I tried to decide whether to mention Ingrid's name. Felicity knew Ingrid; she'd been a freshman with us at USC. 'I just came to town for a drink,' I said. 'The clients I'm staying with had other things to do this evening so they gave me a car.'

'I don't use a car in this town anymore. Have you seen the way they paper parked cars around here? I'm living way out near the airport. You can give me a ride home if you're going that way. It will save me cab fare.'

'Okay. Sure you don't want a real drink?'

'We'll have a nightcap at my place,' she said.

'Sounds good,' I said. 'Let's go.'

'Down, boy, down!' she said.

I smiled and drank real slowly, and we exchanged small talk for half an hour. Her boozy work mates cheered as we went out together. We eased our way through the Saturday-night people and out into the street. Felicity was a neat person. I wondered if she had enough old friends with cars to manage permanently without a rental.

I wasn't prepared for the neat little house she was occupying. Not very big and not very fancy but in this town – even out near the airport – buying a place like that wouldn't leave more than small change from a million dollars.

'What kind of budget you got on this movie?' I said, settling down on the velvet-covered sofa and eyeing the fancy light fittings.

'Don't be dumb. This pad has nothing to do with the production. It belongs to my sister, Sheree. You never met her, did you? She's a lovely girl.' Felicity didn't really mean 'girl,' she just didn't like to face the fact that she was grown up enough for her sister to be a woman. 'Her boyfriend rented this place for her, plus a swanky apartment in New York. In the Fifties, looking out over Park Avenue, doorman, heat, and all the bills paid. Can you imagine?'

'Not easily,' I said. 'That kind of thing hasn't happened to me in ages.'

'But she's got her troubles. He's moody and demanding. And he's a cokehead . . . well, I don't have to go on, do I?'

'He's married, this moody cokehead?'

'I always said you should have been a detective.'

'Ha-ha. Give me a drink.'

'Fix it yourself, big boy.' She slumped down, closed her eyes, slipped her shoes off, and sighed.

I got up and went across to the Art Deco bar. There was every kind of drink on the mirrored shelves. I poured a ready-mix Manhattan and found ice in the refrigerator that was fitted under the sink. With the drink in my hand I looked around. On the piano there were photos, lots of photos, all of them in silver frames. Some were group photos and some were newspaper glossies and always somewhere in the picture were the same man and girl, always smiling and beautiful: Sheree, I guessed, with her cokehead.

'Do you come to Aspen a lot?' I asked her. 'Even when you're not working here?'

'To ski sometimes; it's glorious skiing. But for the likes of me it's expensive.' She came around behind me to see what I was looking at. It was the photo of a gang of people crowding around a wedding cake. 'That's Sheree, and that's Frank Sinatra,' she said, tapping the photo.

'It just looks like someone's arm,' I said.

'It's Frank Sinatra's arm,' said Felicity.

I tapped another section of blue serge suiting and said, 'Could that be Michael Jackson's ass?'

'You're a miserable bastard, Mickey,' she said, smiling, but not smiling so much as to show she didn't mean it.

'It's the altitude,' I said. 'I'm real nice at sea level.' I spotted the smiling face of Zach Petrovitch in another one of the photos: a big melee of guests at some kind of function where everyone was wearing tuxedos, fixed smiles, and tiaras. 'Know that guy?' I asked her.

She looked at me as if I was crazy. As if she were answering the big question on a game show, she said, 'Zach Petrovitch. He's married to your Ingrid. Sure I know him.'

My Ingrid? Oh, well. 'He's my client. That's where I'm staying.' I sat down and rested my feet on a stuffed pig of polished leather. It creaked.

'I wondered about that. Ingrid told me you were working for Petrovitch these days.' She spread herself across the sofa, letting her skirt ride up like wanton women do in movies.

'You see them?'

'Sure. Off and on I've seen a lot of Ingrid. For a couple of semesters we roomed together. We kept in touch, like I kept in touch with you and Betty. I kind of reach out for old friends. I was with Ingrid the day she went to see her astrologer about getting married again.'

'And the astrologer okayed it?'

'No. The astrologer said the signs were real bad. Zach Petrovitch is not really Aquarius: he's born on the cusp. That's part of their problem.'

'That's too bad,' I said. 'And not much anyone can do about it.'

'Ya, looks like. I haven't seen much of her lately. She got a charge account with Gianni Versace, and I found myself cutting the Saks labels off my favorite dresses, and I began to think this maybe wasn't a healthy relationship for either of us. Know what I mean?'

'It's called status anxiety.'

'She'd insist we go to fancy places for lunch, and then she'd keep looking over my shoulder to see who was coming in. I felt kind of uncomfortable with her. I guess she felt the same about me. We never had a row or anything; I still call her regularly and see her. We had coffee together only a couple of weeks ago, and she came down to watch the shooting, but Ingrid's different nowadays. She's not our kind anymore. She has that big house along the road, she has all kinds of celebs out there to stay, but she's never invited me there, not even for coffee.' She grabbed at her arms and hugged herself. 'It's getting chilly in here.'

'Ingrid's all right,' I said. 'She's maybe lost her way.'

'She could always wind you around her little finger. You were bewitched.'

'We were young.'

'Maybe marrying Petrovitch wasn't smart, not if she wanted the kind of care and attention we both know she demands. Petrovitch is a loner.'

'Did you tell her that?'

'No. I was happy for her. They were in love and he was rich and owned half the world.'

'They seem happy,' I said.

'They come from different worlds; they want different things.' Felicity opened her purse and looked inside it as if she was going to get a cigarette. Maybe she was, but if so she changed her mind and snapped it shut and put it aside. 'When she started to feel neglected she drained me, Mickey. I helped her all I could, but she took me to the cleaners emotionally.' Maybe I didn't look convinced because she went on. 'One night

109

in LA she came around to see me and said she was frightened. I spent half the night talking to her. Finally she went back home happy and reassured, and slept till noon, and had her maid bring her brunch in bed. Great, except that I grabbed two hours tossing and turning, then went to work bushed. I can't be a stand-in for her emotional wear and tear. She doesn't understand what it takes out of me.'

'Frightened of what?'

'Frightened of Petrovitch. It's all nonsense, of course. The truth is she's become a neurotic woman; she needs counseling.'

'Maybe she gets lonely.'

'We all do. It's okay for you, you've got your lovely son.'

'I haven't got my lovely son. He's living with a Gloria Steinem look-alike near Paramount Studios. The last time I went to see him he was brandishing a Browning automatic and telling me how much he could hock it for. I haven't got my son.'

She continued as if she hadn't heard me. 'But what has Ingrid got? Dinner parties and charity committees.'

'She's got her husband,' I suggested tentatively.

'Oh, boy, isn't that a man's answer. A husband! Let me tell you something: her husband takes balance sheets to read in bed. Ingrid told me that for a fact. He takes his accounts to read in bed.'

I didn't like Petrovitch, but that didn't seem like a fair comment. 'The guy is working his butt off to make money so she can take a gold charge card to Rodeo Drive, and you bad-mouth him.'

'Talk to Ingrid.'

'I was talking to her this afternoon,' I said.

'Did she bend your ear with her problems?'

'No,' I said.

'Well, maybe you're the one person she should have laid it on. You're a lawyer. You're paid to give people advice.'

'Thanks, Felicity. Can I give you half a dozen of my business cards?'

'My, my. Did I touch a nerve?'

'So you're in special effects? That sounds interesting.'

She grinned. 'Don't press your luck, buster! As a matter of fact I've been developing a subject for nearly two years. I got a script written, paid for the first draft, and then decided I could get it into better shape myself. I took journalism and English at college, so I know how to write. Special effects? Hell, no, that's for the birds. I'm going to direct the next one.'

'Direct? Could you handle that?'

'Half those jerks get director credits for standing around while the crew makes the movie. I can direct. Yes.'

'When?' I wasn't convinced, and neither was she.

She tugged at the hem of her skirt. 'Good question, old buddy. When I can get someone excited about my script, that's when. You know the problem with Hollywood?'

'I've been waiting to hear.'

'Nepotism. The whole lousy industry is packed with the cousins, brothers-in-law, and children of the guys at the top. Run the credits of any new movie, and you find the greatgrandchildren of the guys who were running the industry back in the thirties.'

'It's not so easy,' I said. 'There's a lot of competition, even for people with the right family.' I have movie clients, plenty of them. Getting from being an outsider with a script under your arm to being a director with a few million bucks to make a picture is a leap that few wannabes made. I hoped she wasn't going to ask me to twist the arm of someone I knew.

'And too many kids from film schools. Every last lousy college in the country has got a film school. Usually run by some dumb nerd with a subscription to *Variety* who learned about movies by doing the Universal Studios tour.'

111

'You should see the guys teaching law,' I said.

'They know all the shots: "We'll take the umbrella scene from Hitchcock, the baby carriage sequence from Eisenstein, the sunrise from David Lean, the horsemen from Peckinpah." The trouble is they haven't got one original idea in their head; all they know is camera angles.'

'Can I have another drink?' I said, getting up to help myself.

'Too many goddamned car chases,' she called, waving her empty glass at me.

'And not enough sex and violence,' I said, taking the glass and pouring her a refill.

She looked at me for a moment and said, 'You're all right, Mickey.'

'If you say so, Felicity.'

'You got a football scholarship to college, didn't you?'

'When people say that to me in that tone of voice, I know it means: I can believe you're brainless enough, but do you have the build for it?' I gave her the drink. 'That's right. I was lucky. They needed people on the team that year. The Marine Corps had kicked me out with an injured hand after ten months of service. USC was awarding football scholarships, and as a disabled vet I hit the spot with the board.'

'You don't have to apologize. It's just that you never did look like one of those football dudes.'

'I was on the team with Budd Byron. He switched from Political Science to Theater.'

'I see him all the time. We were on a movie together last summer.'

'Yes, he keeps working.'

'He's a fine actor and still gorgeous-looking. I could go for him.'

'Lucky Budd.' I sipped my drink and then put it down. I didn't want it anymore. The mood had changed. When we first

112

came back here I had the feeling that she could hardly wait for us to tumble into bed. But the moment had passed.

Maybe she saw that and wanted to make a preemptive strike. 'I really must get some shut-eye.'

'Yep, I must be getting along,' I said. 'I've got a meeting with Zach Petrovitch in the morning, and I have documents to read.'

I guess we were both putting Band-Aids on our egos. 'And I have to be on location by six-thirty. There's a lot of preparation for tomorrow's shoot, and we've got an eight-year-old director who throws tantrums if he's kept waiting.'

I kissed her decorously, once on each cheek the way the beautiful people who'd been to Europe did it. And then I drove back to ranchero Petrovitch. It was a wonderful night and the mountains gleamed in the moonlight. I didn't see anyone as I parked the car, but there were several little buzzes as the security cameras turned and focused and checked out who I was and where I went.

It was still only a little past midnight. I didn't look in on Vic Crichton, in case I got a fusillade of lead. I decided to do half an hour's work, and while I was tapping away at my laptop I heard cars coming and going. While working I kept thinking of Ingrid, trying to decide if she was really happy or not. I couldn't tell. Feeding chocolate bars to your husband's favorite filly sounded like something a shrink could make a saga from. Jealousy? Hatred? Indulgence? I gave up on it and switched to TV. I could only find electronic snow: maybe nighttime TV in Aspen was always that way. I felt tired. I'd fallen into some kind of generation gap, I guess.

I went and opened the window to breathe some of that clear Colorado air. On the mountainside, like strings of amber beads, the lamps of Sno-Cats crawled across the slopes, reupholstering the ski runs for morning. I closed the window tight. You can have too much of that kind of fresh air.

113

Finally I went to bed and read a book I found on the shelf: *Selected Letters of Ernest Hemingway*, the author. Oh, boy, and I thought lawyers had problems! After I'd switched off the lights I lay in bed listening to the owls hooting and that wild-life ruckus. Out here in the Colorado mountains all the animals came out after dark; in this respect it was a lot like Los Angeles.

I was awakened by voices. At first I couldn't hear what they were saying; the sounds were muffled by the deep snow. But I recognized the voices as the folks who live on the hill: Petrovitch and Ingrid. Then I heard Ingrid say, 'Maybe you get too emotionally involved with them.' Petrovitch said something about 'I'm not going to shoot her, and that's final.' And then the door closed and silenced the voices.

It was almost dawn; it probably would have been dawn but for all those lousy mountains blocking the light. I guessed they'd been holding hooves all night. Instead of quarreling over kids they quarreled over horses; maybe the nags answered some kind of need for them. Or maybe not. In any case, what business was it of mine? I turned over, thumped the feather pillow, and went back to sleep.

Next morning a phone call from some in-house female secretary told me that Mr and Mrs Petrovitch would both be sleeping late. I could fly home. They'd contact me next week when I was needed. Okay, folks, no offense taken; everything is itemized and on the bill. I gave Vic Crichton a miss. I had breakfast in the morning room, just me, seated, and two servants pouring coffee and orange juice. Before me there was a bowl piled high with watercress and grapefruit salad, two small oatcakes, and muesli with yoghurt. It was delicious and healthy, but I couldn't help hoping that on the plane they'd serve fried eggs, crispy bacon, and pork sausages.

The man in the woolly hat was wearing his Eddie Bauer

fur-collared parka when he took me to the airport via downtown Aspen, where vital errands had to be done. He was a taciturn fellow, and I didn't ask him whether Aunt Jemima had gone to that big racetrack in the sky. After he'd picked up a package from a laboratory and posted some mail, we crawled through downtown Aspen in heavy traffic until halted by some kind of private cop brandishing a stop sign and a walkie-talkie. 'Hold it, buddy.'

The mountains shut the light out. The gray snow-packed sky made the street shadowless and drained the world of color, except that small section of it the camera crew saw. For them a searchlight – the gigantic kind of carbon arc lamp that the movie world calls a brute – flooded the street with an oval lake of yellow light and ridged the houses with gold trim. Aspen's main street, usually a set piece of ordered car parking, was now crammed with vehicles strewn around like forgotten toys at bath time. Not just cars: bulldozers and station wagons, vans and buses, trucks and cranes.

Downtown Aspen was a scene to behold. In a mad reversal of normal life, snow was being trucked down from the mountain and shoveled into the street from the backs of slowly moving dump trucks. They were bringing snow into Aspen! Aspen, which had its every last street swept clean of snow every night: what kind of kooks were these movie folk?

'No cars – not until we get the shot.'

'We'll be through and away in ten seconds,' I said.

He smiled to reveal broken teeth. 'This is eighteen eighty-two, mister. No cars, get it? We don't want the camera to spot the tracks of your deep-tread Michelins, do we?'

The street was crowded with people: some of them were in costume, many of them were drinking coffee and eating dough-nuts being dispensed from an open-sided van marked KING KONG LOCATION CATERING. Tracks had been laid along the sidewalk, and on the camera dolly a bearded cameraman in a fur hat was bent over to peer through the eyepiece of the camera. Two powerful grips were flexing their muscles, ready to push the dolly backward along the tracks.

'Mickey! Mickey, hurry. What luck: you're just in time!' It was Felicity. She was wearing a bomber jacket with a fur collar. In her hands she had two steaming Styrofoam cups of coffee. She was smiling and bright-eyed, as though working on the movie energized her.

'In time for what?' I opened the car door. It was cold out there.

'Have coffee and come see what I do for a living.'

'I've got a plane to catch.'

'They'll hold the plane.' She gave me one of the coffees.

'For me they won't hold the plane,' I told her.

'We have some film that must go to the lab. The LA flight won't leave until it's on board.'

'She's right. It will be okay,' my woolly-hatted friend agreed.

'Movies rule the world,' I said. But I got out of the car and plodded behind her to a place where a row of folding chairs had been arranged for the technicians. The director was huddled on a high stool. He was dressed in black: black pants, black boots, black windbreaker, black turtleneck, and a black fur hat. He was a big fellow for an eight-year-old.

'Be quiet. Sit here. Want more coffee? A doughnut?' She indicated a canvas chair with SPECIAL EFFECTS stenciled on the fabric.

I shook my head. 'Are you sure about that plane?'

'Sure, I'm sure. Watch! Watch the actor in the middle, the one with the big Stetson. They're just about ready to go.'

I'd had dozens of movie clients. Watching movies being made was no big deal. 'Where's the focus puller?' I asked her.

She was up to that. 'It's a tracking shot at walking speed.

They won't need to change focus; the distance between the actor and the camera dolly remains the same throughout.'

'Um,' I said, and drank my steaming coffee while one of the assistant directors bull-horned everyone into silence. Then the script girl snapped her Polaroid shot and clipped it into the book for continuity.

Felicity leaned across to say, 'It sure would be great to get it in one shot. It's a lot of work setting it up. See the other cameras? This is a key shot in the story, and the director wants it covered from a lot of different angles. Mute camera for this one; no need to hold your breath. The airport being so close by makes location recording impossible here.'

'Let's go. Camera! Action!' called the assistant director.

The camera dolly rolled back, keeping always about ten feet away from the three cowboys, who came stomping out of the saloon and through the snow, cursing and waving their arms in anger.

'Come out, gunman!' shouted the director. From the same doorway behind them came a man with a rifle. He put it to his shoulder, aimed, and fired. I heard the faint whine of some sort of radio-controlled gadget. Then I was stupefied to see the tall cowboy's skull explode in a great thick cloud of blood. *Pow!* Brains, blood, and skull fragments rained down upon the snowy street as the figure crumbled, flailed his arms, and collapsed into gore-encrusted snow.

It was horrific. His head burst open so that imitation blood, gray brains, and torn pieces of Stetson were scattered everywhere. For a moment even these hardened movie people seemed stunned by the sight of the mess, and then the director shouted, 'Cut! We'll do it again.' He was angry as he called to some unseen special effects guy who'd triggered the explosion. 'Alan, I don't want to see damage to the Stetson. That wouldn't happen in reality, would it? Can we fix that?'

117

Felicity waved a hand in the air, and the director nodded.

A bulldozer roared in to scoop up the bloodstained snow and the bits of skull and brain. As the actor was helped to his feet by a special effects man and a wardrobe girl, I could see the way in which a false head had been fixed to a frame he wore. He was a double: really some six inches shorter than he would seem to be in the film. A girl stood by, holding a new head complete with radio antenna that would be hidden by the Stetson. A second hat, exactly like the previous one right down to the last stain and crease, was also ready.

'Pretty good, eh?' said Felicity. 'I told them to put reinforcing in the Stetson, but that dumb director said it would be okay without.'

'It's disgusting,' I said. I spoke with great feeling.

'You've turned white,' she said. She chortled. 'You're really going to enjoy your airline breakfast.'

'What kind of mind dreams up a sequence like that?' It would have served her right if I'd thrown up my grapefruit-and-watercress salad.

'You're upset, Mickey. I'm sorry,' she said, without sounding very sorry. 'I didn't know what a sensitive kind of guy you are, or I would have warned you.'

'All us footballers are like that,' I said. But I'd heard something in her voice that betrayed her delight. I knew then I had misread the entrails last night. She'd felt rejected by my getting up and going home, and she didn't like to be rejected.

But she wasn't going to let me get away so easily. Hanging on my arm, she said, 'I couldn't sleep last night. You made me feel guilty . . . about Ingrid, I mean. I shouldn't have said she was neurotic. Maybe deep inside I was a tiny bit jealous. I'll go talk to her and cheer her up and be a little more supportive.'

'They're sleeping late. They had a sick horse up there last night,' I said.

118

'She didn't feed Jemima candy bars again, did she?' When I didn't reply. Felicity said, 'She swore she wouldn't. I guess things must be bad between them. She does it to punish him, of course.'

'You're doing a great job, Felicity,' I said. 'See you in LA sometime.'

She let me get into the car before replying. 'Yeah, sure,' she said. I heard a very loud maybe.

Once in the car I sat back in the leather and fought down waves of nausea. I opened the window and waved as the car drew away. I needed air. 'Did you see that stunt?' I asked the driver.

'Yeah. Great, wasn't it?'

'Maybe Mr Petrovitch would like to come down and watch,' I suggested. 'They're blowing heads off all morning.'

7

Flying back from Colorado was not a pleasure for me, but at least I was heading in the right direction. When I'm working and a client foots the bill, I have my secretary arrange a car for me, but this had all been planned so hurriedly I took one of those door-to-door buses for the outward journey and on my return flight I just walked out bag in hand and flagged down the first cab I saw.

'You want to go to Woodland Hills?'

I asked him because some of those guys are choosey about journeying into the sticks. This one even helped me with my bag; there must be a recession or something.

'Sure, that's my kind of habitat.' The driver was a short fat Armenian with a curly gray mustache, a worried face, and a tire lever under his seat. He saw the label on my bag. 'You been in Aspen, huh? How is the snow?'

'I couldn't tell you, buddy. I was there on business.' I didn't want him to think I was some rich jerk who could go to Aspen for a weekend and tip with my eyes closed.

'Are you a travel agent?' He jumped into the driver's seat, revved up, and tore away like we were doing the Indy.

I held on tight as he went around the airport feeder road on two wheels. 'I'm a lawyer. I was with a client.'

'Lawyer, huh? So what do you think the jury will do? Will

you look at that guy!' He gave a blast on the horn, went through the changing signals, and tore up the hill at full speed.

'What jury?'

'The Simi Valley trial. The amateur video.' He said it like I must be a visitor from Mars. 'The cops and the black guy in Foothills a year ago. Don't tell me you haven't seen the tape?'

'I've seen it.' Who hadn't seen the blurred pictures of the figure on the ground and the baton-wielding policemen? The Rodney King beating was prime-time TV. Every talking head in the world collected fees for discussing it under lights.

As we fed into the traffic and slowed to its speed, the driver leaned back. 'I had a fare who'd just arrived from Taiwan. Oriental guy but perfect English, hardly any accent. First thing he asks me is what's happening to those cops on trial. This guy travels all the time. He told me that video clip has been shown on every TV station in the world.'

'I guess so. Even in Aspen.'

'Is that so? Do you think they pay a fee to that guy every time they use it?'

'I'm not sure.'

'So what will the verdict be?'

'I never predict verdicts; you're safer guessing what the horses will do at Santa Anita.'

'Not guilty. Mark my words. That's how the verdict will come in.'

'You think so?'

'And you're a lawyer? Sure. Not guilty. You know what the law says. It's a crime to resist an arresting officer. It's in the code: submit, it says. Resist having the cuffs put on, and a cop can club you senseless. That's what the law says, Mac. You going to tell me I'm wrong?'

I said, 'The law says reasonable force can be exerted until an arrestee is restrained.'

He nodded sagely; he'd had this conversation before. 'Okay. Maybe you like it, maybe you don't, but it's the law of the land. No way that jury can find those cops guilty. No way! You're a lawyer, you know that.'

'You can never tell what a jury will do, believe me.'

But he gave no sign of having heard my caution. 'They got to have the law framed that way. A cop is often alone in the car when he confronts a perpetrator. No way a single cop can cuff a huge guy like that if the guy is determined not to be cuffed. No way, except being able to club him senseless if he resists.'

'Reasonable force,' I said. 'Not club anyone senseless; just use reasonable force.'

He wasn't listening to me. He was like all my clients. They come to you for advice and never listen to what you tell them. He said, 'You want to do the Coast or the One-oh-one?'

'Whatever you say.'

'Let's try the One-oh-one. Yep, that guy is a bodybuilder. I have those guys in the cab sometimes, but when I spot that kind of muscle flagging me I keep going. I don't slow for them guys.'

'Why?'

'Why? Why?' His voice rose. Overcome by my ignorance and foolishness, he swiveled in his seat to get another look at me. 'Are you kidding? Because a black guy built like the Bonaventure Hotel is likely to have done his long stint of muscle-building at government expense, that's why.' We bumped over a series of potholes. 'I don't know why they let them have all that expensive gym equipment in prison. Bodybuilding – shit! All those cons should be fixing the roads . . . Look at that son of a bitch!' There was another jolt.

'How do you know so much about the law?' I said. 'I mean about cuffing perps.'

'Cabbies have to know the law. Let me tell you, my son is a cop and it's tough being a cop in this town. Okay, some towns are worse, but do you know how many LA cops have been blown away in the last ten years? He's twenty-one years old. I begged him not to do it. He says he wants to help people. My old lady worries every night about the kid. Did you see those figures *Time* magazine got from the county DA's office? We've got thirteen thousand hard-core killers walking the streets in this city – and a lot of those goons are fresh from Asia, straight out of the jungle.'

'It was a woman,' I said, remembering the newspaper account. 'The one who pulled that guy over for speeding and driving under the influence – that was a woman CHP officer who started the whole business.'

'Jesus.' He shuddered. 'Am I glad no daughter of mine rides these streets through the night. If you saw the things I see when I'm on late shift. Pushers, pervs, psychos. I'd rather she was a twenty-five-dollar hostess in Dreamland. There are people out there on the street who will kill for the price of one fix. Ever been to Little Phnom Penh in Long Beach, the Cambodian section?'

'I've heard of it,' I said.

'Stay away; it's a battlefield. I won't go there anymore. Gangs run that neighborhood. There are drive-by shootings every day. No one is safe.'

'It's the next ramp,' I told him.

'What? Oh, sure, no sweat. I know Woodland Hills. This is a nice neighborhood. Good schools and decent people. Respectable white European people, not like all this foreign immigrant shit we got downtown. You're lucky.'

By the time I reached my home it was getting dark, but the sun's got visiting rights to Southern California and we see it on a regular basis. I walked around the house feeling good and went out on my deck to watch the sunset, smell my little orange trees, and listen to the traffic pounding down the freeway.

I made sure that Mrs Santos, my Mexican cleaning lady who is really from Colombia, had given Rex his canned food. Although his water bowl was not empty, I poured more into it. He wagged his tail.

'It's good to be home, Rex,' I said. He smiled and drank some water just to show me he needed it.

I sat down on my big chintz sofa with a chilled glass of one of those low-cal no-alcohol beers. I had a selection on the fridge door and was working my way through them. One day I was going to cut out alcohol altogether – the cops had been leaning on drunk driving lately and the courts seemed to single out lawyers for punitive sentencing. In fact, some of these lead-free brews were actually drinkable. Yum-yum.

I hit the button of my phone to take the messages. It was all routine except for a long message from Jo-Anne, a nice girl I'd been dating off and on since Thanksgiving, when I met her at a cookout in Palos Verdes. She worked as a broker in the stock market, and the message said she was going to Chicago Monday morning to visit with her mother and would be back midweek. We'd both been getting pretty serious lately, but I didn't want to talk with her right now. Meeting Ingrid again had jolted my mind in a way I didn't think was still possible. I wasn't about to try and explain any of that to Jo-Anne. Not even the most understanding of women is going to nod through the notion of being put on hold because I'd had a cup of coffee with a married woman who gave me the brush-off more years ago than either of us cared to calculate.

I hadn't been back home for half an hour when the door buzzer sounded. It was a little late for social calls. I squinted through the viewing lens in the door and switched on the light that illuminated the entry porch. The light seemed to startle

124

him, and he jumped back. It was no one I recognized. I opened the door as far as the safety chain allowed.

'I'm a friend of Betty, your wife,' said the guy on the doorstep. This character must have been waiting outside in a car, and seen me arrive, and waited some more. Can you beat it? It's sobering to find out what kind of guys your ex-wife attaches herself to. This greasy-haired individual in his natty suit, a cigar between his teeth and a ready-made floral-pattern bow tie, was straight from Central Casting: the crooked fight manager in a black-and-white B-movie who wants his boy to take a dive.

'I'm a friend of your wife,' he said again, in a New York accent. 'No need to be scared.' He plucked the cigar from his face and gave me an unconvincing smile.

'Scared? I'm relieved,' I said. 'I'd figured you for a talent scout from the IRS.'

'Yeah, well, as a matter of fact, I want to talk about money,' he said, and waited for me to release the chain and ask him in.

'Talk on.'

'You want to let me in?'

'I got a fierce dog,' I told him. 'And he hasn't been fed yet.'

'You've got to let Betty have more money,' he said. 'She can't manage on what you give her, and she can't work.'

'Why can't she work?'

'She's not strong. You know that.'

'I don't know anything of the kind,' I told him. 'You can take it from me, Betty is strong. She may not be muscular, but she is one of the strongest women I ever wrestled with.'

'Cut the comedy,' he said. 'She can't manage, and you've got to give her a cash settlement out of all that dough you're getting for the sellout.'

'Beat it,' I said.

'Ten thousand.'

'Get out of here. I'll have you arrested for demanding money by threat.'

'She said you were an asshole.'

'Look, buddy, if you feel the dough I give her each month is inadequate, you give her some of your own moola.'

'Ten thousand, and she'll never bother you again.' He removed the cigar from his mouth and tapped ash onto the ground.

'I said beat it.' I closed the door.

Boom, boom! My visitor delivered a succession of blows to the door panels. It wasn't a very good door: the lock had been forced three times over the years, and one of the hinges was very shaky. And this guy was heavy-duty, a veritable steam shovel. 'Let me in!' He was shouting and hammering on the door so the whole house shook.

I figured any minute the glue around that panel was going to give, and then those big hands were going to come groping through the door for me. Where the hell was Rex? He always went and hid when I needed him. 'Rex! Rex!' I called in a low confident voice. 'This is a ten-thirteen, Rex, old buddy: officer requires assistance.' No sign of the mutt. Just a couple of growls and a bark would have been backup.

Lacking Rex, I had to cool this maniac before he leveled the house. I shouted, 'Stop that and get out of here, greaseball, or I'll blow both your goddamned heads off.' That got his attention, all right. 'With this Magnum,' I added, although all I had stashed behind the door was a rain hat and a dated certificate from the termite and pest control inspector.

He stopped pounding on the door and shut up, maybe to snatch a drag on his cigar. Then he shouted, 'I'll be back, Mickey Murphy. I'll be back!'

'That's right, it's been lovely, let's do it again,' I said. 'Go home and take your vitamins.' Jesus, what did I do to deserve this panorama of life in a great city? I went into the family room

– family room: that's a laugh; the last time a family was in this room was when my cleaning lady brought her two cousins and her husband to get the cobwebs from the higher reaches of its cathedral ceiling.

I sat down and clicked my way through all thirty channels offered by the cable company. Then I riffled through my videos without finding any Hollywood musical I wanted to see for the hundredth time. I was hungry. I got a *pollo alla cacciatore* from the freezer and slammed it into the micro. It wasn't bad; not like the picture on the package, of course, but there was an element of excitement as I sifted through the thick red sauce, encountering pieces of olive, tomato, and mushroom until I discovered the elusive piece of chicken.

After I'd eaten this spicy mixture I made a really strong brew of coffee in the automatic, sat down, and slipped off my shoes while it hissed and bubbled. I seemed to be having a lot of arguments lately. This is not you, Mickey, I thought as I saw my bulbous and distorted self reflected in the dark blank screen of the TV. You are arguing with cops doing their duty, firemen trying to save lives, your son's charming and beautiful girlfriend, and even the well-meaning associates of your dear ex-wife. Come to think of it, maybe a Magnum would not be such a bad idea. And a shoulder holster. There was that Browning my son Danny kept wrapped in a half-eaten burrito, or maybe some friendly neighborhood gun store would sell me an M60 on time.

I looked at my mail. I already had it in my hand. Mrs Santos put newly arrived mail – together with her itemized bill – in the plastic jug of the coffee machine. It had to be removed before coffee could be made. And since last month, Mrs Santos had been using her son's computer to print out her bills: tracking paper and that crazy expanded lettering that some of them do. She couldn't read, write, or speak the language but on that computer she was a regular Horowitz, and her counting was unassailable. Don't get me wrong; we're all immigrants, and I like her. Mrs Santos caught on fast, and I admire that: it sure was taking me a long time to adjust to life in the U.S. of A. If Mrs Santos stood for public office I'd vote for her, because put her in the White House with her son's computer, and this nation would not have a four-trillion-dollar deficit for long, believe me.

Mail. More two-for-one coupons for the giant-size tubs of fried chicken pieces. But I can't get through one of those giant-size tubs before my skin goes yellow and I get broody. One dollar off the new Lightfinger car wash, and a one and only chance to invest in real estate. The only real letter, with hand-written address, was from Danny. It said BY HAND across the top and had a stamp that looked like it had been soaked off some other missive. I opened it. There was a folded sheet of lined yellow paper from a legal pad and a Polaroid photo of a lovely old motorcar. On the yellow paper, Danny had written:

> If this is the one you want, it's in a lockup in Topanga Canyon. It belongs to a guy named Panter who's had it for years. He doesn't drive it much on account of it's too valu-able but all the car buffs know about it. I'll have his address late Monday or, failing that, Tuesday morning. Did you say one hundred bucks?
> Yrs, Danny

It was a lousy photo, but it looked like a Packard Darrin, all right. That was a valuable car: if a Bugatti wanted to give a Ferrari a fancy motorcar it would buy a Packard Darrin. I tried to decide where the Polaroid shot had been taken, but there was so little background it was difficult to be sure. A palm and a section of sidewalk with a yellow painted line on the curb

128

and a traffic signal in the background. It wasn't Topanga Canyon; Malibu maybe.

Panter, Pinter, Pindero. I'd buy any of those. These guys never changed their name drastically. Some of them kept the same initials so their monogrammed shirts, flatware, signet rings, and silver hairbrushes didn't look like they all belonged to someone else.

So it seemed I had found Mr Pindero. Chasing that Packard Darrin was a lucky shot. I guess this guy Pindero was attached to that buggy the way I was to my vintage Caddie. Well, if he wanted to disappear he was dumb to keep such a tight hold on that car. Car freaks notice every such machine on the streets. Riding around in a conspicuous car is no way to go into hiding; you may as well get yourself paged in the Polo Lounge. Topanga Canyon? Well, that might tempt a guy with the heat on him as a place to go and avoid the scrutiny. It was worth a try. I burped. Maybe I should warn you: there is a lot of garlic in chicken cacciatore.

It rained all through the night, which gave the raccoons a bad time. They kept me awake scampering about and trying to prize off my roof shingles. If they were building some kind of home up there I would have to do something to evict them; they're destructive little critters.

By morning the rain had stopped, the clouds were broken and scattered, and there was sunshine. Topanga Canyon connects the 101 to the Pacific Coast Highway, but it's not like the other canyons. Its steep sides are green and rugged, and everything sparkled after the rain. You can't drive Topanga without being reminded of all those cheap movies made when Hollywood belatedly discovered there had been a war in a place named Viet Nam. Its hills are scrubby and steep, its roads narrow and winding. But it's not all greenery. You can find just

about anything you want in Topanga. It's a wacky stretch –
Sunset Strip served country style. Hot-dog vendors, car
wreckers, antique dealers, saddlemakers, college professors,
vagrants, and movie stars all call Topanga home.

Trails ascend on both sides, and all the intersections are
adorned with dozens of hand-painted signs to help find the
homes of residents. I found a fingerpost bearing the name of
Panter and turned onto the narrow side road. It took every last
cubic millimeter of the big V-8 to pull my Caddie up that steep
stretch of slippery surface, muddy hairpin after hairpin, to the
hilltop where Albert H. Pindero, aka Panter, had stashed
himself.

My Caddie is big, and negotiating such bends, with other
drivers coming down, was a hair-raising experience. There were
narrow entranceways every few yards, to add a little extra terror.
Twice I was nearly run off the road: once by some swimsuited
kids in a pickup and the next time by a frizzy-haired woman
in a dented Honda who nearly hit me while I was stopped and
asking directions from a man pruning his roses. She waved her
fist at me as she went past pounding the horn.

The top of the hill was heavily wooded and there were more
road junctions, and more signs, together with dented and rusty
mailboxes: conglomerate and glistening in the rain and looking
like the sort of well-kept abstract sculpture that rich insurance
companies enshrine in their lobbies. But none of these signs
said Pindero or Panter either. I reached a dead end at wide
wrought-iron gates with an ARMED RESPONSE keep-out notice
and an empty trash bin.

I switched off the engine, got out of my car, and took a deep
breath. I looked around, but the trees and undergrowth were
enough to conceal any houses nearby. It had become a glorious
day. The sun was slanting through the trees to speckle the
rock-strewn soil. The air carried a spicy scent of freshly cut

timber, and from somewhere out of sight came the cruel growls and gasps of a chain saw. There is always the noise of construction out in those green canyons. Houses bulged with extensions, new decks, pools, jacuzzis, carports, and guest accommodations.

As I went to unlatch the iron gate a man emerged from behind the trees. 'What do you want, mister?' Forty-ish, he was wearing a new checked shirt, clean jeans, and sneakers. Quick-eyed, freshly shaven, with good lace-up shoes and two hundred pounds of muscles. In my book that added up to an ex-cop who worked out.

'This is a beautiful spot,' I said.

I wasn't jesting. The sky was deep blue instead of khaki, the smell of sage and eucalyptus outbid the smog, and the birds were singing instead of coughing. It was hard to believe we were only a few miles from the big La-La. Maybe I would move out this way when I no longer had to commute every day.

'I'm looking for the owner of a big old Packard Darrin,' I said.

He tossed a cigarette butt to the ground, crushed it into the mud with his heel, and looked at me. 'What about it?'

I knew that saying I wanted to buy the old car would invite the reply that it was not for sale, and that would terminate the conversation. 'My name's Murphy. I'm a collector – Murphy's Vintage Automobiles of Bakersfield. Maybe you've heard of me. I possess an even finer example of elegance. A real collector's item, a jewel. Maybe your boss would like to buy it.'

'Got ID?'

'An out-of-date Price Club ticket, and an Amex card cut in two pieces.'

He came through a wicket gate to pat my jacket with a casual touch to see if I had a gun. I had the feeling he'd done it often. Up close he smelled of fried onions. It wasn't a very thorough search and I was grateful: I never did like snorting fried onions on an empty stomach. 'So who are you really, buster?' he said, after giving up the search for a gun.

'Who do you think I am, the Avon lady? Take a look at that car I'm driving. I'm a dealer. Museum-quality antique cars. I'll write what I'm selling down for you. You tell your boss.' I tore a page from my notebook and wrote in block capital letters the name of an ultra-desirable motorcar.

He took it from me and, before reading it, leaned down to look inside my Caddie. He opened the glove compartment to see if I had artillery stashed there. Finding nothing, he picked up the photo album in which I had put part of my big collection of car photos. He flipped its pages without responding to the glorious pictures. Bored, he put it down and looked in the back seat. 'Is this jalopy some kind of antique?' he said as he straightened up. He stared at me. A hungry-looking Doberman came out of the woods to look at me too.

'You bet your ass it is,' I told him. 'This baby is a 1959 antique that goes from zero to sixty em pee aitch in ten seconds.' He gave no response to this. I said, 'Go down to your friendly neighborhood BMW dealer and get a brand-new 525i and see if you can get that shiny chunk of imported machinery to do that.'

He nodded. I think I impressed him. 'That good, eh?'

'You betcha.'

While he was reading what I'd written on the slip of paper, I looked around and noticed that several of the nearby trees were chipped and gouged and some were adorned with paper targets peppered with bullet holes. I guessed it was just for appearances. As a way of keeping trespassers at a distance, it had a lot to recommend it. I retrieved my photo album and made sure he hadn't left finger marks.

The big man read the note I'd written, looked again at the

car, and then pulled a cellular phone from his pocket and pushed its buttons. 'Got a guy out here with a big old Caddie, boss. Antique job,' he told the phone. 'Says his name is Murphy. Says he's got an antique car to sell. Better than yours, he says.' He read from the paper I'd scribbled out for him: '1933 Packard Twelve Special – Tailback Speedster with a custom body by Darrin.' I heard some kind of unintelligible splutter that I hoped was amazement, and then without hurrying the big man unlatched the gate and pulled it wide open. 'Drive on up to the house.' As I started up the motor he reached into the car, grabbed my arm tightly, and said, 'But if you are any kind of process server, rent-a-cop, or lawyer you'll be riding back down with the paramedics. Got it?'

As a fully paid-up member of the county bar I felt discriminated against. What was a kindhearted Irish attorney doing at the bottom of the popularity stakes? That was a spot reserved for realtors and politicians. But I didn't say anything like that to this big guy. I smiled and, tapping my leather-bound photo album, said, 'Don't worry about that, buddy. When your boss sees these pictures he's going to have you take that old Packard of his down to the nearest wrecker's yard and cube it.'

The man's crooked smile said he didn't think so, but he waved me through and pointed up the steep muddy track between the trees. Two young, fit, sleekly groomed Dobermans rushed out, shouting abuse at me as I drove past, angry at having missed their chance of pissing on my wire wheels.

At the end of the roadway a house of dark timber fitted snugly into the wooded landscape. With its picture windows and shallow-pitch roof it was the sort of mountain cabin you can only build somewhere winter never comes. Parked outside was a new Ford pickup and a well-used Jeep. No sign of the Darrin, but there was a garage big enough to hold one. The house door had a brass knocker and a BEWARE OF THE DOG sign – now he tells me!

'Anyone at home?' I called from the entry. No reply. I walked in and along the corridor. Through an open door I saw a neat kitchen brightly lit by fluorescent tubes. Piles of dishes occupied both sinks, a compactor bin was piled high with the wrappings from TV dinners, and the air was heavy with the carbonized smells of fried chicken and boiled coffee. He must have dined on *pollo alla cacciatore* too. I hope he enjoyed it; I could still taste mine.

I walked to the end of the corridor, where it opened up onto an interior balcony. From there I could see that this house wasn't the simple single-story structure it had seemed from outside but was nestled artfully into the hillside. The front door opened onto the top floor of a three-story building. From where I stood, I could look down into a big family room with brightly colored rugs and leather furniture arranged to face a massive stone fireplace. No fire: just ashes and half-burned logs remaining from some ancient conflagration. At the far end of the balcony, a stainless spiral staircase led down to the main room. But the facing wall consisted mostly of tall bronze-tinted windows, providing a dramatic view along Topanga Canyon. Far below me I could see cars moving on the winding road that led to the Pacific Ocean.

It was all tastefully done, with abstract art on the walls and glass-beaded cushions on the sofa, but there was something suggesting that this was a house furnished for some other people and some other time. Rented; or maybe a turnkey deal that included everything but a wife and kids. Along the wall there was a six-foot-long brightly lit aquarium, where tropical fish of improbable colors dashed around, playing tag between the shells and rocks.

While I was still leaning on the wooden-railed balcony, taking it all in, a gruff voice from behind me said, 'So you are Murphy?'

I turned. It was gloomy where he was sitting. He'd arranged

134

a desk in the shadow of an old upright piano at the end of the balcony. It was an elaborate instrument, its front ornately carved in oak and its ivory keys exposed like yellowing teeth, curiously resembling the man sitting near it in his swivel chair. Hidden in the shadows, he could see the room below us and the magnificent view through the windows. There was a pair of binoculars on a shelf, just in case he wanted a closer view of anything.

'Murphy. Yes, that's me,' I said. 'I've got a car to show you.'

'That Caddie outside?' He had a small black-and-white monitor balanced on his desk, and he could see my car from some kind of video security camera on the roof. He must have watched my arrival.

'No, another one.'

'A 1933 Packard Twelve Special – Tailback Speedster with a custom body by Darrin?' he said, quoting my message.

'Not exactly,' I said, hesitating.

'Well, I thought it wouldn't be exactly,' said the man in a lazy drawl. 'Because there ain't no such animal.' The phone rang. It was someone he called Hamp. They talked briefly about whether he was comfortable and about paying money by bank draft. I guessed it was the owner of the house calling to check up on things.

'That's right, sir,' I said when he'd finished his call. 'I wanted to get your attention.'

'You got it, wise guy. Who sent you?' Long pause. 'Petrovitch?'

'I'm here on my own account.'

'So what kind of shakedown is it?'

'No kind of shakedown. I'm an old friend of Mrs Petrovitch, a close friend. She was worried about you. She said you'd disappeared.'

'I haven't disappeared; you found me.'

'She wanted to be sure you were safe and well. That's all.'

'Mrs Petrovitch did?' He rubbed his chin. 'She's always got a new surprise for me.'

'Ingrid considers you a personal friend; she was worried about you. She discovered that your apartment on Wilshire was vacated and then couldn't trace those phony companies you gave as references.'

'Is that right?' He got to his feet and stepped into the sunlight. Ingrid thought this guy looked like a college professor? Man, I've been away from school too long. He was tall and slim, a big old-fashioned Wild West-style mustache dominating his face. He had that man-living-alone look: a chin grizzled and stubbly with several days' growth of beard, frayed carpet slippers, and a clean denim shirt that had come straight from the washing machine without being ironed. And he had that man-living-alone fragrance on his breath; he'd been drinking.

'Known her long?' he asked, and picked up his coffee mug and drank from it. His other hand he hooked into a wide leather belt that had the sort of ornate brass buckle they sell in Wild West stores.

'A long time,' I said.

'Me too. Know her husband? Her first husband, I mean.'

'No,' I said.

'I knew him. He was at State College in Urbana; my brother's roommate. First time I ever met Ingrid she was with Jack Piech.' Then suddenly, in that way a drunk gets sober and suspicious, he said, 'So what is a long time? And what's your angle?'

'I was in high school with her,' I told him. 'Alhambra. She lived with her folks on the next block. She asked me to find you, that's all.' I smiled my best friendly smile. 'I've got no angle.' So this guy knew her first husband; Ingrid hadn't told me anything about that.

He nodded and relaxed for a moment and resumed his

position on the swivel chair behind his desk. It creaked as he sat down. 'Okay. Yeah, I did a little business with her first husband, Jack Piech.'

'I never knew him.'

'Jack and his father had a little savings and loan. They must have made a lot of dough.' He upended his coffee. 'You want some coffee? It's on the hot plate. Grab a mug from the hook.'

Why not? I went across to the hutch, chose a mug, and poured coffee for myself. It was a dark and bitter-smelling brew. I took a tall carton of Ralph's Mocha Mix Lite – 'half the fat and calories of regular mocha mix' – and poured a lot of it into the coffee, together with two big spoonfuls of sugar. Sugar: this was not a guy who used low-calorie sweeteners.

'Come here,' he said, and when I went across to his desk he already had the cap off a bottle of Chivas Regal. He poured a slug of whisky into my coffee. 'It gives it a little flavor,' he explained, and poured a hefty measure into his own mug.

I nodded and sipped at it. Phew! Flavor it already had, but that whisky would certainly kill the germs. I looked up and smiled. 'That really hits the spot,' I told him.

'I know,' he said and swallowed some whisky from the bottle. He tried to replace the cap on the bottle but had trouble doing it. He was drunk, but he'd spent a lot of time learning how to conceal the effects. 'Look, even if Petrovitch killed Jack Piech I don't want to get into it.' Drunk and very talkative. I'd come at the right time to get an earful.

'Killed him?' I said. No reply. For a moment I thought he'd dried up. Drunks do that sometimes: they talk like there's no tomorrow, then suddenly they seize up like an engine filled with sand. 'Killed him how?'

'Didn't Ingrid tell you? Petrovitch bought his way into Piech's savings and loan. That's how he got started in the big time. Made five million, Ingrid said.'

'Ingrid said?'

'Maybe it wasn't Ingrid who told me. She's kinda discreet about money.'

'I don't get it,' I said.

'No, Petrovitch got it.' The big guy laughed hoarsely.

'How?'

'The S and L. I don't have to draw you a diagram, do I? They set up a lot of phony accounts: always a few bucks under a hundred thousand so as to get the federal insurance. Then they loaned the assets on the security of land deeds for upcoming deals.' He stopped as if exhausted, but another swallow of booze got him started again. 'I don't have to tell a smart young guy like you how it works. The land deal goes sour – the local authority won't give permission to build some big office building or shopping mall. The S and L is left with the deeds to a lot of parcels of land no one wants. The government pays out, the savers lose a little dough, and Petrovitch sits back and counts his money. The federal government sorts out the mess of debt and pays him all over again. That's what those boys in Washington do all day. Did you think they were there to make laws to protect the Constitution or something?'

'Killed Jack Piech?'

'Don't get me wrong. Piech was loving every minute of it until he saw how deep they were going.'

'Who killed Jack Piech?'

My question didn't register. His mind was still on cruise control. 'Sweet, eh? Even the dumbest insurance company would only pay off a percentage of insured loss – sixty cents on the dollar or whatever – but Uncle Sam pays off one hundred cents on every dollar. Limit: one hundred K per account, so they fixed all the accounts at ninety-five grand!' He laughed. 'Those Washington fat cats have got the Mafia beat when it comes to thieving.'

'Killed Jack Piech?'

He looked at me and frowned as he tried to remember who I was and what I might be doing there. Then illumination came to him. 'Yeah, yeah, yeah. Jack had to be wasted. Jack was going to tell the bank inspectors the whole story. He was going to spill to the SEC. Jack and his dad had lived in that neighborhood all their lives. They were the leaders of the country club set: five hundred-a-plate dinners for a new hospital, a committee to buy valuable paintings for the county museum. Maybe it was all too easy or they got religion or something, but these dudes suffered a sudden fit of remorse. They had a family confab with Ingrid sitting in, and then Jack and Ingrid flew to New York to break the news to Petrovitch. Jack told him the Pieches were going to undo the whole thing. Repay everything. Keep the bank solvent. And they had stock enough to force the decision.'

He sighed, and his head lolled back and his mouth slightly opened. He stayed that way, and for a moment I feared he'd slumped off into a drunken sleep. Then he belched mightily. That seemed to awaken him.

'What happened to Jack Piech?' I said.

'A beer truck hit him as he was crossing Sixth Avenue. Died on his way to Bellevue.'

'Are you telling me Petrovitch arranged that truck?'

'He sure didn't drag him out of the way. Ask Ingrid.'

'And Ingrid married the man who murdered her husband?'

'It was an accident,' he said sarcastically. 'Petrovitch went into deep mourning, paid for a fine funeral, and gave an Oscar-winning display of grief and mortification. He consoled Ingrid. Ain't that the way it goes?'

'Who told you all this?' I said. 'Did you get this from your brother?'

'Or was it Ingrid who called the shots? Maybe she enticed

139

Zachary Petrovitch into the deal. Maybe she urged Jack Piech to go into the swindle and then – when Jack got cold feet – conspired with Petrovitch to kill him. What do you think? Could the little lady be that scheming?'

I didn't answer. I could see he enjoyed the bewilderment that must have showed on my face. He was in the kind of mood where he'd say anything to get a reaction.

He waved a finger at me. 'Ask Ingrid; she knows. It took me a little time to figure her out, but figure her out I did. She is one dangerous little lady. Excuse me, will ya?' In a remarkable display of displacement activity, he reached for the phone and called someone to ask the price of spark plugs and a muffler. He was a compulsive telephoner. Hollywood is full of them: men who can't sit still for five minutes without making a phone call.

'How do you know all this?' I said.

'I used to be a hit man. Ingrid tried to hire me; I turned her down. I don't get into family fights.'

'Cut the bullshit and tell me. I want to know,' I said.

He looked up at me and grinned. 'I told ya: I used to be a hit man. For the mob. You meet a lot of influential people that way. The trouble is, you lose contact with them again.' Another big grin.

Why was I listening to all this drunken babble? This guy was flowing with venom, and I wasn't smart enough to turn off the tap. 'The things you're saying—'

Pindero held up a hand to hush me. He listened to the phone and wrote down some prices and then put the phone down. After a long silence while he studied the bottom of his mug of whisky as if trying to read his fortune there, he looked up. 'That's the way Petrovitch does things. That's the new way to do business. Speedy, smooth, and without a great deal of paper-work. You murder the opposition.' He laughed. 'Murder them. It was a marriage made in heaven.'

140

'You're crazy.'

'I'm not crazy. You'll find out one of these days. It's people like that who are putting us hit men out of business.' He shifted in his chair and fixed me with an intense stare. 'You tell Ingrid you couldn't find me. I'm not about to hurt her; tell her that. But she has to solve her own problems.' I was near him and he reached out to grab my arm, but I stepped out of the way. 'Never get into family fights. First law of survival, right?'

'Did you get all this from Jack Piech's dad?' Sometimes a grieving relative will find a scapegoat and dump all their misery there.

'Naw! It's like I told you. Jack's dad signed the whole shebang over to Petrovitch. Now he's living in a trailer in El Paso, scared of his own shadow. I went there and saw him: he wouldn't hardly talk to me. Scared shitless. He insisted he was happy with the Petrovitch deal, but that old man was looking over his shoulder the whole time. While we're sitting there in the trailer, a guy calls by to deliver a repaired set of dentures. Can you imagine? After all the dough they had, he's sitting there and can't even afford some new false teeth.'

'And how do you figure in all this?' I said.

He looked at me as if staring into a bright light. 'I *don't* figure in it; I'm retired. You tell Mrs Ingrid Petrovitch I'm just fine. But don't tell either of them where to find me. I'm planning to stay just fine. I don't want no part of her deal. If she takes my advice she'll just disappear too. You can't fight the whole world.'

Forgetting for a moment what it tasted like, I gulped down a mouthful of the coffee and booze, spluttered, and got to my feet. 'You got a great car, Mr Pindero,' I said. 'But it makes you too conspicuous. If you're hiding from the world, you'd do better to sell it to me and get out of town for good.'

'You really want to buy it?'

141

'I sure do.'

Very slowly, as if committing it to memory, he said, 'It's too darn conspicuous. You're right about that.' He took a little time to arrange some pencils on his desk. 'I might take two hundred thousand bucks for it.'

'It's worth more than that,' I told him.

'Who are you, Mother Teresa on vacation? Yeah, it's worth more but I don't want the ads or the dealers and all that hassle. You bring me two hundred grand in cash and we'll talk. But I mean cash: used hundred–dollar bills.'

The notion of owning a real museum piece like that car brought out all the worst kind of covetousness in me. With the money I'd be getting from the Petrovitch deal I could afford it. 'Hold it for me,' I said. 'I'll put together the money somehow, even if I have to take out a second mortgage. Hold it for me.'

He smiled to see my excitement. I couldn't tell whether he was just stringing me along or not. 'You bring me cash. But don't come back here hand in hand with the Petrovitch family.'

'No.' It was no good trying to conclude a deal with him in his present condition. I felt like telling him to sober up, but I knew that's one of the most dangerous things to say to a drunk. 'I hate Petrovitch. He's buying my firm. When the deal is finalized, I'll keep well away from him.'

'Finalized,' he said contemptuously. 'Didn't they teach you anything at college? Shit! I've laid it out for you as clear as I can make it.' He held up his hands like a kindergarten teacher taking a class in rhythm. Fingers splayed, he tapped an index finger against his palm. 'Petrovitch doesn't finalize deals. He finalizes people.'

From outside I heard a sound like twigs snapping. I guessed it was the guy at the gate putting more holes in a paper target. Maybe they were not just for appearances.

8

I went home to Woodland Hills and shuffled through some newly arrived bills. After opening a can of dog food for Rex I told him about my trip to Topanga Canyon. Rex was mad because I hadn't taken him along, but I explained there were other dogs there, big critters that might have torn him to pieces. Rex wagged his tail; he saw the sense of that.

I switched on the TV. There was a talk show about fathers who don't spend enough time with the kids. What about mothers who come into a guy's office and pretend they're going to leap off the window ledge?

I switched off the sound. I have this large-screen projection TV. People look almost lifesize. With the sound turned off it provides all the companionship of friends and neighbors with none of their demands for food, drink, and flattery. I sat watching this silent show. A sleek-haired guy with a microphone was running around lithely and blithely, selecting mothers and kids in the audience who stood up on cue, opened their mouths, and waved their arms around. It was restful to watch.

And I thought about the old man of Topanga and his lovely car. Sometimes when you get away from a meeting you see it all in a new perspective. Of course Pindero was stoned out of his mind, but that didn't explain why he was moving around, covering his tracks and giving out false names. And would

Petrovitch really want to push Jack Piech under a beer truck? It was all crazy talk, but almost anything is possible. Just sit in my office for a week and you'll believe it.

I had been thinking of Ingrid a lot. I loved her. I really adored her. I even found myself reluctant to go out of the house on errands just in case she phoned me and I wasn't there to take the call. I know that's teenage stuff, but meeting her again had renewed all the adoration I stored up over the years. Even the prospect of speaking to her was enough to give me a glow. I phoned Ingrid at the Aspen house. 'I think I found your guy,' I said, after she'd given out with a cautious hello that made my scalp tingle.

She said, 'You must have the wrong number. Please check your phone book and don't call this number again.'

She'd recognized my voice okay. Ingrid was scared or I was very much mistaken. Very very scared, if her voice was anything to judge by. And that gave me a sick feeling in the stomach. You know what it's like when you love someone desperately and you feel they are in some kind of trouble.

I replaced the phone and sat there thinking about it. Poor Ingrid. No one except me understood what she was really like: vulnerable and childlike. I made coffee and watched some more lousy TV; that always helps me think. Talk shows, more about the Rodney King trial, a Cosby rerun, and then the news came on. I switched up the sound. Two guys had got themselves on prime-time TV by holding up a liquor store equipped with a video camera. See you around, guys! A 'gang-related' drive-by in South Central and a member of the City Council talking about increasing the sales tax. I guess that was to pay for some of those fancy foreign trips by the mayor's appointees. I hit the mute: life was sometimes better with the sound off.

The phone rang. Rex barked to show me what a grand house dog he was. I keep saying I'll send him to one of those training schools for dogs, but I'm not sure Rex has the right SAT score. And, as he said once when we talked it over, would I like to have a week with the Marine Corps on Parris Island?

'Hello?' I said cautiously.

'I'm sorry I hung up on you.' It was Ingrid, with a different voice. She must have gone to another phone. 'So you found him?'

'Pindero? Yes, that's right,' I said. 'It wasn't too difficult. He's okay, really okay. But you didn't level with me, Ingrid. You didn't tell me you knew him in Chicago.'

Long pause. 'I know. Maybe I should have told you more. What did he say?'

'Don't sound so worried, honey. He didn't say much. He was boozed. I just made sure he was okay, like you said.'

'Are you seeing him some more?'

'I can if you want. He's not far away.'

'Where?'

At first I wasn't going to tell her. Then I thought what the hell. 'Topanga Canyon. The only reason you couldn't find him is because he's calling himself Panter. The house is signposted Panter – the Pacific Ocean end of Topanga.'

'You're so clever, Mickey.'

'It was easy,' I said, bathing in the warm admiration. 'Wrought-iron gates, TV camera, and some kind of security guy roaming around the grounds. But I talked my way in to see him. He's okay; or he will be when he recovers from his hangover. Are you coming to LA?'

'Yes. Let's meet. I'll be in town this weekend. Would Sunday, sometime around noon, be okay?'

I'd promised to take Danny for Sunday brunch at the Beverly Hilton. It was stylish, sophisticated, and the biggest spread in town, and Danny went for it. I couldn't put him off again. I said, 'Beverly Hilton – brunch at noon. I'll be with my son, but we can talk while he's at the counter refilling his plate. He does that quite a lot. No need to book, just come along and find me behind a stack of Irish bagels.'

'That's wonderful,' she said. 'Thanks. You didn't tell me what Mr Pindero said when you found him.'

'Like I say: not much, except that he knew you in Chicago. You should have told me, Ingrid.'

'Why?'

I was bursting to ask her if Petrovitch had been with her first husband when he died, but this wasn't the right moment. 'I don't know.' She was right. She wasn't on trial or even my client. She didn't have to tell me the whole truth or even a large part of it.

'You're a wonderful friend, Mickey. There is no one quite like you. I do adore you.'

'Yeah, I know.'

'The only real friend I've got. I've got to go, dearest. 'Bye now.'

''Bye,' I said. She hung up immediately. I wondered where she'd had to go, to find a phone she'd feel easy about using. Poor Ingrid. I worried about her.

It's a lousy reflection on human nature that while I was mightily concerned about Ingrid, and about her friend Pindero, a great deal of my thinking had been on the prospect of buying that magnificent Packard. See, it was the sort of opportunity that only comes once in a lifetime, and coming when I was about to pocket a sizable sum of money, seemed to be a sign from heaven. It was a museum piece; I even dreamed about that Packard.

It was Saturday when, after an appointment in Santa Monica, I finally succumbed and headed toward Topanga. I took the

Pacific Coast Highway. You can get into the canyon from that end, and on a nice day you have a swell view of the ocean. This wasn't a nice day. A film of high clouds reduced the sun to gray shadeless light, while beneath them ragged scud came hurrying in from the ocean. On the PCH it was chilly, and I kept the roof closed.

It wasn't so hard to find Pindero's place the second time, but the wrought iron gates were locked with one of those fifty-dollar steel padlocks that resisted all my efforts to get it open. So I left my car and clambered over the fence to walk the rest of the way to the house. The hungry Dobermans were nowhere in sight, and there were no sounds from construction workers. The wind had dropped, but a night of steady rain had left puddles, and there was a smell of damp earth. Even up here on the hilltop it was humid and airless.

There was no sign of life anywhere: no Ford pickup, no Jeep. I pushed at the big paneled front door and stepped inside. It was darker today, and airless, and the kitchen smelled worse. I didn't need to go farther to decide that Pindero had taken off. I had a spooky gooseflesh-making tingle that is nature's ingenious way of telling you you're scared shitless. Even in the gloomy light I could see that the furniture and all the junk – right down to the cushions – was unchanged, but there was no sign of Pindero. The ornate piano was still in the same place, and the fish tank, although unlit, was bubbling away like freshly opened champagne. There were screwed-up papers all over the floor. I opened one; it was a bill from the company that hauled the trash. This time his name was Pinter. There was no fire in the big stone fireplace, just ashes carelessly strewn all around the hearth and spilling out across the rug. I stared out of the double-glazed windows. Down below, a long line of traffic crawled along the canyon road like a column of ants.

I looked all around the place in case he'd left a clue about a forwarding address. I even hoped there might be a message for me about his car, but there was nothing like that. Maybe I should have guessed he'd been giving me the runaround.

I went back to the desk. On the wall beside it were some outlets with a crazy cluster of electric plugs that would have given a fire chief apoplexy. I hit the light switch and there was a sudden jangle of sound, loud piano music, animated and discordant. The sound went through my head so I shouted aloud. One of the electric plugs belonged to the player piano, and its whole keyboard had come alive, vibrating with a fast Scott Joplin solo. I switched it off quickly and the music stopped and the light went off. I breathed a sigh of relief. The second switch I tried controlled the fish tank lights. Startled fish awoke and darted around the carefully arranged stones and came close to the glass to mouth obscenities at me. I picked up the packet of fish food and tapped some out so that it spread over the water. The fish upended themselves to gobble it.

I searched through all the desk drawers. There was nothing in them, except some giveaway ballpoints from Citibank, a dog-eared Heritage paperback dictionary with the back cover missing, and – in the deep bottom drawer – some more piano rolls: Lehár, Gershwin, and Strauss.

Maybe if I'd been a trained detective I might have spotted something of significance, but nothing I could see meant anything except that Pindero – or Pinter or Panter or whatever his name really was – had taken off in some haste. Such a sudden departure looked like he was running scared; I wondered if my visit had done that.

I went into the kitchen and touched the stove the way they do in movies. It was cold. Groceries were piled high on the table: two six-packs of Coors, a quart-size carton of milk, a tub of margarine, a small plate with an opened can of cat food on it, and a box containing some pieces of fried chicken. None of

148

it was so chilly that it had recently been in the cold. It was all neatly stacked inside a cardboard lid, as if someone had cleaned out the refrigerator before leaving. The refrigerator's glass shelves, stained with rings of spilled food, had been put in the sink, ready to be washed. Nice going, Mr Pindero, old buddy. I wouldn't have had you down for a Domestic Science major.

It all looked okay and the kitchen was purring contentedly. I went into the bedroom. The bedclothes, expensive-looking pink sheets and pillows with flower prints, had been stripped off the mattress and thrown onto the carpet. The whole place bore the signs of a man who had learned how to housekeep without assistance. On the table by his bed were a reading light and some detective-story paperbacks, one of them half read and face down. Alongside the book stood a glass tumbler and an empty bottle of Chivas Regal, with seven more full bottles of the same brand in a cardboard box on the floor in the corner. On hangers in the closet were some unironed shirts, denim pants, and a leather jacket. Clean underwear was stacked on the closet's shelf, while discarded socks and handkerchiefs had been tossed into a basket on its floor. A wastebasket in the bathroom contained nothing except empty cigarette packs and discarded razor blades. Above the sink a razor and a can of shaving foam had been abandoned. Why did a guy leave so hurriedly that he didn't even grab his soap and razor?

There was the sudden sound of thunder, or it may have been a plane; the way the sound reverberated through the hills and valleys made it difficult to distinguish. Either way it made me jump. I looked up at the sky but the plane must have been above the clouds. Whatever I did, it was impossible to shake off a feeling that I was not alone. I became convinced that I had arrived to interrupt Pindero's packing and he was watching everything I did and waiting for me to depart. Why else would his soap and razor be there?

149

I went to the back door and stepped outside to walk around the house. It wasn't raining, but the air had that silky dampness that is the sign of rain to come. I tried to decide what had prompted my deep feelings of unease. I'm not the sort to tap into the supernatural for guidance; I always left all that stuff to Betty. I inhaled the pine-scented air. The house was built on what I estimated to be an acre of steeply sloping hilltop. I walked across the brown lawn to peer through a dusty window into the neat clapboard garage. There was a car there; not the Packard Darrin, it was one of those fancy British four-by-fours, a Range Rover. An array of hammers and tools were clipped on the wall, and the shelves held sprays and old cans of ant killer, stain, and paint.

None of the buildings here were old, they just looked old, the way people like things to look when they move out of town. As I strolled, other houses came into view, dark wood with gray roofs, cunningly landscaped into the trees. When I got down to where I had left my Caddie I stopped. There was no movement anywhere. Even a big blackbird at the foot of an oak was standing very still, watching the ground so attentively it failed to see my approach. I wondered what it could see. A small rodent? A snake? In the heat of summer a stretch of rock-strewn ground like this would be alive with adders and rattlers but now even the worms kept deep under cover.

I turned around and looked back at the house. Everything told me to get in my car and leave, but I could not do it. There was something unusual in that house. Leaving before I figured it out would keep me awake all night, wondering what I had seen and yet missed.

So I walked back to the house and went inside again. It was the kitchen that drew my attention. I sat down at the table and fidgeted with the beer and stuff that had obviously been taken from the fridge. I had the feeling that a skilled investigator would have found some clue to reveal where Pindero had gone. Car. Car. Car. Since talking with him, the idea of buying his Packard had hardened in my mind. If I could find him again I felt sure I could talk him into selling that car. With the cash in hand he would succumb. I'd bought a lot of cars. I could tell when a man was in a selling mood. Pindero would sell; I was convinced of it. I had to find him.

With these thoughts reeling in my brain I went back to his desk and sat down as he had been sitting, within an arm's length of the piano. What a view! As the afternoon turned cooler the canyon was filling with white mist that rolled down from the hilltops. Maybe it had been thunder I'd heard; we'd had rain four days in a row. Perhaps Pindero was only away on a brief errand; maybe he'd be back any moment. I could leave a note for him. It was a stupid thought; so much of what I was looking at said he'd taken off with no thought of ever returning. Maybe he had another house, a beach place or ski resort that was complete with razor and soap and clothes and stuff.

It was that damned sound that was troubling me. There was something unusual – if not to say unnatural – about it. I mean, the sorts of whining and buzzing noises that all kitchens make falter, stop, and start, don't they? They don't go on forever unless someone has gone out leaving a tap running or a mixer or something switched on. I went over to the shiny black glass-fronted oven and touched the door, opening it so that the interior light came on: nothing. The dishwasher was off. I looked at the overhead light, thinking it might be a noisy transformer, but when I switched off the fluorescent tubes the buzzing continued. I touched the microwave and the coffee machine and the compactor, but none of them seemed to be the source of the noise.

Only then did I locate the sound and realized there was no mystery after all. It was the compressor of the Admiral side-by-side refrigerator-freezer that was making the sound. I had the same two-door model at home. But even the compressor of a big refrigerator is switched off by the thermostat when the food inside is chilled. I stroked the heavy door and looked at the sink, where the refrigerator's glass shelves, marked by spilled food, waited to be washed, and pulled open the fridge door to look inside.

It seemed as if the lightbulb had failed, for the interior was dark, but then I saw that the whole gloomy interior space, some eighteen cubic feet, was crammed with a huge parcel wrapped in black plastic. As I stood looking at it, it moved. With agonizing slowness, the whole shiny parcel came tumbling out of the refrigerator.

I staggered back to avoid it as it fell with a crash onto the kitchen floor, moving and spreading out like shiny molten lava. But it wasn't any kind of liquid that spread across the floor; it was Pindero's legs and arms. His hands, cold and gray, came reaching across the floor as if trying to grasp my ankles. His feet were bare and blue, his toes shiny and red. Still moving, the parcel gave the sound of tearing plastic, as Pindero's body came bursting out of the improvised body bag that had been made from black plastic trash bags. I could see one eye and a section of his face as he peered through a tear in the ripped-open bag. He was dead, very dead. His eyes were wide open, and his lips were drawn back over a half-opened mouth to make a fierce smirk on his pale and waxy face, and tiny flakes of frost had begun to form on his curly mustache.

I touched the body. It was cold but maybe not cold enough. I put my fingers into the bag until I could reach to his armpit. He was not completely cold. Jesus! I jumped to my feet and looked around. No wonder I had the feeling I was being watched; if the body was still warm, his killer could still be in the vicinity. How long had Pindero been in the cold compartment? I stepped back. I had no intention of even trying to shove him back into that cramped space.

Almost without knowing what I was doing, I found myself with a kitchen towel in my hand, wiping the long smooth plastic handles of the refrigerator. What else had I touched? All the appliances and the doors. I went back over my steps, using my pocket handkerchief instead of the towel. I wiped everything I might have touched, including the light switches and even the piano keys, and made sure there were no muddy footprints on the carpet for forensics to spot. What else? I backed down the hall very slowly. When I got to the front door I went through it carefully and pulled it tightly closed until I heard the latch snap. Wipe the handle. The door was firmly locked. The next person inside would have to force an entrance.

Without hurrying I went back along my trail to the car and wiped the fence where I'd climbed over it. Then I got into my car and sat for a moment, putting my thoughts together. My hands were trembling, my mouth was dry, and I felt sick with the unmistakable nausea of fear. Wouldn't it be better to go back up to the house and call 911? Like hell it would. I'd seen people get caught up in murder investigations. The one who found the body remained the prime suspect until the perpetrator was tried and convicted. If the cops never found the perpetrator, or if the courts failed to convict, the one who found the body had to live with suspicion forever. Maybe a happily married bookkeeper in Jackson, Wyoming, could shrug that one off and even enjoy the notoriety a little, and parlay it into a social advantage. But a lawyer in downtown La–La might find his day-to-day life, supporting the forces of law and order, becoming a little complicated. I didn't relish the prospect of going into a courtroom to be torn to pieces by some young ambitious prosecutor in an intrepid demonstration of how the law extends no privileges to its own.

I closed the car roof and put the radio and the heater on. It had become much colder and was getting darker every minute. All those trees that look so green and welcoming in daylight look like the backdrop for *Macbeth* when the sun goes behind a cloud. I started up the engine and turned the car around. For just one moment, as I stared in the direction of the house, I considered going back there one more time. Then I spotted the blackbird, still motionless at the foot of the oak. It wasn't waiting for anything that was nice to have. From here I could see the blackbird was dead, no more than a bundle of feathers, its insides a cavity hollowed away by termites. Let me get out of here!

I went down that hill like I'd never traveled before. Those branches really reached out to get me. It was all in my mind, I know, but that didn't help me stop shivering. The gray clouds sagged over me like a bulging wallpapered ceiling when the upstairs bath is overflowing. As I got down to the bottom of the canyon it dripped. Big isolated blobs at first, but as I swung onto the canyon road the paper really ripped apart. The wipers couldn't cope with it, and the windshield made the landscape dissolve into jelly. My wheels hissed like snakes, the canvas top was drumming, and the paintwork on the hood was pounded to make prickly white spray. When the storm comes up like thunder out of China 'cross the bay, you really know you live on the edge of the mighty Pacific Ocean.

In the canyon the rain came sluicing down from on high, making waterfalls that became muddy brown rivers as they hit the roadway and scattered stones and litter everywhere. Huge palm fronds lay like dead alligators on the wet roadway and scrunched under my wheels. At the end of the canyon I met the sight of the Pacific Ocean and the teeth of the storm. The world went shiny, and the steel-colored ocean looked fierce.

I took my Caddie to a Hand Wash in Marina del Rey. The

guys working there were all sitting around laughing and joking. They must have thought I was crazy to wash a car in the middle of a rainstorm, but I wanted to make sure there were no leaves, twigs, or mud traces on bodywork or tires, nothing that would connect me to Pindero's hilltop hideaway. They did their special interior cleaning, vacuuming every part of the floor and the upholstery. Only then did I drive home. And when I got home I soaked in the tub and then took every stitch of the clothing I'd worn to the local dry cleaners. I wanted to put that trip to Topanga out of my mind completely.

Except that putting things out of one's mind is not so easy. I spent that evening with the sight of Pindero's body engraved in my brain. I watched TV without knowing what was on the screen. I fixed a steak and salad for myself, charred rare just the way I like it. I touched my toes and tapped out my dance routine until the sweat ran off me, but no matter what I did I couldn't shake the idea that the buzzer would sound and I would find some cop standing in my doorway. I wondered how Pindero had died. I wondered if I had been observed all the time I was up there, or whether it was just my nervous disposition. I wondered to what extent the killer was still depending on that refrigerator to keep the body cold and out of sight. With the corpse spread out across the kitchen floor and decomposing in the California air, the schedule would change dramatically.

9

Next day was Sunday. From the very back of my walk-in clothes closet I selected a green linen leisure suit. I'd bought it with a fat fee I collected for getting an elderly studio executive out of a nasty drug bust that could have seen him charged with dealing. Six months later he was arrested in Atlantic City with a suitcase filled with the stuff and went away for five years.

Pale green: I wore it a few times for the St Patrick's Day lunches a gang of us mick lawyers used to celebrate at Jimmy's. Then wives started to come along too, and it was staid and different and sober, and everyone was careful about what they said, and after a couple of dull gatherings there were no more of those frolics. The recession started to show its teeth, the pale green leisure suit went into the back of the closet, and from that time on I celebrated St Pat's with corned beef on rye at my desk.

While dusting off my green suit and feeling low, I found myself looking out the front window and noticing a strange-looking plastic bag propped against my mailbox. It was shiny black, doughnut-shaped, and secured with wire. No sooner did I start cursing the disposal company for not taking my garbage away than I was struck by the absence of Rex. 'Rex! Rex!' None of my neighbors had black plastic bags, trash cans, boxes, or anything else obstructing the sidewalk in front of their homes.

It was then that I realized the black plastic bag had a shape I recognized. 'Rex! Rex! Come here, boy!'

I grabbed a knife from the drawer in the kitchen and ran out through my front door. 'Rex, Rex, Rex!' I tried to lift the dead weight and then broke a nail as I tried to undo the wire that secured the top of the bag. 'Rex!' I cut into the black plastic to make a gap big enough to get my fingers into and then ripped the plastic open. Pouring out all over my feet came grass and twigs and leaves and other rubbish that the gardeners should have taken away with them.

'Rex!' There was a happy bark and Rex came bounding out of the house, laughing and waving his tail. 'You goddamned useless mutt!' I aimed a kick at him but missed. He jumped away and circled me to come back and nuzzle into the grass cuttings and spread the mess farther across the sidewalk. 'Where you been?' I could see lint on his coat. 'You know the linen closet is off limits, you cur!' Rex cowered down, one ear pressed hard against the ground, like I'd thrashed him. That was his cunning way of trying to get sympathy. He knew that damned linen closet was a no-no, and yet as soon as he saw me go to bed he went there and snuggled down in the best place in the house. 'First chance I get I'm going to trade you in for one of those stuffed leather pigs,' I told him.

It was a cloudless Southern California day. Brunch at the Beverly Hilton was a dressy affair: my suit still fitted me and I felt good in it. Ingrid showed up on the dot; she was always on time and made me glad to be looking my poshest. She arrived looking great in a smoky gray silk two-piece with real pearls. We had one of the window tables that line one side of the restaurant; there was a view of the blue pool and the palms. The sunlight came into the room to shine on her hair and through the water glasses to make intricate patterns on the tablecloth.

Life was good. 'My name is Vicky, and I am your waitress.' It was not true of course, the girl hovering over us was no more a waitress than any other young actress and model to be found waiting tables in the restaurants of Los Angeles, but she smiled sweetly and poured champagne for me and Ingrid and poured orange juice into the glasses where Danny and Robyna would be sitting when they came back from the buffet.

'You're looking great, Ingrid.'

She waited until the waitress was out of earshot. 'The first time you phoned I couldn't talk.'

'Sure, I understood.'

'I hear clicks on the line when Zach picks up the other phone, but the second call was okay, I think. I can never be certain.' She looked at me. 'What did Mr Pindero say?'

This was what I feared. I had no intention of telling her the truth about my second visit up there. 'Not much. He'd been drinking. He wasn't in great shape. I didn't spend much time with him.'

'He was alone?'

'A cat, two Dobermans, and a chorus line of tropical fish.'

She put down the champagne she'd been toying with and looked at me, smiling dreamily as if coming awake. 'He's a nice man,' she said.

The sight of Ingrid's lovely face, and the sunny scene behind her, suddenly faded, and I could see only a colorless view of Pindero's body splayed across the floor tiles. I pushed it from my mind. I didn't want to think about it or what had happened up there.

Perhaps she saw some aspect of that fear in my face, for she became serious and said, 'I didn't want to get you involved, Mickey. I really didn't. But there's no one else I can turn to.' She looked at me, gave a bleak little smile, and turned her head to see Robyna and Danny at the buffet counter, piling food onto their plates. I suppose it wasn't a good idea to invite her to a brunch with Danny and Robyna. Ingrid needed a chance to talk to me in private.

'I'll help all I can,' I told her.

'I think I'm in danger,' she said. She reached out and touched my hand, and just that light physical contact made me shiver. Maybe she noticed, for, as if regretting the gesture, she withdrew her hand and looked away.

'Danger how?'

'I can't explain . . . not now.'

'From this Pindero guy?' I said.

She shook her head and looked out the window. The pool was rippling in the sunlight. You know what it's like when you build a pool in Hollywood; before you've even got it full of water, guys are sitting around it discussing their contracts. There was a lot of self-promoting activity out there today: sun-bronzed workout artists oiling their biceps, guys on phones, and, nearer to us, a tycoon wrapped in a towel watching a short fat guy in jogging clothes and a ponytail kneel down to walk a pencil through the floor plans of a mansion.

Ingrid studied them all and looked around constantly with furtive movements that took in everything. I guess she was afraid of being followed. She fiddled with her knife and fork. Neither of us had been up to get food yet. 'From Zach,' she whispered. 'Danger from my husband.'

'Danger? Why?'

'Maybe I shouldn't have said danger. I can't explain.'

'Try.'

'I'm an encumbrance to him. He'd like me out of the way.'

'Zach? Your husband?'

'Yes.'

I tried to remain calm. 'Do you have any evidence to support that idea?'

159

'No. None that would convince a lawyer.'

'Ingrid,' I said, ignoring the jibe and trying to smile, 'maybe you are just going through a bad patch. Marriages do. I know all about that.'

'No. Mickey, I'm not a hysterical or neglected wife, if that's what you're thinking.'

'You told me he loves you and I believe it. I saw the way he looks at you. I'm sure he does.' It hurt me to say it, but it was the truth as I saw it. 'Do you think there's another woman?'

'There's got to be. He's so mysterious and I'm so trusting. All those weeks when he was having an affair with Felicity, I never even suspected.'

'Felicity Weingartner?'

'If she hadn't confessed I wouldn't have found out. I never could really confide in her after that.' She looked into the distance. 'Zach never tells me anything at all. After I spoke to you on the phone, he suddenly told me we had to come to LA. Then yesterday, when I'd booked a table for lunch at a perfectly lovely place, he suddenly remembered someone he had to see. He returned in the afternoon so nervous and flustered and guilty I'm sure he has another woman here.'

'What time yesterday?'

'What time? Oh, I don't know. It was while I was having my hair fixed. I got back all ready to go to lunch and there was this message saying he had to go out on business.'

'Maybe he did.'

'When a husband is being unfaithful a wife can tell, Mickey. He was so hyped up. When he returned he gave me a peck on the cheek and went straight to his study. I could hear him pacing up and down. Then in the evening he said that if anyone started asking questions, I was to say he'd been in all day.' She drank some champagne. 'Who would want to know where you've been? I said, somebody's angry husband? But he just gave a little smirk and said it was nothing like that. It was business, he said.'

'Does this mean you're going to divorce him?'

'I can't, Mickey. I have a son by my first husband. Zach is his godfather and his principal trustee. If I went for a divorce I could lose my son. You know what the courts are like, and Zach gives John so many expensive presents he's sure to want to stay with him.'

'I didn't know you had a son.'

'He's a lovely boy. He's at school in Connecticut. Zach has mixed feelings about him. He hates me having pictures of John Junior around the house. I have to hide them.'

'That's terrible.' Even Felicity didn't know Ingrid had a child, or was she keeping Ingrid's secret?

'No, it's very human. Zach so wanted a son of his own; he loves John Junior, but he also sees my child as some kind of reproach to his manhood. If only we'd had a family of our own it might have been different.'

'There's still time.'

'No. We've seen all kinds of specialists. Zach can't have children.'

'That's tough.'

'It affects him, there's no denying it. You know what he's like, he's macho. He fights for everything he wants, and he has to win.' She drank some champagne. 'I can't desert my son . . . Jack's son. Jack was a good husband, and he adored that boy. I just have to tough it out, but at times I get really low.'

'How did your first husband die?' I asked.

'A truck hit him when he was crossing the street. He was a lovely man.'

'That was lousy luck,' I said.

'At one time I almost confided some of my problems to that lovely Mr Pindero, but I suppose the poor old boy didn't want

161

to get mixed up in my troubles. He's not like you, Mickey. You really care, I know you do.'

'Where is Zach now?'

'He's talking to lawyers in Sacramento. I wish I knew who he was with yesterday. If that woman knew what she was doing to my marriage, she wouldn't torture me this way.'

I looked at her. Now I knew who was spying on me up at Pindero's place the other day: Zach Petrovitch. He must have listened in on the second phone call too, heard me describe where Pindero was living, and acted. I said, 'Don't put anything in writing that would give your husband an alibi for yesterday, Ingrid.'

'You always talk like a lawyer.'

'I'm serious. If he was doing anything criminal at that time you could find yourself indicted as an accessory.'

'It's not anything criminal, it's another woman. Don't you see?' She wrestled with herself before saying: 'Zach is convinced it's my fault we've not had children.'

'Danny's coming,' I warned her as I saw him approaching.

'The shrimp is real good,' said Danny, as he plonked his plate on the table and sat down. 'And they have great-looking prime rib and the best cheesecake in the world.' Robyna's plate contained a modest serving of salads, nuts, and grains. She sat down and looked at Ingrid with unabashed interest.

Ingrid smiled at her. When he was given a chance to eat as much as he wanted of all his favorite foods, Danny reverted to being a child. Looking around the restaurant, I thought maybe everyone did.

'Our turn now, Ingrid,' I said with forced cheeriness.

'I can't wait to try the cold cuts,' said Ingrid politely, but it didn't sound very convincing. I caught an expression on Danny's face that said he found Ingrid an object of curiosity and admiration. Her expensive clothes and careful makeup marked her as an out-of-towner. They were unusual here. This was the edge of the world, a place where the beautiful people went to the beach in designer sun tops, not to the opera in Chanel suits with pearls.

I'd told Danny that Ingrid was the wife of a client, but I could see they were both convinced she was a fancy lady friend I was parading for them. Danny didn't look too pleased about this. He wasn't prepared to believe that anyone could replace his mother. As I got up to follow Ingrid to the food counter, I gave him a fixed stare. I sure hoped he wasn't going to say something stupid to Ingrid. He could be rude if he felt his mother's place threatened.

I watched Ingrid while she put some poached salmon on her plate and took oak salad and grated carrot and jalapeño olives and stuff and arranged it all to look good. I took herrings in sour cream with smoked eel and potato salad.

Ingrid pretended to be studying the buffet thoughtfully; when she was sure no one was within earshot, she took me aside and said, 'About six months back I went down to get a drink from the fridge. We were in the house in Aspen. You know where the kitchen is situated. I could hear Zach talking with people sitting around in the bar. I heard him say something like "you make sure he's dead, really dead." Goldie was there too. He kind of frightens me, that Goldie.'

'He has that effect on a lot of people.'

'Yes. Well, Goldie said, "We don't want another foul-up like last time." The other man – I didn't recognize the voice; he wasn't one of Zach's regular friends or anything – said, "This is what I do for a living, Mr Petrovitch." Zach said, "Next time I do it myself." I'm maybe not getting the words exactly right, but that was what they said in essence.' She stopped as two people came past, heaping smoked salmon and cream cheese on their plates.

163

I said, 'It's easy to misunderstand overheard conversations. In the courts there are examples every day.'

'You don't believe me.'

'I'm trying to put your mind at ease,' I told her. She was mad at me because she thought I wasn't treating her seriously enough. 'I'm just trying to get at the facts.'

In a troubled and impatient whisper she said, 'I know my husband is planning to kill me. The only "fact" that will prove it is my dead body.' Despite her agitated manner, she still had her emotions well under control.

'It won't come to that.'

'Why won't it? What are you going to do to prevent it? I'm scared, Mickey. I've never been frightened of anything before in my whole life, but now I'm scared.'

'Maybe you should take your son and leave home. Separate.'

'That's dumb.' Her profound desperation could be heard in the flat way she said those words. 'I've explained all that to you. John Junior has no passport, and Zach as guardian would have to submit the application. If I ran away, Zach would apply to the court for custody on the grounds of my being nuts, or an unsuitable person to be a guardian, or some other legal trick that would give him the boy. I'm trapped.'

'Perhaps there's a chance of compromise. Shall I talk to your husband, tell him you're desperately unhappy? Ask him to let you go?'

She looked at me with contempt. 'If Zach knew I was talking to you this way, he'd get rid of you too. I pretended I was asking you more questions about the charity regulations.'

'I'm not frightened of him, Ingrid.'

'Well, I am.' She looked at her watch. 'The car will be waiting. I must go.'

'You can't,' I said.

'It's okay for the next week or two. I'm safe. Nothing will

164

happen to me until I've signed over the companies he's so concerned about. He's fixing up some kind of nominee holding; he told me that. He wants me to go to South America with him and sign a whole lot of documents in what he calls the appropriate jurisdictions.' She looked at the door. 'There's Goldie,' she said. She put her half-filled plate down on the table. 'I must go. It's a wedding anniversary; people I've known for ages. And I promised to look in for a moment at Budd Byron's party. There are no friends like old friends, Mickey. It's taken me until now to discover that.'

'Wait a minute,' I said. Her cutting away at this moment of high stress was unbearable. To persuade her to stay I felt like telling her what I'd found in the icebox on the Topanga hilltop, but I'd resolved to tell no one; I still had no evidence that Petrovitch had murdered Pindero and stuffed him in the fridge. On the other hand I really was worried about her.

'I know what I'm doing,' she said. She made a sudden effort to change the mood. 'Maybe I'm exaggerating. Zach's a darling most of the time.'

Across the room Goldie was standing in the doorway with his hat in his hand, a faithful retainer look on his face and Ingrid's fur coat over one arm.

'Call me anytime,' I said.

She gave me a peck on the cheek. 'Don't look so solemn. It will be all right.'

I watched her go. Women like Ingrid should display a warning from the surgeon general: Associating with this woman will impair your powers of reasoning and lead to insane actions that endanger your health.

I went back to the table and sat down with Danny and Robyna. 'Are you going to Budd Byron's party?' said Danny.

'How did you hear about that?'

'He sent me an invite but we can't go. I've got a test tomorrow morning and I need to improve my average. Will you give him this?' said Danny.

He brought out a printed yellow sheet of paper and smoothed it on the tablecloth. It was a pawn ticket with *This is a pledge and not a sale* and a five-digit number printed sideways along its edge. It took me a moment to decipher the computer printout: THREE HUNDRED AND TWENTY-FIVE DOLLARS. 9-MM HANDGUN. BROWNING MODEL 35. DANIEL M. MURPHY. SEX: M; RACE: W: HAIR: BRN; EYES: BLK; WEIGHT: 150; BIRTH DATE: 01/23/70.

'You pawned the gun!'

'Don't get excited, Pop. The pawnshop has a back room filled with them.'

'Don't fool with guns, Danny. Didn't I tell you that a thousand times?'

'This pawnbroker preferred the gun to the stereo. He said customers always come back for their guns, but stereos go out of style.'

'Let me look at that again.' I picked up the pawn ticket. 'That's not your date of birth. Did you show him fake ID?'

'All the kids at school have them.'

'You walk in there with a heater. You have your name and address filed into their computer. And you use fake ID. Are you out of your mind?'

'I needed the money, Dad. My brakes needed relining.'

'Didn't any of those street-smart friends of yours tell you that the Police Department has a pawnshop detail where they file all routine reports about suspicious merchandise? The police clerk will take the counterfoil, bring your name up on the computer, read off your driver's license, and see you've given a false age.'

He wet his lips nervously the way he'd done as a small child. 'I'm sorry, Dad.'

'I can't straighten this one out for you. This is not like a speeding ticket.'

'My brakes needed relining.'

I'd always told him that maintaining the brakes and steering and other vital parts of his car was top priority, so he invariably used that as a defense. I picked up the pawn ticket, folded it into two, and put it into my billfold. 'I'll redeem it.' I felt like driving down to the pawnshop right away.

'You don't need to redeem it. Budd wants the gun. He's going to buy the ticket from me and collect it himself.'

'He can't do that, can he? It's illegal.'

'Sometimes you talk like an out-of-town hick, Dad. Why wouldn't it be legal? I just have to sign the form, that's all.'

'Okay, I'll tell Budd to redeem it tomorrow without fail, before the cops get interested.'

'Budd wants a gun real bad. He said it gets scary up there.'

'Don't call him Budd when you talk to him. It's better to call him Mr Byron.'

'He said to call him Budd.'

'Scary? He's just highly strung.' Danny was looking at my billfold longingly. I said, 'You want me to advance you the money? Is that it?'

'Budd will pay you when you give him the ticket.'

'How much?'

'Four hundred.'

'Four hundred! What kind of a loan shark did I raise?'

'Budd insisted.'

'Okay.' I tossed four bills onto the table. 'You stay away from that pawnshop. Let Budd redeem the gun; at least he can prove he's over twenty-one.'

'Thanks, Dad.'

'Let me tell you something, Danny. Until last year the cops used to collect the counterfoils every day. Now the pawnshops

167

mail them in. Thank your lucky stars that we'll probably just be able to get out of this before the shit descends on your head.'

'Where has your friend Ingrid gone?' said Danny.

'She had to go to a meeting.' I let him change the subject. I didn't want to give him a bad time.

'Is she on the sniff?' said Robyna.

'How's that?' It was Robyna's way of getting under my skin.

'I thought she was spaced out,' said Robyna. 'She's kind of odd, isn't she?'

It's true that Ingrid has a calm and inscrutable manner. She'd been that way when young. I'd always thought of it as a legacy from her mysterious Scandinavian forebears: the result of endless expanses of snow and ice and unrelenting melancholy. I had a weird idea about what Sweden was like back when I was in high school and had never been farther from home than Lake Havasu. 'No, she's not spaced out, Robyna, she just has a lot of worries. Now, is there anything else I can do for you?'

'You bastard!' said a voice from behind me. I looked up and saw my wife, Betty. Ex-wife, I mean. 'I knew you had a fancy woman, Mickey. Why do you always lie to me?'

'What are you talking about?' I said, although I knew she must have been spying on me and watched my tête-à-tête with Ingrid. 'That was a client—' Realizing that Ingrid wouldn't want anyone to know she was consulting me, I amended it. 'The wife of a client, I mean.'

Betty's face registered anger and satisfaction in equal amounts. 'Now the truth is coming out,' she said. 'You're carrying on with the wife of a client. I hope you're proud of yourself.' I looked around. Where were the kids? They'd made themselves scarce. The people at the next table were all looking at us, but when I stared back they went back to eating their brunches.

'Felicity knows her,' I said. 'You ask Felicity.'

'You two-faced bastard. You should be disbarred.'

'Get yourself under control, Betty.'

'To think of the way you lie to poor little Danny . . .' she said, and dried up as if thinking about it were too much for her. So that was it. Danny had invited Betty to eat with us. It was another of his endless attempts to reunite his parents. No wonder he went so pale when he saw me with Ingrid. And no wonder he was staying out of the way now. 'Womanizer!' said Betty. She turned and marched out to the pool as if she was about to throw herself into the deep end. In a way, I couldn't help feeling sorry for her. At least, maybe I would feel that way tomorrow. I watched her choose a seat by the pool and sit down.

Danny was watching her too as he returned with his plate. 'Did you invite your mother along?' I asked him.

'She said she had to see you. She was worried about the cops digging up the yard.'

'What?'

'She's renting that house on Mulholland where you lived way back. The cops came and dug up the yard, looking for a dead body. She wants to know if she can make them reinstate the flower beds and stuff.'

'Wait a minute, wait a minute. Cops looking for a body? What is all this?'

'I told her you'd probably know all about it.' He looked unconcerned. 'And the waitress said, Are you four brunches or five?'

'Tell the waitress I don't know how many brunches I am. Tell her I'm coming back to sort out the bill in a minute.'

I got up and hurried out to where Betty was lolling back on a lounger. She was calmer now.

'I'm sorry,' she said. 'I'm really sorry, Mickey. And I apologize.'

'Have you been drinking?' I said. I'd never heard her apologize before.

'Of course not.' She held up a glass of orange juice from the breakfast jug.

'What's this about cops digging up the yard?'

'Yes, that's what I wanted to ask you. Can I charge the city for the flower beds? You remember those two lovely camellias? They'll never recover.'

'What did they say, the cops?'

'It's a homicide investigation. They came with a crew and equipment. They asked for you, and when I said you weren't there they said they wanted to dig. What could I do except say yes? Now the landlord wants to replant and make me foot the bill.'

'Asked for me by name?' The idea that the cops thought I was dead and buried in a backyard on Mulholland Drive was nothing less than horrifying, but I didn't want Betty to see I was worried. She talked too much.

'They thought it was your home. They said, Was I Mrs Murphy?'

'What did you tell them?'

'What am I going to tell them? I said yes.'

'Didn't you tell them we're divorced?'

'They didn't ask.'

'You let them think it was my home?'

'I didn't let them think anything. They came in like they owned the place and searched the closets and everywhere. They put it all back, but when you're not expecting it—'

'Did they take things away?'

'What did you bury in the yard, Mickey?'

'I didn't bury anything in the yard. I haven't been up on Mulholland in ten years or more.'

'They took away samples of dirt and stuff in evidence bags. They were looking for a body.'

'What is going on?' I said to the world in general.

170

She smiled at me as if I were joking. She never did take things seriously. 'It was Danny's idea,' she said. 'My coming to brunch with you was Danny's idea. I thought we'd be alone. Just you and me and Danny. I have a favor to ask you.'

'I can't keep shelling out more dough. Times are tough. There's a recession, remember. No matter what the White House spokesman says, I've got a real-life recession down here in the savings account, where it hurts.'

'It's not about money,' she said.

'Not about money?'

'You don't have to be sarcastic,' she said.

'Give me a break, will you? I send your money regularly. You don't have to tell some has-been prize-fighter to try and lever more out of me.'

'Prizefighter?' She wrinkled her brow and then she laughed. 'Prizefighter!'

'What's funny?'

'That "has-been prizefighter" is Juan, my astrologer.'

'I should have guessed. Juan, the only astrologer in town with oiled biceps: oh, boy. That's where my money goes. It's always a mystic or a guru or a fortuneteller or some other kind of phony. Why don't you grow up, Betty?'

'He just wanted to help me. He's not a moneygrubber. He's a sweet man.' She was defensive now.

'Oh, sure. I knew he was some kind of altruist when I saw him drive off in that metallic-silver five hundred SEL. Do you know what an import like that costs?'

'Don't start going on about imports. You sound just like your father.'

'So what's wrong with that?'

'Nothing. I liked him, you know that. In his last few months I visited the hospital more often than you did. You always had urgent work on Sunday mornings.'

171

'I guess so.' That knife went deep. She knew how to get between the ribs. Dad was a great guy, but I was a less-than-great son; I didn't make enough effort. I said, 'Remember the surgeon's face when they fitted his pacemaker and he asked if it had a lifetime warranty?'

Betty said, 'Sometimes I wonder if I'll stay as cheerful as that if I wind up in some old people's home, hoping Danny won't find urgent work to do on Sunday mornings.'

It was a chilling thought. Ten minutes with Betty, and I needed to go lie down in a darkened room. She really knew how to get to me. 'Yeah. It's how we get punished, I guess. I miss him.'

'Danny or your dad?'

'Both,' I said feelingly.

'Danny has his own life, Mickey. When he was just a kid we were all together, like we were on the dock or something. But suddenly he takes a short step and he's on a boat. At first it doesn't seem so different, but then boat and dock are moving apart. There's water between us. And all of a sudden his boat is almost out of sight and he's off to live his own life. Married soon, maybe, with kids of his own. And he won't be a part of our life anymore. Does that sound flaky?'

'No.'

'I tried to do a little poem about it, but I couldn't get the rhymes right.'

'It doesn't sound flaky, Betty. I guess all parents find it tough.'

'That's what Felicity said.' She drank some orange juice. 'Felicity got together with Paul again.'

'Is that right? She was looking very detached when I saw her in Aspen.'

'Could we try again?' she said. 'Sort of a second honeymoon? You know: go somewhere and try again. You and me, like it was in the old days. We had some laughs, didn't we?'

'Go where?' I wasn't about to schlepp across to Vegas again.

172

One honeymoon in Vegas is more than enough. How many gambling games can you lose in one weekend? 'I'm busy; I couldn't get away if I wanted to.' Any flicker of interest, and she'd have us sharing a thatched hut in Kauai or renting a drive-yourself gondola in Venice, Italy.

'It doesn't have to be anywhere special. We could go to the Hilton in Anaheim.'

'The Hilton in Anaheim?' I couldn't keep my voice level. My surprise didn't register with her. 'I'll book it and pay. They do a special weekend rate at the Anaheim Hilton with a complimentary champagne breakfast. Saturday and Sunday.'

'I don't care if they give us complimentary mouse ears in Disneyland and a free pie at Knott's Berry Farm, the answer is no. No, Betty, no.' I said it with conviction. Maybe you think that sounds cruel, but you have to be very careful with Betty. Any other response and she'd start thinking I was hankering to strap on the harness, blinkers, and reins again. 'Like I say, I'm locked into work right now.'

'Felicity and Paul patched things up at the Anaheim Hilton. They're really happy again.'

A fat guy with tattooed arms ran past us, feet slapping, and jumped into the pool, arms flailing: *splash!* It made Betty jump and sprayed us with water.

'That's great,' I said dabbing water from my arms. Now it was all explained. Felicity Weingartner had a big reconciliation with her live-in boyfriend at the Anaheim Hilton, so we have to go to the Anaheim Hilton. For Betty it always had to be metaphysical. It had to be good omens or vibes, something in the lines of your hand or in the stars. Or numerology: what was their room number?

'Come and have dinner tonight. Baked sea bass with black bean sauce. I'm using that recipe we got from the waiter at the Mandarin.'

173

'It's Budd's birthday party.'

'Yes, I was invited too,' she admitted. 'For lunch.'

'I told him I'd be late.'

'He's weird.'

'I saw him on TV last week. He was a cop who got gunned down in *Miami Vice*.'

'I saw it. He came on with the titles, read out Miranda, and then he gurgled and was gone.'

'He looked really great,' I said.

'Because they're reruns; that's why he looked great. That was years back, when he was younger. What has he done lately?'

'He's working his ass off. I know that for a fact.'

She looked at me to see if I was sincere. 'You're always so loyal to him,' she said, in a voice that wondered why I wasn't similarly loyal to her.

'You used to keep on about how handsome he was.'

'Did I?' She lifted her eyebrows and gave a faint reflective smile as she remembered. 'Maybe I did.' She looked pretty – almost beautiful when she smiled. It was easy to remember meeting her and thinking she was the only one for me. She got up.

'Are you going to Budd's?' I said.

'I've got guests for dinner. I have to cook.'

I nodded. I wasn't going to press her to come and see Budd with me. An evening with a roomful of movie actors was a heavy enough prospect without having Betty along to give a running commentary.

'I'll call you,' I said.

She put up her hand and gently ran her fingers through her hair to loosen it. 'Forget Budd Byron. He'll have all his actor friends with him. Let's you and me have dinner instead. Tell him you're sick or something.' She looked great; she must have been doing her exercises again.

174

'I thought you had people coming to dinner. You said you had to cook.'

'I can rearrange it.'

'No,' I said.

'Honey . . . being together again would save you money,' she said.

'No. Lay off me, Betty, will you? I'm real low on conjugal motivation these days.'

'What's that mean?'

'It means we're through. It's all over.'

10

Budd's party was not the sort of Hollywood celebration that Betty had been so caustic about. There were no megastars parading complete with an entourage of press agents and gofers, no studio executives with ponytails and designer stubble chins, no fashionable catering, no upstairs rooms where pretty young boys, shapely girls, and little bowls of white powder were arrayed for guests to help themselves.

For nearly twenty years Budd had owned this rickety old house perched up in the Hollywood Hills near the Laurel Canyon intersection. It was only a stone's throw from all the litter, traffic, and panhandling horror of Sunset, but it was a world apart.

Manderley. What star-struck romantic had named it? It was an old house by Hollywood standards. You could tell the age of these houses in the hills by the mature trees that were part of their landscaping. Manderley sheltered under the canopies of three horse chestnuts. Inside it was crammed with Asian carpets and heavy furniture that Budd bought cheap back in the seventies, when cash-hungry studios turned their back lots over to the speculators and opened their property warehouses to the auctioneers. Okay, so it was a film set: an incongruous clutter of orphaned furnishings that would never get along together. But all his friends and visitors escaped their chaste design-conscious interiors to revel in the novelty of his cluttered home.

And who wanted to go inside anyway when, with a chilled drink in your hand, you were standing in the warm sunshine exchanging jibes with a crowd of old buddies and marveling at a view right across the city? Budd had set up an elaborate portable bar, fashioned like one of those old New York ice-cream carts. There was every kind of drink you can think of; chips and nuts from Trader Joe's and warm popcorn and cheese straws, and those tiny Japanese snacks that look like plastic and taste like seaweed.

I arrived late. It was long past lunchtime, and the Weber barbecue was cooled and closed down. Beside it there were toasted buns, mustard, and a huge floral-patterned plate of hamburgers and franks that had been left to go cold. Champagne was being served while, for those who didn't like bubbles, half a dozen bottles of Mondavi Chardonnay stood in a plastic tub of ice and bottles of Beaulieu Cabernet Sauvignon were lined up ready to uncork. This was all set to go on late. But I stood there that afternoon transfixed by the view. The storms had gone; the ragged clouds were dipped in gore, and the sun was dropping out of them like a silver dollar coming out of an upended collection box.

'You never get used to it,' Budd said. Having greeted me and brought me a drink, he answered the question I'd never put to him. Budd had broken free from a group of open-mouthed thespians – mostly young – who were listening to Pop Pedersen, a redfaced fifty-year-old raconteur who had been Budd's agent ever since he started work.

'It's a great spot, Budd,' I told him. 'You got the most spectacular home in the city.'

To the standard compliment he gave his regular reply: 'It's my million-dollar view.'

177

Budd was looking great; the big fellow always looked great. He was wearing a custom-made tuxedo – white jacket and black pants – with a fashionable high-collar shirt and wine-red bow tie. Budd did not subscribe to the rule that a host must not outdress his guests. 'It's good to see you, Budd.' We didn't have to say much to each other; we were pals. 'Danny had to study. He's sorry not to be here. I brought you a pawn ticket.'

'What do I owe you?'

'Happy birthday,' I said. Behind him, Pop Pedersen was responding to his appreciative audience. He mimed some business with a door and a girl and a bed. Show-biz agents are all actors at heart, how else can they stay in that stressful business?

After a moment or two of scanning the ticket to be sure it was signed, he stuffed it into his pocket. 'What a wonderful birthday present. I knew you'd come through, Mickey. When you told me Danny had a gun, I could tell how badly you wanted someone to take it off his hands.'

'Oh.'

'Did I get it wrong?'

'Did I say Danny had a gun, Budd? I don't remember that.'

'Maybe Danny told me. He phoned to thank me for inviting him.'

'Maybe that was it,' I said.

Behind him Pop was ending his story by grabbing the lapels of an imaginary hotel manager and shouting, 'Rule number one for beach hotels, you son of a bitch – print the do-not-disturb notices in some language the chamber maids can understand!' They all laughed while Pop drank his wine and bathed in their reaction.

'I'm glad you could get away,' said Budd. 'You more than anyone.' I knew he meant it. He had this big wide sentimental streak.

'Everyone always turns up, Budd. It's an event,' I said. 'Did Ingrid look in on you?'

'Just old friends,' Budd said, nodding and looking around. 'Round up the usual suspects. That's it, right?' And then, in belated reaction to my question: 'Ingrid? Yes, that's right, she did.'

I watched him in surprise. I would have thought a visit by Ingrid would have brought a stronger reaction. As well as being a minor celebrity, Ingrid was someone Budd adored almost as much as I did.

I looked around at the mutual friends: college buddies and Budd's actor friends. No one there looked like they were seeking asylum from the autograph hunters, but I recognized a few faces that regularly uttered lines in the soaps. And scattered around the patio were plenty of beautiful young women. Some were in faded designer jeans and T-shirts, while others wore snazzy low-fronted audition dresses. Long-legged girls with good teeth and chunky jewelry always went for Budd. With his broad shoulders and wavy blond hair, he was the ultimate fashion accessory.

'Happy birthday, Budd,' called another latecomer. It was a homicide detective named Felix Chiaputti who'd been a history major with us at college. He never looked like a cop; I suppose that was how he came to be a detective. He was wearing a dark-blue polo shirt and a light-blue cotton cord suit, with the jacket draped over his shoulder so that a short-barreled Smith & Wesson could be seen in its holster on his belt.

'Felix! Just the man I want to see,' I said. The news that the cops were digging up the yard at Betty's home in Mulholland had alarmed me, but it was better to get around to it gradually. 'How's the homicide business?'

'Frisky,' said Felix, after he'd gulped down a lot of his bourbon. 'How are things with you?'

'Mustn't grumble.'

'I needed that,' he said, finishing his drink with a second swallow and stepping aside to pour himself another from a bottle he grabbed from the bar.

'Tough day? I didn't know cops worked on Sunday.' He turned on me with pointing finger, opened mouth, and narrowed eyes. I knew how to get to him. 'Only kidding, Felix,' I added hastily.

'I spent the afternoon discussing sailing boats and catamarans and where best to take them in the Caribbean.'

'You've got a boat now?'

'Plump little guy with very white front teeth and golden molars . . . way-down-south accent. Boat? Are you kidding? I've got trouble meeting the payments on my condo.'

'So?'

'This guy says he likes Haiti best: lots of quiet little beaches and clear water you can snorkel in. That's why he bought a holiday home there, but then he likes unspoiled places. He's not looking for caviar and nouvelle cuisine; he's just plain folks. He's like you and me, except he's got a thirty-foot trimaran named *Pegasus* and knows all the little islands in the Caribbean better than I know the singles bars in Santa Monica.'

'Is that right?' Why would Felix know the singles bars? Was he cheating on his wife, Maureen? I noticed that Felix was combing his hair forward from the back of his head, to hide his balding crown, so maybe the answer was yes. I said, 'What does this guy have that I don't have?'

'Resources, Mickey, that's what he has. He married the heiress to a pantyhose fortune.'

'What's your connection with this guy?'

'On his last voyage he chopped his wife into bite-sized pieces with a cleaver he bought in a Chinese market on Broadway and fed her to the sharks. They have a lot of sharks around Haiti, and bite-size pieces for sharks are pretty big. They get used to the idea that boats throw garbage over the side, and they follow them. I put that to him. He agreed. He had books about sharks and their habitats on his bedside table. He said they're an endangered species. He seems to have lost the cleaver. It must have gone overboard with the garbage, he says.'

'Jesus. What will happen to him?'

'He'll inherit ten point seven million dollars from his wife. It's mostly in T-bonds, but a guy with chutzpah like that will switch to equities unless I've got him all wrong.'

'I mean, what will he get?'

'Get? He'll never go to trial. If I asked the attorney's office for a grand jury, my boss would send me off for counseling and then fire me. All I've got as evidence is a lady's Rolex with a gold wristlet that forensics says was sliced right through with a heavy steel blade. On the gold there are minute traces of a distinctive low-quality steel exactly like that of a Chinese cleaver I got from the same store. With no more than that I couldn't even get the bastard for polluting the ocean. We'll never be able to hang it on him. He's done everything right. He even asked me for his wife's watch back. He said it had sentimental value and implied some cop might steal it. I don't know how I kept my hands off the little bastard. He used to be a doctor, can you believe it?' Felix shook the bottle to get the last drop. 'It was almost empty when I took it,' he said, meeting my eye.

I said, 'Judging from the bills my doctor sends me, I don't know why he doesn't have ten million dollars of his own.'

'Maybe he has.' Felix stepped across and found another bottle of bourbon and poured some and drank that pretty swiftly too.

I said, 'If you're driving home, I'd take it easy.'

'*Pegasus*, he calls the boat. I looked it up. It was an immortal winged horse that sprang from the blood of the slain Medusa. Then I looked up Medusa and found she wasn't a god, she was a mortal woman.'

I looked at him. 'That's cute,' I said, 'even for a history major. Are you saying this guy named his boat with murder in mind?'

'It's a thought, isn't it?' He looked around. 'We're all getting older, I guess.'

'Speak for yourself,' I said. 'Say, does this happen a lot – men killing their wives and getting off scot free?'

'You're not remarried, are you? You're still divorced from Betty?'

'Take it easy, Felix. I'm asking because I have a client who feels threatened. She thinks her husband is going to kill her.'

'Maybe she's nuts,' he said.

'You're a hard man, Felix. But what kind of advice can I give her if she isn't nuts?'

'Why doesn't she just take off?'

'There is a custody dimension. If she takes off she figures her husband will say she's irresponsible and mentally unstable and persuade the court to give him custody of her kid.'

He looked at me and rubbed his face for a moment before answering. 'Fifty-eight percent of all murders in the U.S. are done by close friends or family. Family and workplace: it's where it all starts. Not many wackos go out and kill someone they don't know for no reason at all. Statistically she's got more chance of being wasted by her husband than by anyone else. And if there's money in the offing the chances go up. Say, is this someone I know?'

'No, it's a client.'

He looked at me suspiciously. 'You're not another of these people with a secret film script going the rounds, are you? This town is full of them. You and Budd maybe? Budd was

182

asking me exactly the same kind of questions only two weeks back.'

'Budd was?'

'Okay, so it's secret. I won't tell on you.'

'Listen, Felix. I'm not writing a film script. I've got problems and I need your advice.'

'Go!'

'Betty is living in that old house we used to rent on Mulholland. A team of homicide guys went up there the other day. They searched the house and dug up the yard. Do you know anything about that?'

'Not a thing. What were they after?'

'You tell me. They asked for me, Betty says. That's all I know.'

'No messages? Nothing in the mail? Nothing by fax? They didn't contact your office?'

'I haven't been to the office for a couple of days.'

'These things always have a simple explanation,' said Felix, as if cops were constantly engaged on surprise digging raids in yards all over town. 'You know what the mail is like these days.'

Before I could say anything more, his wife Maureen arrived with three mini hot dogs. I knew her. She was a determined thirty-year-old talent agency executive with beady blue eyes and fashionably frazzled hair. Cute in a ferocious kind of way. 'I'm telling Mickey about the wife murderer.'

'Felix was hoping for an expense-paid trip to the Caribbean,' said Maureen. 'When the guy returned of his own volition, Felix was determined to put him into the gas chamber as revenge.'

'Maureen's never lost her great sense of humor,' he said. 'That's what holds our marriage together. Right, Maureen?'

'I've never been more serious in my life,' she said, offering me a hot dog on a bun. I wasn't hungry, but it was so friendly of her to include me in the logistics that I took one.

'Did you put mustard on this, sweetheart?' Felix asked her.

'Would I shortchange you after all these years of slaving for you?'

Felix bit into his hot dog and then closed his eyes and pursed his lips as he savored it. 'Gelson's.' He pronounced his verdict on the hot dog. 'My favorite: with Safeway's as runner-up. Maureen's got her own outfit now. Did you know that?'

'Agenting?' She certainly never pushed any of her legal work my way.

Maureen nodded. 'Yeah. Mostly writers and directors. I'm planning to package producers too, when I get a development deal that's right. I'm staying clear of actors for the time being: too temperamental.' She had a low, clear, attractive voice. At one time she'd been in radio, a kid's story program, but when they refused to give her her own show she left.

'Congrats, Maureen,' I said. 'Are you putting on a little weight?'

'Yeah, I am, you bastard.' She stopped eating her hot dog and stared at it accusingly. Maybe she read my mind about her never giving me any legal crumbs swept off the agenting table. 'I'm a victim of the Hollywood business lunch. But I've been doing real well, and it's good working for yourself.' So there!

'You should see the office, Mickey,' said her proud husband. 'Santa Monica Boulevard, near Rodeo. Oak paneling, carpets up to your ankles, hand-painted art on the wall; we should live so well at home!'

'Don't be mean, honey,' said Maureen. 'I've got to have a neat place to take executives and the talent. Clients need the reassurance prosperous-looking representation provides. The kind of clients I'm interested in don't want an agent who works out of a cocktail lounge with a mobile phone.'

'Let me know when you get a vacancy,' I joshed.

'Right now,' she said. 'I need someone right away.' She plucked the hot dog from her roll, ate it, and dropped the roll into a nearby bin.

'What kind of a someone?' I asked.

'Someone prepared to pound shoe leather. Someone who can figure a percentage without a Japanese calculator and knows his way around the studios and the eating places. I'm eating two or three lunches some days, and it's killing me. You got any ideas?'

'My ex, Betty, is available; she's looking for a job.' This was not exactly true. Betty had given no indication that she was looking for a job, or even that she'd take one if it came along. But Betty in paid employment sounded good to me. If she had some kind of income it might get her off my back.

'Betty? Betty Murphy that was?' She looked at me quizzically. I guess she could see what was in my mind.

'Betty Murphy that is,' I said. 'She likes my name better than her own, Vanderbilt. People in credit departments were always making jokes about repayment plans.'

'Does she have any experience?'

'Of eating three meals a day? Sure she does. Four, some days. Refrigerator raids in the A.M., too. I'll show you my check stubs.'

'You louse! Are you serious?'

'Betty could do it,' I insisted. I was getting keen now.

'I need a negotiator. A catalyst; a mediator. Agenting is not the breeze some folk seem to think it is. It's very tough, and you have to be quick on your feet with these film deals.'

'Negotiator! She negotiated me into the poorhouse.'

'And she was your secretary at one time, so I guess she can write letters that sound legal.'

'She can draw up an agreement. She worked for Pop Pedersen back before Danny was born.'

185

'If you're kidding me, Murphy—'

'I'm telling you the truth.'

'Is Betty here?'

'No. But I just lunched with her. Give her a call. She'd be great for you. Very tenacious, if you know what I mean.'

'I know Betty,' said Maureen, in that resentful we-girls-stick-together kind of voice. 'You're a bastard, Mickey. I can see why she left you.'

'Give her a call. This is where you can reach her.' I scribbled Betty's number on the back of a business card and gave it to Maureen, who put it away in her smart alligator purse.

'Maybe I'll give Betty a job and she'll make you eat your words.'

'Just as long as she picks up the tab for them.'

As I spoke, Budd yelled from the far side of the patio, 'Felix! Come over here and arrest this guy!'

Felix smiled at me, took his wife's arm, and began to move off.

'I've got to ask you something, Felix,' I said. 'See me before you go, will you?'

He nodded and moved away. But I had the feeling he didn't want to take up the conversation again.

'Not many people here,' said a man Budd had introduced as a famous movie producer. I'd never seen him before. He was a tough-looking little guy with very wide shoulders. Close to, you could see he'd had a face lift at some time. Now he needed another. His hair was perfect, wavy and graying at the temples, and his face was craggy and distinguished. 'Harold Torvik.'

'Good to know you, Harry,' I said. 'My name is Mickey Murphy.'

'I don't know any of these people,' he said.

It was hard to tell whether he was complaining or boasting. I looked across the patio with him and studied the other guests. 'It's just close friends.'

'That's the way it looks,' he said. He adroitly snatched a newly poured glass of champagne from the tray of a passing waiter. 'Are you an actor?'

'An attorney. I was at college with Budd.'

'He told me he went to college,' he said, as if it was difficult to believe.

'A football scholarship,' I said. 'Budd and I were both on football scholarships.'

'Football? Did he get a letter?'

'He did all right.' It wasn't exactly true. I always suspected that Budd got the scholarship more because he looked like a football star than because he stood any chance of becoming one. To see Budd so carefully groomed, dressed in his uniform, helmet under his arm, shy smile, and determined distant stare, inspired us all. He personified the love we all had for the game.

'But he didn't graduate?'

'He got so many movie offers he left.'

'His agent sent me a video of his acting work. Has he ever had a star role?'

'Sure, lots,' I said. This guy was bugging me, but if Budd was being considered for something important I felt I'd better stay there and sing his praises.

'I mean in a big production.'

'Oh, sure,' I said loyally. 'He's done everything. For sample videos,' I said, improvising desperately, 'actors like to show a wide variety of minor roles to emphasize versatility.'

'Tell me some titles.'

'I've got a terrible memory,' I said. 'And to tell you the truth, I'm not a big moviegoer except for musicals.'

'Me neither; movies are a load of shit. I never go to movies; never watch them on TV or on videos either.'

'I thought you were a movie producer,' I said.

'No, that's just Budd's flight of fancy. My line is bowling

187

alleys. I've had a lot of people try to get me to invest in movies. I wouldn't touch them.'

He paused and waited. 'Why?'

'Because movie bookkeepers can show you a grievous loss on a gold mine. I've got eight bowling alleys: Chicago, San Diego, Dallas . . . right across the country. You want to make a little extra dough, let me put it into bowling. It's a wonderful investment, and I guarantee you won't get gypped. My books are open to every investor. I run a clean business, and it pays.' He produced an expensive-looking leather wallet and gave me his card. 'Budd will be my guest when we open the newest and biggest one in my group: Albany.'

'Congratulations.'

He gave the ghost of a smile. 'I thought your pal was a big movie star, but I'm beginning to think he's a wannabe.'

'You're wrong, Harry. Budd Byron is a well-known face,' I said. 'You don't see many movies, you told me, but movie buffs will know his face, even if they don't recognize the name at first. And he's a very fine actor.'

He looked at me. 'Is that right?'

'Yes, it is. Budd is one of Hollywood's most famous personalities.'

He looked at me. That was going too far and we both knew it. He sniffed and took a gulp of champagne and then dabbed his mouth with a spotted silk handkerchief. 'Maybe you're right. Anyhow, Budd's price is all I can afford – I can't splash a fortune on an opening – and shit, what do bowling freaks in Albany know about film stars?' We both stood there while he scrutinized the other guests. Then he suddenly moved off to talk to a young girl in a see-through blouse who was trying to open a can of 7-Up all on her own. She saw help coming and beamed at him. I guess she spotted the can opener in his pants.

Budd was doing the rounds; he was a conscientious host.

To round off the party Pop Pedersen was taking Budd and a bunch of the guests to Morton's. Budd asked me to join them but I said no. I could see it was going to be one of those evenings that ended up in some little bar in Santa Monica with a lot of guys smashed, maudlin, and sitting around with their cellulars on the counter promising to produce a dozen gorgeous sexy girls who never answered the phone.

'Another time, maybe. I've got things to do at home.'

'Come on, Mickey! What kind of things?'

'What kind of things? Listen, either I stop off on the way home to buy more chinaware or locate the owner's manual for the dishwasher. My tumble dryer is on the blink, and I'm up to here in dirty laundry. My cleaning lady is home nursing a sick daughter, and if I don't start cleaning up soon, the board of health will cite me for trying to start a cholera epidemic.'

'Come on, Mickey. Forget those chores. Pop would love to have you along.'

Budd didn't believe me, I could see that. He thought I was rejecting him and our friends. 'Look, Budd,' I told him. 'The real story is that I've lined up a big-titted blonde in Marina del Rey. Her husband's at a paint manufacturers' convention in Dallas, and this could be my big chance.'

'Gotcha,' said Budd and gave me a fixed, uncertain smile. He didn't know what to believe. He couldn't even distinguish what I wanted him to believe. And that was good. The beneficial interactions of urban American life only succeed because we don't know what to believe. If we knew what to believe, we'd be beating our neighbor's door down.

'Well, you're welcome to join us if you change your mind,' Budd said. 'Have you got a drink?'

'I've had enough to drink.' I quite liked Pop Pedersen, but he was one of those guys who has got to convince you of his unquenchable libido, and I couldn't face an evening trying to laugh at funny stories that would all end with Pop performing energetically in bed, beach, or back seat with some beautiful starlet.

The sun was fast disappearing now, and the light was golden. I moved to the terrace rail and sat down on one of the loungers. What a city it was: the biggest collection of strangers in the world, people from every part of the globe with nothing in common but a belief that making money in the sunshine was no more strenuous than making it in the rain and snow. The city was laid out before me. From up here you could see that most of it consisted of low hutlike prefabricated buildings giving the effect of a vast army camp. Standing around awkwardly, like tall grown-ups at a children's party, were some elegant glass skyscrapers: a cluster of them glinting in the distant haze of Century City and more around City Hall downtown. And everywhere, marking the grid patterns made by the long avenues, were spiky rows of palms reaching high into the smog. And when the sun was very low like this, its rosy glow came through the haze so it looked as if the whole city was ablaze, from Pasadena to LAX.

It was dusk when I left Budd's party and drove over to my office. I went upstairs and sat at Miss Huth's desk to go through the mail and messages. There was nothing there to explain the cops digging holes in Mulholland.

While sitting there I heard voices from the next office. It was Billy Kim talking to Vic Crichton. I'd not seen my partner since he was discharged from the hospital in Phoenix. I had a lot to say to him, so I rapped on the door and went in.

'Billy,' I said. 'Why didn't you tell me you were back?'

Billy looked at Vic Crichton and Vic looked at his shoes. The quality of the ensuing silence and the stance of the two men told me I'd interrupted some kind of argument, one of those fierce arguments that are conducted in low voices.

'Hello, Mickey,' said Billy Kim softly. He was standing behind his desk. In greeting he held up his left hand, clad in a plaster cast. 'When this comes off I'll be in good shape. I was planning to see you.'

Vic Crichton was sprawled in an easy chair with a drink in his fist. 'I'm glad you've come, Mickey,' he said. 'Talk to your partner and get some sense into his head.'

'Mickey is not a party to what we are talking about, Vic. Leave him out of it.'

'Don't give me that shit,' said Vic, his face reddened by emotion and exertion and maybe by the alcohol too. 'I talked to Mickey in Aspen, didn't I, Mickey? He took the stiff to the mortician. Do you think I don't know that? We own that mortuary; we know what's happening.'

A bottle of brandy was on the desk in front of Billy and there was a glass there too, but Billy seldom drank alcohol and his obvious anger was not brought on by drinking. 'I don't need you, Vic,' said Billy Kim slowly and deliberately. 'You need me, but I don't need you. It would serve you well to remember that.'

'There's no shortage of stiffs,' said Vic, spitting out the words like pips from a papaw. He got up from the chair and walked across to the window. It was dark outside, and the lights of the city – the billboards and advertising signs, the movements of cars along the elevated freeways – sparkled like scores on a pinball machine. 'Walk across this city in the early hours of a chilly morning, and you'll trip over a dozen dead 'uns. You can take your pick for shape and size before the city comes to collect them.'

'Maybe you forgot that you need a certified death certificate for U.S. Customs,' said Billy Kim, with that oriental calm I knew to be the precursor to a display of violent temper. 'I have to pay the doctor for the certificates. I have to pay all of them.'

191

'Listen to me, you creep,' said Vic, swinging around from his position at the window. 'The airline won't accept a dead body for carriage except from a mortuary.' He went up close to Billy. 'And before you tell me how easy it would be to fix one of the airline guys, let me remind you that it has to be consigned to a mortuary at the other end, and the law says the foreign mortuary has to send someone to collect it.' He raised his hand to point a finger in Billy's face. 'Your contribution was minimal. Maybe that auto accident shook your little oriental brain more than the medical tests revealed.'

Billy blinked as the finger almost touched his nose. He struck Vic's hand aside and I was fearful that the Englishman would reach for that gun he liked to carry under his arm. But Crichton showed no fear. He stepped back, raised his arms a few inches in a gesture of surrender, and grinned defiantly. 'I thought there was some kind of Chinese saying that a fight means a fool has lost an argument.'

'I'll kill you, you bastard,' said Billy.

'No, you won't,' said Vic cheerfully. 'I'm calling your bluff and you'll have to back off.'

I said, 'Listen, you dumb bastards. Getting a new identity for Sir Jeremy seems to have gone to your heads. But too many people know what you did. You should be covering your tracks, not fighting about money. Stojil obliged you by selecting a suitable shape and size of dead vagrant, and he got a passport and whatever else Sir Jeremy wanted. But that doesn't mean Stojil will sit still and take the rap for you if the cops go sniffing around the Rainbow Rooms. Neither will Vic's obliging mortician protect you, even if he *is* on the payroll. If you two have an argument about money, it will be cheaper and better to settle it quietly and quickly.'

'Don't kid around, Mickey,' said Vic. 'Is this the next scene in the shakedown? Did you arrange this between you?'

'Wise up, Vic,' I said. 'The alarm bells are ringing and you've got everything to lose. How much money are you guys arguing about?'

'I don't like being swindled,' grumbled Vic. But there was a change in his manner. Maybe he was the one who had been bluffing.

'Listen carefully,' I said. 'The cops have been up to a place I used to live on Mulholland. They've been digging up the backyard. Any guesses about what they were looking for?'

'What do you mean?' said Billy.

'My guess is that the British cops have got wind of your racket. If they did a postmortem on that body you air-freighted to London and compared the dental X-rays with those of Sir Jeremy, they will be asking who this corpse is and what happened to the real Sir Jeremy. It seems they've opened a homicide investigation that will lead them to Stojil.'

The sirens screamed from somewhere on the other side of the city. 'Murder?' said Vic, his brow furrowed and his voice croaking. 'Arrest Stojil for murder?'

'If your pal Sir Jeremy is in hiding somewhere on the other side of the world, it might be tricky for anyone to prove he's still alive,' I said. 'If Stojil convinces them he isn't the perpetrator, the cops will start looking at us.'

'Is this on the level, Mickey?' asked Billy Kim. 'Were the cops really looking for a body?'

'You'll find out when they come sniffing around *your* backyard. Meanwhile, you'd better get rid of any evidence you wouldn't like to see passed to the jury for closer inspection. Kiss and make up, guys. Close ranks, sit tight, and pray.'

'You're right, Mickey,' said Billy Kim in a chastened way. Vic nodded. By the time I left the office I believed I'd managed to make them see sense. In fact, they were waiting for me to go away in order to plan their next escapade.

11

When my next-door neighbors, the Klopstocks, had people over, they always parked their own three cars along my curb. This way they had their front and their ramp for parking the cars of their guests. There was nothing I could do about it, but looking out the window and seeing the Klopstocks' big white Mercedes sitting outside my front door exasperated me. They knew how I felt about imports. Sometimes I wondered if they did it deliberately, but there were no city ordinances or local regulations to prevent people from parking anywhere in the street they wanted, except when the disposal trucks came to collect the garbage on Friday mornings. But with those cars positioned at my curb it was tricky to steer a course into my own garage, and that bugged me.

So I was mad a few days later, when I got home very late, to find the street looking like a parking lot. It was a clear moonlit night with just a slight breeze, and I could smell charred chicken and hot wine punch. I'd suspected that morning that one of the Klopstocks' fancy barbecue parties was coming on-line. Suddenly the trees in their yard were strung with colored lights, and stacks of rented chairs and tables were being delivered. Now here it was.

'Hi there, Mickey honey!' Binnie Klopstock was standing outside saying good night to some guests.

Henry Klopstock was there too, wearing a tuxedo – a tuxedo! – and helping a tipsy woman into her Lexus. 'Do you really have to leave so early?'

I watched him as he wrapped her long fringed coat under the seat so it didn't get caught in the door. She was giggling, and the driver of the Lexus – her husband, I guess – said, 'Pull yourself together, Fleur' in a voice amplified by alcohol and, when it had no effect, said, 'Pull yourself together and say we had a great time.'

Binnie and her daughters were all wearing short 1920s-style dresses glittering with sequins and glass fringes and bugle beads. Binnie came across to me as I drove slowly onto my ramp. I was trapped.

I brought the window down. 'Hi, Binnie!' I said.

'Working late at the office again, you toiler?'

'How did you guess?'

'I could tell by your go-to-work outfit. You should get out more. Spoil yourself.'

She had some nerve. Go-to-work outfit. This was my best suit; a dark wool three-piece I'd bought to wear in court. I smiled and pressed the garage-door opener. My overhead door rolled back with a crash to expose the terrible disorder in my garage. Apart from oilstained newspapers all over the floor, the rear section had become a storage space for old dusty broken things: a bicycle Danny had outgrown, a stuffed toy lion my folks had given him for his ninth birthday, some tires with a lot of mileage left on them. It was stuff I didn't need but couldn't throw out.

Binnie looked sadly at the mess. The Klopstocks were obsessionally well-ordered: they even stored their paper Christmas decorations. 'I knew you wouldn't mind about all the cars,' she said. I kept the smile coming, but it wasn't easy. 'Now your wife has left and Danny has flown the coop, there's plenty of room.'

195

'Yeah, yeah,' I said in my usual cowardly way.

'And it gives the old shack a touch of class having the five hundred SEL standing outside, right?' She'd turned around and said it loudly so her friends could hear.

'Have a good evening, Binnie,' I said and rolled forward into the garage.

'Come and have a drink,' she called.

'It's past my bedtime.'

'We'll go on for hours yet,' she threatened. Oh, my God. I pressed the garage control so my door came down with a crash.

As I stepped through the garage into the house, I switched on the light in the hallway and spotted a sheet of orange-colored paper. It had been pushed under the front door instead of into the mailbox. I picked it up and read it. A drawing of palm trees framed a hand-lettered invitation to a party at the Klopstocks'. Today's date: a last-minute resort. *Dooo come Mickey dearest!* Binnie had scrawled in felt pen along the margin. Well, every inhabitant of suburbia knew what kind of ultimatum that was. As the hands of the clock came creeping around to zero hour, my neighbors had decided on a preemptive strike that would deprive me of any chance of complaining about 1,000 watts of Japanese woofer and tweeter that would bring Cher and her greatest hits into my home with me. The music was still going. Cher had now given way to heavy metal, a tuneless *boom boom boom*, Cole Porter on a life-support machine.

I sat down and listened to the messages on my phone, hoping Danny had called. I liked to hear his voice. But there was nothing from Danny. I made myself coffee and started to load the dishwasher. I hadn't been kidding Budd about the state of the house. I needed Mrs Santos real bad. I wondered how fast her daughter was recuperating, but I couldn't think of a tactful way of calling and asking. Did she really have a sick daughter?

196

Maybe that was just her Latin way of saying she was going to work for someone else for more money. Maybe I should advertise. Maybe I should throw a cleaning lady festival: hot Latin music, polish as a floor prize, and everyone brings a bottle of Palmolive.

I went to bed and read until midnight; then I turned off the light and worried. I do that sometimes when I take in too much caffeine. When finally I did drift off to sleep, the phone rang. I was going to let it go, but then I thought maybe it was Danny and Danny didn't like leaving messages.

'Yeah?'

'Mickey?'

'Yeah, Mickey. How are you?'

'It's Ingrid.' Her voice was thin and strained.

'Sure it is.' Did she really think I wouldn't recognize that velvet voice?

'What's that noise?' she said. 'What's going on with you?' The noise from next door was number six on the Richter scale and was getting down the wire to her.

'I've rented my spare room to the Philharmonic.'

'I need your help, Mickey.' She sounded very shaken.

'What is it?' I switched on the light, looked at the time, and yawned nervously.

She didn't answer. It was like she was having second thoughts about calling me and was debating whether to hang up.

'What can I do for you, Ingrid sweetheart?'

'Mickey . . .' I let her pause, and she said it in a rush. 'Would you drive out here and pick me up?'

'Where are you? I mean, sure I will; but tell me where. You're not in Aspen?'

'I'm standing outside Alice's.'

'Malibu, on the pier?'

'Yes.'

'Alone?'

'Yes. No. There are people fishing.'

'Is Alice's still open?'

'I don't think so. The windows are all dark. Why?'

'How did you find a phone?'

'In my purse. This is my own phone, silly.' It was the first time her voice lightened. She almost laughed.

'Malibu pier?'

'Don't keep asking the same questions, Mickey. Can you come or not?'

'Sure, but it will take me thirty minutes. Maybe more.'

'I can wait. Just do it, dearest.'

'Are you all right?'

'I don't want to talk on the phone.'

'I'll be there.'

I hung up and shivered. I dressed hurriedly, sorting out a turtleneck pullover and a green nylon flying jacket that belonged to Danny. I looked like hell, but I couldn't spare the time to shave. As I rolled out of the garage the music from next door was making the tarmac tremble.

Topanga and Malibu are both winding and inconvenient on a dark night, so I went up the 101 through Kanan, which is wider and straighter. Stabbing my way through the buttons I found a late-night station playing hits of the fifties: I guess geriatrics just can't sleep.

Soon the ocean came into view. There is something awe-inspiring about being on the rim of the Pacific at night. The black sky reaches down to join the black ocean so that it is like a ride through space. Jammed tightly together along the Pacific Coast Highway at Malibu stand the million-dollar hovels of the rich and successful. Facing them on the other side of the road is a diverse collection of eating places, stores, motels, and gas stations.

The lights never go out on the PCH, but right now there was little or no traffic. Standing under a restaurant's flashing neon sign, revelers in furs and tuxedos stood by their shiny new light-dotted cars saying protracted farewells. They stopped talking and turned to watch as I cruised past looking for Ingrid. What a scene it all made: like one of those big outdoor Italian operas they stage for the tourists in Verona: the star-littered sky, the battlements dotted with stagy lights, the costumed chorus carefully posed and silent, staring out into the hushed auditorium and waiting for the dramatic entrance of the prima donna. And there she was.

Ingrid was waiting for me at the side of the road. Dressed in an ankle-length green Loden coat, hair tucked into a black beret pulled down tight on her head, she looked like Marlene Dietrich in an old black-and-white spy movie. She was barefoot, holding her expensive shoes in her hand, and a cellular phone stuck out of her pocket. An old recording of 'Perfidia' was playing softly on my car radio as I opened the car door, and the roar of the ocean came flooding in to overwhelm Dorsey.

'Jump in!' I said. She brought in a draft of cold air. 'What are you doing out here alone at this time of night?'

She slammed the door and didn't answer, just dropped her shoes on the seat beside me, flicked the heater fan full on, and held her hand against the outlet to feel if there was warm air coming. I waited there for a moment to let her catch her breath. Across the road the chorus split up and drove away. A moment later the neon sign was extinguished and two waiters came out to stack bags of garbage at the roadside. The opera was over.

'Are you all right?' I asked her.

'No, I'm not all right.' She was hunched on the seat, massaging her bare toes.

'Where do you want to go?'

199

'Can we go back to your place, Mickey?'

'If that's what you want to do.'

'I need time to think,' she said. She opened the glove compartment and looked inside.

'Whatever you say, Ingrid.'

'Have you got a gun?' She closed the compartment.

'No, I haven't got a gun.'

'Budd is getting a gun,' she said.

'Wasn't that some party the other day? I'm sorry I missed you there.'

'Budd says everyone should have a gun,' said Ingrid. 'He says this is a dangerous town.'

'It will be when Budd gets a gun,' I said.

'Thanks for coming to get me, Mickey. You were the first person I phoned. I thought of phoning Budd, but I phoned you.'

'I'm glad you did, Ingrid. Budd is in Albany.'

The party next door was still going on. A little group of unsteady guests had gathered on the sidewalk, saying a noisy good night to the Klopstocks. The Klopstocks were saying good nights back to them. The Klopstocks were the noisiest people I ever encountered. They couldn't toss a tissue into the trash without creating a racket loud enough to raise the whole street. But what could I say? Danny had strummed mega-decibel guitar for years. I couldn't suddenly start playing Mr Hush-hush-whisper-who-dares.

Binnie Klopstock saw me, of course. You can't avoid that woman's gimlet eyes. She waved and bent down low to see who was in the car with me. When she saw it was an attractive woman, she leered and waved those long spindly fingers at me.

When we got inside the house, Ingrid just stood there, blinking in the light and holding her arms across herself like someone who has just been rescued from drowning. She went to the window and pressed her nose against the glass, trying to see into the yard. There was nothing to see beyond the lights strung across the next-door yard.

'Coffee? A drink?' I asked.

She remained where she was, face pressed against the glass. 'Where are we?' she said at last.

'What do you mean? This is my home.'

'This is not Mulholland. You can see right across the valley from Mulholland.'

'I live in Woodland Hills,' I said.

'I thought you lived in Mulholland.'

'That was years ago. Coffee?' I flicked the switch of the coffee machine. 'I need a hot drink.'

She turned around to face me. 'Yes, coffee. Thanks, Mickey. Did I get you out of bed?'

'Ingrid, did you tell anyone else that I lived on Mulholland? I mean, did you give anyone that address recently?'

'I may have.'

'Who?'

'I can't remember.'

'Try. Please try.'

'Poor Mickey. I'm a terrible trial for you.' She came away from the window. 'I'm so cold. May I take a bath? Is the water hot?' She was moving around restlessly now, gripping her coat in front as if all the buttons had come off.

'You want to take off your coat? Sit down? The coffee will come through in a minute. Shall we phone Zach and tell him you're safe and well?'

'He's in Minneapolis, a business trip. You see, Mickey . . .' Again there was the awkward pause. She was standing under the light, holding her coat with both hands and looking very disheveled, very vulnerable, and very beautiful.

201

'What's wrong?'

'I haven't got any clothes on,' she said in a little-girl voice. 'I'm naked under this coat.'

'Are you kidding?'

'I wish I were.'

Oh, my God, how did I get into this situation? 'What were you doing naked out there on the pier?'

'I've just got a coat on . . . and these shoes.' She raised a foot in a childish gesture.

'What's going on, Ingrid? Tell me who you gave the Mulholland address to. It's important.'

Deep sigh. 'I was going to drown myself tonight.'

'You were what?'

'I worked it all out. I threw my clothes into the ocean as soon as I got there.'

'What for?'

She turned away and spoke over her shoulder. 'It was like the point of no return. I figured I'd never have the nerve to walk back along the pier naked.' She came closer to me.

'I mean, why would you want to drown yourself? You said you had John Junior to care for.'

She reached out for me, putting her arms around my neck like she was in the ocean and going down for the third time. 'But I just couldn't do it. I'm a coward. I didn't have the nerve to go through with it. It was so cold, Mickey. Hold me tight.'

I held her tight and felt the warmth of her body.

She whispered, 'There was a wind off the ocean and I looked down at it, and it looked so gray and rough. I just couldn't jump in. I just couldn't. Don't laugh at me.'

'I'm not laughing.' Her face was very cold, and I could smell her perfume and the ocean smells in her hair.

'Ingrid,' I whispered, 'did you ever try to kill your husband?'

202

I thought she might react fiercely to such a suggestion, but she remained very still. 'I have thought about it, Mickey. May God forgive me, I thought about it a lot.'

'That bomb in the phone, the night of the party . . . remember?'

'You found it.'

'Yes, I found it. I've thought about it a lot. Who do you think put it there?'

'You don't think I did that?'

'I've been thinking about it. Whoever put it there would have had to get your husband to use the phone. Who could have persuaded him to go up to that office? Someone close to him, I think.'

Without letting me out of her tight embrace, she twisted her head to see my face. 'Goldie? Is that who you mean?'

'Goldie could have arranged it. But Goldie spotted the wiring. You see, Ingrid, you could have found some way of getting your husband there.'

'How?'

'You could have invented some reason.'

'You're not serious?' Her eyes looked directly into mine.

'I'm trying to show you how an investigator could make out a strong case against you.'

'But it's *Zach* who wants to get rid of *me*,' she said angrily, tears welling up in her eyes.

'Take it easy, Ingrid. I want you to remember who you gave that Mulholland address to. These things might be connected.'

'You don't want me to just make up a name, do you, Mickey?'

'I want you to remember who it was.'

'Give me time and I will,' she promised. 'But let me take a tub bath. Once I'm really warm again I'll be able to think properly.'

'Take the master bathroom. On the left. There are clean towels right there in the closet. I don't use the other one since Danny left home, so there's no soap or anything.' The coffee had dripped through, and I poured some for us both.

'Am I being a dreadful nuisance?' Between sips of coffee she looked down at the little gold watch on her wrist. 'Look at the time; it will soon be daylight. Can I sleep here? I've got to think this problem through, Mickey. You're the only person I could turn to and know I'd be safe.'

What kind of rep have you got, Murphy? If the word ever gets out that a beautiful naked woman said that to you in the middle of the night, you're going to have to move to another town.

But I was still dopey about Ingrid. I couldn't think straight. Having her here like this was everything I'd ever dreamed of, but this crazy situation was everything I didn't need. 'Sure, Ingrid. I keep Danny's bed made up. You can sleep in his room if you can find a way past the airplane models and amplifiers and broken clocks he's going to fix someday.'

'Thanks, Mickey. You always were a darling.'

'There are clean pajamas in the closet, and I'll find you a sweater.'

She went into the bathroom, and I heard the water running. As I sat down and tried to get my thoughts in order, the phone rang. It was a woman's voice. 'Mr Murphy?'

'That's right.'

'Michael Murphy? Attorney?'

'You got it.'

'Sheriff's office, Malibu, here, Mr Murphy. Would you have Mrs Petrovitch come to the phone?'

'She can't come to the phone right now,' I said. 'I'm speaking on her behalf. What can I do for you?'

'I have her physician here. He says his patient is in a disturbed state of mind and needs medical care.'

'Is that right?'

'Yes, it is,' said the woman in the sheriff's office.

'Well, you tell him I'm her attorney, and I think she's fit and well and perfectly capable of deciding if she needs medical treatment, of choosing a physician, and of phoning for one if she feels she can afford his fees. So tell him good night.'

'Don't hang up, sir. Did you collect this lady from the pier tonight?'

'Why?'

'Someone did. Someone in a 1959 Cadillac Coupe like the one registered in your name.'

'Okay, so you've got a line into the motor vehicles computer. Yes, I collected her. So what?'

'Mr Petrovitch will be coming to your home to pick her up. Can I assume you will cooperate? I don't want to send an officer with him unless you are going to make difficulties.'

'Now?'

'That's right.'

So Zach Petrovitch wasn't in Minneapolis after all. 'I'll be home. It will be okay.'

'Thank you, Mr Murphy.'

I went and beat on the bathroom door. 'Your husband's coming to collect you,' I called.

I was frightened that she might take that idea badly, but judging by her tone of voice she accepted it mildly enough. 'He'll notice I haven't got any clothes,' she said.

'Yes, I thought of that too,' I said.

'I remembered about the Mulholland address,' she called through the door. 'Zach copied it from an old address book of mine. He said he had to send you some legal documents.'

I don't know if you have ever delivered a naked woman to her husband in the hours of darkness, but it's not something I'd recommend to the fainthearted.

'I borrowed a pair of your pajamas,' she said while we sat waiting.

'Yes, I see.'

'And this lovely sweater. It's cashmere, isn't it? I'll send it back, of course.' She had the innocent sincerity of a small child. And like a small child she seemed unable to understand the unkind and cynical world around her.

'Ingrid,' I said, 'do you often get depressed to the point where you go to the ocean to drown yourself?'

'It's all right for you, Mickey. You're the outgoing cheerful type. You're strong and aggressive and independent. You always have been. Not everyone can be like you.'

'But are you content to go back home with your husband?'

'It's my problem, and I must just work it out my own way.'

It was the white stretch limo that arrived for her. Goldie was sitting in front alongside the driver. Petrovitch was sitting in back looking mournful. I went out first to speak with him.

'She's okay,' I told Petrovitch. He sat very still. There was a bag at his feet, a smart Louis Vuitton bag that a woman might take on a weekend. He had a drink on the little refrigerator table in front of him. His face was set like a granite portrait bust, but there was no sign of anger. He was a man who knew how to keep his emotions suppressed – or at least concealed. That's the secret of big business, I suppose. Maybe it should be illegal; carrying a concealed emotion makes it tough on those who want to know what's coming.

'You picked up Ingrid at the pier?'

'She was distraught,' I said. I was waiting for him to blow his top, but it was a look of suffering rather than anger that passed across his face.

He reached for the bag and passed it to me. 'Here are her overnight things. Tell her to get some clothes on,' he said.

'You know what happened?'

'She phoned me from the pier,' he said.

'She knew you were here in town?'

'You mustn't believe everything Ingrid tells you. She's a sweet girl, but she suffers from a highly developed sense of melodrama.' He smiled. This guy was indomitable. Given this situation almost any husband in the world would be fragmenting. Petrovitch was reserved and rational and almost able to grin.

'Ingrid said you sent some legal documents to a place I used to live on Mulholland,' I said.

'I don't send legal documents to private addresses. You've got an office, haven't you?'

'That's what I thought. I'll fetch her.'

'No need,' he said. He was looking beyond me. I turned to see Ingrid standing in the doorway. She was carrying her shoes, and now she supported herself with one hand while she slipped them on.

I said to Petrovitch, 'I'm worried about Ingrid. How are you going to look after her?'

He looked at me without replying.

I said, 'She has a lot of friends. If anything happened to her, a lot of people would be very troubled. Know what I mean?'

'I know exactly what you mean, Mickey,' he said.

I stepped back to let Ingrid climb into the back seat alongside Petrovitch. He grabbed her and hugged her tightly to him. 'What have you been telling this man about me, baby?'

'Nothing, darling. Just that you're a sweetie.' She gave me a big smile and then kissed her husband on the cheek.

'I'll look after her, Mickey,' said Petrovitch. 'You can depend on it.'

'Good night, Ingrid,' I said, as I closed the door, but she gave no sign of having heard me.

As the car moved away I saw her clinging to Petrovitch like a teenage kid in a drive-in. I mean they were embracing! That Ingrid must be the greatest actress since Sarah Bernhardt. But that still didn't explain how the cops got that address of mine in Mulholland or what they were looking for. And what was all that stuff about hearing clicks when Zach picked up the extension to hear what she was saying on the phone? She had her cellular phone.

12

My secretary, the indomitable Magda Huth, came running out of the office to intercept me in the corridor. Her accent was more pronounced than ever. 'She's here again, Mr Murphy. The window woman. I couldn't stop her. I tried but I could not.'

'Is Mr Kim here yet?'

'No.'

'What did you say about the window?'

'That woman.'

'What woman?'

'The one who throws herself from the window. She is here again. She's in your office.'

'That's okay, Miss Huth,' I said, showing more composure than I felt.

'You want I call the Fire Department?'

'Not for a moment. Get me the usual.' I went and looked in Billy Kim's office. It was empty. The idea of any sort of combination of Vic Crichton and Billy Kim made me uneasy. Although they came from opposite sides of the earth they were very much alike: highly intelligent womanizers looking for shortcuts to fame and fortune. Such people make dangerous associates.

'Two Toni–chinos and two almond croissants?'

Every morning she double-checked the order.

209

'Tell them it's almond croissants or nothing. No more stale Bear Claws.'

Miss Huth was watching me anxiously as I opened the door of my office and went inside to greet Betty.

'Hello, Betty,' I said. She was standing waiting for me. I was tired. I wasn't getting enough shut-eye. I watched her warily as I settled behind my desk and flipped through my mail. 'Sit down, Betty honey,' I said but she remained on her feet.

'I didn't recognize Ingrid Petrovitch. She had about six pages in *People* magazine last year. I was on the phone to Felicity Weingartner, and then I remembered. Ingrid Petrovitch was at school with you . . . You were sweet on her, weren't you? I don't know why I didn't recognize her.'

'What is it, Betty?' I said impatiently. 'Have the cops been back digging again?'

She shook her head. 'Do you like my outfit?'

I had been wondering why she was standing in that funny way; she was posing like a model so I could admire her new suit. It was dark green, the jacket fashionably oversize and the tight skirt too short. 'It looks great,' I said.

'I had to have a whole new wardrobe and a new hairstyle. What do you think?' She turned so I could see her bubble-cut hairdo. It made her look like Shirley Temple.

'Just great,' I said vaguely, and then I took in what she had said. 'Why do you have to have a whole new wardrobe?'

'My job with Maureen.'

'Maureen Chiaputti's agency?'

'Lebovitch Talent International. Lebovitch is her real name.'

'Is that right? I thought she was married to Felix. I thought Chiaputti was her real name.'

'You are the archetypal pig,' said Betty. I saw Miss Huth peeking over the frosted glass partition, and when I met her eyes she raised her eyebrows. I beckoned her to bring the coffee in.

210

'And Maureen's paying you real money?' I asked, determined not to get sidetracked.

'Not yet. I'm on retainer, with a bonus payment for any deals I make. I work hard over there. I'm showing her how to put the accounts on the computer and setting up proper filing systems. And I'm out talking to clients too. I like it.'

'That's great, Betty,' I said, as Miss Huth placed the coffees on my desk. She did it with that kind of deferential care she showed only when there were visitors present. She smiled at Betty and then tiptoed out again.

Betty said, 'Coffee for *me*?' in a coy way that suggested she was some little orphan child whose birthdays had never been remembered.

'Grab what you want,' I told her.

'We'll be putting together the stars, story, screen rights, script, and director to sell the whole deal to a studio. Packaging. That's where the real money is.'

'Star? Wait a minute, these are not almond croissants.' In mid-bite I picked up the phone. 'These are not almond croissants.' Almond croissants have marzipan filling.

'They are hazelnut croissants,' admitted Miss Huth.

'With jelly filling.'

'With jelly filling, yes.'

'I don't like jelly. I don't like it in Bear Claws and I don't like it in hazelnut croissants. Now do you understand? Don't eat it, Betty! They'll have to change them.'

'I like it fine,' said Betty, nibbling away contentedly.

'I shall tell them right away,' said Miss Huth, swooping in to take back my pastry.

I watched her go. I said to Betty, 'I'd really like to know what *she's* eating out there. I'd bet a million dollars it's an almond croissant.'

'That's because you are paranoid,' said Betty calmly. Having

211

eaten half her croissant, she delicately wiped her fingers on the paper napkin. 'We haven't got any actors. That's the next step.'

Red lights flashed and a loud bell started ringing in my ear. 'Is this something to do with your visit?'

A soft and wonderful loving smile. 'We'd love to sign Budd Byron.'

'Budd has been with Pop for years. You know that.'

'We'd split the commission with Pop.'

'And Pop would get half instead of a whole commission? Why are you telling me this?'

'Because Budd is coming here this morning, and I want you to help me.'

I confess to a sinking feeling at the imminent arrival of Budd. I'd forgotten he was coming. 'Is Budd big enough?'

'Maybe not. But he's well-known around town, and other actors like him. We've got some name directors and good writers, but we can't put deals together without actors. Signing Budd will break the deadlock.'

'No, no, no,' I said. 'If it all went wrong I'd feel guilty.'

'You've never felt guilty about anything in your whole life,' she said. 'You mean, if anything went wrong it would be bad for business.'

'That's another reason,' I agreed.

'I'll wait outside and catch him as he's coming out.' Betty was looking good these days. I guess the new outfits and changed hairdo had put fresh life into her. She always said her dress allowance wasn't big enough. 'I'll take off and come back after Budd is closeted with you. I'll make it look like I just blew in.'

I picked up the phone. 'Where the hell are those almond croissants?'

Miss Huth said, 'They were all out of sweet croissants. They could do plain croissants or Bear Claws. I said you didn't want them.'

'How do you like that!' I put the phone down.

'What's wrong?'

'Nothing,' I said. 'Have you abandoned that croissant?'

'Yes,' she said, and passed it to me. She got up to go.

Between bites I very casually said, 'Someone was telling me Felicity had an affair with Zachary Petrovitch.'

Betty looked at me, trying to discern a purpose behind my remark. 'Petrovitch? And Felicity? Don't make me laugh. Who dreamed that one up?'

'I don't remember. One of the guys I work out with, maybe.'

'He's out of his mind.'

'Yeah, that's what I told him.'

'If she'd been to bed with Petrovitch, I'd have heard.'

'That's what I figured.'

Budd arrived on time. He always did. He was in California casual clothes: tailored pants in wide blue and white stripes, a soft dark-blue suede jacket, and Ferragamo moccasins. He was carefully tanned, and the arrangement of his wavy hair might or might not have been the result of an hour with the hairdresser.

'That was some party,' I said, coming forward to greet him. Before I could shake hands, he embraced me in one of those two-arm show-biz body hugs that make you think the other party is going to sink his fangs into your neck.

'Good to see you, Mickey!' he said loudly into my ear, as he held me captive and slapped my back. His voice was low, vibrant, and carefully modulated. It was an actor's voice, and his timing was an actor's timing. He held me tight and he was strong. He was always boasting about the hours he spent with the weights and the rowing machine.

He released me, and I reeled away to catch my breath. 'Drink?' I said and went into a bout of coughing.

He watched me, bent over and coughing, with the restrained

interest that actors view all human activity they might one day be called upon to simulate.

'Perrier water for me,' he said, when I had finally recovered and straightened up, breathless, blinking, and watery-eyed.

I got him his fizzy water and sipped some myself to relieve my throat. Budd was seated in the client's chair when I got back behind my desk.

'Yes, some party!' I repeated softly when I felt fully recovered.

He half turned in his chair and, in a practiced movement, flipped back his suede jacket to reveal a shoulder holster under his arm.

'Jesus!' I said. 'Is that Danny's gun? Are you crazy? Save this kind of stuff for the movies, Budd. Carrying a concealed weapon will get you into a lot of trouble, and I won't be able to get you out of it.'

He buttoned his jacket to hide the gun. 'I want to talk to you about Ingrid. We've got to help her.'

'Help her do what?'

'You think she's blissfully happy,' said Budd accusingly, 'but her life is a misery. That husband of hers is a gangster. Someone should knock him off.' It came out in a rush; then he looked at me and waited for my reaction.

I said, 'You don't mean that.'

'I do mean it.'

'Look, Budd, there have been a couple of attempts to murder Petrovitch. Someone put a wrench in his airplane and a bomb in his phone. I'm your attorney. I don't want you ever saying anything like you just said, to anyone at all, again. Never ever. Do you understand?'

'I put the wrench in his airplane engine.'

'You what?'

'Don't get mad. Someone has got to do something before he kills Ingrid.'

'You put a wrench in his airplane engine?'

'I went out to Camarillo last month. His plane was in the hangar. I tossed a wrench into the intake. They found it. I knew they would. They have to do a preflight check. Relax, Mickey. Nothing happened.'

'Did you leave your prints on the wrench?'

'I'm not stupid.'

'On any of the doors or gates?'

'I wore gloves.'

'I can't handle this sort of stuff, Budd. Maybe you need an analyst.'

'I won't do it again. I just wanted to throw a scare into him.'

'Does anyone else know about this?'

'No one.'

'You didn't put the bomb in the telephone?'

'No. I heard about that, but it was nothing to do with me. I think that may have been some kind of business vendetta.'

'So it was just the once you tried to kill Petrovitch?' I tried to keep my voice level and normal.

'You don't have to look at me like that,' said Budd indignantly. 'This guy is going to kill Ingrid. Maybe you don't care about that, but I do. I was hoping for some kind of help and encouragement.'

'Help and encouragement to kill Petrovitch?'

'Do you know he pushed Ingrid's first husband under a truck?'

'Believe me, Budd, when guys like Petrovitch waste you they don't fool around wrestling on pedestrian crossings. Stay clear of him.'

'I'm telling you he did it.'

'Someone told me that story, but it's not so easy to arrange for an articulated truck to hit someone crossing the street. Can you imagine how many times you would have to drive around the block to hit a nimble pedestrian who is not going to cooperate?'

'I should have known better than to talk to you, Mickey.' His sudden loss of faith in me was evident in his slumped shoulders and deep sigh.

'So why did you?'

'Because you're my attorney.'

'I'm not your nurse,' I said.

'I don't need a nurse,' he said. *Cut! Take two*: Budd swelled up, smiled, and beamed the full Budd Byron charm in my direction. 'How are the trips to Marina del Rey going?'

'Marina del Rey?'

'You and that big-titted blonde you got lined up in Marina del Rey. Her husband was at a paint manufacturers' convention in Dallas the night of my party. Wasn't that where you were rushing off to?'

You couldn't make any kind of joke with Budd. He took everything literally; that's how he was taking Ingrid's problems with her husband. 'That's going just dandy,' I said.

'Can I come in?' called Betty in her little-girl voice.

Betty had of course chosen exactly the wrong moment to crash into the room. Budd shriveled. He smoothed his jacket into place over the gun and jumped to his feet.

'I only want to say a little hello to my lovely friend, Budd,' she said, as though she was always in and out of my office and noticing who was doing business with me. She flung herself into his open arms, kissed him, and proclaimed, 'I caught *Fire and Fireflies* and you were marvelous.'

'It's not showing yet,' said Budd.

'Westwood. It started yesterday.'

Budd looked at her with profound respect. Betty went on, 'I can tell you the scene with the girl on the fire escape had the audience rocking. That was your picture, Budd.'

'I haven't seen it yet.'

'Go,' said Betty. 'This is a classic.' She turned to me. 'You saw it?'

'No,' I said. I hadn't the slightest idea what she was talking about. 'You said it only started yesterday,' I added defensively.

'Saturday, as a matter of fact,' said Budd. 'It's a week of previewing.'

'A classic,' said Betty. 'Have you ever thought of going into more substantial roles? Star parts, I mean. You could be a major star – a Cary Grant – if that was the way you wanted to mold your career.'

'You think so?'

'Listen,' said Betty. 'I'm developing a story about an insurance salesman. I'm talking heavy drama.' After Budd nodded she continued. 'I'm with Lebovitch Talent International these days. Mean anything?' Budd nodded. 'I have a truly wonderful script, and a certain big-name director is reading it now. This is a story about a guy who sells life insurance door-to-door, but he's also a vicious serial killer who dismembers his victims. Psychotic. Bizarre. And yet it's all done in a light comedic vein. It's a comment on the world we live in.'

'Wonderful,' said Budd. 'That sounds wonderful.' His muffled anger was a declaration of the stand he was prepared to make against the world we live in.

'I can see you in that role, Budd,' said Betty.

'Betty. I had no idea you were . . .' said Budd. Still on his feet, he paused for a moment and pirouetted with his hands aloft. I knew it was some bit of business he'd done in the movie.

Betty glowed. 'That's it!' I remember the way Betty had been bowled over by Budd the first time they met. Budd had the same effect on every woman in the world. He was the clean-living college-educated all-American quarterback who looked like he'd know what to do in bed. Ingrid was not immune to his charms either. The first time Ingrid saw Budd she could talk of nothing else for ages afterward. Lucky for me that Budd had never tried to take any of my girls away from me. He could have had any of them by raising an eyebrow.

Betty smiled. She was looking at Budd as if he were a new St Laurent gown she'd just discovered was part of a fire sale. She stood against the wall under the expensively framed steel engraving of Cork, with one hand on her hip and the other raised and gesturing extravagantly. 'I wish you'd told me you had that kind of talent. It's the rarest thing to find in this town. One in a million actors have that – well, let me come out and say it: comic genius.' And then in a lowered and more reverent voice she added, 'It's precious. Very very precious.'

'You are too much,' said Budd, thrusting his hands deep into the pockets of his pants, hunching his shoulders, and staring at the toes of his shoes. All he needed was a straw in his mouth.

I was watching Betty's performance with great interest. If there was any acting genius in evidence, it was in Betty's effortless handling of Budd. This was Betty's forte. And there was something sensual, if not to say sexual, about this dance they did. The more she excited Budd, the more excited she became. I'd never seen this side of Betty. Maybe that's why our marriage collapsed.

Betty said, 'Is there any chance you could spare five minutes one day this week? I'd love to talk to you about the project and maybe get your views and advice on some other deals I'm doing.'

'What about Pop?' I said. I wasn't going to have the story going around that my ex-wife stole Budd away from his agent right there in my office. You could bet that some smart-ass would embellish the story so that I was standing by with a fully filled Montblanc and the contract and got a large slice of the action.

218

'Pop?' said Budd innocently, as if he'd never heard the name before. Right before my eyes I'm watching my wife fitting the glass slipper on this guy's foot. I looked out the window, just in case the golden coach and horses were having problems parking. What were those two middle-aged ugly stepsisters calling themselves, Lebovitch Talent International? Maureen and Betty should be sitting back worrying about their kids' midterms and waiting for the menopause. Instead, they were screaming around the studios, coming on like a couple of speed-happy teenyboppers. My God, what this town does to people!

They both looked at me wide-eyed. 'Pop Pedersen,' said Betty in a low reverential voice. 'A professional of the first magnitude! I love that man. I learned everything I know from that gentleman. He was a mighty big man when I worked for him. I was just a baby in those days, but how I learned! The industry should have put up a statue to that guy years and years ago.'

Well, *requiescat in pace* Pop Pedersen. At least she hadn't called the poor old bastard a wonderful human being.

'He's getting on now,' said Budd, who hadn't missed the implication that Pop was aged and past it.

'A gentleman,' said Betty reflectively. She turned to me and said scornfully, 'Do you think I'd do a deal like this with Budd and not include Pop in it?'

'I figured it might slip your memory that he has Budd signed,' I said.

'I love him,' Betty proclaimed to the world.

'I can come back with you now,' said Budd. 'Where is your office?'

'Close by. We'll be there in three minutes. I'm going to show you some videos. I want you to see what magic this director gives to his actors. And have you meet my partner. No chance you can do lunch, I suppose? Tokyo is socked in, and my guy from Sony had to cancel everything he'd set up.'

'I'm free for lunch,' admitted Budd.

'You get a fun crowd at the Grill at lunchtime.'

'I'd like that,' said Budd.

'Then let's do it,' said Betty. She turned to me and said softly, 'I charged all my new shmatte on your plastic, so don't go ape when you get the bill.'

'You did *what*?'

'Things are going great for me, Mickey. Big, big deals. If I'm going to become independent, the way you say you want, I must have good clothes.'

Budd had discreetly moved away and was studying with an almost unnatural intensity a steel engraving of Limerick, one of a series of six prints of Irish cities that the interior decorator said was right for my image. It was brilliant of Betty to time this revelation of her extravagance so that Budd was there to witness me going red in the face and inhibit me from beating her over the head with my leather-bound edition of *American Jurisprudence*.

'I'll see,' I said. 'But this is instead of the dentistry, not as well as.'

She looked over her shoulder to see how far away Budd was and lowered her voice accordingly. 'Can you advance me a fifty?'

'You're not going to cuff the Grill, are you?'

She grinned wolfishly. 'Maureen has an account there. But I'll need small change for tips and the powder room.'

'You'd pull a routine like that with no money at all? What would you have done if I'd said no?' I gave her five twenties.

'You're a darling,' she said, and gave me a peck on the cheek to which I did not respond. 'Let's go, Budd darling,' she called.

Budd stared at me from the far side of the room. 'Are you okay, Mickey?'

'Sure I'm okay.'

'You don't look good.' He flicked his hair back. He looked very handsome. Maybe he *could* be another Cary Grant.

'I'm okay,' I said.

'You drink too much coffee,' he said. 'It does the same thing to me.'

I sat down behind my desk and smiled at them as they left. 'Miss Huth,' I said into the phone, 'can you let me have fifty from petty cash? I'm going to treat myself to a nice lunch.'

'You'll have to pay me back this afternoon, Mr Murphy. This is the day I do my bookkeeping.'

'Come to think of it, I'd rather have a pastrami sandwich from Tony's. On toasted rye. Put it on the account.'

13

A week later a call from Felix Chiaputti brought a date for lunch, but when Felix is involved even the most workaday encounters can go out of control. Either he's decided it's a great day for the beach or he drags you along to a hotel room in Century City to sit in on a poker game that's been going for three days and nights. Or he arrives with two exotic dancers and comps for a matinee, or he's waving invites for a press junket with giveaway rock videos. What I'm saying is that Felix is a man of infinite resources. He was always like that. Even at college he knew places where he could eat on the cuff or drink booze without showing ID.

Now Felix was sitting in a booth in Cy's Steak and Sandwich on Pico, within walking distance of my office. It was as normal as any lunch I'd ever eaten; I knew there would be an added dimension. Felix lifted the upper bread slice from his rare New York steak on toasted rye to inspect his grilled beef very carefully. Felix never did anything without checking it out, not even taking a bite out of a steak sandwich.

'Budd was looking great, wasn't he?' I said.

'He's a crazy guy. These sudden enthusiasms he has . . . Suddenly he's into guns. Do you know he's at the gun club almost every day punching the centers out of targets?'

'Did he tell you that?'

'About the gun club? Cops are always in and out of gun clubs. Most of my guys know Budd and know I know him.'

'Something wrong with your sandwich?'

'No, it's great.'

The decor in Cy's is Route 66 but the prices are Century City. The walls are crammed with ancient out-of-state license plates, fifties newspaper front pages, and photos of slick-haired trendsetters such as James Dean plus a bulbous jukebox lighted up and belting out such discoveries as 'Rock Around the Clock.' But Felix showed an interest in the pictures and artifacts on the walls to an extent that was unnatural.

'What do you keep looking around at?' I asked him.

He smiled. 'Looking around?' He took the head off a Coors and wiped his lips delicately.

'Yes,' I said. 'Looking around.'

'There's a guy might look in and say hello.'

'I thought this was just a spontaneous notion, this steak sandwich at Cy's.'

He smiled. 'Yeah, well, this is a drinking buddy of mine. I thought you might want to talk with him.'

'Me? What's he going to talk about? Selling insurance?'

'Talk off the record. He doesn't know you're a lawyer.'

'Thanks, buddy. I'll do the same for you sometime.'

'Don't get emotional, Mickey. It will be better if you talk to him off the record.'

'Better? Better?' I bit into my sandwich.

'Cy's got a little gold mine here,' said Felix, looking around again. He said old Cy was a friend of a friend, but for all its folksiness I think Cy's is an artfully designed fast food franchise with outlets throughout the nation and a quote on the New York Stock Exchange. Felix is inclined to embroider the facts sometimes. It was the proximity of the movie industry: it happened to everyone, particularly the witnesses I questioned.

I said, 'I wish you'd tell me what this guy is going to be talking about.'

'He'll be talking about a homicide investigation,' said Felix through a mouthful of steak. 'Good, huh?'

'The guy who fed his wife to the sharks?' I drank some of my Coors. Beer is fattening. I was rationing myself to one per day.

'Nothing to do with that.' Felix opened his sandwich and put more mustard on his steak. 'You asked me about the guys who were digging up your old place on Mulholland. An old buddy of mine is in charge of that investigation. I asked him about it, and he wanted to meet you. You might be able to help him.'

'Help him how?'

'Just talk to him, Mickey.'

'Why?'

'Because it's better that way.'

'Better than what?'

'Better than having him haul you down to the station to quiz you. Right?'

'Sounds kind of threatening.'

'It wasn't meant to be. I don't know anything about it.'

Felix could be the most exasperating man in the world. I flagged down the waitress and said we'd like apple pie and coffee right away. 'What's the big secret?'

'Routine. Get yourself eliminated from the blotter over a sandwich and beer.'

I looked at my plate and took a deep breath. 'If you say so, Felix.'

'Trust me.'

'What alternative do I have?' The waitress arrived with the apple pie and brandishing two carafes of coffee. She looked disappointed that I wanted decaf. Felix had the real thing and she brightened.

'We're practically family,' said Felix, in what I took to be a curious and oblique reference to Maureen and Betty. When the waitress heard him she looked from him to me, smiled, and nodded knowingly.

When she had moved on I said, 'Bring him on, I'll talk to him. Where and when?'

'He's waiting outside.'

'I thought he might be.'

Felix got a little excited. 'Don't start acting like it's a sting, Mickey.'

'Bring him on. What are you guys looking for, a confession to the Hoffa killing?'

Felix beckoned, and his buddy, Lieutenant Pete Laird – who'd been peering in through the window – came and sat in the booth with us. Laird was a tall thin forty-year-old with a cream-colored zip-front golf jacket over a red shirt, white pants, and speed-cop glasses. His hair was black and neatly combed, and he wore a signet ring and a gold wristwatch.

'Hi, Mickey,' he said. He sat down and rubbed his hands together. 'With you being Felix's pal, I figured we could get this over with as fast as possible.'

'What's on your mind?' I said.

'Do you use Topanga on your way home?'

The alarm bells were ringing. 'Not often, not on my way home I don't. What you make on the PCH you lose in the canyon. I stick to the One-oh-one. If that gets overloaded I come off and drive Ventura Boulevard and maybe stop for a coffee.'

Laird nodded. As an explanation it was far too long. After the number of times I'd told witnesses to keep their answers short, you'd think I'd do the same myself. A long explanation sounds like guilt to a cop. 'Know a guy named Pindero? Pinter, maybe. Lives up the hill not far from the ocean.'

'Know him: no. I went to visit him. He has a car I'd like to buy.'

'A car?'

The waitress came. 'Are you all on the one check?' she said.

'Separate bills,' said Felix.

'Just regular coffee for me,' said Laird, but she gave him a menu and he sat reading it as though engrossed.

'A very special Packard,' I said. 'I like Packards.'

'Is that what you drive?'

'No,' I said. 'I drive a 'fifty-nine Caddie Series Sixty-two.'

'You mean you're a collector? A dealer?'

'I have been known to buy and sell. I like old Cadillacs.'

'Except when you like Packards,' said Laird.

'Right.'

'We got a witness to your being up there,' said Laird.

'Witness? Who needs a witness? I just told you I was up there.'

'Driving your Cadillac?' The waitress came with Laird's coffee and refilled my cup from the orange-top decaf pot. She smiled at us and told Laird today's special was a meatball sandwich that came with coleslaw and pickle. Laird said he'd have it on toasted rye.

'No, I was in my silver Mercedes Five hundred SEL,' I said sarcastically. 'It matches my wife's nails.'

He let it go. 'You met with Pindero?'

'I heard he was likely to be putting a nice old car on the market. When I talked to him, he said it wasn't for sale.'

'How long you stay?'

'He was very drunk. I could see there was nothing to be gained from talking more.'

'You drink with him?' said Laird.

Shit! Fingerprints on the coffee cup. 'He gave me a cup of coffee and poured whisky into it. I didn't finish it.'

'On account of having to drive this silver Mercedes of yours back down the hill?'

'You got it.'

'My witness says you were in there for an hour.'

'Well, you tell your witness to buy himself a new plastic Casio.'

'Anyone else up there?'

'There was a guy on the gate.'

'You get a good look at him?'

'Clean-shaven, short brown hair. Forty. One hundred and eighty pounds, maybe: in good shape.'

'Okay. We located that one already.'

'Do you want to tell me what this is all about?'

'Pindero was wasted up there sometime between Friday eleven A.M. and nine A.M. Monday.'

'Between cleaning-lady visits, huh?'

'You don't seem too upset about it.'

'You want me to go into deep mourning? I told you, it's just a guy I visited to buy a car. How was he killed?'

'An intruder put a plastic bag over his head.'

'You kidding? I thought that was just for geriatrics.'

'The M. E. thinks the guy was probably paralytic. His blood levels were out of sight. A helpless drunk like that would offer no resistance to a determined man with a plastic bag.'

'How about a determined woman?'

He looked at me. 'No, not unless she was a big strong woman. The killer did a lot of lifting and moving up there.' He didn't mention the refrigerator. I guess he was hoping I'd say something that revealed more knowledge than I was admitting to.

'Tell me the truth. How did you come to drag me into this investigation?'

'I told you. A witness.'

'Okay. If that's the way you want to play it.' I knew a witness

227

would be sure to have seen my big Caddie. Laird would not have nodded through my jokes about the silver Mercedes if there really was a witness. But if not a witness, how did they know I'd been up there?

Laird's meatball sandwich came, and he bit into it as though he hadn't eaten for days. I let him eat in peace. Cops and lawyers learn to gobble on the run like that; that's how they get ulcers.

'I was hoping you would be able to help,' said Laird. I watched him swallow the last of his sandwich and push aside the coleslaw and pickle. I eat slowly nowadays, and it all tastes better.

'Well now, you know I'm not about to break down and confess. You should take a look at his phone bill; that would maybe show the time of death more accurately. This guy was making calls all the time I was up there. And don't ask me who he was calling, because I don't know.'

'Okay, Mr Murphy. I hope we won't have to bother you again.' He changed his mind about the pickle and bit the end off it.

'Has this Pindero guy got a sheet?' I asked.

'What do you know about that?' said Laird.

'What do I know about it?' I snapped. 'I know nothing about it, that's why I'm asking you.'

Felix tried to lower the temperature. 'Yes, Pindero was a small-time hoodlum. He did five years for turning over a warehouse: there were five of them; the night watchman was badly crippled. The word was that Pindero had long ago been an explosives expert for the mob. Someone said that he blew away some bookies by putting bombs inside their phones. But we've got no record of that and he was a loudmouth. It maybe was all talk. You know the way some of these small-timers like to build a rep.'

'You got some kind of tip-off about me, is that it?'

'Why do you say that?' asked Laird calmly, very calmly. I knew I'd hit it.

'What else can I conclude? You haven't even got a license number to find me on the computer. Then you go and dig up the yard of a house I haven't lived in for years. It was an anonymous phone call, right? Someone's trying to finger me. If I've got it wrong, tell me.'

'There was no informant, Mr Murphy.'

'Level with me, lieutenant,' I said. 'If you were acting on information from some troublemaking kook, would you admit it?'

'I might,' said Laird. Using the tip of his wetted finger, he picked crumbs from his plate until the last one was gone. 'I figured you'd want to help us.'

'Yeah, well, if I think of something else I'll let you know,' I said.

Laird brought out his wallet and gave me his card with the Police Department badge on it. 'My son will be graduating from UCLA this year. Theater Arts with a minor in Journalism. The project he did for his screen-writing course would make a great vehicle for Harrison Ford with Shirley MacLaine as the young grandmother.' He must have seen the look on my face, for he added hastily, 'I know you do a lot of business with the studios—'

'Every bum in this town wants to be a movie producer.'

Laird's expression didn't change. 'I'm talking about a chance for my son,' he said. 'It's a great script. It's got pace and sensitivity. You could at least read it.'

'You guys don't know the difference between an investigation and an audition,' I said.

'Well, thanks anyway,' said Laird and got up. So did Felix.

'Are you going my way?' Felix asked Laird. Laird nodded. They must have arrived in the same car. That Felix! He was so devious.

Felix leaned over and tossed two tens on the table. 'You'd better be innocent, pal,' he said quietly, in a voice that was both compassionate and ominous. Then he followed Laird.

As they went through the door, all the tension and fear came bubbling up inside me so that I was suddenly very angry. I put down money for my food and followed them to the door. I watched them walking to Laird's unmarked police car. 'Hey, *compadre*!' I shouted to them.

Laird ignored me until Felix tapped his shoulder, whereupon he looked up and, squinting into the sun, cupped his ear.

'What about getting your kid to write a real story for the movies . . . something maybe I could get them interested in?'

'For instance?' Laird shouted. People were turning to watch.

'A story with a lawyer as hero. A hard-working California attorney with the cops on his back, who nails a killer or gets all the women or saves the world or something.'

'A lawyer?' said Laird, frowning hard with the effort of thinking about it.

'A lawyer. A California lawyer.'

'You must be out of your friggin' mind,' shouted Laird angrily. He got into the driver's seat and slammed the car door.

Felix looked at me and shrugged.

While I was standing there watching them drive away into the traffic I heard a woman's voice calling, 'Hey, dude! What's with you, Perry Mason?'

I looked around and at first couldn't see who was shouting, but then there came a loud shrill laugh and I saw it was a woman in an open-top canary-yellow sports car that had pulled in to the curb.

'Perry Mason,' she shouted again as if very pleased with her joke. 'See you in court!' She hit the horn several times and shouted 'Mickey!' very loudly.

When I'd put on my shades I could see it was Felicity Weingartner sitting behind the wheel of a mean-looking Corvette.

'You want a ride to your office, Mickey?' She was wearing a checked suit with a gold brooch and fancy wristwatch: the Hollywood career woman as dreamed up by Central Casting. She gestured with her mirrored Ray-Bans so I could see her new nails.

'In this jalopy? How can I decline?' I opened the door and got in beside her. She must have been coming from the beauty salon: her cheeks were carefully shadowed, her eyes had copious mascara and false lashes, and her hair glinted with a bronze tint that had never been there before. I stroked the dashboard. She put on her shades and tapped the gas pedal so that the V-8 launched us into the traffic like a shot from Cape Kennedy. 'Take it easy, Felicity,' I said, as I strapped in tight. 'This is not like pedaling along in your Beetle.'

'You pig. I never had a Beetle in my life. That was a Rabbit.'

'Those German domestic animals all look the same to me. How long have you had this machine?'

'Three days and four hours. My press agent said it would be good for my image.'

'Your press agent said that?'

'Didn't you hear?'

'About your press agent? Does he have a car for my image?'

'This one used to belong to Robert Redford.'

'Did it?'

'Or was it Richard Gere? One of the two. At least that's what the salesman told me. But it was the color that sold me. What do you think? It goes well with my hair, right?'

'Dark at the roots and splitting at the ends?'

'Bastard!' She aimed a blow at me and connected. 'I'm into preproduction. For my movie. I got a deal. Producer: with a single-name card on the credits and a shared script credit too. Didn't Betty tell you?'

'Your movie?'

'Twenty million dollars below the line. I've even put Sheree on the production at one grand a week.'

'I thought you disapproved of nepotism. Sheree? Doing what?'

'She can scout locations or something.'

'Will she know what to look for?'

'It will give her a chance to break up with that married man,' said Felicity. 'He's a bastard.'

It was the kind of nutty irrelevant answer a woman gives you. 'Twenty mil. Wow!'

'Below the line. Add the stars and so on, and I'll have nearer thirty.'

'That's real money. Is this the movie you told me about in Aspen? The one you were going to direct?'

'I can't believe you don't know.' She shook her head to emphasize this disbelief. With palms pressed on the steering wheel, she wriggled her fingers to show her wonderful crimson nails. 'Everyone in this town has heard about what Betty got for me. There was a whole page in *Billboard* and a big ad in *Variety*.'

'There was nothing in the *Law Gazette*.'

'You should buy the trades; then you'd know your wife is hot, and I mean hot!'

'Ex-wife,' I said automatically. 'Betty got this deal for you? This wouldn't be the door-to-door insurance salesman who turns out to be a psychotic serial killer, with Budd Byron as the salesman?'

'So you do know!' She chortled with relief. 'I guess Betty's success is pretty hard for you to handle. You always were a male chauvinist pig.'

'It's not hard for me to handle,' I said. 'I've always had a yen for rich women. Watch out for that truck, Felicity! He's going to change lanes.' Ahead, and towering over us, was a huge truck, its cabin bright and shiny like a Cours d'Élégance contender. Its driver had a tattooed arm and an exhaust pipe on the roof from which he could spray black clouds of diesel over the traffic following him.

She swung around to make an agonized face at me. 'Yeah, poor Budd. We had to let him go.'

'But it was all being set up around Budd. Betty made a big thing out of talking him into joining her.'

'Yep, that's the way it goes sometimes. But once we heard Meryl Streep might be interested, we had the script rewritten for her.'

'You mean she's going to be the serial killer?'

'She's not signed yet.' Felicity crossed her fingers and held them up as we were overtaking the truck. The truck driver, perhaps misunderstanding this gesture, made a wholehearted attempt to crush the Corvette against a line of parked cars. But Felicity hit the gas and we leapt ahead of him, squeezing through the narrow gap with a roar and a squeal of rubber. I closed my eyes, but Felicity's voice betrayed no alarm. 'In the new script she's a very lovable unemployed Russian nuclear scientist, single-parenting in Baltimore. Betty says Streep will love the challenge of the accent.'

'Poor Budd. He ratted on his agent to go for that one with Betty.'

'He'll get over it,' said Felicity callously. She came to an abrupt stop outside the door of my office.

I could hear something in her voice. 'Are you telling me he's fighting mad at you both?' I wanted to be prepared for Budd's storming into my office, wanting me to enjoin or sue or picket the studios. I knew from past experience that any kind of rejection could make Budd very emotional.

'We'll write in a cameo for him. He could be a plainclothes cop, couldn't he?'

'He could be a cop,' I agreed. As I was opening the car door I said, 'Felicity, you know Ingrid very well. Did she have any children by that first marriage?'

'To Jack Piech? Of course not. She's never had any children. That's why she's always so sorry for herself.'

'You're sure?'

'Of course I'm sure. Why do you ask?'

'I have a lot of old toys in the garage,' I said.

'Why can't you ever tell the truth, Mickey Murphy?'

'The truth always makes me look like an idiot,' I said.

'Yes. Well, there's nothing I can do about that,' she said, and blew me a kiss before driving away.

Felicity and her car caused a minor sensation among a gang of kids who use my entry as a hangout. They ran after her as she accelerated away and argued about whether or not she was Diane Keaton.

I checked incoming calls with Miss Huth. So far there were no urgent messages from Budd Byron, which was a great relief. I continued my final sorting of the papers concerned with Vic Crichton's company. Now that I had told them to find another attorney, the sooner I got rid of them the better. I was determined to have everything ready so that as soon as they paid me off and gave me the details of their new lawyer I could kiss them goodbye forever.

But there were documents to be signed to confirm and make legal the new arrangements. Also, there was the new offshore company in Lima, Peru. These guys follow each other like sheep. Do you know that? Petrovitch decides to use nominees – people signing things on behalf of other people – as signatories for the holding company and its negotiable assets. The next thing I know, Crichton decides they want their holding

234

company's negotiable assets put into a newly formed company in Lima with nominees holding a big chunk of stock. Then, when the Petrovitch-Westbridge deal goes through, they use nominees again. As I say, they follow fashion like sheep. I always advise clients to avoid documents with nominees empowered to sign. It's like giving someone a blank check; it's asking for trouble.

At four o'clock I was looking at the clock and waiting for Victor Crichton, who was supposed to go through the amalgamation paragraph by paragraph. It would be the last job I would do for them, and I didn't want any last-minute wrangle to keep us from closing. Vic was late. It was arranged as a three-thirty appointment, but Brits are always late. I was mad at myself. I should have just made the appointment for half an hour earlier than I wanted him to come. 'Crichton didn't call, did he?' I asked Miss Huth when she came in with letters for me to sign. She'd spent all day transcribing them from her machine.

'How is this, please?' she said. My God, why can't I find a secretary who can speak and write the English language?

'Is this the best you can do?' I said, looking at the letters. She couldn't work the word processor, and her typing was patterned with white-out and littered with misspellings.

'You want I should do them once more? I will do them again and again until they are right.'

'Some of these you already typed twice. We'll run out of paper if you keep doing them till you get them right.'

She smiled as if that was a wonderful tribute to the German work ethic. 'That is true,' she said.

The phone rang; it was Vic calling. 'Sorry I'm late, chum,' he said.

'What delayed you this time? Were they polishing your star on the Hollywood Boulevard sidewalk? Or were you rescuing a small child from drowning?'

'That's next week,' said Vic. 'Right now I have a little problem with my transmission. I'm waiting for the tow truck.'

'What are you driving?' I said, making it casual.

'Ahh! I knew you'd ask. I'm in my late boss's BMW.'

'Serves you right,' I said.

'I knew my having a breakdown in an import would warm your heart, Mickey. Put you in a good mood.'

'So what's happening?'

'I'm at Wilshire and Westwood. I can't get a cab, and I must find somewhere to rent a new car.'

'I'll come and get you,' I said. 'Give you a ride in a real automobile. Are you at the intersection?'

'I stalled at the traffic light, and then it just seemed to seize up,' said Vic.

'Stay there.'

As soon as I put down the phone, Miss Huth buzzed me. 'Mr Byron is on number three,' she said.

'Tell him I'm in a meeting.'

'I told him you were in conference. He says it's very urgent.'

'Oh, no. Tell him I'll call him back as soon as I get five minutes to myself.'

'He sounds very worried.'

'Maybe tonight from home, tell him. Tell him right now I have a dear friend injured in an auto crash, and I have got to rush to him.'

'Is that true? A crash?'

'Just tell him, Miss Huth.'

Westwood at Wilshire is the only section of Los Angeles that looks like downtown New York City. Glass-sided skyscrapers and pedestrians complete the illusion. Crichton was waiting there, making the inter-section look even more New York with his English wool suit and striped school tie.

He climbed into the car. 'I wish I hadn't sold my old Range Rover, it never let me down. Get me to Santa Monica, and I'll find a rental company in one of the hotels.' I pulled away into the traffic. Santa Monica was becoming jammed as more and more commuters were bunching up to get onto the San Diego Freeway and go home.

'If you don't want to come back to the office, maybe we can sit down somewhere quiet. I brought all the papers with me.'

'Before we start talking about the amalgamation agreement, are you wired, old pal?'

'Wired? What do you mean, wired?'

'You know what I mean,' he said.

'Wired? No, and I'll tell you why. That Scotch tape tears all the hair off my chest.'

'I'm serious, Mickey.'

'Are you? I thought you were trying to make me laugh. No, Vic, I'm not wired, if you mean strapped into a concealed recorder. I don't spy on my clients. And I don't report what they say to the Justice Department. Do you?'

He was unabashed. 'No, in England we haven't got the technology. You have to stick a quill pen up your ass and wriggle.'

'Are we talking about the cops?'

'I thought they might have got to you.'

'Who?'

'Forget it. I've got a lot on my mind these days. Is everything ready?'

'Let me tell you once again,' I said. 'I don't like these setups with nominees to sign and bearer shares.'

'I know, you've told me that ten thousand times.'

'Once Petrovitch and you and the other signatories have signed, witnessed, and completed, you become vulnerable.'

'Stick to what you know, Mickey. This is out of your league.

Let me tell you how it works. I sign everything away and I am divested of all assets; same thing with Petrovitch. Everything valuable is in those bearer shares and they are in a drawer in some offshore bank. No one owns them. Now I go to Peru a pauper. I find the bearer shares in a drawer. I now control a vast company, but the wealth arose in Peru and so is subject to no more than nominal tax.'

'We're talking about almost a hundred million dollars,' I said. 'It's safer if you have a fully notarized power of attorney, just in case some other clown opens the drawer before you get to it.'

He thought about it for a moment and then nodded. 'Whatever the instrument, make sure it gives me the right to take possession in any name I like.'

'The power of attorney will come from you and from Ingrid. Signed at the same time as you divest yourself of the assets. You'll have the power of attorney in your pocket, never mind about some drawer in a faraway land.'

'Why are you acting so nervous?' Vic joshed.

His little smile irritated me. 'I'm giving you professional advice,' I said.

'I know, Mickey, I know. And I appreciate it. But we're not doing anything we haven't done before. It will be all right.'

'They probably have a car rental desk at the Santa Monica Loew's,' I said. 'We can sit in the lobby and go through it all.'

'This bloody business with the stalled motorcar has made me a bit tight for time. Is there any need for me to go through it line by line? You've checked it through, haven't you?'

'There is a lot of it,' I said. 'Amendments and letters modifying some of the conditions. It's very complicated.'

'We'll do it when my mind is clearer,' he said. 'Meanwhile don't let them scare you, just stand your ground.'

'I've nothing to worry about,' I told him.

'Don't get shirty, old mate. When someone discovers that

the federal government has got its figures wrong, the bureaucrats shrug and say no one gets it right all the time. But when the federal number crunchers find that your secretary mistyped the date, or you described a witness as a blonde on the day she became a redhead, the feds yell criminal conspiracy and toss you into the cooler for twenty-five years.'

'No one is going to be going through our confidential files,' I said. 'There's a little matter of client-attorney confidence. They'd be in violation of the Fifth and Sixth amendments.'

'Your faith and erudition do you credit, old boy, but that won't stand in their way, believe me. Nothing does nowadays, not even double jeopardy. The Supreme Court has made sure that if the state don't get you, Uncle Sam will.'

'First you tell me I've got nothing to worry about; then you tell me they're going to throw me in prison.'

'I want you to see how serious it is. Then you will see how neatly it will be solved by torching your office. Billy Kim says it's okay by him.'

'Arson?' I could hardly believe it.

'No papers, no nothing.'

'Do you know the penalties for arson?'

'No, what are they?'

'I don't know,' I admitted, 'but that wouldn't be the end of it. They would get me for concealing evidence, being an accessory . . . I'd be disbarred. It's a crazy idea and I don't want any part of it. Petrovitch virtually owns that partnership. He'd take you apart if you tried anything like that.'

'I don't think he would,' said Crichton.

'Have you talked to him about it?'

Crichton looked at me as if I were an idiot.

'Is this what it was all about? Did Petrovitch buy me out in order to burn down the office, destroy the paperwork, and leave no trace?'

'You'll have to ask him about that,' said Vic. 'But I would have thought it was obvious. Petrovitch is up to his fanny in lawyers; he doesn't need you. He only started groping you because you were acting for us and it could all be done under the one roof.'

'No.'

'So what did you think got his attention? Your natural Irish charm? Your experience with big international corporations? Or maybe your luxurious downtown offices?'

'I'm not your pet poodle.'

'You're in this too deeply to walk away from it now.'

'Drop dead.'

'I haven't got time to argue. I must rent another car and get back on the road.' He beamed at me as if one big smile would seal our friendship forever. 'What can you tell me about Mrs Petrovitch? Ingrid Petrovitch?'

'I know her. We were at college together.'

'She's signing for Petrovitch. Does she have the authority? Did you check all that?'

'Of course I did. She'll have forty-nine percent, like you, with two percent held by the partnership against a voting deadlock.'

'Sounds workable.' He opened the door, got out, and gave me another of the cheery smiles he specialized in. 'Thanks for the ride, chum. Nice car.' A significant pause while he stroked the paintwork of the door. 'It's a lot like one I saw recently outside a hilltop house on Topanga.'

'This time rent a domestic,' I said. It was only after he'd walked away that I realized what he'd said. I was going to chase after him, but I figured that would be playing into his hands.

I must have sat there in the car for ten minutes or more. Then, instead of heading up the Pacific Coast Highway and home, I drove back to the office and sitting at the word processor

I brought the documents up on screen and read them through. Then I drafted a power of attorney for the two principals, Vic and Ingrid, to sign. It would leave the whole fortune floating in the air for that short period when the Peruvian company was formed, but I suppose everyone concerned knew what they were doing. Then I printed out four copies of the agreement and all the other documents. I shredded all the old paperwork. I felt better after that; I hate bearer shares.

Late that night, at home, I got a call from Goldie. 'Mr Petrovitch is arriving in town tomorrow. The car will collect you at noon. Shall I send it to the office or your home?'

'Wait a minute, Goldie. I'll need to look in my appointments book.'

Sarcasm was always lost on Goldie. 'He's flying directly to California.'

'So what?'

'Direct. He's catching a flight from Rome and not going to New York. He's coming out just to talk with you.' Goldie said this in a voice charged with awe.

'What's he want to talk about?'

'I'm not sure,' said Goldie, in a voice that told me he knew darn well. 'But he'll see you at the mansion. That's quite an honor.'

'Don't let's wade out of our depth, Goldie. This is a meet with Zachary Petrovitch, not an audience with the Pope.'

'Listen, you dumb Irishman. The boss never flies from Europe to California without breaking his journey in New York. And he's canceled a board meeting and a briefing with the lawyers who have already flown from Washington to New York and are waiting there for him, clocking up expenses like there's no tomorrow.'

'You sound a little frayed, Goldie. You got something on your mind?'

There was a long silence. Then Goldie said, 'Mrs Petrovitch is on my mind. Her social life is such that she's lost in a blur. She's an ingenious and energetic lady. I can't keep up with her, and neither can the boss.'

'She'll have to be here to sign. There is a newly drafted power of attorney that Mr Petrovitch or one of his people should read through. It's instead of the bearer shares. I've explained it on the fax.'

Long silence. 'I sure hope we've spelled your name right, Mickey. I've always gone out on a limb for you, but when you pull these dumb routines with me, I wake up screaming.'

'Routines?'

'Don't overdo the injured ingénue, Mickey, or you'll be tired out for tomorrow's matinee.'

'Send the car to the office,' I said.

'Noon,' said Goldie. 'And no hardware.'

'Take a couple of Librium tablets and lie down in a darkened room. It might pass off.'

'I mean it. No hardware. You'll be searched.'

'Good night, Goldie. It's always nice chatting to you.'

14

Petrovitch had a place up on Hillcrest, where the folks from Bel Air go and live when they get rich. The electric gate opened to let the car through. A twelve-foot outer wall, marked with fidgeting video cameras, surrounded two or three acres of well-irrigated lawns, ornate renaissance fountains, and the sort of shrubs that get replaced when they are not flowering.

It was a sunny day with the weatherman predicting highs in the seventies, touching eighty in the valleys. These sprawling mansions looked right across the city, and there was a breeze from the ocean that sometimes caught the water in the fountains and flicked it across the grass. At the base of the nearest fountain, three brawny men were standing around trying to look like gardeners, but they didn't bend down to weed in case the machine guns fell out of their work shirts.

The house was neo-classic Disneyland: six tall fluted columns supporting an ornate pediment, with marble steps to the ten-foot-high front door. A four-car garage was arranged alongside it, a more pagan shrine for lesser gods. The driver flicked a button, and an overhead garage door swallowed the white limo with a *whoosh* of machinery and the creak of straining woodwork. As it crashed closed again, the darkness lasted no more than a moment before fluorescent lights flickered on to reveal a large concrete garage area, with two more cars, a repair bench, and stacked bundles of paper and boxes marked GLASS and PLASTIC for recycling. The doorway that led to the house was lined with a metal detector. Goldie was standing there grinning at me. 'Hi, Mickey! So you tore a piece out of your busy schedule?' he said sarcastically.

I smiled and went and stood inside the frame of the metal detector while he made sure I wasn't armed. I let him gloat. This was his territory, and he wanted to make sure I knew it.

The Roman theme continued inside, where a large foyer featured the lifesize busts of pale emperors on red marble columns set between uncomfortable thrones. Swagged drapery on every side introduced a disturbing and prescient note of Napoleonic France.

Beyond the lobby a grandiose staircase swept up to a long balcony. Goldie led the way up to a room on the first floor that Petrovitch had converted into a study. The Roman theme was somewhat modified at this point, which was just as well because I didn't fancy having my conference with old Petey sprawled on the terracotta in my toga and vomiting after every roasted peacock. A large sitting room held two soft leather sofas, a liquor cabinet, and four busy paintings depicting, according to the engraved brass tags, four decisive battles of imperial Rome. The windows over-looked the garden; as is usual in houses built for Southern California's mega-rich, no windows faced toward the street, where there might lurk kidnapers and tourist buses.

The long wall without windows held two oak display cases in which Roman coins were arrayed on red velvet cushions under tiny spotlights. Between the cases stood a glass-fronted cabinet where a polychrome drinking vessel, an Etruscan statuette, a bronze portrait head, fragments of marble, and similar priceless treasures were arranged with the studied disregard with which decorators display the possessions of millionaires.

Petrovitch was standing at the far end of the sitting room.

244

Behind him, through the double doors, I could see a metal L-shaped executive desk with seats for master and secretary. Within reach of both was a computer keyboard with a screen on a lazy Susan so it could be swung into position either way. On the desk were a dozen or so silver-framed photos of Ingrid and Petrovitch and some elderly folks whose prominence there would seem to owe more to kinship than to physical beauty.

'You're looking great, Mickey,' said Petrovitch in a husky voice. He was cool and good-tempered, affecting a British style with his red suspenders, shirt with broad blue stripes, and cutaway stiff collar with club tie. 'Drink?'

'Coffee.'

'Get Mickey a cup of coffee, will you, Goldie?' As Goldie disappeared into the study room, Petrovitch sat down and stretched out his long thin legs to admire his patent leather Gucci loafers. Above his head, Marcus Aurelius was expelling the Germans from the Danube provinces; the river was very blue, the way Johann Strauss always liked his Danube. 'Are you a gambling man, Mickey?'

'No, I'm not.'

'Neither am I. I figure I take enough risks all day without going to a middleman for more.'

Goldie brought me a cup of coffee. I guess old Petey didn't want me snooping around in his study.

'But I've wagered Goldie one hundred bucks on the way you'll answer a question.'

I looked at him and drank coffee.

'Goldie says you won't answer truthfully; I say you will. The trouble is, I don't know how we're going to settle the bet. We won't be sure if your answer is the truth or not. Right?'

'The same as being in court,' I said.

'What I want to know is, do you hate me, Mickey?' He smiled.

'Hate you?'

'Don't play for time. Just tell me.'

'Why should I hate you?'

'Maybe you just despise me?'

'Don't put me on the spot, Mr Petrovitch,' I said.

'Do you hear that, Goldie? Mr Petrovitch, he calls me now. Is that a sign of something?'

'You're my client,' I said. 'I work for you as a lawyer; I don't run a dating agency.'

'You mean you don't give a shit about me either way? You do your job, file your time slips – in six-minute segments, I notice; I guess that makes it easier to calculate from a per hour time base – and hope for the best.'

'If you want to work with another attorney—'

'Not at all. You've got all the attributes I'm looking for.'

'For instance?'

'I want advice from someone who doesn't give a shit about me. I got so many people playing the angles, it's getting hard to distinguish friends from enemies.'

'I don't hate you,' I said truthfully.

'You've never done much to conceal your dislike of me, Mickey. I didn't pay much attention to that, but then I got around to figuring that your casual hostility was part of your aggressive disposition, and maybe a reliable indication that you were not plotting against me.'

'I'm not plotting against you,' I said, looking into his face and trying to decide what kind of paranoid personality I was dealing with.

'No, if you were plotting against me you'd be smart enough not to let your hostility show.'

'How did you eliminate Goldie?' I asked.

Petrovitch looked at Goldie and then looked back at me again. 'I had to start somewhere. And Goldie and I have been together a long time.'

'What kind of plots are you suffering under?' I asked him.

'I don't have to tell you someone is trying to kill me; you found the telephone bomb yourself. My wife is involved.' He said it evenly and coolly.

'What kind of evidence you got for that?'

'Tell him, Goldie.'

Goldie coughed and cleared his throat. 'Mrs Petrovitch hired a hit man,' he said awkwardly.

'How do you know?' I said.

Goldie said, 'Don't screw around. You know all this. She knew Pindero back when she was young. When she met him again on this charity committee she's so dedicated to, she tells him some yarn and he tells her he was a hit man. She pays him five grand as first installment on a hit. He planted the bomb in the phone but when that didn't work he took off. You went and found him for her. Don't screw around.'

'I didn't know all that,' I said.

'You talked with the law, didn't you?'

'Laird? That was just routine after some louse phoned my name in to them. Was that you, Goldie?'

'Don't let's start playing Truth or Consequences,' said Goldie. 'There's too much at stake.'

Petrovitch said, 'Ingrid went up to Topanga Canyon with someone, and when they came down again Pindero was dead and stuffed into the icebox. We figured you were the helper.'

'Jesus!' The painting over my seat was a turbulent version of Rome's Capture by the Goths, the dark flames reaching into the sky. Treachery by slaves decided the fate of the city.

'Didn't Ingrid ask you to waste me?' said Petrovitch.

'No. At least not in those words,' I said.

'She said I was trying to murder her, did she?' I didn't respond. 'That's probably the way she's using her new assassin,' he said. 'That makes it easier for them, I guess. And she plans to go away with them . . . plans it down to the last detail.'

'But now I'm in the clear?' I asked.

'We heard Ingrid give your name to the cops. She told them you went up to Topanga.'

'And gave them my address in Mulholland? I wondered about that.' I looked from one to the other and tried to hurry them along. 'So who else was there with her?'

'We don't know,' said Goldie and bit his fingernail.

'She has more than one accomplice,' said Petrovitch. 'That's what had us puzzled at first. We couldn't pin down any one person who could have done all the things that were being done.'

'Where is Ingrid now?'

'She's coming back here this evening.'

'Well, I guess you have nothing to fear from her directly,' I said. 'If she went to so much trouble to get someone to kill you, she's not likely to do it herself.'

'No, she needs to be a long way away when it happens. The insurance company will put her under the microscope.'

'How did it ever get to be like this between you?' I said. I got to my feet and walked across the room, desperately needing to stretch my legs.

'She's sick,' said Petrovitch. 'It's my fault, I guess. I neglected her when she needed care and attention.'

'Is it the money?' I asked. I looked at the coins in the glass case. The Roman emperors were all frowning. I think maybe the spotlights were getting in their eyes.

'She feels rejected, and it's eaten into her soul. She's devious and manipulative. At first I even liked that, it seemed very female, very childlike. But when she started doing bad things I couldn't handle it anymore.'

'Has she seen a shrink?' I said, abandoning the ancient world for more urgent problems.

248

'She refuses. But her regular doctor is a shrewd old guy. He's helped me a lot.'

'No drugs?' I sat down alongside him with my feet stretched out. We compared shoes.

'Not for her, only for me.' Rueful smile. 'I'm in analysis. He's arranged counseling too. It's kind of traumatic.'

'I imagine it is.'

'The thing that torments me is the murder of the old guy in Topanga. Did she kill him, or was she just around when it happened?'

'Maybe we'll never find out,' I said.

'Goldie, would you go find the driver?'

It was a neat way to tell me the audience was at an end and tell Goldie that the master wanted a word with me in private.

I got to my feet. Petrovitch got up too. Take away the curly beard and the noble-looking horse and a distinct likeness to Marcus Aurelius was apparent. Of all the Roman emperors, here was the one to resemble: humane, studious, unassuming, and ready to share power. Good old Zach Petrovitch, he certainly chose the right decorators.

'This signing,' said Petrovitch, as if it was just an afterthought. 'Have you arranged the witnesses and whatever we need? Is the other side ready?'

'It can be ready tomorrow,' I offered. 'Vic Crichton is in town, and I'd like to get the whole thing off my hands. It's to be done by means of a power of attorney. I guess you got my message.'

'That's okay. Tomorrow will suit me fine. Any time in the P.M. Line it up. Your office?'

I was about to tell him what a dump it was and suggest some other venue, but with him in the middle of paying good money for those premises that seemed inappropriate. 'Great,' I said. 'Great.'

As he shook hands and said goodbye he said, 'I still love

249

her, Mickey. You'll understand that, I know. That's why I'm taking such a hit.'

'I know,' I said.

Goldie reappeared and escorted me down to the garage and told the driver to take me wherever I wanted to go. 'Mexico City,' I said. 'Do you know a good whorehouse?'

After I got into the back seat of the white limo, Goldie followed me, leaving the car door open to show that he was getting out again.

'It's straight stuff,' said Goldie. 'No matter what you think, it's true.'

'Is it, Goldie?'

'I'm not going to sit around and let it happen. It's not just a matter of being on his payroll; he's the guy I look after. I like him: he won a Silver Star flying a chopper in 'Nam. It's my rep too. Am I getting through to you?'

'You still think I'm a part of it?' I said, trying to repress any sign of panic. 'You think I'm trying to knock off my own client?' I forced a smile. He reached out very slowly and took my arm in his gorilla hand.

Goldie had cold gray eyes, and looking into them wasn't comforting. 'I'm not sure,' he said. 'But I'll tell you this, Mickey. I'm on the way to finding out, and when I find these people I will blow them away.'

'Like you blew away Pindero?'

'I think we both know the son of a bitch I'm talking about,' he said.

'Did you give my name to the cops, Goldie? About Pindero?'

'I told you, it was Mrs Petrovitch did that.'

'Yeah, I forgot. You told me.'

'I'm going to blow that bastard away. I mean it, Mickey. You're a buddy, but it won't make any difference.' He let go of my arm and stepped back out of the car, still watching me.

250

'Tell me something, Goldie,' I said. 'What charity is it that Mrs Petrovitch is so dedicated to? I mean the one where she met brother Pindero, who got so tragically dead?'

Asking Goldie even the simplest kind of question brought a suspicious frown to his face, like I knew the answer already and was trying to needle him. 'Rainbow Stojil,' he said. 'The Rainbow's End Shelter for Homeless Men. Don't tell me you haven't heard of it.'

'Heard of it? I gave them a big donation only recently.'

He closed the car door with more force than it needed. Stojil? Ingrid? More than one helper? How much of Petrovitch was real life? None of it, maybe. None of these rich people were real – they were just poor folks acting.

'Where did you say, buddy?'

'My office,' I said.

'That's a lousy neighborhood,' said the driver.

'What are you, a realtor?'

I sank back in the leather and thought about Zachary Petrovitch standing there in that room full of Roman pictures. From a paranoid like that I would have expected a mural of Julius Caesar being stabbed to death on the steps of the capitol building, but I guess that wasn't one of the decisive battles of imperial Rome. It was just a felony.

15

The trial of the policemen accused of beating Rodney King was being aired on the Fox channel. The transmission was live and screened all day. It had been going for weeks. The evening news often featured day-by-day clips from the trial, but I didn't watch the news regularly. Maybe I should have, but like most people in Los Angeles I figured a trial out in Simi Valley, Ventura County, was not something to miss the sports for. And for the likes of me, seeing the law in action was too much like work.

The verdict came through about three in the afternoon. I had been at LAX and was on my way from the airport to my office to keep my appointment with Mr and Mrs Petrovitch and Crichton. We were to read through and then sign the agreement and the other papers.

The sun was shining, and I'd had a good lunch at the airport with a satisfied client who was in transit. When I have meetings there I like to use the main restaurant because they have valet parking and I can be back on the road more quickly. The airport traffic was light, and I came under the 405 with the car stereo playing a tape of Mercer, feeling that everything was just fine. That's always a dangerous state of mind.

The first time I became aware of something unusual was when I spotted a crowd standing watching the window of a TV store where dozens of TV screens were tuned to the Fox live transmission. It took me a moment or two to guess what was drawing these little crowds.

Once the verdict was brought in, the news spread through the city like a tidal wave. People who had shown no interest in the trial all week were suddenly inflamed or indignant or excited.

My first evidence of the city's hysteria came a block or two later, when half a dozen black kids – big guys about eighteen or nineteen years old – came running out to my car when I stopped at a red light. There were four of them; they began beating on the glass with their fists and trying to wrench the doors open. I maybe would have toughed it out but a fifth guy arrived waving a baseball bat and swung it at my windshield. I shouted abuse at them and jabbed the gas pedal so that the car shot forward and the baseball bat hit metal instead of glass. Traffic coming across the intersection had to swerve as I went weaving through the cross-street traffic. There were yells of anger and a dissonance of horns, but I got through to the other side and kept going.

I began to realize I'd not encountered just one freak gesture of hostility. I could see other signs of agitation. People were arguing and shouting, and a fleeing figure – a young white guy – was chased across the street in front of me, so I had to brake to avoid him and his pursuers. I kept rolling and figured that as long as I didn't stop I'd be safe. I saw a black-and-white coming the other way with beacon flashing and siren on. I switched my radio from station to station without finding any news bulletins. At the next intersection I slowed and took the right-hand lane. I found myself saying a prayer of thanks to that unknown guy who wrote into the traffic code permission to turn right on a red signal. It gave me a chance to keep moving, and now there were crowds gathering at every intersection to molest and attack any motorist who stopped for a light.

253

It was a rough district to drive through. Had the traffic in town been heavy, I might have been tempted to route myself from LAX to my office by the freeways, but that's a long detour. The noon radio bulletin promised traffic everywhere was light, so I had taken the most direct route. No one had confided to me the fact that the city was about to disappear in smoke and flame.

As I turned the corner and neared my office, I saw a group of men in T-shirts and jeans smashing the windows of a dry cleaners I'd used from time to time. The Korean proprietor and his two muscular sons came out the door wielding shot-guns. The men smashing the windows ran off, shouting and laughing. All along the street, shop windows had been broken. The sidewalks were marked with white puddles of broken glass, and at the end of the block there were flames billowing out of the little mom-and-pop grocery store.

My car phone buzzed. I thought it would be Miss Huth, complaining again about the social decline of the neighborhood, but it wasn't.

'Murphy?'

'You got it,' I said. I recognized Goldie's voice, so I guessed what was coming.

'Mr Petrovitch for you,' said Goldie.

Without preamble, Petrovitch said, 'Where are you, Mickey?'

'South Central, and it's very active. You?'

'I'm on the Harbor Freeway heading north.'

'You have a good view from there,' I said.

'There are fires all over South Central – to the right and the left of us. Is your office okay?'

'I'll be there in a couple of minutes,' I said. 'But it's not a choice location for a meeting. Stay on the freeway and keep going; it's not healthy down here in the streets.'

'I can't reach Ingrid,' he said. 'I missed her at the restaurant.

She's driving over to your office, but she's not answering her phone.'

'I'll go to the office and wait for her. It's better I'm there. My secretary will be popping her rivets: she's never seen our lovely city *en fête*.'

'Ingrid may have heard the news on the car radio and gone straight home.'

'You go home too,' I said. 'I'll ask Ingrid to call you if she arrives at the office.'

'Do that,' said Petrovitch and rang off. He wasn't a man noted for his lingering goodbyes.

I saw a gang of about a dozen men in a parking lot, systematically smashing the cars, levering the trunks open, and ransacking them. Then I saw the first of the many looters. Dodging through the traffic came individuals, then streams of men, women, and children, every last one of them laboring under the weight of some item or other, from car batteries to sewing machines. The looting had started; political science gave way to economics. Seeing so many shiny possessions cradled in the loving arms of new owners, the gangs roaming the streets were irresistibly diverted from violence to theft.

As I neared my office the sky became darker with smoke and I saw more violence. Bloodied people rushed past. A white man was on the ground bleeding, and a woman was standing over him sobbing. From an overturned car, its doors opened wide, papers, hats, shoes, a newspaper, an umbrella, and broken glass had spilled onto the road. Many LA drivers regularly carry handguns in their glove compartments; today guns were what everyone wanted. Above the noise of the engine I heard the regular crack of gunfire. Everywhere I looked, there were indications that attacks had been made on shops and people who just happened to be in the wrong place at the wrong time. Some of the business premises had BLACK scrawled or sprayed across doors and windows, but that had not always saved them from smashed windows or fire bombs. As I got to the office and turned into the garage I saw that the van parked across the street selling tacos and soft drinks had been wrecked and set afire. It was now just a blackened shell with blistered paint and smoldering tires. There was a stink of burning in the air, and the crack of gunfire was growing more frequent.

I breathed a sigh of relief as I went down the ramp and into the garage under my building. It was gloomy. The fluorescents were off so that the only light came through the windows along the sidewalk. There was no sign of the janitor; the little glass office he called home was locked up. I went around my car and examined the dent the kid had made in my paintwork; it was as big as my fist, but the paint was intact and with luck it wouldn't flake before I got it fixed.

Not all the building's tenants had fled for home. There were half a dozen cars there still. I saw Miss Huth's old Buick, and on the far side of the garage I recognized a white BMW and knew I had a visit from Budd.

On the stairs I caught up with two of my neighbors. Karen, a big earth-mother Nicaraguan nurse from the single mothers advisory center, had a shotgun under her arm. Clive, the architect, was nursing a big machine gun with a curved magazine and wooden stock. 'Jesus Christ!' I said. 'What are you doing with an AK-Forty-seven?'

'Don't you have a gun?' said Karen in surprise.

'Not like that, I don't,' I said.

'You'd better stay with us,' said Clive. I looked at him. His bold-patterned bow tie and neatly trimmed beard looked incongruous with the battle-worn old gun. 'We're going on the roof to protect the building.'

'I'm expecting visitors.'

256

'They won't be coming,' said Clive. He looked out of the window. The street had become quiet.

'I'll be okay. You go ahead,' I said. 'And be careful. You'll kill someone.'

'*Tacka tacka tacka tacka tacka*,' he called. Oh, my gosh, every man is a Rambo at heart.

'Is that thing loaded, Karen?' I couldn't believe that my neighbors were all armed to the teeth.

'Of course it is,' she replied, pushing her long black hair back with her free hand. 'I keep it under my desk. I'm always having people threatening me and trying to steal the cash.'

'In the prenatal advisory bureau?'

'You're a lawyer,' she said. She was touchy in the way people get when they are nervous or frightened. 'So don't pretend you don't know what goes on in this neighborhood.'

'Okay. Well, take care, you two,' I said.

'You should have a gun in the office,' said Clive. 'It's not fair to your staff to leave them unprotected.'

'I'll see about it.'

'*Tacka tacka tacka tacka tacka*.' His voice echoed in the narrow stairwell as he trotted up to the roof brandishing his machine gun. He put an arm around her protectively, but I figured Karen's dark skin would keep her safer on the streets than Clive and his AK-47.

When I opened the door to my office I saw Budd facing me with an apprehensive look on his face. In his hand he had Danny's Browning, and it was pointing at my belly. When he saw it was me he said, 'Oh, I'm sorry, Mickey. I didn't see your car arrive.'

'You want me to go out and drive in again?' I hate having guns pointed at me.

He'd been sitting in the room that used to be Korea Charlie's office, alternately looking at the TV and then out the window and exchanging his thoughts with Miss Huth. I could see her

257

now, standing on tiptoe to see over the frosted glass partition. I wiggled my fingers at her.

'What are you doing here, Budd?' I asked as I gently nudged the gun aside so it didn't point at me.

He ignored my question. 'Holy shit! Have you seen what's going on out there?'

'Have I seen it? I've just driven through it, buddy.' I went to the phone and dialed Danny. After a few minutes with the busy signal I put the phone down again.

Budd was watching me. 'I've never known anything like this,' he said. 'Were you here for the Watts riots?'

'I was only fourteen years old,' I said caustically. 'You must have been twelve.' I wasn't in the mood for another of Budd's flights of fancy.

Now that she was quite sure my arrival wasn't a visit from a friendly neighborhood riot mob, Miss Huth emerged from her den to greet me. 'We were worried about you, Mr Murphy,' she said.

Budd said, 'Miss Huth said you'd be here anytime. She said you had an appointment at—' He looked at the clock.

'Sit down,' I said. 'You're making me nervous striding around with that gun in your hand. Put the damn thing away.' To Miss Huth I said, 'Is the coffee machine working? Have you heard from Mr Kim or Crichton or anyone?'

'I'll make you fresh coffee, Mr Murphy. I am so pleased you are safe. Mr Kim is at the Rainbow Hostel.'

'How do you know?'

'He just phoned from there,' she said, 'and I had to phone him back to tell him Mr Crichton's date of birth.'

'Did he take any money from the safe, do you know?'

'Yes,' said Miss Huth. 'Twenty thousand dollars in cash. I had to get it from the bank. I am worried about him with all this trouble in the streets.'

The TV in the corner was babbling away. I was thankful I'd kept that ancient set although I seldom looked at it except during some really important football game.

By now most of the TV channels had suspended normal programming. The newsrooms were permanently on the air, bringing minute-by-minute reports from their mobile camera teams using vans with portable antennas. It was a hell of a scene to watch when you knew that the real thing was going on in the street outside your door. Most of these transmissions from the battlefront were shaky and wobbly. Sometimes the picture collapsed completely and the anchors in the studio had to ad lib their way through the break or find some earlier footage to transmit. In the back rooms of the TV stations every telephone was in use, as reporters heard – and tape-recorded – reports of fires and violence across the city. Other staff members were using the phones to locate politicians, sociologists, writers, and academics: instant-wisdom talking heads always ready to give a TV camera their views on the world.

The choppers normally assigned to spotting traffic conditions on the freeways were providing live pictures of Central Los Angeles, with columns of smoke ascending vertically into the air. I was looking out of the window as Miss Huth came in bearing a cup of coffee, and a chopper came roaring over at rooftop height, its rotor blades thudding heavily against the still air. It circled a couple of times, and then there was a burst of smoke and a rolling ball of fire appeared just a block away. The chopper went in close to shoot pictures.

'It's a paint store,' said Budd, who by watching TV had become an expert. 'Until now most of them have been hitting the liquor stores and getting smashed. But if they start torching the paint stores and lumber yards, they'll turn the town into a fireball.'

'If they start on the gas stations the explosions will tear

259

whole blocks apart,' said the ever-cheerful Miss Huth. 'Already there are many dead.'

'Calm down,' I said. I was looking out the window. Moving along on the other side of the street were some kids who hung around on the corner. Four of them were staggering under the weight of a glass-fronted commercial refrigerator filled with beer.

'These blacks are torching their own neighborhoods,' said Budd. 'Are they crazy?'

'They are not blacks,' I said. 'Not all of them, anyway. Look in the street there. Watch the TV. Take a ride around the block. At least half the rioters are light-skinned – Latinos and whites too. It's not a race riot, it's just a riot.'

'Could this spread across the whole state?' said Miss Huth.

'Not at the rate these guys are boozing and looting,' I said. 'By tomorrow morning those without a hernia will be too hung over to riot.'

'I hope,' she said.

Budd was glued to the TV again, his fear mingled with pride. 'Hollywood! Where else in the world could you have half a dozen airborne cameras filming killings and arson from just a few feet away from the action? This is terrible.'

'Look what's happening across the street,' called Miss Huth.

On the opposite sidewalk and in the parking lot a crowd had gathered. Most of them had bottles in their hands and drank contentedly. The crowd was watching some men in baseball caps, shorts, and T-shirts battering at the door of Graham's discount store. The active looters weren't kids, they looked like men in their thirties, and neither did they look particularly impoverished. They had already smashed the glass doors, and now they were using tire levers to break open the grille. There was a crash, and one of the men overbalanced and almost toppled over as the gate broke open. The crowd cheered and laughed and slapped one another on the back. Then, politely, without pushing, they went scrambling one by one through the gap made in the grille and through the doors. More looters came, picking their way over the shards of glass and disappearing inside the darkened store.

There must have been a dozen or more inside when a black-and-white bumped up over the curb and stopped at the broken doors. A cop got out. For just one moment the looters froze like a film stopped in mid-action. A middle-aged Hispanic woman with a bandanna around her head was emerging with a small TV set in her arms. She put it down on the ground and stood by it possessively. The second cop got out of the car, and cops and crowd looked at each other.

'What are they going to do?' said Budd.

'What can they do?'

'Nothing,' said Budd.

The cops evidently came to the same conclusion, for they got back in the car, and it edged forward and ran across the sidewalk and back onto the road again. As the car went around the corner the looters came back to life suddenly; a film restarted.

'Is that what we pay the police for?' said Miss Huth. I looked at her. I'd always had her down as an illegal immigrant, but maybe I was wrong.

I said, 'The cops are always being told not to provoke ethnic crowds. They probably have direct orders to play it cool.'

'Play it cool?' she said. 'What is to play it cool?'

'Not get involved,' said Budd over his shoulder.

Miss Huth shrugged. She didn't understand any of it. 'You want me to try phoning Nine-one-one?' she asked.

'No,' said Budd. 'They've got a police radio in their car. They're not in trouble. We don't want cops here.' He looked at the clock. 'Where are your visitors?'

261

Before I could reply, Miss Huth said, 'Something is happening at the warehouse.' We went to the window but could only see the flat gray roof of Graham's warehouse, the place we bought all the fittings and furniture after our office was vandalized at Christmas.

I could see an unnatural and slightly bluish haze rising from the building.

'They're inside Graham's,' said Miss Huth.

'What are they after there?' said Budd.

'Looking for cash in the office maybe,' I replied.

'There is heat coming out of the roof,' said Miss Huth. 'You can see it.' The haze, growing more dense, made the building wobble gently.

'Shit!'

There was no warning. Graham's pipes and tubes and air-conditioning plant, which make the flat roofs of Los Angeles so ugly, suddenly snaked and ripped open and the whole roof blew off with a mighty explosion that came booming into our ears and rattled the doors and windows.

'Oh, my God!' said Miss Huth. 'What ignited?'

'Were there people inside?'

'I guess so,' I said. The whole scene was now enveloped in smoke.

'Should we phone the Fire Department?' said Miss Huth.

'I don't imagine we can tell them anything they don't already know. They must be getting reports from all over town.'

Miss Huth wrung her hands. 'That woman Karen came in here. She had a gun. So did the architect.'

'I know.'

'The architect! He had a machine gun.' She was generating anger within herself, and her voice became shriller. 'It's not right, an architect.'

Still looking at the TV, Budd suddenly produced a snippet

262

of the new wisdom he'd gleaned. 'Those fires where the oily black smoke is turning gray: that's a sign they've got hoses directed on the fire.'

'It won't be long before it's dark,' said Miss Huth. 'Should we wait until dark to leave? Or would it be wiser to drive in the light?'

I thought about it. In the distance I could see that traffic on the freeway was moving. Moving fast as hundreds of drivers made for the routes out of town.

'Once it's dark we stand a better chance,' said Miss Huth, making up her own mind. I'd never seen her nervous before; I'd never seen her anything less than ferocious.

'I'm not sure about that, Miss Huth,' I told her. 'It may be better if you can see where you are going. By nightfall the streets are going to be littered with all kinds of junk that would bring a car to a permanent stop.'

Budd kept ducking in to watch the TV, and whenever he did he emerged more nervous. 'Did you see that piece of film taken from the chopper? They were dragging guys out of cars and beating them to death.'

'I'm sure it is spreading all over the state,' said Miss Huth. 'The TV says they are getting calls about riots in places way out in Ventura and fires in Huntington Beach.'

'Then switch the goddamned TV off.' I went to the window and looked out again. 'Stay calm.' I hadn't reckoned on its getting worse. I thought it was just a local disturbance that the cops would contain within an hour or two. Now the whole city seemed to be engulfed. There were more and more columns of smoke reaching into the blue sky. Not many of them were turning gray.

'Stay calm! Are you crazy?' she said. 'Do you want to know what Mr Byron and I just saw on TV?'

'No, I don't want to know. It won't help to get emotional,' I told her.

263

'It won't help to sit here refusing to face facts either,' said Budd.

I stayed by the window, but I turned around to see him. 'I know the facts,' I said. 'I can guess at them, anyway.'

'Then tell me,' he said.

I waited for Miss Huth to go back to her office. 'You're waiting for Zach Petrovitch, aren't you?'

'I'm taking Ingrid away with me,' said Budd. 'We'll find a place no one can find us.' He had thought about it a lot, I suppose. I felt sorry for him. No one knew better than I did what it was like to be in love with Ingrid.

'Conspiring to murder is a capital offense. In this state it carries the death penalty.'

The phone rang. It was Vic Crichton. 'I've got myself a rented chopper. What is it like where you are?' he asked.

'Not healthy,' I said, 'but momentarily quiet. Do you want to do it next week?'

'No,' said Vic. 'I am heading in your direction. Better everything is signed today. Is Mrs Petrovitch with you yet?'

'Not yet.'

'I'll land in that empty lot across the street from your building. Is it all clear?'

'It's empty.'

'Bring the documents across when I land. My pilot is getting jumpy about the fine print on his insurance policy.'

'Anything you say,' I told him, and hung up.

'Was that your son?' asked Miss Huth.

'No. Where did Budd Byron go?'

'I don't know,' she said. 'Everyone is acting strangely today.'

'You can say that again.' I put the four copies of the agreement and the powers of attorney and other papers into the impressive leather folders that we use to make clients feel important. Everything was quiet on the street outside. All the activity had moved over to the next block, where the serious looting was going on.

Mrs Petrovitch arrived on time. I saw her at the wheel of a Honda as it turned into the ramp and disappeared into the garage. 'Stay here and take care of things,' I told Miss Huth. I got the gold-plated Parkers that we always use for signings, put the leather folders under my arm, and went down to meet Ingrid. She was wearing a belted trench coat and looked beautiful, although somewhat subdued.

'The other party is coming in by helicopter,' I said. 'We'll do it all as quickly as we can.'

'Good,' she said.

'Your husband wants you to phone him,' I said. 'He's worried about you.'

She looked at me and nodded.

No sooner did I put my nose out on the street than I heard a helicopter circling the building as the pilot of Crichton's rented chopper took a look at the empty lot. The explosion had completely destroyed Graham's. There was nothing left of it but a smoldering shell. And it seemed to have chased bystanders away too, for the whole parking lot was empty. On any other day a helicopter landing there would have been a sensation, but today choppers filled the sky everywhere you looked.

As the helicopter landed and kicked up dust, I took Ingrid's arm and hurried across the street. Vic Crichton was ready and waiting for us. He got out, and after hurried greetings he put the leather folder I gave him on the seat in the helicopter and bent over it to sign the papers.

'Sign where I made pencil marks,' I said, giving Ingrid the other folder. 'It's already witnessed.'

It took only a couple of minutes for all four documents and the letters and amendments to be signed and complete. 'Why don't you come with me in the chopper, Mrs Petrovitch?' said Crichton, in that fancy British voice of his. He got back inside but held the door open.

'Can I leave the car with you, Mickey? I'll come and get it tomorrow.'

I looked back toward my building. I could see Clive and Karen on the roof brandishing their guns and watching our activities.

'I need my two copies of the agreement,' I said. 'You keep your powers of attorney. You have now assigned your assets and neither of you have any holdings in any of the companies named on the schedule. Helicopter? Sure, Ingrid. The way things are today that makes good sense.'

Budd came running across the lot, expecting no doubt to find Petrovitch sitting at the controls of the helicopter. When he saw Vic Crichton sitting next to the pilot he halted suddenly. 'What's happening?'

'Save it for another time, Budd,' I said. He turned to Ingrid, who tied the belt of her coat in an agitated gesture that a shrink would have called self-abnegatory.

'It's all over, Budd,' she said hurriedly. 'You and me, it's all over. I love my husband. Zach and I are reconciled. It would never have worked out.'

Budd's face registered amazement. He looked at me and then at Vic and then at Ingrid again. 'Are they making you say this? You're being threatened?'

Ingrid gave me the briefest of glances, wet her lips, and said, 'No, Budd. It's entirely my own decision. I've been ill, and now I'm going to be all right.'

'I can't believe it,' said Budd. 'You mean we're not going away together? You promised.'

She looked at me again and bit her lip before telling him. 'You'd better know I've sworn out a complaint before a magistrate.'

'You've what?' said Budd. He waggled his head violently, like a dog shaking itself dry or a man trying to unhook his head from his neck. 'What am I supposed to have done?' His movements were clumsy and awful to see. There was none of that detached skill that actors use to convey grief. Budd was flapping around, crippled and uncoordinated and out of control.

'There will be no indictment unless you try to make contact again,' said Ingrid calmly.

'Wh-what?' I'd never known him to stutter before. 'What for?'

'Trying to persuade me to help you,' said Ingrid.

'Help you what?'

'Kill my husband.'

I looked at Vic Crichton. He was crouched in the front seat and holding the headset to his ears as if totally oblivious to what was going on behind him.

The gun was still in Budd's pocket and I thought he would reach for it, but in his anxiety he seemed to have forgotten about it. He stepped toward her and, without touching her, said softly, 'How can you do this to me, Ingrid?'

'It's my marriage,' she said. 'I had to do everything I knew to save it.'

She swung around and climbed up into the back seat of the chopper. Then she clipped her seat belt together as if she'd done it many times before. I guess rides in helicopters were nothing new for rich ladies like Ingrid.

'I can't stand the stink,' said Budd, looking up at her, his face contorted with rage. 'It's the smell of treachery!' he yelled above the sound of the engine. 'You're a rotten whore!'

Ingrid looked at him eye to eye without blinking. 'Once an actor always an actor,' she said, and closed the door and locked it.

I'll never forgive her for that final jab of the knife. Like a rich kid who couldn't learn the value of money, Ingrid had become a spendthrift with love. Her supply was infinite. She'd never had to crave it and cherish it the way the rest of us did. All her life she'd been showered with love from every side. There were always men around who would die for her. Budd was no more than the next in line.

'Let's go,' said Vic to the pilot. 'Goodbye, old chap!' he said politely to Budd through the open window. 'See you next week, Mickey.' The pilot speeded up the blades to a scream, and the shiny machine lifted into the air.

'Don't promise,' I told him. A flicker of a smile went across Ingrid's face, but she wasn't looking at me.

'Come back to the office, Budd,' I said. I put my hand out to touch him. 'I'll tell you all about it.'

'No, no, no!' he shouted, his eyes wide and his hair blowing crazily in the downwind of the blades.

As the chopper was in that tilted-forward attitude they assume as they ride the air cushion, Budd went running after it across the potholed empty lot. He pulled the gun from his pocket and was firing it as fast as he could pull the trigger. Over the rough ground he couldn't keep up with the forward speed of the chopper, and it drew ahead of him. At that range, and on the run, he would have had to be Annie Oakley to hit anything. The chopper rose majestically into the sky. There was no sign that pilot or passengers were aware that they were being attacked. I saw Vic calmly turning his head as if asking Ingrid if she was comfortable enough in the back seat.

I watched Budd as he went running off down the street, still waving the gun. I called after him but he seemed not to hear me. When it was obvious that he would not return I went back to the office and dialed Danny's number again. It was still busy.

268

I began to wonder what kind of signal I'd get if Danny's building was in flames.

Miss Huth heard me trying to use the phone and came in to ask who I wanted to call.

'Keep calling my son, will you, Miss Huth? I'd like to know he's safe.'

I looked out the window. There was a sudden flurry of traffic. Some cars, obviously stolen, were crammed with drunks who went past shouting and singing. Once a black-and-white went past at speed. It took some ill-aimed rocks, and a bottle hit its roof and bounced off to smash in the street. But most of the attention of the lawbreakers had turned to looting, and the streets were filled with people carrying their plunder home and coming back for more. It was stores rather than homes that were being broken open. People didn't want used items when they could get them in their original cartons complete with warranty. TV sets were favored, along with VCRs and stereos. Camcorders, computers, and fax machines were also of a tempting size, weight, and shape. Anything fitted with wheels was vulnerable to the covetous ambitions of someone or other. A long leather sofa, a huge freezer, and a large photocopying machine had all been manhandled past by means of the tiny wheels fitted to them.

It was tempting to glue oneself to the TV. Watching the tube converted it all into entertainment and made the immediate environment seem less dangerous, and yet new fires were cropping up in all parts of the city as fire bombs were lobbed into shops and hotels from passing cars.

Miss Huth said, 'There is always the busy signal from your son. Now I am going home.'

'Will you be all right?'

'Of course I will be all right.' She put a cover on the typewriter, put the lid on her tin of cookies, locked the petty cash, and went off as if nothing unusual was happening. But from the way she made her exit I had the feeling that she was holding me personally responsible for the riots.

There were new fires and plenty of wrecked cars, some of them stolen ones deliberately wrecked by drunken drivers. The hospitals were now providing the numbers of people injured and killed by the rioters, but I drove across to Danny's place without seeing anything life-threatening. Of course I was worried sick that something had happened to Danny, but when I got to his apartment I found Betty there already. She was sitting on the sofa talking to him.

'Mickey, darling! How wonderful!' She was looking terrific: the combined effects of losing about fifteen pounds and an unrestrained rampage through the designer boutiques of Rodeo Drive. 'I was worried about him,' Betty told me, stroking Danny's head. Danny usually objected vociferously when she did things like that, but today he smiled. 'I guess you were worried too,' she said.

'No, I just happened to be passing,' I said.

Danny said, 'Robyna will be back in a minute.' He got to his feet and looked out the window to see if she was coming.

Betty looked at me. I shrugged. 'I didn't come to see Robyna,' I said.

'It's getting worse,' said Danny, looking through a pair of Zeiss binoculars he'd got in exchange for the fancy sports shoes his Uncle Sean had sent him. Was it a college or a garage sale that he went to every day?

Robyna arrived, her hair awry, huffing and puffing and cuddling a bag of groceries. 'You're still here? Good,' she said. Without even acknowledging my presence she went and kissed Betty on the cheek. I could see Robyna got along just fine with

Betty. Robyna went into the kitchen, set out some cups and saucers, and started making tea.

'None for me,' I called. 'I'm just passing through.'

'It's getting worse out there,' said Danny again. 'The next-door apartment is empty. We have the key; you could stay there. It's real nice inside.'

'Stay next door?' I said. 'When I've got a proper home to go to?'

'I'd love to stay, Danny,' Betty told him. 'I'm nervous with all these fires and shootings.'

'I'll look after you, Mom,' said Danny, and went and put his arm around her.

I said, 'Okay, I'll have some tea as long as I don't have to drink it with milk.'

'I thought you Irishmen all loved tea,' called Robyna from the kitchen.

'No,' I said. 'You're confusing it with boiled cabbage. It's the Brits who like tea.'

Robyna came in with a huge wooden tray. On it was a brown teapot, and a cake decorated with pecans and icing. Danny was waiting with a knife to cut the cake. Robyna held up one of the teacups and said, 'A house present from Betty. Aren't they cute?'

The cups and saucers were very ritzy: fat little blue Chinese guys on a rickety bridge. A house present! I hope this wasn't a sign that Robyna was starting to build a nest.

'It's like a celebration,' said Betty, as Danny cut slices of cake and handed them out on matching little blue Chinese pattern plates with silver-plated forks.

'It's just a frozen Sara Lee,' said Robyna. 'All the best stuff was gone.'

I was biting into the cake when I realized what she meant. 'Wait a minute, Robyna,' I said, swallowing hard. 'Did you just go out and steal this cake we're eating?'

271

'There's no other way of shopping, Mr Murphy,' she replied calmly. 'The shops are all closed because of the riots.'

'The shops are closed because of the riots,' I repeated. 'So you go out and loot the goddamned markets?'

'Don't go on at her, dear,' said Betty, in that dreamy tone she adopts when she's not been listening to what I say. 'The cake is lovely, Robyna. It was so considerate of you to fix something for us.'

'It's like an English tea,' said Robyna. 'I was going to do cucumber sandwiches too. One of the girls in my chemistry class is English. She's a nutrition major.'

'A nutrition major!'

'Eat your cake,' said Betty, 'and be grateful your son is sharing with such a sensible girl.' Oh, they were thick, very thick. Poor Danny.

'What do you think of Mom's new career?' said Danny, reaching for another piece of cake. 'Pretty nifty, eh? You heard she packages productions: stars, writers, directors, the whole schmear.'

'Do I hear a career in philosophy creaking at the foundations?'

'Well, I've always been interested in directing,' said Danny.

'Of course you have,' I said. 'Being interested in directing is as near as anyone can get to being jobless without the stigma of unemployment.'

'I'll find a place for him,' said Betty, giving him an affectionate pat on the arm. 'Just as long as he graduates, I'll find something for him.' Danny smiled smugly. Telling him stuff like that wasn't going to motivate him.

'He could handle the power lunch,' I suggested.

'Why don't you stay overnight too, Dad?' Danny coaxed. 'I could put your car in my lockup.'

So he'd noticed the way in which I was going to the window

272

regularly to make sure those bastards hadn't zeroed in on my car.

'Maybe,' I said. There were developments along the Robyna–Danny axis I didn't care for. I didn't want Betty there brainwashing him, or plotting with Robyna, without me being able to put in my point of view. Betty's new career in movies seemed to have turned the kid's head.

16

Like most of the city's inhabitants, I spent many of those early hours of the riots comparing the TV coverage with wary glances out the window, until eventually I could hardly distinguish between those two distorting sheets of glass. The denizens of the news-rooms welcomed a seemingly endless stream of professionals. Reporters and camera teams, they came wide-eyed and excited and gleefully overloaded with news that was theirs for the taking on every street corner. And by nightfall my memories fused with theirs, and I indiscriminately looted their stories and carried them off to tell them as my own.

'Come away from the TV, Danny. Robyna has helped me, and I've fixed corned beef hash the way you like it.'

The smoke-darkened blue sky changed to night. When the sky had disappeared, the city was criss-crossed with the orange-colored dots of sodium streetlights, which became blobs as the cameras tipped and joggled to get a new angle. A camera follows the crowd: *bang!* you almost feel the fist that strikes it. Race down the street, camera running, people screaming. Is it television, is it reality, or is it neither?

'There is someone on the roof. Jesus, there is someone on the roof!'

'It's okay, Dad. It's just my neighbor.'

'He's got a gun, Danny!'

'All my neighbors have guns. We're doing two hours: turn and turnabout. I said I'd spell him at midnight.'

'Stay out of it, Danny.'

'They might try and torch the lockups,' said Danny, guessing that concern for my Caddie would help me see it his way. 'That's what they did across the street. Folks use them for storage.'

'I'll come up with you,' I said.

Those night hours on the roof with Danny will never fade from my memory. The view across the burning city was awesome. Sometimes for an hour or so Los Angeles seemed to be going to sleep, and then the sudden glare of red and yellow flames tore holes in the night to show where another building had been ignited and blown apart. What a panorama – with the city twinkling like fairyland and large sections of South Central totally dark as electricity outages severed the power connections.

It was cold on the roof, but it was a chance to talk to Danny in a way we hadn't talked in a long time. He was a good kid. We talked about football and automobiles. We talked about politics and his allowance. We talked about everything except the riots and his grades; he made sure of that. 'Did you see where the police seized a Packard Darrin? Sounds like the one you were looking for.'

'How do you know?'

'It was in the paper. The owner was murdered in a house in Topanga. I was going to send you the clipping, but I figured you'd have seen it. You didn't read about it?'

'I haven't got time to read the papers.'

'What happens to stuff like that? Will they sell that car at auction?'

'I don't know.'

'I thought maybe you wanted to buy it.'

'At one time I did. But I lost interest in it. I like my Caddie.'

After I sat on the roof with Danny for an hour and a half I was almost frozen to death. Two of Danny's neighbors came and took over from us, and brought us hot soup.

The apartment next door to Danny was surprisingly comfortable. I guess the residents – an Iranian couple plus a brother-in-law who ran a plush nail and beauty salon in Beverly Hills – made a good living, but they were smart enough to hide all signs of it until you were inside. Then, *pow!* – there was booze and cigarettes and silk walls and shag carpeting everywhere you looked, and no matter where you strayed there was an ashtray within arm's reach. Were they smokers! You could smell it everywhere. And there was every kind of ashtray you've ever seen. Brass ashtrays and ceramic ones, Mickey Mouse ashtrays and thatched cottage ashtrays and ashtrays that played a tune. Some tobacco kooks they must have been. They'd all gone to Vegas for a vacation and given Danny the key so he could look after the apartment for them. The Iranians had called Danny at midnight. They were watching the LA riot scenes on TV in a hotel room in Vegas and worrying.

When I came down from the roof shivering and frightened and burping with the taste of tomato soup, Betty was already in bed and asleep in the big master bedroom with its fluffy carpet and deep pile bedspread. I must have made a noise or something; she woke up when I came into the room.

'Hello, Mickey,' she said. 'Is Danny okay? The poor baby.'

'He's a grown-up now,' I said. 'We can't keep calling him baby. You got to let him go, honey.'

She sat up in bed. She was wearing one of Danny's striped shirts as a nightdress. It looked good on her. 'We never talk anymore,' she said.

'You're looking swell these days, Betty.'

'I wish I could say the same about you, Mickey. You look like hell.'

'It's cold out there.'

'I told you not to go. You want me to make you a hot drink? They got everything here.'

'Neighbors fixed tomato soup for us.'

'Tomato soup doesn't agree with you, Mickey. It gives you indigestion.'

'Now you tell me. Maybe I'll just close my eyes for a minute.'

'It's nice here . . . this apartment, I mean. Did I tell you? I've got to get out of my place. The landlord wants it for himself.'

'You can use the Woodland Hills house if you want.'

'Can I really, Mickey? I'll pay rent. I'm earning big bucks now.'

'You don't have to pay me anything. That place is too big for one person.'

'You'll be there too? Is that what you mean?'

'I've nowhere else to go,' I said.

'We'd need a new bed,' she said. 'One like this would be just great, wouldn't it?'

'I'll let you know in the morning,' I said.

'Oh, Mickey. I do love you.'

I never did get up to switch off the TV. It was going all night. All normal programming was dumped, and the major local channels went over to a minute-by-minute news service. More and more pictures came in from the helicopters that now had the sky to themselves.

As dawn broke over the city, the cameras revealed empty streets littered with unimaginable amounts of debris, wrappings, rubbish, and discarded loot. Hundreds of fires were burning in the city, and they'd produced a fairy-tale gauze over the whole basin as far as the Hollywood Hills. The smoke rising from the fires was solid and black, and the TV news desk reported that there was intermittent gunfire and snipers so active that Fire Department personnel were no longer willing to enter South Central without police escorts.

The looters showed a considerate willingness to plunder only in regular shopping hours, and only when daylight was fully switched on did the TV vans get their cameras rolling at some of the most popular scenes of pillage. Men, women, and children were clambering out of smashed stores, laughing and joking as they staggered away under black plastic trash bags bulging with stolen goods. The supply of booty was dwindling now, but there were still TV sets to be found by the venturesome. Others had to be content with Teflon pans, toaster ovens, and blankets; from one store came a dozen gleeful kids bowling brand-new car tires along. Housewives were shopping without tears, coming out of a Hughes Market with bags filled to overflowing with frozen pizzas, steaks, Daz, Palmolive, and ice cream. The violence and hatred of yesterday seemed to have been largely replaced by relief and good humor. The cops were obviously under orders to stand back, and they were doing so. The looters were summoning that gleeful hysteria that marks the finale of a hit show.

Suddenly I woke up fully. The bed was empty.

The door opened suddenly. 'Mom! Felicity is here,' announced Danny. In the other direction, Betty's head emerged from the bathroom. 'She wants to see you,' Danny told her. 'And there's fresh coffee next door. How did you two sleep?'

'That's none of your goddamned business,' said Betty and disappeared back into the bathroom. I could hear the water running fiercely.

Felicity pushed past Danny and came into the bedroom to look around at the furnishings. 'Hey, not bad!' she pronounced. I pulled the bedclothes up to my chin. She laughed.

'Felicity wanted to see the apartment,' Danny explained, when he saw I was mad at his letting her in like that.

'Is Betty up and about?' she said.

'Hours ago,' said Danny before I could answer.

'I didn't get a lot of sleep last night,' I said.

'What do you think? What do you think?' Felicity kicked the mattress under me to get my attention. She was like that.

'Think about what?'

'About me, Rambo!' She was pirouetting around with her arms held high.

I recognized a cue when I got one. 'You look sensational, Felicity. Sensational!'

'Bastard!' she said. I guess you can't do anything right for some people.

'You're thinner, more lovely, and rich. What do you want me to tell you?'

'I've had it done.'

'What?'

'Do you want coffee, Dad?' said Danny, a sure signal that he didn't expect me to escape in a hurry.

'Cream, no sugar.'

'Tummy tuck, nose job, cheek implants, new eyebrow line. My sign was in the ascendant; the numerologist said the numbers figured, so I said, Do it all, baby, do it all!'

'Great, great,' I said. 'But stop spinning around, will you, Felicity honey? I've just woken up and you're making me dizzy.'

'Can you smell all that burning and stuff? The whole city stinks of smoke and ashes this morning.'

'In this apartment who would notice?' I said. I suppose I should have noticed all that cosmetic surgery when I was in her car but I spent all my time with my eyes on the road.

Danny brought two cups of coffee. I took them both,

pushed Felicity gently out of the bedroom, and knocked on the bathroom door. 'Your coffee is here, lover,' I said.

Betty came out again, this time wearing a clinging pale-blue silk robe. She smiled, downed her coffee, and went off to find Felicity. It was like the concourse of Union Station.

'Felicity is up and about early,' I said when Betty returned. Betty looks good in pale blue.

'She brought my overnight bag. I've been staying with her the last week. We've been going over the preproduction on this movie.' She sipped her coffee. 'What did you do to Budd?'

'What did I do to Budd?'

'You got it word perfect: now answer.'

'I didn't do anything to him. What's wrong with him?'

'He called Maureen last night. We're his agent now, you know. He sacked Pop Pedersen.'

'So I heard.'

'He says he's looking for mature roles.'

'Aren't we all,' I said.

Danny popped his head around the bedroom door. 'The TV just showed a guy arriving outside a store in South Central in a Yellow Cab. He looted himself a microwave oven, put it in the cab, and then drove away. They showed it happening on TV. Can you beat that?'

'Stay at home today, Danny,' I said. 'There's going to be a lot of reaction out there.'

'The cops are doing nothing,' said Danny.

Betty said, 'The cops are mad at everyone from the mayor to the President of the United States of America. The cops figure the hell with the public.'

'Wait a minute, Betty,' I said. 'You are a liberal. Aren't you the one who collected nearly a thousand signatures petitioning Chief Gates about police brutality?'

She was looking at her toenails. 'A man on TV said the

President should be talking to the arsonists, not complaining about the verdict the jury brought in. What's the goddamned Constitution all about anyway?'

'I don't know,' I said. 'I need at least four cups of coffee and a shave before I can discuss the Constitution. Anyway, what was all that stuff about Budd?'

'He's writing a screenplay. He says you gave him the idea. Some kind of screwball story about a loopy rich housewife planning to knock off her husband while telling everyone that *he's* trying to kill *her*. He was a bit incoherent over the phone, but I go for it. Maybe it's for Greta Scacchi. All I remember is Budd says he wants to play the heavy.'

'Budd wants to play the heavy?'

'He made it sound like you knew about it,' she said.

'Not me,' I said. 'I never heard of any loopy housewives, let alone rich ones.'

'He wants me to be the executive producer. He said the time has come for Hollywood to make a movie with a lovable villain. Do you think he's on to something?'

'You'd produce it?'

Betty smoothed the robe over her hips. 'To tell you the truth, Mickey, I was thinking of getting myself an Equity card.'

'Equity card?'

'What was that step you used to teach me, Mickey? Hop, shuffle, step. Heel, heel. Toe, heel; toe heel. Is that the way you do it?'

'Hey, Betty. That's not bad,' I said. 'Hop, shuffle, step.' I could see she'd been taking lessons.

I remained at Danny's all that day. It was late afternoon when Zachary Petrovitch located me. He came buzzing in at the yoke of his own bright red chopper and landed in the road outside. Goldie was with him, of course, sitting up front toting a Skorpion machine gun. They'd both been up all night, hopping around from spot to spot, trying to locate Ingrid, and now their faces were drawn and gray.

I climbed up into the chopper and Petrovitch took off immediately. The blades beat the air to a fury; beneath us gangs of looters waved at us and grinned, thinking we were a TV camera crew. Petrovitch and Goldie had discovered the whole scam: Vic Crichton and Ingrid had been close for a long time, and now they had assumed new identities with the help of Rainbow and departed to collect their loot.

'I never thought this would happen,' said Petrovitch. 'She outguessed me.'

'She's an unusual woman, Mr Petrovitch,' I said. 'You figured that the one she persuaded to murder you would be the one she ran away with. It was a natural mistake.'

'What else do you know?'

'I suppose she's gone with Vic Crichton. Budd Byron, the guy she was making a fool out of, was the one trying to kill you.'

'I covered everything except the possibility that she'd change her identity. They'll get away with it. I can't stop them. They've got real passports and Amex cards and everything. That company in Lima will yield anything up to a hundred million in negotiable assets. I can't even sue them or sue the bank. I chose Peru because it has no effective treaties with the U.S.'

'It was Vic Crichton who was with her at the house in Topanga. He killed the old guy,' said Goldie.

'Is Crichton in love, or is it the money?' said Petrovitch.

'I don't know,' I said. 'Crichton is a Brit. The Brits never fall in love; it's against the law.'

'When they get to Lima they're sure to use their authority to transfer the assets to another bank or into another company. Has Crichton set up anything like that down there?'

'Not to my knowledge,' I said. 'I guessed there might be

something like this in the works, but I couldn't see exactly how it would operate.'

'If you guessed, why didn't you do something about it?' said Petrovitch with an uncharacteristic bitterness. 'You're an attorney, aren't you? You're supposed to protect the public from swindlers.'

'I *did* do something,' I said. 'I got them to agree to having the power of attorney instead of bearer shares.'

'What are you getting at?'

'The assets went from your company and the Westbridge company to Ingrid and Crichton. They then signed powers of attorney. They fly to Peru and then reacquire everything in the new jurisdiction.'

'Don't remind me,' said Petrovitch.

'They knew they would change identity. They agreed to the powers of attorney because that would enable them to receive the money for themselves in their new identities.'

'I know all that.'

'But they can't get it,' I told him.

'Why not?'

'Because the authority vested in a power of attorney ends at the death of the signatory. Ingrid Petrovitch and Victor Crichton are certified dead by the Los Angeles County Coroner, and you can't be deader than that. That's why Rainbow makes so much money: those death certificates are one hundred percent kosher, just like the passports and social security numbers he provides.'

'Wait a minute,' said Petrovitch.

'You make sure the people in Lima, Peru, know that Ingrid Petrovitch and Victor Crichton are dead. Fax them copies of the death certificates, and there is no way the powers of attorney can be used to do anything.'

'I believe you're right. But I have no way of preventing the transfer of funds.'

'With the two beneficiaries dead, all shares except the

nominal two percent held by the partnership against voting deadlocks revert to you in effect. They will be held against your instructions by the bank.'

He looked at me. He got it of course, but apart from a brief and mirthless little smile he didn't show the tumult that must have been in his mind.

'And Crichton didn't object to any of that?' Petrovitch was giving all his attention to flying the chopper. There was a lot of smoke, and three TV choppers were flying around in tight circles, risking everything for close-up pictures.

'Vic Crichton read it very hurriedly, and Mrs Petrovitch didn't read it at all. Crichton was mainly concerned with being able to pass the power on to his assumed identity; he didn't remember that the power of attorney would end on the date of Rainbow's death certificate. People never are scared at the sight of their own names anyway. It wasn't easy for them to see that, out of all the names in the world, theirs were the only ones that would spoil their plan.'

'Will you look over there,' said Goldie. 'It looks like your office is burning, Mickey.'

I looked; he was right. 'I'm not surprised,' I said.

'No,' said Goldie, trying to be very subtle. 'I guess with all this rioting there'll be no difficulties with your insurance company.'

'Nor with the cops, the county, or the Securities and Exchange Commission,' I said.

Goldie looked at me and then at Petrovitch, who became very concerned with his piloting. 'So what's happened to them?' said Goldie, who had not followed the conversation because he was so eager to look down at the riot-torn streets. Now, having seen what he wanted to see, he relaxed. 'Tell it in plain English, so I can understand.'

'Vic Crichton and Ingrid Petrovitch are officially dead,' I said. 'The certified death certificates will by now have been supplied by the county. The doctor who attended them for the mandatory ten days prior to death will have signed to say their deaths were due to natural causes. Two bodies, of approximately the right size and weight, will have been embalmed and hermetically sealed into caskets and put on a plane to London.' I looked at my watch. 'Collected at the other end by now, if my calculations are right and LAX is open again.'

'Quit kidding,' said Goldie.

'They can't get the money,' Petrovitch told him. 'Murphy has completely snookered them. They can't collect the money or exercise any authority. They're dead.' He nodded. 'You took a mighty big chance on guessing right,' he said reflectively.

'Not much risk,' I said. 'If the two of them didn't plan to cheat you and die the way 1 suspected, the powers of attorney would still be current and effective.'

'So we didn't lose the money?' said Goldie.

'You made three million,' I said. 'Ingrid and Crichton were insured for one point five million each while they were acting as principals.'

'We can figure out the details while we're flying to Lima,' said Petrovitch. He'd already pointed the chopper in the direction of Camarillo airport. 'Mickey had better come along. He's the only one around here who hasn't made a dumb move.'

I could feel Goldie bristle at that verdict. To change the subject, I said, 'By the way, Goldie, that's the neatest rug I've ever seen. I've been admiring it ever since the night of the party.'

Goldie ran his fingers across his head. 'It's my own hair, you creep,' he said awkwardly. Goldie never was able to take a joke.

285

Len Deighton's masterly novel *Faith* is also available from HarperCollins and marks a return to the shadowy world of Bernard Samson, the hero of *Berlin Game, Mexico Set* and *London Match*, and *Spy Hook, Spy Line* and *Spy Sinker*.

'What is she really like, Bernard? What was she like in bed?' Such questions torment the mind of Bernard's wife Fiona who cannot reconcile herself to his love affair with the youthful Gloria who now works alongside them both. 'She's determined to get you back.'

But Bernard has other things on his mind.

Len Deighton's *Faith* takes up the story where the *Hook, Line and Sinker* trilogy ended. It is 1987 and Bernard has flown from the comforts of California to the grim and grimy streets of Magdeburg, and the closely guarded sanctum of the secret police apparatus. Within hours of getting on the plane in Los Angeles he finds himself in a shoot-out with Stasi agents on a dark country road in East Germany.

Bernard's best friend Werner is exiled and in disgrace, and his arrogant father-in-law has grabbed Bernard's beloved children. His boss Dicky is determined upon promotion and Bernard's job is on the line.

Ask no questions, Bernard, whisper the top brass of London Central as they struggle to avoid the consequences of the worst and most dangerous scandal the department has ever faced. 'Middle management' such as Bernard are expected to shoot first and *not* ask questions later, or be content with hints, half-truths and downright lies. The cold war turns to ice and nothing is quite the way it seems. Bernard Samson, caught between two women, finds there is no one he can confide in, and nothing to depend upon, except his own faith.

Is there hope and charity round the corner?